FIVE PLANES

THE RULE OF FIVE SEASON 1

by

Melissa Scott & Don Sakers

FIVE PLANES
copyright © 2018, Melissa Scott & Don Sakers

Published by
Speed-of-C Productions
811 Camp Meade Rd
Linthicum, MD 21090-3030

First edition: November 2018

ISBN: 978-1-934754-19-1

PRELUDE

<u>SECOND PLANE</u>

At this hour of the night, the main deck of *Broad Increase* was all but empty, the lights and music dimmed, and Imric bin Marrick made his way through the relative quiet, grateful for the faint hum of the ship's systems to remind him that he was not somehow abandoned and alone. The shops were dark—not that they had passengers who could afford to buy, not this trip —and only the all-hours bar that occupied the central podium showed any sign of life. A single tender perched beside the machines, but she was buried in a book. Only two of the tables were occupied, each with a solitary drinker, staring into the cylinder that purported to display their progress through the void. At the moment, they glowed blue, turquoise strands writhing against cooler clouds, a single point of purple at its tip: no other ships in firing range except for their companion, *Iridium Azimuth*.

Of course, the passenger display didn't mean much, wouldn't show anything until it absolutely had to, but it seemed to provide a certain amount of reassurance.   The trouble was, the pirates knew they were there, had picked them up the minute they'd left Nelson's Keep without Issandro Lasser's Letters of Passage—the new ones, anyway, the ones that doubled the cost of the voyage and that the captain refused to pay. It had been a short and nasty meeting, the crew gathering in the large mess, three decks below cargo and one above engineering. Lasser wanted new Letters, a new bribe to let the ship pass, and even if they pooled their pay and doubled the passenger fares, they couldn't come up with the cash in hand. Already there were ten multiplanars in orbit around Nelson's Keep, and rumor said there were still more at Hag's Rock and Carolinia. On top of that, there were a good thousand refugees in port, all looking for some way off the Second Plane: presumably there was some political upheaval going on, which Imric guessed was the reason for the increased fees.

"He wants an excuse to gut some ships," the captain had said, which to Imric's mind didn't seem to preclude politics. Still, they had all agreed that they could neither pay nor stay in orbit until things got better, and if they traveled in company with *Iridium Azimuth* there was a chance that the pirates might prefer to concentrate on the bigger, newer ship.

"Of course," Mac Cattal said, as they were leaving, "*Azimuth* is probably hoping the pirates will go after the easier target, and leave them alone."

"Well, one of us is going to be right," Imric had answered, and they had both laughed. It had seemed like a good idea at the time.

He wished he could afford a glass or two of something soothing—nothing fancy, just a nip of whiskey to take the edge off—but none of the crew could afford to drink during a transit. During the drop, sure, there was nothing you could do then, but in the run up to the Mouth of Hell, the blazing nebula that surrounded the entrance to the Drop from the Second Plane to the First, everyone had to be ready to act on seconds' notice. He threaded his way through the tables anyway, the flickering blue lights like reflections on water, and leaned against the serving ledge while the tender put aside her book and came to join him.

"Evening," she said, though it was well past ship's midnight. "Tea? I've got some of that ruby-drop you liked last trip."

"Thanks." Imric laced his fingers together, afraid that they might shake. The pirates were after them, that was an absolute certainty, and every prediction showed that three ships would miss and the fourth and fifth would come into range just as they were lining up for the Drop. At that point, it became too close to call, all a matter of which ship the pirates chose to chase, and how closely they were aligned to the grain of space when they reached the Mouth. And there was nothing, nothing at all, that he could do to affect that.

The tender scooped ice into a tall cup, poured streams of two different teas and added syrup with a flourish, then lidded the cup and shook it briskly. Imric admired her detachment: there was even less she could do about the pirates, she or any of the service crew. He accepted the cup, touched the screen to put it on his tab and to add the usual friend's-tip to the account, and she leaned toward him.

"How long?"

She didn't need to say until what; there was only one countdown that mattered now. "Less than forty hours. Unless Lasser's figured out how to bend physics, there's only one of them left that can catch us." Or unless he had other ships on converging courses, out of range or hidden in the gases of the Mouth until they got a good deal closer.

The tender's smile was wry, and he guessed she had made the same calculations. "Trust physics," she said, and the old catchphrase sounded less useful than ever.

Imric turned away, twisting the lid to open the seal, but he barely tasted the sweet tea. In forty hours they would know, one way or another, and until then there was very little they could do except wait. He should head down to his own quarters, he knew, try to get some more sleep so that he would be in the best shape possible when the attack came, but he was too keyed up to sleep easily. Drugs were out of the question, just in case something went wrong with the systems; perhaps the sleep-wave machine would help, but he'd never had great results. He paused at the edge of the central space—the Promenade, it was called on fancier ships—and stood staring blindly at the fountain's cascade of blue-toned light. If he was honest with himself, the problem was that he didn't want to climb down through the refugee level, where Cargo Two had been converted to barracks for over a hundred souls. The rows of curtained cots were depressing, and frankly terrifying when you added them to his responsibilities. Maybe he would finish his tea, and then make his way down to the crew deck by maintenance tubes.

He had drunk the last of the tea, and was rattling the ice against the sides of the cup as though that would force more to appear when he caught the movement among the giant ferns that divided the Fifth-Plane coffee lounge from the rest of the Promenade. The lounge was closed, its service counters sealed tight, but sometimes passengers preferred to use its more comfortable chairs. He pasted on his most neutral expression as he turned.

"May I help you, Sen?"

He recognized her by sight, though he didn't remember her name: one of the actual paying passengers, and one of the Fifth-Plane suites, too, a tall woman with unusually pale skin and hair bleached snow-white. He guessed she was somewhere in her forties, though from the way she leaned on an ebony cane she might be older.

"The Chief Data Engineer, is it not?" Her voice was Fifth-Plane, too, mid-range and accentless, educated to be unremarkable.

"Acting Chief," Imric corrected. He remembered now, he had spoken to her briefly at the departure dinner—the captain had been determined to preserve as many of the amenities as possible—but he still couldn't dredge up her name.

"The original chief chose to stay behind?" It was just barely a question, and Imric sighed.

"Yes, Sen." It was a tricky topic, particularly if she wanted to talk about the reasons behind that choice, and it was somehow worse not knowing her name.

She smiled as if she guessed his dilemma. "Llian ap Farr."

He blinked, for a moment unable to match the spoken words to the printed list of names that rose obediently in his memory, then realized that the sound he had heard as an aspirated L had been transcribed with the double letter. On the Second

Plane, they would write it with a dotted H, and on the Third and Fourth with an apostrophe… He forced a smile. "Imric bin Marrick."

She folded her hands and made a politely social bow. She was dressed very plainly for the Fifth Plane, her ankle-length gown dark-blue and unpatterned, though he guessed that the fabric was polished linen—not exactly cheap. "I wonder if I might ask you a question."

"Of course, but I may not be able to give you an answer if it's ship's business."

Her smile widened. "My question is more of a personal nature. Though of course I will understand if you don't choose to answer."

"Very well."

"You were one of the crew bringing refugees aboard."

Imric nodded.

"I had already come aboard by then—already booked my passage," Llian said. "But I couldn't help watching. There was a family, a man and two children. You turned them away."

"I didn't turn them away. I got them passage on *Iridium Azimuth* instead." He glanced sideways to see her regarding him politely, her expression unreadable. "They—Milos is one of my ex-husbands. I divorced them five years ago, pretty much amicably. It was a large household, and I didn't really get along with the person they voted in after Zofia was born. And I'm vertically born anyway, and wanted to go back to space—" *And why am I telling this perfect stranger my life's story? Other than to keep me from thinking about worse things.* He put on his company smile, the one he used for dealing with passengers. "It seemed like a better idea."

Llian's eyebrows rose. "You couldn't bear to be on the same ship as your ex-husband and his children?"

"No! No, I thought—" And there he stopped, because the true answer was entirely too revealing. He had called in favors to get them onto *Iridium Azimuth* because he thought they had a better chance of survival there.

Llian nodded as though she'd read his thought. "You thought they'd be safer there."

"You know I can't say that," Imric answered.

"No, I suppose you can't," Llian said. "Well. If we're taken…"

For the first time, her voice faltered, and Imric took a careful breath. If they were taken, any passenger who could afford Fifth Plane passage stood a good chance of being able to pay their ransom. Except that Lasser seemed to have stopped doing sensible things, or asking for possible ransoms. "We may yet get through ahead of them," he said, but the words were hollow.

The alarm came just as he was preparing to go on watch. He didn't need to wake the screens to know what it had to be. Instead he grabbed his crew jacket—its pockets already stuffed with mobile and ID and cash-equivalents and a handful of ration bars—and flung himself into the emergency lift that would take him directly to control. There were others ahead of him, he could see boots and legs ascending in the column of light, and at the top Mac Cattal was waiting to grab an arm and steady him off.

"Pirates?" Imric dropped into the data engineer's seat and unfolded the keyboards, already typing access codes.

"As predicted," the captain said loudly, overriding the rising mutter of questions and answers, "we've got the Mouth in sight, and two pirate ships are coming into range. *Iridium Azimuth* is ten seconds ahead of us and broadcasting course corrections."

"We've had it," Mac Cattal said under his breath, and dropped into the seat next to Imric. He was internal systems, and *Broad Increase* was already in optimum defensive configuration: nothing for him to do until the shooting started.

He was right, too, Imric thought, opening input screens and setting them aside as quickly as he could rouse the ship. The AI was dumping data into his channels without screening, all its processing power turned to calculating their approach. If they could make the Drop, the pirates wouldn't pursue—but if *Iridium Azimuth* was ahead of them, her passage would change the coordinates fractionally, and make it impossible for them to make the Drop after them.

"Engines," the captain said, his voice tight. "Decrease power point two percent."

"Decrease?" the engineer echoed, and the captain's voice rose to a shout.

"Yes, decrease! Point two percent—now, damn it!"

"Decreasing power point two percent," the engineer said. "Confirmed."

Trying to buy time for the AI to recalculate after *Iridium Azimuth* dropped, Imric knew. His screens were steady, primaries showing nominal and secondaries coded green to let him know he could ignore them for now. A new window opened, the AI dumping supply and noncritical internals to his control, freeing up processing power for the last-second calculations.

"Damn, it's close," Mac Cattal whispered, but Imric couldn't spare a glance for the main display. He touched keys, prioritizing the messages and clicking off the ones that could be delayed, diverting the passenger systems to lockdown mode and setting the control linkages to their compartmentalized versions. Light flashed on the main screen, a flare of color washing through the room.

"*Azimuth*?" Surely that had been the Drop.

Mac Cattal shook his head, his face ashen. "They're shooting. The pirates."

No hits yet, or at least none that registered on Imric's systems. There was a brighter flash, blue-white and blinding even with his head down, and someone said, "*Azimuth* has Dropped."

"Recalculate!" the captain called, and another set of Imric's windows flashed from yellow to red: the AI had dumped the rest of the internals into his lap, but they should stay stable a little longer.

"Incoming communication," Pedra said. "The pirates are trying to contact us."

"Don't answer," the captain said. "Buy some time—"

The ship shuddered, like a speeder crossing rough ground, and somewhere in the outer structures a depressurization alarm began to sound. A window shot to the top of Imric's screen, messages cascading down the screen: breach in the outermost hull by the X-positive engine. That area had been evacuated long before, and Imric touched keys to tell the automatics to shut down the alarm and seal the affected corridor. It wouldn't even be that expensive a fix, if they could just make it to the First Plane...

Broad Increase jolted again, a heavier blow this time, and new alarms sounded: local depressurization again, power loss, environmentals. Imric's screen filled with windows, each one competing for priority. He flicked the least important away, trying to focus on the things that would slow the ship, things that would kill crew and passengers, but the others kept struggling back, demanding attention even as he dismissed them. "Captain! Sound general stand-by?"

That would tell the paying passengers to seal themselves into the bunks that doubled as escape capsules, and send the refugees scrambling for the lifeboats. Of course, none of those were safe unless the pirates decided to pick up survivors, and he was not surprised to see the captain shake his head.

"Negative. No alarms yet."

"Copy that." Imric bent over his keyboard again, shuffling through menus. Power was starting to fluctuate, the engines pushed beyond capacity; if the oscillation wasn't damped down, he was going to trip the breakers and lose control of the secondary systems. He brought that window to the foreground, its warnings strobing scarlet, and began working his way down the fault chain. Shut down the weakest links and damaged sections, route everything through the heavier boxes at the ship's core—that would hold, but now four other systems were screaming for attention.

"Drop calculation?" the captain called, but there was no response from the AI.

Active environmentals screamed at him, warnings scrolling across the bottom of his screen: one of the shots had taken out a central junction box, and the feedback was threatening to overwhelm the rest of the system.

"I'm shutting down active environment, going to stand-by!" He typed the commands without waiting for acknowledgment: they'd have about two hours' control from the stand-by system, and if they made it to the Drop they could worry about it then. Half a dozen screens vanished, but they were instantly replaced by a dozen more. "Damn it…"

He grabbed the internal network screen as marginally more important than the rest, began working his way down the failure tree. Before he could clear the first round of error messages, the ship shook again, the hull groaning, a dark, ugly sound just at the edge of hearing. His screen filled again, red on red on red, too many messages to sort. He shook himself, tried to isolate something, anything, and heard the captain swear.

"That's it, people. We're fucked. Engines, close her down. Comm, tell them we're heaving to."

Imric sat back, unable quite to believe what he'd heard, and saw the same expression on Mac Cattal's face.

"We are so screwed," Mac Cattal whispered, and Imric could only nod.

1.01 IRIDIUM AZIMUTH

FIRST PLANE

Iridium Azimuth was on the last day of the transition clock, finally aligning ship's time to the planet's, and that meant that was the last time the secondary bridge was likely to be unoccupied during his free watch. Val Millat let the door close silently behind him, and only then took a step forward to wake the local systems. Lights flickered across the screens and the work lights strengthened, forming a ring that echoed the broken circle of consoles. Val settled himself in the navigator's chair, frowning at controls subtly shifted from their usual positions at the pilot's station, then entered his personal key to light the screens. That was a risk, of course—there would be no pretending he hadn't been here—but he hoped no one would bother to look. And, after all, it wasn't unreasonable of him to want to know what had really happened on the Drop from the Second Plane to the First…

Except, of course, that he'd been told to let it go. But surely Captain Turan wouldn't object to his reviewing the data tapes; that was hardly the kind of public speculation that had brought down the captain's reprimand. And that was two reprimands this trip, both posted formally to his professional factum. Any more, and he'd start having trouble finding decent berths, never mind his outstanding marks in most other categories. For a moment, his hands hesitated on the keys, but then shook his head. He couldn't stand not knowing, not for another Drop, and he entered the next command, calling up the data from the next-to-last Drop.

The primary screen filled with codes, file names and references, while a secondary screen produced an image of twisting cloud of light, *Iridium Azimuth*'s simulation of the surging transdimensional energies that surrounded it and carried it through the Drop. And that, of course, was part of the problem: there was no way to record those energies directly; various programs translated sensor readings and field fluctuations into a guide for the human pilots, who processed data more efficiently as shape and pattern. But that meant that what he had seen in those patterns would not appear in the simulation: there was no precedent, no previous experience to draw on, and so the ship would smooth it out of sight.

Or, of course, it had never been there at all. That was what the captain said, and what most of the bridge crew at least claimed to believe. Even Izanagi was back-tracking as fast as he could, agreeing with the captain that it must have been a hallucination, a trick of light and stress and the weird energies of the Drop.

I know what I saw. Val closed his eyes, the image still solid, unmistakable: another ship, riding the hyperspatial currents, leading *Iridium Azimuth* through a nasty knot of unphased currents, pointing the way toward safety. And not just any ship, but a giant, massive and beautiful and unlike anything that had traversed the Planes these last thousand years. Five generation ships had settled the Planes; four had been dismantled over the generations to build their new worlds, but the fifth ship... The Fifth Ship had vanished sometime before good records had been kept, before the Planes had been understood, never mind explored. Vertical legend, spacefarers' legend, said that she still traveled the Planes, a threat to those who would do ill and an occasional rescuer of ships in trouble. Val had never believed the stories until now.

But it had happened, the Fifth Ship had appeared out of the maelstrom of energy, pointing—perhaps even creating—the way through. If he could just find real proof... His fingers moved on the keys again, entering commands. He knew the minute when the Fifth Ship had appeared; if he searched all the sensor inputs for data from those sixty seconds, surely there would be an anomaly—

"Sen Millat."

"Sen?" Val swung to face the hatch, schooling his expression to mild surprise. Inwardly, he was cursing. The databanks had to have been set to register this kind of search, and he should have thought of that, negated it before he started his own queries.

The first officer, Espelt Hillard, frowned at him as she let the hatch close behind him. "Sen Millat, I believe the captain gave you explicit orders about pursuing this."

"I know what I saw," Val said. If he was going to get another reprimand, he might as well go all in. "I know you saw it, too. Sen."

Hillard sighed, and leaned one hip on the environmental station. "Val, I've seen the Fifth Ship four times in my life, and, yes, this was one of them—but it was a hallucination. Humans are pattern-making animals, give us random movement and we'll make a design out of it.There's even a word for it— apophenia. It's something humans do, not something real."

"If it was a hallucination," Val said, "how did it get us out of there?"

"It didn't." Hillard's voice was flat. "It wasn't there."

"I'm a good pilot, but that was a real hell ride." Val shivered, terror still too sharp in memory. *Iridium Azimuth* had taken fire just as they Dropped, suffered damage to the field screens and the void projectors; he had barely had steering control as they fell into the Fracture, alarms shrieking from every console. He could still taste the fear, still felt it when he closed his eyes at night, the screens swirling blue and turquoise and no safe path visible anywhere... "I couldn't have gotten us out without the Fifth Ship's help—and why the hell would I say that if it wasn't true?"

"Maybe because you're stupid?" Hillard answered. "You tell me."

"Sen, if I hadn't seen it—" Val shook his head. "Look, why does anyone care what I think?"

"Captain Turan doesn't believe in superstition," Hillard said. "The Fifth Ship is a particularly dangerous superstition, because you start to rely on it." She pushed herself away from the console and gestured to the door. "I'm not making this official, Sen Millat, not this time. But you'd be very wise to leave this alone."

Val rose to his feet and preceded her out the door. He knew he should agree, promise to let the whole thing drop, but he couldn't bring himself to do it. Hillard sighed as though she'd guessed his thought.

"I'm warning you, Val. One more reprimand on this subject, and the captain's going to put you out. And I don't know what kind of recommendation she'll be offering."

Iridium Azimuth was an excellent ship, good pay, good crew, good passengers, and a company that actually managed to protect its people more often than not—not something to be lightly thrown away. And yet. The Fifth Ship rose in memory, a towering shape against the void. "I understand," he said at last, and saw Hillard's mouth tighten, but turned away before she could say anything more.

———————

When Nalani Lotuma stepped onto the deck of *Iridium Azimuth*, the first face she saw was that of the Captain, Elizavetta Turan. A rather short woman, Turan had the commanding presence of a stubborn bulldog. With high cheekbones, short straight blond hair, and pale skin just starting to show a hint of the wrinkles to come, she stood in contrast to the tall, dark, nearly bald Nalani.

Nalani smiled and bowed. "Permission to come aboard, Captain?"

Turan returned the bow. "Permission granted, Supreme Justice." She smiled. "Welcome back. It's been, what, five years?"

"Nearer to seven."

"I put you in your usual cabin. But before you settle in, I thought we could have a quick drink and catch up?"

Since Nalani had last been aboard, the Captain's Club had been redecorated in bamboo and teak; the rattan chairs were slightly uncomfortable and the tables too low. It was worth it, however, for the view: with the ceiling irised open, the surface of Capital provided an ever-changing panorama just five hundred kilometers away. Once the ship left orbit, she knew, the view would be less spectacular.

Nalani ordered invertase wine, while Turan chose fizzy water. "I'm on duty for departure," she said, "although I might as well not be. Until we leave the system the Capital AIs will be doing all the work."

When the drinks arrived Turan lifted her glass. "To you, Sen, and the pleasure of having you aboard."

Nalani chuckled. "Oh stop. To the *Iridium Azimuth*, long may she fly."

After they drank, Turan settled back in her chair. "I heard some silly rumor that you retired."

"No rumor. A few years ago." Nalani took a sip of wine. "Not that any of us truly retire. We're like ship captains in that."

With a barely-raised eyebrow, Turan asked, "So is this a pleasure trip?"

"Mmm, some of both. I'm on a mission for myself. But not one so urgent that I couldn't wait for a comfortable ship."

Turan frowned. "You almost didn't have us. As it is, the ship's going to need an extensive overhaul once we reach Dzamglin on Fifth."

"Bad Drop? I know that *Quartz Phantom* and *Floriture* both left the Second Plane after you, and arrived sooner."

Turan's eyes turned upward, looking into the past. "Bad Drop, yes, but that's not why. Trouble with pirates on Second. Worse than usual." Her eyes refocused. "Much worse."

"In what way?"

"Something's going on among the pirate combines. Power's shifting. Have you heard of Issandro Lasser?"

Nalani made a face. "I had dealings with Sen Lasser the last time I was on Second. A decade and a half ago, easily. The encounter left a bad taste in my mouth." She stroked her bronze arm cuff.

Turan nodded. "Longer ago than that, Lasser took control of the Mouth of Hell. If you wanted to Drop to First, you did it with his permission. The rates were reasonable, no worse than the gang that had control before. Then..." She spread her hands.

"Then what?"

"Lasser jacked up rates, again and again. Worse, Letters of Passage wouldn't be delivered, or would be revoked without warning. Rumors of another faction, either within Lasser's organization or outside it." She twirled her tumbler. "We only made it through because we partnered with *Broad Increase*." She set down the glass. "I don't think she made it."

Nalani regarded the Captain for long, silent moments. "El, why are you telling me this?"

Turan's face was pained. "I guess I'm hoping you'll tell me that the Judiciary's going to take action. This isn't a matter of internal governance, it's a threat to multi-planar commerce."

"You've made your concerns known?"

Turan nodded. "To the Commission, to all our reps, to every Judiciar I can find." A wan smile. "You're the highest-ranking Judiciar I know."

Nalani sighed. "Give me what information you have."

Without a word, Turan handed her a data flake.

Nalani touched the flake to her cuff, then handed it back. "I promise you, I'll review this before we leave this Plane, and I'll make a recommendation." She finished her wine. "I don't have to tell you how reluctant the Valley is to get involved with the Second Plane. You know yourself how difficult it is to get from First to Second; the logistics alone are a nightmare. Vault to Fifth, then drop to Fourth, Third, and Second..."

"You're saying I shouldn't hold out much hope." Turan rose. "Thanks for doing what you can."

"I didn't say to give up hope," Nalani said. "Rather, you might want to put your hope in something other than the First Plane. Local solutions are often the best."

"Said like a true Supreme Justice. I'll ponder that." Turan bowed. "Thank you."

Nalani stared after Turan's departing form, then shrugged and ordered another glass of wine.

SECOND PLANE

The pirates took control of *Broad Increase* with callous efficiency, sending a team to secure the refugees and passengers before attempting to take control of the crew. The internal screens showed the thirty-one passengers lined up on the Promenade in the stark emergency lighting, a hostage team covering them with pulse rifles conspicuously placed on the "lethal" setting. Whoever was in charge had an excellent grasp of commercial realities, Imric thought, as he followed the rest of the bridge crew through the ship's corridors under the watchful eyes of another hostage team. The captain was far more likely to worry about the paying passengers than about anyone else, or about the cargo.

The hostage team brought them out on the north end of the Promenade. Engineering and Services were already there, lined up hands on heads under the watchful eye of a third set of guards, and the control room crew fell into place beside them. The bar was between them and the passengers, but Imric craned his neck to see anyway, hoping no one had been stupid enough to resist. He could see only a ragged line, men and women in a mix of sober business robes and brighter traveling clothes. A child was crying somewhere, but he couldn't see where.

The hostage team prodded them into line with the rest of the crew, and took up positions where they could easily cover the entire group. They were all lightly armored, with full-face helmets that had only a narrow vision slit, deliberately and effectively intimidating. Imric glanced at the captain, wondering how much it was going to cost to buy them out, and how much would be taken out of their voyage share—or out of their pay, if they were spectacularly unlucky. Surely that was all Lasser wanted, well, money and maybe some of the cargo. Imric couldn't remember what was in the holds besides the refugees. The Second Plane was beaming more and more of a bottleneck for goods carried between Planes; more than once he'd heard someone say that the Planes would have to band together to do something about it. It hadn't happened yet, though, and seemed less likely with each passing year.

"Attention!" That was one of the hostage team, the helmet amplifying and distorting their voice. The rest of the team straightened, not crisply military, but certainly not without discipline, and a man in armor stepped out of the cage elevator that brought passengers up from the deck below. He had tucked his helmet into the crook of his arm, and his rust-colored hair was sweat-damp, the tight curls plastered close to his scalp.

"Which of you is the captain?"

Canalda hesitantly lifted his hand. "Here."

"Name?"

"Jorde Canalda."

"Full name," the pirate said, patiently enough, and Canalda swallowed hard.

"ACU Jorde à Kesar Canalda Sanrosa."

"I'm Mac Braith Bain," the pirate said. "You're not on our list of ships, so… It's time to pay now."

"We're not a wealthy business," Canalda said. "We're a Class Three, cargo with some passengers. I'm willing to pay what we can, but…" His voice trailed off, and Mac Braith sighed.

"You should have thought of that before you left Nelson's Keep."

"We thought of it before we reached Nelson's Keep," Canalda answered. "We had letters of passage, paid out good money for them—"

"Which I expect you recouped with a surcharge on the tickets," Mac Braith interrupted.

"Not all of it." Canalda glared, and then thought better of it. "We couldn't afford to pay out again. Not right away."

"So you decided to make a run for it," Mac Braith said. "Only that didn't work out so well. We'll take ten thousand cash, or equivalent value in cargo, parts, and indenture."

"We haven't got the cash." Canalda's voice was barely a whisper.

They didn't have it in cargo, either, Imric thought, not this trip, and he doubted they had the parts, either, even if Mac Braith stripped them bare. He glanced at Mac Cattal, and saw the other man lick his lips.

"Cargo?" Mac Braith looked over his shoulder, and an unarmed woman handed him a mobile. He paged through the screens, shaking his head. "Not looking good."

"It's all we have," Canalda said.

"You have crew and passengers," Mac Braith said. "And a hold full of refugees, but they haven't got a pot to piss in, we'll let them go for a token fee. How about your passengers, anyone there likely to pay out promptly?"

Canalda hesitated, visibly tempted—there were Fifth Plane passengers who could probably afford the loss—but shook his head. "I don't know."

"You won't get a decent fee," a woman said, brushing past two of the hostage team. "They're none of them particularly well off, and Lasser and the captain between them cleaned them out."

The voice was familiar, and Imric blinked hard, unable for a moment to believe what he was seeing. But that was Llian ap Farr, cane in hand, moving freely among the pirates.

"You're better off claiming crew indenture. I've made a list."

She gestured to Mac Braith's mobile, and he nodded, running his finger down the screen.

"You're with them?" Canalda gave her a wounded look. "I discounted your fare."

"Which I have taken into account," Llian answered. "And the service was impeccable."

Mac Braith nodded again. "Right. Captain, I'm giving you and your crew one chance to buy yourselves out of this. The people on this list can accept an one-year indenture, and you'll turn over our choice of your cargo, and we'll let the rest of you —and all passengers—continue to the Drop."

"Why the hell would we do that?" someone asked from among the service crew, and Canalda said, in the same instant, "Who's on the list?"

Mac Braith glanced toward the service crew. "You'll do it because otherwise we'll just take everything, including the people we need. As for who—" He raised the mobile. "JP Farren bar Genrys Sanrosa. CEV Eleicia Marievna Escarrey Sanxing. A A Imric bin Marrick Roeland Sanxing."

Imric hissed and heard Mac Cattal swear under his breath. Why would pirates need a data engineer? No, that was a stupid question, they needed data engineers for the same reason any business did; the real question was why they'd chosen him, and the answer was probably just that he was the highest ranking DE on the ship.

"Why me?" That was the bartender from the late night shift, her voice wavering. Presumably she was Eleicia Escarrey. "What do you want with me?"

"You have certificates in FTJ Foodservices maintenance and repair, plus training," Llian answered briskly.

"Well?" Mac Braith demanded, and Canalda nodded.

"We agree."

"Wait just a minute," Mac Cattal said, and there was a mutter of agreement. "Seems like you don't have the right to answer for them."

Mac Braith shrugged. "Suit yourselves."

"Hold on," Imric said. He had been born on the Second Plane, he had heard enough stories to know that the majority of the pirates kept at least the letter of their agreements— otherwise the other Planes would have banded together generations ago and cleared out the entire mess. "What are the terms again?"

Mac Braith moved down the line until he was standing in front of Imric, and Imric clenched his fists to keep his hands from shaking. "One year indenture, during which you will be treated as crew with full rights of protection. At the end of that year, transport to Nelson's Keep and no further obligation."

One year. Five hundred days. It wasn't that long, not really, but he would have made a full transplanar circuit in that time, Fifth Plane to First, following the Great Circle, with all the pay and profit that implied. He took a breath, and was amazed to hear his voice steady. "What about pay?"

"No pay," Mac Braith said. "Your pay's going to this ship's debt. But I'll give you a tenth share—point-one share—in any bonus payouts."

From any other ships taken like this. Still, it would mean that they wouldn't be dumped on Nelson's Keep without any cash to their name. And they wouldn't have to depend on *Broad Increase* turning up to rescue them. He nodded slowly. "All right. I'm willing."

"I suppose I am," Escarrey said, and Farren bar Genrys nodded as well.

"Done," Mac Braith said, and turned away.

Canalda babbled something that might have been thanks but certainly wasn't a promise of recompense. Imric ignored him, his eyes fixed on Llian, who smiled coolly at him.

"The team will escort each of you to your cabin to collect your belongings. Behave sensibly and you won't regret your choices." Her smile widened as she looked directly at Imric. "You might even come to like it."

1.02 BETWEEN PLANES

BETWEEN PLANES

On her way to breakfast, Nalani saw a man leaning against a door, sobbing.

He was young, mid-thirties she estimated, with olive skin and dark, wavy hair that had gone a few weeks since its last styling. His clothes were plain, dark tunic and kilt, both worn but clean enough. He sagged against the door, one hand half-hiding his face.

At the man's feet, a little girl clung to his kilt, hair mussed and cheeks streaked with tears. Nalani guessed that she was no older than five.

In spite of herself, Nalani sighed. It had been a long night. She never slept well on multi-planar ships, and after less than a day aboard she knew that this was going to be a rough voyage. All that got her through the night and up this morning was the thought of hot coffee and unlimited breakfast bar in the Zephyr lounge.

Well, it looked like breakfast would have to wait.

When she came close enough, she heard the man pleading in a ragged whisper, "Dav, you must reach higher. You can do it."

Nalani cleared her throat. "Can I help at all?"

The man spun, startled. "Oh." He looked her up and down. "I'm sorry, Sen. My little boy's in there. Th-the door snapped shut, and he can't reach the plate to open it." His accent, although faint, was Second Plane. "I don't know why it won't open for me."

Nalani gave a soft smile. "Lavatories are like that. It's a one-person facility, and it knows it's occupied." She allowed her brows to contract the slightest bit. "It should recognize you as the lad's parent, though."

He lowered his eyes. "Sen, I don't know that we're exactly...registered with the ship's systems. At least, not on the upper levels."

She nodded. Refugee, then. "I understand. That's why you haven't called for crew help."

He looked up. "I j-just wanted my children to be clean and feel safe. You don't know what it's like on the lower decks."

Before Nalani could answer that she did, in fact, know what it was like—had traveled on those decks more times than she cared to remember—they were interrupted by a scream from beyond the door, a shriek of distress that clutched at her heart. Inside, the little boy wailed in a voice that would credit an opera diva.

That set off the girl. At once Nalani crouched down, took the girl's hands and looked right into her eyes. "Don't cry. Dav's going to be all right." The girl stopped crying. "Good," Nalani said. "What's your name?"

"Zofia."

"Zofia, I want you to tell Dav everything is okay. I figure he'll listen to you. Can you do that for me?"

Zofia nodded and, with a sniff, turned to the door. "Dav. Dav, shut up! A nice grownup is here to help. Stop crying."

It worked; Dav's noise stopped. Nalani figured she had about thirty seconds before he started again.

She stood, pushed back her left sleeve, and tapped the bronze cuff on her forearm. Her codex answered at once through her neural link, its voice soft but insistent. ("Yes, Nalani?")

("Tell me what you know.")

("All is as he says. They're on the ship's manifest as refugees, came aboard on the Second Plane 108 days ago. You're picking up strays again, aren't you?")

Nalani ignored the taunt. ("Well, open the door, then. And without alerting the crew, thank you.")

The door snapped open and a small boy tumbled out, shin-high and with a mass of dark curls. His father fell to his knees and gathered the child in a tight hug. He looked up at Nalani. "Thank you, Sen. H-how did you...?" She saw his eyes dart from her arm cuff to the fine iridescent tracery that ran up her left arm, then to the insignia pendant around her neck. He jerked to his feet. "Your Honor, I'm sorry, I didn't—"

She offered her most comforting smile and her hand. "No offense. Professionally I'm Thurgood IX, but socially it's Nalani."

He blushed and shook her hand. "Milos Savoie. This is Zofia and Dav. But you knew that. I'm sorry."

Her codex had already dredged up all the ship's information on Milos and his family, feeding it into her short-term memory in a steady stream. No need to let him know that. "After such an ordeal, I hope you and the children will be my guests for breakfast."

He looked down. "Your Honor, we couldn't."

"You're not going to make me order you?" She winked at Zofia, who hung on every word. "My orders have the force of law, you know. And I've experienced ship's rations; you must be ready for a real meal."

He met her eyes, as she knew he would, relief on his features. "Thank you."

Coffee and food calmed Nalani, although an incipient headache still hovered just above her temples. Watching the gusto with which the children attacked the food bar, on multiple trips, brought a smile to her face.

Milos Savoie, however, didn't even fill his plate. He picked at his food and ate like an automaton, face blank and eyes glazed.

("Tell the Purser I want to see him,") she told her codex. Then she leaned forward, resting her chin on one hand. "Tell me about yourself, Milos. How did you get...here?"

He shrugged. "I'm a data archaeologist. That is, I was, until the pirates came." He looked up at her. "My family had a data business on a Second Plane settlement called Kuala Domal. We thought we were in a safe zone. Turns out it wasn't so safe." He took a breath. "I g-got away with Zofia and Dav. The others didn't make it."

"I'm so sorry." She shook her head. "So that's how you came to be aboard the *Iridium Azimuth*?"

"We had nothing left. Not even money, the pirates jacked our accounts. We got on board, and barely made it through the pirate blockade to drop to the First Plane." He wrinkled his nose. "It was a long drop. More than a hundred days."

Their table was on a balcony overlooking *Iridium Azimuth's* passenger decks. Cabins lined the faces of the great pyramidal space, with the vast open interior ringed by balconies. Below the pyramid's base was another, inverted pyramid—crew spaces, cargo holds, and the great multi-planar hyperdrive engines that propelled the vessel.

Nalani followed Milos's gaze. Twenty floors below, at the base of the pyramid, were the decks reserved for refugees: a broad expanse of flimsy cots and chairs, blankets hung as makeshift walls, and everywhere bodies clothed in rags and tatters. At least they were far enough up that she couldn't make out the despairing faces.

Milos whispered, "They kept telling us there weren't enough supplies, that food was running out. Rations got smaller." He closed his eyes. "Some people stole what others had. I made the kids eat what we got right away, all of it, because I didn't want to take a chance on losing food." He opened his eyes and they met hers. "I-I don't know how I can thank you for your kindness. It means so much...."

She rested one hand atop his. "Well, you could try to eat a little more yourself."

"Habit. I'm so used to eating less so they could—" He choked and looked away.

("The Purser,") her codex alerted her. ("XUA Ghazan bar Huisak Sanxing, goes by Ghazan bar Huisak. Sixteen years in current position, record fine but undistinguished. A safe by-the-regs bureaucrat.")

("So I'll just have to shake him up a bit. Be ready to locate the Captain if I need to go over his head.") She stood just in time to greet bar Huisak, a dour round-faced man with a regulation mustache and long goatee. A data monocle clung to his left eye.

The Purser bowed. "I am so pleased to make your acquaintance, Supreme Justice."

Nalani matched his bow. "The pleasure is entirely mine, Sen bar Huisak. Thank you for making time to speak with me." She gestured to Milos, who sat open-mouthed and frozen to his chair. "My associate, Milos Savoie. Milos, Purser bar Huisak." She took her seat; the Purser settled into a waiting chair.

"Supreme Justice Thurgood, I am ecstatic to be able to be of assistance. What service can this humble one provide you?"

"I've become aware that—through no possible fault of your department, of course—there has been an irregularity involving Sen Savoie's passage, as well as that of his children." She forced a barely-audible chuckle. "They're listed as refugees, can you imagine that?"

Bar Huisak mimed distress. "Unsupportable. Simply unsupportable. Your Honor, the fault is most certainly mine. Such a grave blunder can never be undone nor forgiven. How can I make proper redress?"

"Nonsense, I'm sure the misunderstanding was mine. However, I might be able to salvage some of my self-esteem if Sen Savoie and his family were moved to a cabin on one of the Fifth Plane decks—and, of course, given full access to all facilities. Any adjustments will naturally be charged to my account."

Bar Huisak shook his head. "I wouldn't hear of it. Since it was my mistake, there will be no charges." He paused a moment, his throat muscles moving as he subvocalized orders. Then he turned to Milos with a tight smile. "Sen Savoie, cabin

1832 has been keyed to your biocodes. If you need any service, please don't hesitate to ask."

("He plays the game well,") Nalani thought to her codex. ("He's a pussycat.")

("No, he's scared to death of offending a Supreme Justice.")

("I like my interpretation better.")

Bar Huisak turned back to Nalani. "I'm happy that this unpleasantness is behind us. Your Honor, how else can I be of service?"

She leaned back, looking over the balcony. "There is one other small thing, but I hesitate to bring it up."

"Don't hesitate a moment. Your smallest wish is my command."

She locked eyes with him. "I understand that the last drop was very difficult on the refugees. I would appreciate it—as a personal favor, one might say—if someone could make their lives a little easier. Extra rations, access to facilities on higher decks, more provision for privacy and security, that sort of thing."

He drew back half a millimeter. "Your Honor, I assure you that we've complied with all the relevant conventions...I don't see how we could possibly—"

"Sen bar Huisak, I was so hoping I wouldn't need to bother Captain Turan with—"

He cleared his throat. "No, there's no need for that. I," he swallowed, "I will make the arrangements. But if this drop proves to be as long as the last..." He spread his hands.

"It won't." She massaged her temples. "Don't you feel it? This is an intense one. The short ones always are."

He nodded. "Such is the superstition among the crew. One can never be sure. How can I assist you further, Your Honor?"

"You've answered my every concern. I don't know how I can repay you." ("Other than not starting an investigation of your handling of refugees, I mean.")

He rose and bowed deeply. "The pleasure is all mine. Now I regret that the press of business calls me away. But if I can do anything else for you, anything at all, I am at your call." He spun on a heel and walked off, not looking back.

Milos stared after him. "I can't believe you did that. I-I can't ever thank you enough."

"When the time comes, you can help someone else in need. That's all the thanks necessary." Zofia and Dav approached, their faces smeared with detritus from the sweets cart. "You'll want to get them settled in your new cabin. I have some work to do, then I'm going to take a swim. Perhaps you and the children will join me, about thirteen o'clock?"

He stood and executed a bow deeper than the one bar Huisak gave. "It will be my pleasure, Your Honor."

She laughed. "For that, you're going to get the splashing of a lifetime." She gave Zofia and Dav both a hug. "Off with you, then, all of you."

Nalani and Milos fell into the habit of meeting for breakfast at their usual table. The children went off to crèche-care, and the adults lingered over coffee, sometimes for hours.

On the third morning, Milos raised the question Nalani was waiting for. "When the drop ends, I guess you'll be leaving the ship?"

"Yes, I will. I have business on the Fifth Plane."

"Nalani, what do you think I should do?"

She took a sip. "I don't usually give personal advice." His face fell, and she added, "In this case I'm willing to make an exception. If you're asking whether I think you should disembark on Fifth and find a place to settle—then yes, I do. You're more likely to find work there than on Fourth or Third."

"Some of the other refugees are talking about staying on until the Third Plane, then starting over as settlers on colony worlds."

Nalani shook her head. "That's a hard life. New colonies aren't launched every day. Most settlers start out indentured. It can take many years to work off the debt." She took a bite from a sweet, delicate pastry. "And I've never known a settler who didn't fill every week with ten days of relentless labor." She smiled. "You can do better than that."

"Finding work on a strange Plane isn't going to be easy."

"Here." She dropped a data stub on the table. "There's a letter of introduction, that should get you an interview at any data firm on the Plane. I'm also giving you letters of credit, drawn on my personal accounts. I don't want those children to starve while you're deciding which position to take."

"Nalani, I couldn't...you've done so much already."

"You can and you will. I'm also giving you a comm code. As long as we're on the same Plane, you can reach me with that code. Use it if you need me." She met his eyes. "I'll also expect you to keep me updated on your situation and codes."

"How long will you be on the Fifth Plane?"

"I don't know. But I'll promise you this: I won't depart until I'm sure that you're settled safely."

"I don't know what to say, except thank you."

She smiled. "That's more than enough."

Back in her cabin, Nalani tapped her codex. ("When we arrive on the Fifth Plane, message Milos's ID to the relevant Refugee agencies. Tell them I want him settled quickly and efficiently.")

Her codex responded, ("So it is written, so it shall be done.")

("Oh shut up.")

Two hours later, as she was just beginning to contemplate lunch, her headache spiked, her stomach knotted -- then just as quickly it all faded and she felt fine. The subsequent announcement that the ship had emerged on the Fifth Plane came as no surprise. Nalani had always been sensitive to the ineffable discord of hyperspace between the Planes; it seemed to bother her more the older she got.

("I want to get to Polo Halau as soon as possible.")

("I'm negotiating.") A multi-planar ship's arrival was always known instantly throughout the Plane; limited hypercomm channels were usually swamped within seconds. And although Nalani's codex could transmit on one of the reserved Judiciary channels, replies had to come via public channels. Until intraplanar ships drew close enough for radio, communications would be slow.

("I'll leave you to it. Let me know the instant you have a booking.")

("There are terabytes of judiciary updates available. I wish you'd let me integrate them.")

("You synched with the central codices before we left. You're the most up-to-date codex on this Plane.")

("But I feel outdated.") The machine seemed almost to whine.

("You'll live. Where's Milos?")

("In his cabin with Zofia and Dav.")

("Tell him I'm coming down there.") She threw her few possessions into her floatbag and signaled for it to follow her and not get in the way. At the door she paused, surveying the cabin. If only for a few days, it was an entirely comfortable home. Of all the multi-planar ships, *Iridium Azimuth* was one of her favorites.

Zofia hugged Nalani, burying her face in Nalani's shoulder. "I'll miss you," she sniffed.

"I'll miss you too, hon. Take care of Dav and your Daddy for me, will you?"

"I'll do my best."

Dav gave her a dignified bow followed by a most un-dignified hug. She squeezed him tight. "Be careful with those lavatory doors now."

"I will."

Milos tried to get away with a formal bow, but Nalani pulled him into a quick embrace. "You know what you're going to do?"

He nodded. "We'll stay aboard until 5GSL3. That's where Themis refugees are to be processed. They said it'll be less than a week."

"Remember to stay in touch."

("A clipper's ready to take you to Polo Halau. Departing in twenty minutes")

"I have to go. Best of luck to you all." A last bow, and she left.

THIRD PLANE

Dilma á Juliano Ramos was usually grateful for an excuse to leave her office, but not this time. Artur Herrera's workshop was clear across town, and reeked of pungent chemical mixtures that would stay in her hair and clothes the rest of the day. And while Artur was a pleasant enough fellow on the phone, face-to-face meetings unsettled her.

No help for it, though. Her mobile assured her that Artur was in, and his workshop door, as always, was open. She didn't bother knocking.

She found him perched on a stool at a workbench, tinkering with a large bank of circuits. His dark hair was tangled and unkempt. The right half of his face was obscured by a set of ungainly lenses, and his right arm—a slender prosthetic of dull gunmetal—branched into a forest of micromanipulators that danced in intricate patterns over the circuits.

Dilma cleared her throat; Artur looked up. "Three seconds," he said, and finished whatever he was doing to the circuit board. The manipulators ceased their motion, and Artur gave her a grin. "What can I do for you, Governor?"

The stacked lenses, she discovered, were actually less disturbing than the prosthetic eye he normally wore. That one, a protruding mechanism that carried within its depths a hologram of a lifelike eyeball, always made Dilma fear it was looking directly into the recesses of her brain.

"Artur, I've been calling you for days. Why didn't you call me back?"

He shrugged, the mechanical right shoulder a perfect mirror-image of his natural left one. "I keep meaning to. Things come up. Like this gizmo here. It lets us tie into cargo reports from multi-planar ships."

Dilma frowned. "How is that useful?"

"First of all, it's an interesting hack. Second, if we know what ships are carrying, we can figure out what's most in demand on other Planes. So we can make better decisions about what to grow."

"Yeah, I see it." Obviously Artur had still not forgotten the spelt-7 debacle five years ago, megatons of unwanted grain rotting in a thousand silos. Well, she hadn't forgotten either. None of the settlers on Coquimbo had. She shook her head. "Don't distract me. What I need to know is, what's the status of the heat shield?"

"You're kidding me, right?"

"No."Her voice fell. "How much longer can you keep it running?"

Artur removed the lenses from his left eye, leaving an empty metal socket. "I've got that thing held together with wattle and daub as it is. I thought you were getting us a replacement." Without the heat shield, the planet's temperature would begin to creep upward—and the recent chain of volcanic eruptions on the western continent hadn't improved the outlook. Coquimbo was a new colony, always on the edge; they couldn't afford more crop failures.

"We've had a setback,"Dilma said.

"Another one?"

"It's not anyone's fault that our first request didn't get through."

"Other than the pirates who took the mail ship, no." The branching manipulators of his metal arm interlaced like fingers intertwining. "Go on, what was it this time?"

"Our request reached the First Plane."She swallowed. "It was denied."

"Why?"

She looked at the floor. "Best we can figure, someone down there transposed letters in our planetary code." Before he could explode, she held up a hand to silence him. "First we knew of it was when we got a call from the Governor's office on 3-3CBV5 —CBV, you see, not BCV. They were wondering why they got a denial for an order they never placed, and some bright character got the idea of contacting planets with similar codes."

For a space of several heartbeats, Artur stared with his one good eye unblinking. Than it closed, reopened. "You're telling me we're back to the beginning? No, not even that, there's eight months more wear on the shield generator, two repairs that I don't even understand why they worked, complete system failure imminent..."

"How imminent? We've resubmitted the request, it should take only a few months this time."

A hundred tiny tools drummed on the workbench like a squall of hail on a roof. "I'd be surprised if the shield lasts another 25 days. We're already planting in the southern latitudes. Less than a month after the thing goes, we'll see drought all through the mideast. It'll just get worse. Without the shield, this planet's equilibrium temperature is 13 degrees higher."

"I know that." It took nearly a decade of planetary engineering before the first settlers could start planting. "Only 25 days? Is there no chance you could stretch it further?"

The drumming stopped. "Maybe. It would help if I could get some specific parts from offworld."

Dilma sighed. This was no time to argue budgets. "All right. Get me a list, and we'll see what we can do for you."

1.03 POLO HALAU

FIFTH PLANE

Iridium Azimuth hung in orbit above 5-3ECK3, a cloud of repair bots and their tenders swarming around the ship's upper levels. They had had to repair the worst of the engine damage on the First Plane, the systems fried when the pirate's attack had hit just as they entered the Mouth of Hell, but the expense had been ruinous, especially after the unnaturally long Drop. At least they'd been able to pick up enough cargo and passengers to afford proper repairs here, but it would take until they reached the Third Plane to stand a chance of recouping the worst of the expenses. Val Millat blanked his cabin screen and rolled onto his back on his comfortable bunk, throwing one arm over his eyes in a vain attempt to make his worries disappear. No bonuses for the First Plane, or the Fifth; that was bad enough, but he was still in disgrace over the Fifth Ship. But there had been no mistaking it, not at the time and not now as he recalled it, the Ship wreathed in blue-green fire, leading the way through the tangle of energies, showing the way back to the safe channel that would take them to the First Plane. Oh, he knew what he was supposed to do: file it and forget it, like everything else about the Fifth Ship. That way lay nothing but trouble, and yet...

The door chimed twice, and he rolled over to see Kiri Sionek's face displayed at the corner of the screen. "Yes?"

"Want to go planetside? They're making shuttle reservations."

Val sat up and waved his hand at the room controls. The door rolled back, and Sionek leaned in, her eyebrows lifted.

"Are you all right? You've been weird since the First Plane Drop."

She was a rigging engineer, she couldn't have seen anything of the Ship from her place in the lower control room. Val shrugged. "It was a bad one."

Sionek glanced over her shoulder, and stepped into the cabin, letting the door close softly behind her. "This is about the Ship, isn't it?"

Val winced. "Is everybody talking about it?"

"No, you've been talking about it," she answered. "And everybody's talking about you."

"That's not fair."

"Probably not." Sionek seated herself in the guest chair, pulling up her feet to sit cross-legged on the broad cushion. "But you've pissed off the captain. Or at least that's what I hear."

"Damn it…" Val shook his head, scowling, and she went on as though he hadn't spoken.

"Is it true you're thinking of resigning?"

"No." But it was true that the thought had crossed his mind, the simplest way out of the situation. He shook his head again, harder this time. "I have no intention of quitting."

"Then come down to Dzamglin with me," Sionek said. "Take your mind off things. Whatever you saw—whatever happened —"

"Everybody on the damn bridge saw the Ship," Val said.

"Yes, but they have more sense than to keep saying it."

"It was real."

"So what?" Sionek leaned forward, her broad face suddenly serious. "I mean it, Val. What difference does it make whether it is or isn't?"

"Because—" Val stopped abruptly, his first answers trying on his tongue. In one sense, she was right: whether it was real and gave real guidance, or it was a hallucination that allowed an over-stressed brain to see the safe path, the end result was the same. Plenty of people in the vertical world accepted it as just that, a wild card that might or might not help in times of danger. It wasn't unreasonable for him to do the same—except that he couldn't quite bring himself to do so. "Because if it's real, there's something fundamentally off in how we understand the physics of space. And that—that we have to fix."

Sionek was silent for a moment. "Well, if you're going to take it that way…"

"Is there another way to take it?"

"Several! It's—nobody's ever had any proof that it's real!" Sionek broke off, shaking her head. "It's got you, hasn't it?"

"I just want to know."

"Well, you're not going to learn anything reading cultist trash." Sionek sighed. "My brother's an academic, Archaic Period, all the way back, none of your early-consolidation stuff. I can give you a list of reliable sources, people who take this seriously but aren't all mystic about it."

"Would he talk to me?" Val leaned forward in spite of himself.

"Probably, but he's off on the Third Plane, go some kind of search-and-study there. But I can give you his advisor's name, she's on Kauhale. Maybe you could get an appointment when we get there."

Val nodded. "That—yeah, that would be great."

"Caridad Sanrosa—LVS Caridad kaQuin Mateus Sanrosa. She was Sami's advanced-degree advisor. She's one of the big experts on the whole First Ships period."

Val reached for a book-board, entered the name. "And you'll give me that list?"

"As long as you promise not to access them through the ship's library."

"Fair enough."

Sionek pushed herself to her feet. "Come down to Dzamglin with me, buy them there—and for physics' sake, keep them on an unlinked board."

It didn't take long to collect his shore kit, and to stop by Sionek's cabin for the list, transferred board-to-board out of discretion, and then they headed for the shuttle bay to cadge a lift to the transfer station. All the disembarking passengers were long gone, along with their luggage; a few passengers with business on the planet were waiting in the lounge, and Sionek tapped on the window of the duty purser's office.

"Any room on the next flight?"

The duty purser looked down at her screen. "Yeah, plenty. You'll be getting in after midnight, though, local time."

"Not a problem," Sionek began, and someone cleared their throat behind them.

"Sen Millat."

Val turned, swallowing a curse, to see First Officer Hillard looking at him over the narrow band of her dataglass.

"The captain and I would like a word with you, please."

"I'll wait," Sionek said, and Hillard gave her an austere smile.

"No need, sen. Sen Millat won't be going planetside this stop."

Oh, won't I? Val felt his eyebrows rise, though he managed to swallow the words. "Is there a problem, Sen Hillard?"

"As I said, the captain and I would like a word."

"I'm right here," Val said, "and apparently not going anywhere."

"I expect you'll want to discuss this privately," Hillard said. "Personnel matters…"

Val shook his head. "As far as I know, I don't have any reason to be private." He knew it was stupid to push this, knew he was taking a stand that was likely to get him thrown off the ship, but he was sick to death of being told what he had to do. "I'm off duty, and was planning to go planetside with my friend, and I'd rather not be delayed."

"Suit yourself," Hillard said. "If you're not willing to let go of this Fifth Ship nonsense—"

"I'm not the one pushing it," Val said, and saw Hillard's eyebrows flick up in disbelief. "I have done what you asked, and if you—if the captain is going to make never mentioning the Fifth Ship a condition of employment, I'm not sure this is the ship for me."

"Val," Sionek said, and stopped, looking at Hillard.

Val glared at Hillard himself, feeling his bridges in flames all around him, but he couldn't bring himself to back down. He knew what he'd seen—hell, Hillard herself had seen it, she'd admitted as much. He couldn't bring himself to lie to everyone, and most of all, not to himself. The silence stretched between them, and then Hillard shook her head slightly.

"If that's the way you want it, Sen."

"Yes," Val said. The word cut like a knife, fear and freedom washing over him—and, physics, what sane captain would hire him if Turan gave him a low rating? Except maybe he was past needing sane captains. "That's what I want. Consider this my resignation."

"Very well," Hillard said, and touched the databoard that hung at her lapel. "So noted. Ship access is revoked except to your private quarters, and we'll waive the pay-in-lieu-of-notice provision. I'll expect you to be off the ship in—" She glanced sideways, calculating times. "No more than ten standard hours. You're of course free to use the shuttles to reach the transfer station, at no fee. The balance of your pay and pensions will be transferred to your accounts before *Iridium Azimuth* leaves orbit."

"Thanks." Val nodded sharply.

"Sen," Hillard began, then shook her head. "I wish you good fortune, Sen Millat."

She turned on her heel and stalked away. Val watched her go, and realized that he was shaking. This was either the best thing he'd ever done, or the worst—and he hadn't even thought to ask about ratings. But it was done, and there was no taking it back, not after he'd broken the contract so publicly.

"Val, are you crazy?" Sionek laid a hand on his shoulder. "You don't have to do this."

"Too late now," Val said, and thought his voice sounded strange.

Sionek sighed. "I'll help you pack."

Polo Halau—officially 5-2NKW3, formally The Polo Halau
Judiciary Center—orbited a gas giant in the same planetary
system as Kauhale, the Hina Lineage Seatworld. Close to the
political center, yet far enough to demonstrate independence;
that's how Judiciars always liked it. Although born of Hina
herself, Nalani—like all Judiciars—long ago renounced ties to
any of the five Lineages.

The clipper pilot went out of the way to take Nalani directly
to Polo Halau, rather than landing her on Kauhale with the
other passengers to find an insystem shuttle.

There was no hope of sneaking onto the station unnoticed; if
nothing else, the security system would blab to its supervisors
the second she stepped onboard. Nalani allowed her codex to
inform Polo Halau of her imminent arrival, and a delegation
was waiting for her.

The entry hall was a soaring, vaulted cathedral, all but
transparent to show the full glory of the ringed and banded
giant planet that loomed outside. At the head of the welcome
party was a middle-aged man, olive skinned and dark-haired
with tracings of grey at the temples. He wore a severe black
judicial robe with the usual mandarin collar, cut to minimize
his paunch. An elaborate silver cuff hung from his right ear—
Nalani surmised that it was his codex.

("Superior Justice Grotius XI,") her codex told her. ("Full
name VER Thiago Enrique kaBenicio Medina Sanrosa. He's en
counsel with the Gulkisar Codex. In charge here for just under
four years. You've never worked with him before.") Additional
details, everything from Grotius's family to his favorite
comestibles, hovered on the edges of her consciousness.
("Don't be too familiar, he likes to sound professional.")

He bowed deeply. "Welcome to 5-2NKW3, Supreme Justice.
It's a pleasure to have you as our guest."

She returned the bow. "Thank you for the warm welcome, Superior Justice. I hope I won't cause too much disruption while I'm here."

In the endless series of introductions that followed, Nalani tried to greet everyone with a warm smile. She'd served her time—far too much of it—in institutions like Polo Halau. Most of the work, while necessary and useful, was routine, unchallenging. An occasional visit from a big shot was a diversion from tedium.

In due time the crowd dispersed and Grotius showed her to an empty office. "I had quarters prepared for you. Your codex requested chambers. If this is satisfactory, it's yours...or we can find something else."

"This'll be fine." The office included a conversation area with a few chairs; she took a seat and gestured for him to do the same. "I've been in your place, so let me say right up front that I'm not here on any kind of administrative mission to check up on you."

"Thank you. Of course, I want to assist you in your mission however I can."

She leans back. "Do you know what's the greatest thing about being a Supreme Justice? Once you get that last cycle behind you—and believe me, the time passes quicker than you can imagine—nobody can tell you what to do. You've got all that experience, and all the resources of the Judiciary behind you, and you can work on any case you want."

"I'm sure it's a good feeling."

"And you're very polite." Her tender smile fades. "Did you ever work with Supreme Justice Accursius XVII?"

"Just once, long ago. She was my superior in Sanxing territory on the Third Plane when I was just a Judge. Brilliant intellect, and a good sense of humor, as I recall."

Nalani nodded. "A legendary Judiciar, deservedly so. We were good friends." She looks away. "Seven years ago she went missing. I'm trying to find her."

"I understand. Naturally you have the full cooperation of all our personnel." His relief was palpable—did he fear an official investigation that much? Or just a new Superior Justice in his first real command, who didn't want supervisors jogging his elbow? "You need only ask."

"As I said, my intent is minimal disruption. But I'm afraid I can't do this alone. How many Apprentices do you have?"

"Fifteen or so."

"I'm afraid I'm going to have to ask for one or two to be assigned to me for the duration."

Grotius smiled. "It will actually be a pleasure. We have a glitch of a time coming up with enough to keep them all busy."

"Good. I'd like to get started as quickly as possible. How soon can you get them all together for inspection? I'll pick the ones I want." You're not going to stick me with your behavior problems, you old snake.

Not unless they're good.

Grotius coughed. "The workday actually ended an hour ago —we keep Kauhale local time here, simplifies everything. So it shouldn't be too much trouble to gather the Apprentices." He touches his earring. "An hour from now, perhaps?"

"That will be fine."

ELSEWHERE

When the woman entered the compartment and locked the portal, she left her name behind. In this space, she was Hirose. It's the name they gave her, a name drawn from the ancient, forgotten literature of the prelapsarian world.

She sat before a blank screen and composed her thoughts. *Hirose,* she repeated within her mind, for the word was both name and mantra. A special implant, nestled between cerebellum and brainstem, awakened and signaled its readiness.

She touched the screen. "Ready to receive." After a moment the screen cleared, displaying a random pattern of colors. No video—even transmitting coded speech was a risk.

The sounds that issued from the screen were gibberish, grunts and whines barely recognizable as speech: a high-level code unbreakable to anyone without the implant.

"Grumby speaking for Vanderdecken. All agents are to be on maximum alert for an individual named BD Valentyn wa Salim Millat Naksatra, going by Val Millat. This individual is a pilot most recently attached to multi-planar *Iridium Azimuth*, currently located on the Fifth Plane. Millat has evidenced dangerous curiosity regarding forbidden topics.

"If located, observe and assess possible threat level of this individual. Report back to Grumby for further instruction. If events warrant, Millat is to be apprehended or otherwise neutralized. Grumby, speaking for Vanderdecken, end of alert. Acknowledge receipt in code."

Hirose nodded. "Received and understood." With the implant controlling her vocal centers, her response was in the same ever-changing gibberish. "I will be alert for subject Val Millat."

As the screen darkened to neutrality, she silently repeated her name in her head, backwards—*Esorih*—until the implant went back to sleep. Rising, she brushed at her hair, unlocked the portal, and exited the compartment...leaving the name Hirose behind.

1.04 WHEELS OF JUSTICE

SECOND PLANE

Mac Braith Bain had retreated to his private quarters in the northwestern lobe of *Divine Mountain*, stood now beside the narrow bar working his shoulders and trying to decide if he could afford another drink. They were safely in hyperspace, unreachable for the next twenty-eight hours, but that only ruled out outside attack. The situation on *Divine Mountain* was still almost as volatile as the politics of the Second Plane. His muscles tightened, needles stabbing into the points of his spine where nerves were still imperfectly healed, and he grimaced and reached for the second sealed can. He had allowed himself the indulgence of taking most of *Broad Increase*'s stock of Third Plane-brewed ale, and he was unlikely to get a better chance to enjoy it. He snapped open the cap, listened for the gas capsule to fire, then filled the chilled glass that stood ready in its chamber. The liquid was the color of the red gold mined on Foremost, and he allowed himself to admire it for a moment before he retreated to his chair. The cushions moved beneath his weight, shifting him to a position that eased some of the aches: if he'd had his way, they'd have waited another few week before challenging Lasser's letters, but Llian ap Farr had been very definite in her requirements.

As if the thought had conjured her, a light flashed on his control cuff, and Llian's voice spoke from thin air. "A word with you, Mac Braith, if I might."

It was not a request, despite the courtesy. Mac Braith took a deep breath, wincing at that, too, jarred the healing nerves, and gestured at the controls. "Come in."

The door slid back, and Llian entered, a box half-a-meter square floating at her side. Mac Braith tensed, then recognized one of the treat-boxes the liners served to Fifth Plane passengers. Llian smiled, possibly because she had seen him flinch, but her voice was cool and pleasant.

"I thought we might share some of the spoils."

"A kind thought."

Mac Braith didn't rise—she'd been the one to kidnap a Fifth Plane surgeon for him all those months ago, she knew perfectly well how far he had still to go—and she touched the release on the side of the box. A recorded fanfare sounded, and the lid began to fold back as it floated toward him, exposing trays and boxes that in turn unfolded like an entire bouquet of flowers, so that when the music ended, twin bottles rose from a central well, trailing a veil of frost, while a dozen trays offered tiny, perfectly formed delicacies. He only recognized a third of them: the style was First Plane, certainly aspirational for *Broad Increase*, but it annoyed him unreasonably that he couldn't put a name to the bright red objects—vegetables?—carved in the shape of flowers, or the tiny translucent spheres, red, black, amber, deepest green, that filled thumb-sized shells nestled in a bed of shaved ice.

"I've got a drink."

"So I see." Llian nudged the box closer, making it spin so that he could see that all four sides were identical, and reached for one of the silver-banded glasses tucked in with the bottles. She poured a generous measure of the pale liquid—its bottle was larger, Mac Braith saw—then added the other, which hung in coils like purple thread until she swirled the two together. Mac Braith smelled flowers, and realized he was looking at the legendary *jillun-mar*, the hope of heaven. It was made on a single world in the First Plane, and the two bottles cost half a year's salary for a First Plane executive. He whistled in spite of himself, and Llian smiled again.

"I'll save you a glass."

"Very kind," Mac Braith said again, and couldn't keep the bitterness from his voice. He had been born on the Second Plane, and would almost certainly die there: it was only one

Drop from Second to First, but the differences in the technology, in wealth, in everything that mattered, made it like stepping from the ordinary world to the Peachflower Paradise his mother had described when he was a boy.

"I'm not doing this to make fun of you," Llian said. She lifted the hand that held her cane, and a chair slid over to take her weight.

And if she had been, there wasn't much he could do about it, Mac Braith thought. He said, "I'm relieved to hear it."

Llian leaned back in her chair, sipped thoughtfully at her drink. "First, I thought you might enjoy it. I certainly intend to. Second... it's in my thoughts that it might be well for you to be familiar with another style of living."

"Pirate," Mac Braith said. "It's what I am." He studied the trays, trying to find something that he recognized, then gave up and reached recklessly for a small ridged rectangle that might be anything. It smelled reassuringly of cheese, and tasted the same, with a bite of pickle.

"It's meant to be eaten from top to bottom," Llian said. "Light savories at the top, heavier ones and ones with more protein in the middle, and the lowest trays are the sweets. The spheres with the three-lobed leaves on them have soup inside; eat them in one bite or they go everywhere."

Mac Braith nodded, but took a carved flower instead. "You could have had more of these if you'd let me take *Iridium Azimuth*. And our profit would have been considerably higher."

"You've come out well enough."

"I can always use more."

"Touché." Llian lifted her glass to him.

"People will wonder," Mac Braith said.

"You're their captain," Llian answered. "And, with a few more strikes like this, you'll be the dominant power on the Second Plane. Lasser's day is done."

Thanks to her, Mac Braith thought. He wasn't a modest man; no one who didn't understand his own worth could rise to the captaincy of any pirate ship, much less one of the Five Mountains. But he also wasn't fool enough to think that he could have taken on Issandro Lasser without her help, at least not at this stage of his career. He'd only been *Divine Mountain*'s captain for four years; there were still factions on board who missed their former captain. "We're getting there. But it doesn't exactly help our cause if we have to settle for the lesser ship." He paused, gauging her mood. "We could have taken *Iridium Azimuth*, and you know it."

"Shall I tell you it's better to take the sure thing?" Llian smiled again, her pale lips tinged purple from the drink.

Mac Braith snorted. "Just tell me, did you get what you wanted?"

There was a heartbeat's silence, and then she laughed with every appearance of delight. "Oh, very good! Yes, I did. And I'm taking the data engineer for the *Deal*."

The *Last Fair Deal* was the fleet multi-planar she'd demanded as part of the price for her assistance. "All right." He shook his head. "I'm missing something."

"Ah, Mac Braith." Her voice dropped, as sudden and thin as a knife. "I wouldn't tell you if you were."

FIFTH PLANE

Nalani followed Grotius into a lounge, where eighteen fresh-faced Apprentices stood awaiting inspection.

("Was I ever that young?")

("You were even younger when we first met. I didn't think you'd last past your first posting.") Her codex makes an uncharacteristic pause. ("I was glad you proved me wrong.")

("What do you know about them?")

("Two, maybe three are worth any attention. He's got them lined up by seniority; the first three are poison.")

Nalani bowed to the Apprentices. "Good evening all. I'm Supreme Justice Thurgood IX." She gestured, and an obedient chair raced into position. It was hard, institutional, too low for her comfort. "Please, make yourselves comfortable. Take it from me, sit whenever you can—you've got more than a century of standing up ahead of you."

The joke worked; at least there was polite laughter, and the tension broke. The Apprentices sat—although Grotius, she noticed, still stood.

"You wouldn't know it by looking at me, but I remember what it was like to be in your position. Polo Halau is your first duty station. We ease you in by starting you on the Fifth Plane. Some of you have been here less than a year, others nearly five." She took a breath. "What a long, long journey is before you."

She swept her gaze around the rough circle, meeting each pair of eyes once. "At least once or twice in their careers, Apprentices get the opportunity to step off the path and work directly with a senior Judiciar. Those who do, often learn more in a few years than they could in decades." She lowered her tone. "This is reflected in their rankings. I, myself, skipped ten years in rank working under Superior Justice Safa III."

She gave them a few moments to ponder. Then one of them stood, a slender young woman with a thin, pale face and straight, dark hair. Nalani's codex interjected, ("Apprentice Judge Al-Ghazali IV, en counsel with the Bel-ibni Codex. Full name DT Khojin bin Arsi Sanxing. Nearing the end of her fourth year. Her record shows promise.")

Al-Ghazali cleared her throat. "What do you request of us, Supreme Justice?"

"I'm searching for another Supreme Justice who's gone missing. I can't tell you how long the assignment will last, nor where we'll be operating. I anticipate considerable fieldwork. Have your codices query mine for details."

For a few moments the Apprentices sat blank-faced, staring into the distance. It was the sure mark of the Apprentice; sooner or later they'd become more comfortable with consulting their codices. One by one, they returned their attention to Nalani.

She said, "This isn't a mandatory assignment. If you're interested, let my codex know and we'll sit down in my chambers to chat. I'll announce my choices afterwards." She stood and bowed. "Thank you for your attention."

On the way out, with Grotius escorting her, one of the Apprentices dashed to her side. He was half a head shorter than her and gaunt, with high cheekbones and full lips, short black hair, and sandalwood skin. Her codex identified him, ("Apprentice Judge Bhagwati VIII, en counsel with the Nur-Adad Codex. Full name DMC Tua FitzHaku Hina. Nearing the end of his first year. Already several marks for un-cooperative behavior.")

Bhagwati gave a quick, nervous bow. "Supreme Justice, could I speak with you privately?"

Grotius frowned; it seemed a natural expression for him. Some internal matter, then, probably discipline-related. Well, she could give this cub the polite dismissal, if it came to that. Meanwhile, she'd pretend she didn't get it. "I appreciate your enthusiasm, lad. My codex will set up an appointment."

"It's not that, Sen." He glanced at Grotius. "I believe there's been a miscarriage of justice."

Grotius snorted, and Nalani could almost smell ozone. He growled, "Apprentice, we've discussed this. The matter is closed."

Nalani nodded to Grotius, but caught Bhagwati's eye. "As the Superior Justice says." She didn't quite wink at the Apprentice. ("Schedule him for my first appointment.") ("He hasn't registered interest in the assignment.") ("Tell him it's not optional. I'll see him in my chambers in an hour.")

Turning her back on the lad, she let Grotius escort her out. She waited until they were out of earshot, then said, "Is there anything I should know?"

"Let's go to my chambers." Grotius's chambers were about the size of hers, the walls festooned with plaques of appreciation, holograms of him with various Important People, and other flummery. Good conduct ribbons from grade school would not have surprised her.

Grotius sighed and leaned on his desk. "Bhagwati is a troublemaker. I'm sure you know the type: first year, thinks he knows more than anybody else, not willing to listen to reason. Not meant to be a Judiciar. I'll be surprised if he finishes out his five-year hitch here."

Nalani nodded. "I know the type." Both types, she thought—the first-year know-it-all and the Superior Justice with ego problems. "What's his issue?"

"He disagrees with a decision we made a few weeks ago. Claims miscarriage of justice." Grotius tightened his brows. "Of course his claim is baseless."

"Thank you. I'll give it no more thought." She turned to leave, then looked back. "On the other hand, if he comes to me officially I'll have to report that I investigated. Can you open the files on that case to me? That'll make it easier."

"Of course. Your codex should be able to access everything, Supreme Justice."

"Wonderful." She sighed. "Now I have prepare for personal interviews. I hope I can take some of these kids off your back."

Bhagwati entered with his eyes down, arms hanging by his side. One his left hand he wore a fingerless glove of silvery mesh. Nalani stood and walked him over the conversation area. "Thank you for coming, Apprentice Judge. Please sit down and try to be as comfortable as you can." She sat to his side, facing him, and tucked her legs under the chair. "I'm not Superior Justice Grotius, and what's said in this room will go no further."

He raised his eyes. "Thank you, Supreme Justice."

She gave comforting smile number three. "About that. I know Grotius likes his formality; I prefer things to be more casual between colleagues. If you'd like you can call me

Thurgood, or better still, Nalani. How would you prefer I address you?"

He swallowed. "I-I've never thought about it. Call me Bhagwati, I guess. My given name is Tua."

"Bhagwati is a good namesake." She nodded. "Since this is in the nature of an official investigation, I suppose we should stick with Justiciary names." She settled back in her chair, rested her hands in her lap. "Bhagwati, you have a concern about a possible miscarriage of justice. That's a serious charge, and it compels serious investigation. To begin with, let's make sure we're both talking about the same case."

"It's Uenuku Productions v Caridad Sanrosa, Su— Thurgood."

"That's what I gathered. I've done a cursory review, and everything seems in order. Obviously, you disagree. I want you to tell me, in your own words, what's not right."

"I'll try. The verdict doesn't make sense."

"Why not?"

He sighed. "Have you experienced the immersive show *Blind Justice*?"

"That soap opera about a Supreme Justice who goes around the Planes solving crimes? I should say not. It's bad enough that such drivel exists, I'm certainly not wasting my time viewing it."

Bhagwati drew back a tiny bit, tilted his head half a centimeter. "Maybe you should." He blinked. "That's irrelevant, really. Uenuku is the outfit that produces *Blind Justice*. They brought suit against Caridad Sanrosa for copyright infringement."

"I think I see the problem. Bhagwati, Fifth Plane businesses like Uenuku produce intellectual property—not just immersives but all kind of products—that are distributed on all the other Planes. A successful property can be worth as much as a planet. Copyright is serious business around here. You might think it's not a capital crime, but when you look at the big picture—"

"That's not what's bothering me."

"Did you just interrupt me?"

His face paled. "I'm so sorry, Supreme Justice, I don't know
—"

She chuckled. "No, it's a good thing. Means we're finally communicating on the same level. Go on, then, what is your issue with the case?"

"Caridad Sanrosa is an archaeologist with Kauhale University. Uenuku claimed that she appropriated elements from the life of one of their fictional characters, and incorporated them into her own biography."

Nalani frowned. "They identified a persuasive list of correspondences." She scrolled through the list, which formed the basis of the case. "Over fifty unrelated elements in common...that's beyond coincidence." She narrowed her eyes. "The episode containing all these correspondences hadn't even been released, so the defense couldn't even claim unconscious imitation."

"That's just it, Thurgood. Look at some of those particular elements of correspondence." He ticked them off on his fingers. "Born on the Third Plane. Sanrosa Lineage. Archaeologist at Kauhale University. Digging on Kauhale's moon. Vacation on a cruise ship..."

("The case was adjudicated properly.")

("Wait. I think I know what he's groping toward.")

"All those elements predated the episode in question. You think Uenuku's writers based their character on Caridad Sanrosa's life, not the other way around."

For the first time, Bhagwati smiled. "Yes! And the other correspondences could have been legitimate coincidences." He sighed. "You see it, don't you?"

"I...see what you're saying." She took a deep breath. "Lad, Justice doesn't always make sense. Look at the complexity of this case: four hundred terabytes. That's why we have AIs to help us. Somewhere in all that data, in all the facts and their interrelationships, in all the precedents and previous case law, there's something that caused the codices to recommend a guilty verdict."

His eyes, a clear and piercing almond, pinned her soul. "You don't believe that. You can't."

Nalani lowered her gaze. "No, I don't."

"Thank the Fifth Ship! Then you'll reopen the case?"

She looked up again. "If I do, then you'll join me in finding Accursius XVII?"

His broad smile was infectious. "You've got a deal!"

1.05 THE LOST SHIP

THIRD PLANE

With new loads of colonists arriving on Coquimbo every month, Artur found the colony's weekly dance socials indispensable. Just about everyone attended, one Themday or another. By drifting among the colonists, alert to casual conversation and general grousing, he picked up a lot of information about the infrastructure—more than once he'd managed to avert a major problem based on what he heard at the social.

Besides, the social was a great place to meet and welcome new colonists. Case in point, the strapping young farmer's son who danced in the circle across from Artur. Short, dark, curly-haired, and well-muscled, just Artur's type. The lad's name was Graciano; his mother worked a few hundred hectares in the mideast, along with Graciano and his two sisters. They came from an overcrowded world whose code Artur didn't remember, in search of freedom and wide-open spaces. Except that now, after a few weeks, Graciano was discovering how lonely those spaces could be.

The current number, high-stepping and lively, ended with Artur panting and even Graciano breathing heavily. "Let's sit the next one out," Artur said, and the boy nodded agreement. The hall was too warm, the air thick and damp from too many energetic bodies. Artur led Graciano out onto the broad wooden patio that joined the town's boardwalk.

It was cool and quiet. About a dozen shops lined the boardwalk; this late all were closed. They strolled westward, past the beach and onto the town's great pier. Both moons had set with the sun hours ago; the sky was clear and the stars bright. Looking up, Artur felt that if he could just reach high enough, he could stroke the sky and feel its texture like finest sand.

Graciano followed his eyes. "It's beautiful. Back home, we never had skies like these."

"Too many people with too much light, I expect." As they stood together, Artur felt the lad press against his left side, steadying himself. "Hey, want to see something special?"

Graciano chuckled, and Artur shook his head. "Not *that*. Here." He pulled a small data board from his shirt, flicked on a custom subroutine, and handed it to Graciano. "That display's slaved to my right eye. Watch."

The subroutine was one he used often; all the real work was done by his prosthetic eye's sensors and processors. Artur closed his left eye, as usual when doing anything tricky with the right; but tonight he cheated, keeping a side sensor tracking on Graciano's face so he could see the lad's reaction.

On the board and in Artur's perception, the field of view widened to show half the sky, infinite black velvet spattered with myriad gems, each tinier and more delicate than a sand grain. It was the same sky, but sharper, deeper than the human eye could see.

At his side, Graciano drew in breath. "Th-that's so..."

"Wait." With subtle slowness, a completely different set of stars faded into view, crimson instead of white, like the ghost of another sky behind and beyond the one their naked eyes perceived. As the new crimson starfield brightened, the white stars waned, diminishing from view.

Eyes wide, Graciano looked from the board to the actual sky, then to Artur. "What are we seeing?"

Artur smiled. "Technically, that's the sky in polarized microwaves of a very specific frequency set." He slipped his good arm across the lad's shoulders. "That's light from the Fourth Plane, redshifted by bleeding through hyperspace. It takes a lot of processing and cleanup to get a view like this." He felt the lad shiver. "They call them phantom stars. If you were standing in the same cosmographical location, but on the Fourth Plane, that's the sky you'd see."

Graciano turned to face him, ran fingertips along Artur's facial prostheses. "And you can see that whenever you want...?"

They pressed closer. "Not exactly," Artur whispered, feeling his breath on the lad's face. "Conditions have to co-operate. Tonight's exceptionally clear." Their lips touched, then Artur jerked back. Wait a second, exceptionally clear?

"What's wrong?"

Artur snatched the board from the lad's hand and tapped into his maintenance dashboard. There was no mistaking the readouts. "Oh, I do *not* crapping believe this. No wonder the sky's so clear and bright."

"Artur, tell me what's happening?"

"That piece of crap heat shield is down again." He stopped, frozen, then turned pained eyes on Graciano. "Lad, I hate to do this—you don't *know* how much I hate to do this—but I've got to run." He gave the boy a squeeze and a too-short kiss, then backed away.

"Will I see you again?"

"Physics, but I hope so." Artur turned, and set off toward town at a quick trot.

Fifth Plane

Al-Ghazali was Nalani's last interview. Only five other Apprentices had expressed interest in her assignment, all of them uniformly uninspiring. ("I hope this one lives up to her record,") she told her codex.

Al-Ghazali carried herself with precision, spine straight and each movement slow, deliberate. A series of tiny, glittering pinpoints outlined her right eyebrow. Tradition demanded that a Judiciar's codex be visible, but not what form it should take. Few were comfortable drawing such attention to it.

Nalani gestured to a chair. "Sit down, please. I'm sorry this is so late."

Al-Ghazali flashed a smile, just as quickly replaced by the even line of her lips. "I don't mind. I'm a night owl myself."

Nalani settled into her best non-threatening posture. "How would you prefer to be addressed, Sen?"

"I wouldn't presume, Supreme Justice. I'm happy with whatever you wish."

"Sensible. If you don't mind, I'll call you Al-Ghazali and you can call me Thurgood. Does that suit?"

"Of course, Thurgood."

"You've got one more year here on the Fifth Plane, then you move on to Fourth. Why do you want to leave with me now? You must be near the top of the pecking order. Why not stay and enjoy the fruits of your labor?"

Al-Ghazali tilted her head. "As you said, an opportunity like this doesn't come along very often. In the normal order, it could be twenty or thirty years before I have a chance to work directly with someone of your rank." She blinked. "I don't want to flatter, but you're a legend. Your portrait is in the Hall of Judiciars. To serve under Thurgood IX, why that would—"

"Would look impressive on your record? It would."

"Sen, I was going to say it would teach me so much."

"That's fair. To be sure, your record is fairly impressive for a fourth-year Apprentice. Your educational statistics are outstanding, and you've even managed to charm Superior Justice Grotius. No mean feat." She leaned forward. "So that's what *you'll* get out of it. Convince me that I'll gain from taking you on."

Al-Ghazali matched her posture, putting them face to face. "I don't give up. Set me a task and I'll accomplish it. Give me a mission and I'll succeed."

Nalani raised an eyebrow. "A regular bulldog, eh? How can you, specifically, help me find my missing friend?"

"You're looking for Accursius XVII, right? I did my senior thesis on her career. I've read all her books and watched all her lectures. I know her methods and her judicial philosophies. It would be a dream come true if I could meet her in person." Al-Ghazali pulled back. "That's how I can help you. I'm driven by passion."

Nalani grinned. "I'm convinced. I'll have my codex transfer you and Bhagwati to my authority, effective at once."

"Bhagwati? I didn't know he was interested."

"He wasn't, but I persuaded him. Do you disapprove?"

"Not a bit. Bhagwati's got a fine head on his shoulders. It'll do him good to get out from under Grumpius. Ah, I mean Superior Justice Grotius."

"Opinion noted. Professionalism prevents me from commenting on the personalities of fellow Justiciars. A practice you'd be well advised to adopt." Nalani sat back in her chair and folded her hands. "I know, grousing about the boss is timeless. But offhand remarks can be overheard and repeated. Across five Planes and however many worlds, the Justiciary is still a surprisingly small institution." She closed her eyes. "It's worth going out of your way to avoid giving offense, even the appearance. You'll be working with these people for a century, even longer." Opening her eyes, Nalani stood. "That concludes Gran Thurgood's helpful advice for the day. I'll see you back here at nine tomorrow morning. Be prepared to work."

Kauhale's Startown was twice the size of the Startowns on most Third and Fourth Plane worlds, and at first glance twice as elegant, multi-tiered towers rising in neat geometric patterns around hexagonal garden spaces filled with public art. Around the actual port areas, where the shuttles brought passengers and cargo down from transit orbits, there were more buildings and fewer gardens, and the blank reflective surfaces showed only their neighbors' discreet signage and the lights of the traffic in the ground-level travel lanes. Thirty meters above the main thoroughfares, the mass transit tubes strobed slowly, flashing brighter blue as each capsule passed along the

translucent passages. They cast reflections down the side
streets, a steady pulse that made the shadows jump and dance.

Val Millat had followed that safe ring as far as possible, but
now the directions muttering in his ear steered him down a
side street where the buildings were less tall, and the towers'
lowest floors were sheathed in intricate metal mesh, dotted
here and there with the bright red eyes of security watchers. A
little further, barred glass gave way to poured stone, banded
with advertising displays around the third floor, too high up
for any but the most determined vandal to reach; the ground
floors were badged here and there with slashes of paint
imperfectly removed, and any unclaimed space was layered
with cheap paper advertising. This was more like the
Startowns Val had known since childhood, and in the twilight
hours between the end of most day jobs and the start of the
night-work, he felt safe enough. Besides, he looked like what
he was, an out-of-work engineer, and on Kauhale—on most of
the Fifth Plane—that pretty much meant he wasn't carrying
anything worth stealing. It would have been different on the
Third Plane, or even the Fourth, and no one walked unarmed
on the Second Plane, but the Fifth Plane was rich enough to let
the average multi-planar's crew walk unmolested.

The next few blocks grew steadily more lively. The
businesses on the ground floors were open, brief bursts of
music and laughter breaking through the baffles. He passed an
alley that opened into a miniature version of the hexagonal
gardens, strung with multi-colored lamps and already filling
with bright-clad bodies; beyond that, a string of shops were
opening for the night-work, narrow display screens offering
glimpses of clothing and supplies and every small luxury and
souvenir that a traveler might find tempting. The device
tucked behind his ear whispered that the Five Ships was in the
next block, and sure enough there it was, the five great
generation ships that had settled their corner of space orbiting
in hologram above the entrance. Two people in half-armor

guarded the entrance, arms folded on massive chests, and a thin person in an ankle-length robe held up their hand.

"There's an entrance charge after nineteenth hour, sen. Five credits, seven for a seat for the show."

"I was told there was a lecture? A talk?" Val began, the words turning into a question in spite of himself. Surely a nest of Lost Ship cultists wouldn't be quite so obvious as to hold meetings in a club called the Five Ships.

The doorkeeper nodded. "Oh. You're for them. That's ten credits, but that includes the entrance for downstairs, too."

That was a good thing: he'd probably want a drink after the lecture. Why he'd thought this was a good idea—but if he'd been going to let the problem go, he wouldn't have resigned from *Iridium Azimuth*. He handed over his card—loaded with local credits; he'd converted enough of his severance pay that he wouldn't have to worry about conversion charges—and the doorkeeper ran it through their scanner, then held up a glowing tube.

"Hand? Forehead? Wrist? Has to be someplace public for security."

"Wrist," Val said, and let them mark his arm. In the exterior lights, it was barely visible, pale gold against his skin, but once inside, it would glow vivid blue. When he was first serving on multiplanars, he'd loved the Fifth Plane clubs, loved coming home covered in a rainbow of admission marks. At the moment, the back-to-back crescents just made him feel old.

The doorkeeper stepped aside, waving him into the dark. The entrance gave almost immediately onto the casual dance floor, lined on two sides by auto-bars wrapped in glow-tubes. Images from current immersives floated like ghosts over the dancers' heads, a near bald woman in the formal white robes of a Supreme Justiciar striding through a cloud of gesticulating figures, while the music pulsed against his skin. It wasn't so loud that you couldn't make yourself heard, and for an instant he was tempted to stay in the outer bar, see if he couldn't find company to distract him from his own stupidity. Or if that failed, there was always the main room, where the music played at a level that allowed no thought but dancing. He shook those thought away, recognizing them as cowardice, and wove his way through the crowd to the wall where a series of doors led to the club's inner rooms.

He found his way to the mobile stair that led to the third floor, and the room reserved for the lecture. It was smaller than he'd expected, but more comfortable, fitted with padded chairs and couches arranged in clusters that formed a rough semicircle around the display pit, and there was already a server circulating with a cart of drinks.

"Food to follow," she said, when Val waved her to his seat, and dispensed a half-measure of what proved to be decent wine. A few minutes later, another cart appeared with food, and Val collected a plate of small bites. The room was filling up, though the crowd seemed to be divided between quietly-dressed people who sat as close as possible to the display, and people in a wide range of styles who looked as though they weren't sure they wanted to be there. Val allowed himself a wry smile, knowing he fit entirely too well into that pattern. Even outside vertical society, people who pursued the question of the Fifth Ship—the Lost Ship—were considered at best eccentric.

And there were other verticals there. The burly, bearded man might have thrown on a knee-length informal coat, but the boots that peeked out under his pants cuffs were definitely spacer's wear, minus the magnetic plates. The taller man with him moved like someone who spent time in low gravity, and the trio of women on the far side with the pinned and braided hair had the weathered complexions of people who spent a good deal of time under varying solar outputs. The older woman behind them was wearing a vertical-style working jacket. He slumped in his seat, hoping not to draw attention himself, and was relieved when the lights flashed once, then dimmed.

The display space shimmered to life, an empty column that took up about a third of the platform, and a woman emerged from the shadows. She was gaunt and graying, her academic's gown hanging loose on thin shoulders, but when she spoke, her voice was cool and pleasant.

"Sens. It's a pleasure to see so many of you here tonight. Before I begin, I will remind you that the images you are about to see are under copyright, and that piracy will be prosecuted to the full extent of the law."

And on the Fifth Plane, that was considerable. Val wrapped both hands around his wine glass, trying to swallow the sudden excitement. But if there was anything that could explain what he had seen—what he knew he had seen, what had saved them all—this was the place to begin finding it.

"With that out of the way, sens, let us begin." An image thickened in the display column, the familiar cube-on-cube-on-cube shape that had come to be considered the correct form of the Five Ships, and the lecturer raised her hand. "Five generation ships are the foundation of our society and settlement—each of us carries in our very name a link to one of the five: Hina, Naksatra, Sanrosa, Sanxing, Themis. As the first settlements were established, those ships were, by all accounts, demolished to provide raw materials that were otherwise in short supply. Indeed, there is evidence to suggest that this was the Founders' original intentions, that the Ships were designed to be taken apart piecemeal and every scrap reused. Each Ship's population—its lineage—kept relics of the original Ship, and every lineage claims to hold verifiable remnants of their original home.

"And yet. Equally persistent is the story of the Fifth Ship, which somehow avoided demolition and still travels among and within the Planes, a signal of disaster to those who see her, according to some versions of the tale, or sometimes the rescuer of multiplanars in distress, or perhaps just a shape seen on sensors, a ship too large, and entirely wrongly shaped, to be any sort of modern ship. Just as interestingly, authorities on each Plane and within the Judiciary indignantly deny that any such thing exists, but blames any sightings on stress, faulty instrumentation, and gross superstition. I am here to challenge that belief."

Val caught himself leaning forward, and made himself relax, self-consciously sipping at the bitter wine. All he wanted was some indication that he had seen something, that he wasn't fooling himself when he said the Fifth Ship had saved them, had led *Iridium Azimuth* out of danger…

"Let us begin with that most common and most contested category of sighting, those made by trained multi-planar crew in the course of their duties."

An image coalesced in the display, the familiar five-tiered schematic of known space, the Fissure lancing through its layers, and dots began to appear, some brighter than others, creating a cloud that spread throughout the Planes.

"I will begin by conceding that not all of these sightings are in fact real," the lecturer said, "but even after one eliminates the actively fraudulent—" A set of lights winked out. "— the honestly mistaken —"Another set vanished. "— and those that can be explained by other phenomena, a significant number still remain." A third group disappeared, leaving the Known Space Schematic filled with cloud of soft lights. There was no pattern that Val could see, just a haze that spread from the First Plane to the Fifth, and from the Fissure to the edges of the Planes. There were more than he had imagined, more than he would have thought possible, given how eager everyone was to dismiss the stories, and he shook his head. If Captain Turan had seen this, perhaps he wouldn't be out of a job.

The lecturer continued, setting aside more categories as not merely unproven but unprovable—encounters in which the Fifth Ship sent messages that were heard by single parties, sightings from the slow-moving, unidirectional rafts that carried sensoria insufficient to make reliable sightings at any distance—and parsing verified and verifiable sightings into smaller and smaller categories, until Val felt as though he was looking at the subject through the wrong end of a telescope. Everything that he had thought would be clearer seemed more confused than ever, until he wasn't entirely sure the lecturer believed in the Fifth Ship as anything other than an ontological construct. As the lights came up, and the people in the front rows crowded forward to talk to the lecturer, he stood stiffly, and turned toward the nearest exit.

"You're vertical," a voice said behind him, and he turned to see the man he'd noticed before, the one in spacer's boots. A woman had joined him, tall and golden-skinned, her scarlet hair pulled up and back into a high fall, but the taller man was nowhere to be seen. Val looked from one to the other, and decided there was no point in denying it.

"Yeah." He hoped his tone implied *and so are you.*

The burly man grinned, and the woman said, "If you're here for the same reasons we are..."

"How can I know what those might be?" Val asked.

"You've seen her," the man said, impatiently. He paused, then touched his own chest. "Adam Mac Ivan. She's Nanxi Sanrosa."

Val hesitated, but vertical courtesy demanded that he give at least his common name. "Val Morcant."

"If you've seen her," Mac Ivan said, "we'd like to talk."

It was stupid, Val knew. If word got out that he was seriously pursuing the Fifth Ship, he'd never get a job with a decent multi-planar again—more than that, there were gangs who preyed on the credulous, though he didn't think Mac Ivan and Sanrosa belonged to one. But if they had seen her, too... "All right. Where?"

"I know a place," Sanrosa began, and Val shook his head.

"What about here?"

Mac Ivan nodded. "There are some quieter bars on the second level. We can talk there."

1.06 HISTORY

FIFTH PLANE

Both Bhagwati and Al-Ghazali were waiting outside her chambers when she arrived. She ushered them in. "I know Superior Justice Grotius runs things by the codes. You'll find that I'm more informal than that. I expect both of you to operate with a good deal of autonomy—which means I don't want to be bothered coming up with things to keep you busy. When something needs doing, do it. If you need additional resources or help, ask."

Bhagwati shifted his weight from one foot to the other. "Thurgood, what will we be doing to assist you?"

Nalani smiled. "Anything that needs doing. I might give you research assignments, I might send you out on field work, you might be beasts of burden."

Bhagwati grinned. "I was the oldest of three children. I'm used to that."

"Good." She looked from one to the other. "I want you to keep your eyes and minds open. When you think I'm missing something, tell me." Bhagwati opened his mouth; Nalani held up one finger and placed it in front of his lips. *"Silently,* through your codices."

Al-Ghazali crossed her arms. "What's first on today's agenda?"

"Well," Nalani said, "I've just filed to reopen the Caridad Sanrosa case. I expect Superior Justice Grotius will want to speak to me. Accordingly, I'd like to get out of the office." She chuckled. "Let's go interview Caridad Sanrosa."

Polo Halau's detention rooms were among the most civilized Nalani had seen. The furnishings were plain, and exit doors refused to open, but otherwise prisoners were allowed to be comfortable—especially those awaiting execution.

"It could be worse," Nalani said to her Apprentices. "On the Third Plane, they generally keep prisoners in stasis until the review period's over."

A viewscreen outside the detention room showed Caridad Sanrosa sitting at a table, intent on several datapads before her. She was a small woman, shorter than Bhagwati, with bronze skin, the typical Sanrosa prominent cheekbones, and hair a shade between brown and blond. Her eyes were an arresting sky blue under broad brows.

Nalani tapped the door with a finger; the standard chime sounded and Caridad Sanrosa looked up. "Enter."

As soon as they entered, Nalani bowed. She felt the Apprentices, at her side, match her. "Thank you for seeing me, Sen."

Sanrosa stood, returning each bow. "People usually don't knock."

"Please, sit down. I'm Supreme Justice Thurgood IX. Apprentice Judge Al-Ghazali IV, Apprentice Judge Bhagwati VIII." She fingered a chair. "May we?"

"Be my guest."

Nalani took her seat, the Apprentices a second behind her. She flashed comforting smile number three. "I'll come right to the point, Sen. I've reopened your case, due to...several irregularities. I'm prepared to vacate either your conviction or the entire case, depending on the results of my investigation."

Sanrosa froze, a slight frown on her face. "I...wasn't aware that was a possibility."

"Fortunately, a Supreme Justice has enormous discretionary powers. I'd like to ask you a few questions to get the process underway." She held out her left arm, showing her codex. "With you permission, all three of us will record this session."

Sanrosa looked from face to face. "Of course. Yes. I agree."

("Record, sight and sound, beginning now.") "Could you state your full name and professional position, please?"

"LVS Caridad kaQuin Mateus Sanrosa, Professor of History at Kauhale University."

"Can you tell me, in your own words, how you came to be involved in this case?"

Sanrosa's eyes set, sky blue turning to hard steel. "In Septem last year I published a paper on a dig I conducted on Kauhale's Moon. A week or so after the paper appeared, a couple of Judiciary agents came to the University and took me into custody."

Nalani nodded. "According to that paper, the dig you speak of commenced in Quinque, ORC Year 494 and ended in Unum 495, is that correct?"

"That is correct. I have the exact dates if you need them."

"That's not necessary."

Her codex whispered, ("Message from Bhagwati: Uenuku testified that their episode wasn't even drafted until the middle of 495.")

("Tell Bhagwati thank you.") Without a pause, Nalani continued, "Several hearings involved a cruise that you took with a number of other historians. One of them died of natural causes." ("Cerebral hemorrhage,") her codex supplied. "Can you tell me when that cruise took place?"

"It was the second week of Quatuor 498." Sanrosa tapped a datapad. "I have the billing statements and confirmations here somewhere."

"No need. It's all in the case records." The cruise, her codex told her, was a key piece of evidence. Apparently the historian in the show took a similar cruise, one that ended in murder. The fact that Sanrosa's cruise happened after the episode was written was considered an argument for guilt.

("We'll nail this one down,") Nalani told her codex. "When did you start planning that cruise?"

Sanrosa squirmed in her seat. "That's the thing. It came as a complete surprise. Professor Avakian won a drawing at a conference, the whole department got to go."

("Interesting. Remind me to follow up.") "Professor, do you have any enemies? I mean, prior to this matter?"

Sanrosa's brows contracted. "What do you mean, enemies?"

Nalani sighed. "Assuming your innocence—which I do—considerable effort has been expended to remove you from the scene. I wonder who might have made that effort. Naturally the first thought is some personal or professional enemy."

"I've never been asked that before. I can't imagine anything of the sort. I'm an archaeologist concentrating on the archaic period." Her slight, brief smile was the first positive expression she'd given. "I count myself fortunate when people are interested, much less hostile."

Nalani raised a brow. "I have friends in academia. I know that abstract arguments can get very passionate. Is there perhaps a professional rival who disputes your theories, or vice-versa?"

The smile lasted longer this time. "Honestly, Sen, I can't think of anyone."

("Bhagwati asks permission to speak.")

Nalani eyed the Apprentice. Confident and eager...overconfident, if his record was to be believed. Still, the lad had good intuition, and deserved a chance. ("Tell him to go ahead.")

Bhagwati leaned forward ("Remind me to talk to him about aggressive posture") and asked, "What about First Ship cultists?"

Smile turned to frown. "I'm a serious scientist. I don't have any truck with such...superstition."

"But that's your field, isn't it? Artifacts and culture of the Five Ships?"

Sanrosa straightened her back. "*Real* artifacts from an authentic historical period. It's fact that our universe was settled by five original multi-planar ships. It's fact that relics of those ships have been found on all five Planes. Anything else—specifically, fantastic claims that the Fifth Ship is still out there, crewed by ghosts—is pure and utter twaddle."

Time for damage control. "Professor, Bhagwati surely doesn't mean to imply anything about your work. The cultists do exist, and one can see how they might object to your research. Can you remember receiving any suspicious communication? Threats, tracts, anything at all?"

Sanrosa paused. "I don't remember any specific instances. But I do get a lot of mail from cranks and crackpots, I could easily have discarded something like that without reading it."

"We'll check to see if they've made any public statements involving you." ("Search exhaustively. Don't limit it to cults, report all negative correlations with Professor Sanrosa.")

Her codex answered, ("Good, something to fill those long, empty hours when I have nothing else to do.")

Nalani glanced around the table, face to face. "Those are all the questions I have for you, Professor. Thank you for cooperating." She tapped her codex. ("End recording.") She faced Sanrosa. "Sen, I'm afraid that you'll have to stay in detention until I render my decision. I hope that'll be days rather than weeks. Before we go, I want to answer any questions or concerns you have."

"Until you walked in, I thought I had weeks to live. I think you're restoring my faith in the Judiciary." Sanrosa shook her head. "I don't have any questions or concerns."

Nalani pulled herself to her feet; the Apprentices popped upright at once. "If you need me, just ask. The AI here will be able to contact me."

"Thank you, Supreme Justice."

Outside, Nalani walked quickly, the Apprentices half a pace behind her. As she spoke, she issued commands to her codex. "Bhagwati, my codex is searching for hostility toward the Professor, cultists or not. I want you to take over that effort; my codex will report to yours. Acceptable?"

Bhagwati bobbed his head in a nominal bow. "Yes, Thurgood."

"Al-Ghazali, can you follow up on that cruise? I want to know who sponsored those giveaway tickets. Dig deep, find out who's ultimately behind it. Acceptable?"

"Thurgood," Al-Ghazali said, "I don't see how that has any relevance."

"It might not." Nalani stopped, turned to face the Apprentices. "Thing is, in cases of this sort, there are almost always frayed edges. So you pick at them, see what else they're attached to, where they lead. Most aren't useful, but we never know until we look."

Al-Ghazali looked unconvinced, but nodded. "Yes, Thurgood."

Nalani turned and started walking again. Bhagwati said, "Where are we going now?"

Nalani smiled. "I see that Superior Justice Grotius wants to meet with me at my convenience. Which makes this a perfect time to head down to Kauhale and see the folks from Uenuku Productions."

THIRD PLANE

The big multiplanar ships almost never visited Coquimbo; *Melody Amative* was only the second Artur could recall.

The colony wouldn't be forgetting this visit for a long time, mostly because of the big ship's star passengers. Hulda and Eskil Boford were a legitimate entertainment sensation—their unique blend of song, gymnastics, comedy, and impalpable sexuality had made them famous on every Plane. Videos and immersives of their concerts always commanded premium prices. Every one of Coquimbo's ten thousand colonists, it seemed, wanted to see them perform.

Governor Ramos arranged for two concerts, Monoday afternoon and Hinday morning. There wasn't a single enclosed space on the planet large enough to hold them all. Artur and his team worked for two days constructing a makeshift amphitheater in a valley north of the city.

Now Artur was ready to enjoy his reward. After the first concert, the entertainers came down into the audience to interact with the crowd. Artur let it go on for nearly an hour, then pushed his way through stragglers and escorted the pair backstage. "I'm Artur Herrerra, Chief Engineer. You were wonderful. I hope the equipment and crew were satisfactory?"

Both were tall and exceptionally thin, with skin the color of snow and green-brown eyes. Hulda's long hair was bone-white and straight, falling like an icy river past her smooth shoulders; Eskil wore his sky-blue hair in a five centimeter mohawk. It was impossible to guess their ages, although Artur could tell at once that they weren't youngsters.

Eskil grinned and took Artur by the shoulders, kissing the air above both his cheeks. "Sen, everything was stellar. The crew couldn't have been nicer to us."

Hulda repeated the greeting. "They said your people put this venue together in two days?" Artur nodded. "I can't believe that. The sound and vid systems were magnificent. We've played Fifth Plane shows that weren't as well equipped. Thank you."

Artur nodded acknowledgment. "I have good people." He looked the pair up and down. "I suppose you'd like to get some rest?"

Hulda smiled. "Yes, that would be good. We're always energized by a show, but in a little while we'll start to crash."

Eskil retrieved a travel bag and started rummaging through it. "I know the Governor sent us our lodging arrangements, but I've forgotten—"

Exactly the opening Artur was waiting for. "Coquimbo is still a new colony. We don't exactly have commercial hotels or lodges. I think the Governor was going to put you up in her official house." He made a sour face. "It's sterile. No flavor. Now if you'd rather, I have a very comfortable cabin up in the mountains. We can be there in ten minutes."

"That's exceptionally kind of you, Sen Herrerra," Hulda said, licking her lips and taking his good hand. "I believe we'd love to spend the night at your...cabin."

Artur was wearing his social right arm, steel and leather; Eskil ran his own hand down the length. "It sounds the chance of a lifetime. How do we get there?"

Slipping one arm around each of them, he said, "I have an aircar nearby."

On the short flight, he explained more about the cabin. "We have some very temperamental heavy equipment up there—heat shield generator, hyperwave transceivers, seismic monitors, that sort of thing. We put in the cabin as a place for techs to stay rather than running back and forth to town." He shrugged. "Over the years we've added to the amenities."

Eskil chuckled. "I believe we'll enjoy it immensely, Sen."

"Oh, call me Artur."

Hulda gave him a peck on the cheek. "And you must call us Hulda and Eskil."

He detoured past Celestial Falls, a set of lacy waterfalls that sparkled in the late afternoon sun. Eskil whistled. "What beautiful falls. Hulda, don't they remind you of the Iskander Falls at home?"

"Very much," Hulda answered. "We've been away from home for over a year—going on twelve months, in fact. Long enough to start feeling homesick. You can't know what a joy it is to be reminded."

"There's a theory," Artur said, "that every planet has its duplicate on the other Planes. Perhaps your homeworld and Coquimbo are duplicates."

"It would be wonderful to think so."

Climbing toward the high plateau, Artur suddenly frowned. Another aircar was parked at the cabin. Yet he'd told all the boys and girls that he had dibs on the place tonight...who in physics could it be?

Never mind, he'd get rid of them quick enough. He let the car land itself, helped Eskil and Hulda out, and started toward the cabin.

The door opened and Governor Dilma Ramos strode out, trailed by one of her flunkies. "Artur, good. I didn't think you got my message."

Fuming, he waved through introductions. Dilma bobbed her head with a silly smile. "Yes, we've met. I welcomed Hulda and Eskil to Coquimbo right before their concert, don't you remember?" She winked at the pair. "Artur's such a scatterbrain when he's concentrating on business."

With an even tone, Artur said, "Business is exactly what I'm *not* concentrating on right now, Dilma. I brought our celebrities here to enjoy a peaceful night's rest *away from the crowds.*"

"Don't be ridiculous." She bowed to Hulda and Eskil. "We have a lovely suite set up for you in Government House. Our best chef is preparing a special meal; he got your preferences from *Melody Amative* and has a selection of local dishes matching them. And I assure you, lodgings there are far superior to this...shack." She shook her head. "Besides, if I know Artur, he'll be up all night working."

"I will not. Wait just a—"

Dilma waved to her aide. "Take our guests back to Government House and see they're taken good care of."

"But—"

"Say goodbye, Artur."

Before his eyes, natural and artificial, the aide loaded Hulda and Eskil into the other aircar. With barely time for a waved farewell, the car rose and sailed off to the south.

Artur sputtered. "Dilma...those were *the Boford twins*. I'll never get a chance like that again."

She sniffed. "I don't know what you're talking about. Come on, there's work to do."

"*What* work? There's nothing pending. I cleared the whole night and all of tomorrow..."

A frown. "So you *didn't* get my message about the heat shield?"

"What?! No." He punched up his status report, which appeared in the air before him. Everything was green. "The heat shield's working fine, for once. I tell you, I gave it a detailed checkout this morning, it's—"

She chuckled. "Not *that* one. The new generator was delivered half an hour ago." At his confused expression, she elaborated, "It was shipped on the *Melody Amative*. That's why they stopped here to begin with." She waved a hand in front of his face. "Honestly, Artur, are you listening to me at all?"

He glared at her. "Honestly, Dilma, don't you think it's about time the two of us should get married?"

She blinked. "What?"

"The way you keep destroying my sex life, we might as well make it legitimate, don't you think?"

For a moment her face was frozen, then she laughed and slapped him on the shoulder. "Oh, Artur, you always make me laugh." She wiped her eyes. "Now, do you want to see the new heat shield, or not? I wouldn't let anyone open the container until you got here."

Artur sighed. "All right, I guess I ought to salvage what I can from this night. Lead on, Governor."

Next to the fenced-off area of the old heat shield generator, a standard cargo container sat, sunk a few centimeters into the grass. "I'll get a dozer and crane up here to move the thing." He reached up and tugged on the heavy metal handle. "Unf." He pulled harder, and the handle finally moved. "We'll have to keep the old unit going until the new one's on line, it's going to be tricky."

He stepped back as the container opened, the whole end peeling back to reveal the dark interior, as big as a comfortable house. Lights snapped on, and Artur frowned. Instead of the single large piece of machinery he was expecting, he saw rank upon rank of stacked metal cabinets, each with a multitude of small drawers.

"What's wrong?" Dilma said.

"Wait." Artur shot an electronic query to the container: what is your cargo? The answer wrote itself across his field of vision.

"Crap!" With his artificial arm, he pounded the side of the container, producing a teeth-clenching thud and leaving a small dent. "Crap, crap, crap, crap, crap!"

"What's wrong?"

He turned to Dilma. "This isn't our new heat shield."

The Governor paled. "What is it, then?"

He spat the word, "Goats."

"What?"

Artur waved at the ranked cabinets with their thousands of drawers. "Goats. Fourteen million goat embryos. In stasis."

"Why would they send us fourteen million goat embryos?"

"Why are you asking me? Maybe the ship sent the wrong container. Probably not, though, I'm never that lucky."

Dilma touched her ear cuff. "Get in touch with the cargo master on *Melody Amative*. Find out if they dropped off the correct shipment. Contact me as soon as you have an answer." She offered Artur a wan smile. "I'm sure it was an innocent mistake."

"Of course it was. Someone heard 'TC-806 Heat Shield Generator' and typed 'fourteen million goat embryos.' It's an easy mistake to make. They sound so much alike. I can't tell you how often I've said to myself, 'Artur, you'd better make another diagnostic check of those fourteen million goat embryos that are maintaining the planet's heat shield…oh, I mean generator.'"

"There's no need to be sarcastic."

Artur opened his mouth, closed it, then shook his head. "No, I rather think there's *every* need to be sarcastic. I could be sleeping with the Boford Twins, and instead I'm going to be spending the night trying to track down someone's 'innocent mistake.' Not to mention keeping *that* piece of junk running for another month while it all gets sorted out. If it ever does."

Dilma tilted her head, listened for a moment to a voice Artur couldn't hear. "The cargo master confirms that we got the right container. The mistake was further back in the supply chain." She put her hand on Artur's shoulder. "I'm sorry. Do you want to come back to Government House with me? I'm sure there's time to catch dinner."

He took a deep breath. "No. I don't think I'd be good company tonight. I'll just bed down at the cabin." Where, he hoped, the liquor cabinet was well-stocked.

FIFTH PLANE

They settled on one of the smaller bars on the second level, this one decorated in Fourth Plane industrial, all bare metal and carbon fiber and hanging nets carefully arranged to form unexpectedly comfortable lounging spaces. Val steered them firmly away from the netting, and they found an empty table by the wall, far enough from the towering dance stack that conversation was possible. The menu flashed persistently beneath the table's surface, offering drinks and snacks or a seven-credit table charge, and Val reached for it.

"You'll forgive me, I'm sure, but I haven't eaten." It was also a good way to be sure that his presence was noted by the club machinery: there were enough cons and hustlers and just plain irrationals associated with the Fifth Ship that it paid to take precautions. With the same thought in mind, he ordered a single-serve bottle to go with the tapas, and slid the menu back to the others. Mac Ivan shook his head, but the woman made a selection, and after a moment Mac Ivan, too, touched a set of symbols and slid a credit chip across the table sensor.

"So you've seen her," Mac Ivan said again, and Sanrosa laid a hand on his wrist.

"Adam." She looked at Val. "We've both seen the Ship. Not at the same time, and on different multiplanars, but—we've both seen it. You?"

Val hesitated, but he hadn't walked away from *Iridium Azimuth* to run away from even a doubtful contact. "Yes. I've seen it, too."

"It led us home," Mac Ivan said. There was no one within earshot, but he lowered his voice until he was barely audible above the music and the wash of voices. "We'd made a bad jump—this was a pure cargo multi, we ran on a tight margin, and the astrogator turned out not to have the papers she claimed, so she couldn't back up the machines. So we jumped wrong, and got caught in one of the hyperspatial rips you get where the Fissure crosses the Third Plane. I couldn't see a way out, every single eddy was showing more stress than our fields could hold, and then—there it was. Huge, just like in the pictures, cube on cube on cube, never meant for atmosphere or any kind of fluid. I thought we were dead then."

"You were piloting?" Val asked, when it seemed he wasn't willing to continue.

Mac Ivan nodded. "Yeah. I'd been on line for fourteen hours then, I won't lie, but that's got nothing to do with what I saw."

"Never said it did," Val said, though you had to wonder about fatigue at that point.

Mac Ivan eyed him a moment longer. "Well. To shorten the tale, it slowed, took up station in our line of travel, and—I swear to you—she cleared a path for us. She's big enough, you see, she could take the stress when we couldn't, and we could just trail in her wake neat as you please, and the next thing you know, we're through the Drop."

Val made a noise in spite of himself, and Sanrosa's smile widened, showing small sharp teeth.

"It's happened to you," she said.

Val shook his head. "You first."

"We're trusting you," Mac Ivan pointed out, and Sanrosa touched his sleeve again.

"All right. I had something similar happen—and, yes, I was piloting, too, though I hadn't been on as long as Adam. It was on a intra-Plane Jump, though. Third Plane—you know the Meretizia Slide?"

Val nodded. It was a tricky shortcut: if you were successful at factoring its geometry into the Jump calculations, you could cut dozens of hours off a Jump, but the math was complex enough that most ships didn't bother.

"Yeah. We dorfed it totally," Sanrosa said. "Ended up caught in the eddies on the edge of the slide, with the same problem Adam was having, stresses too high for the fields. And then she sailed up right out of the chaos and put herself between us as the worst of the eddies, and we clawed ourselves back into the safe-line. If she hadn't been there —" She broke off, shaking her head, and Mac Ivan leaned forward.

"Your turn."

"Understand, I can't name the ship."

"No more did we," Sanrosa said, with another sharp smile.

Val nodded. "We were attacked coming through the Mouth of Hell. The bolt must have struck just as we Dropped, because we hit the Fissure akimbo, out of the usual range and sliding fast. I tried to correct, but we'd taken up too much potential, and I couldn't pull us back. Then —" He stopped, struggling for the words to encompass what he'd seen. "There she was, ahead and left and a little up, and all I could think was to tuck in behind her, because otherwise we were going to be torn apart in the knots. So I did, and we slipped through clean. And she was gone again."

"And you had questions, and no one had answers." Sanrosa showed her teeth.

"My captain said it didn't happen." Val's tone was flat. "She was there, right next to me, but—it was an illusion. End of story."

"And don't you wonder why?" Sanrosa asked.

"I wonder first if it was real," Val answered.

"It was real," Mac Ivan said, with a heavy sigh. "It was real."

Val nodded in spite of himself. He hadn't really doubted it, in spite of everything. "And, yes, of course I wonder why. But also how. The Ships—historically, they existed millennia ago, and every lineage claims their Ship is accounted for. So how can this be a Fifth Ship?"

"The records are terrible that far back," Mac Ivan said. "And the original Ships were built at the same time, and in the same shipyard."

"According to legend," Sanrosa murmured.

Mac Ivan ignored her. "It's certainly possible that two lineages have laid claim to parts of the same Ship. Settlement was scattered, worlds were lost and found and lost again; it's not really until Consolidation that we've had any clear idea how many planets have been settled on each Plane. For that matter, we don't *really* know that there were only five Ships. Suppose there were six, or seven? One that went missing before we even reached the Planes?"

"The Lineage names argue against that," Val said. "Five Ships, five lineages. It's hard to imagine that people would just forget another Ship."

"There I agree with you," Sanrosa said. "It's also a question I don't think we can answer until we find the Ship—this particular Ship that's making these appearances. And that means figuring out what it's doing, and why."

"Easier said than done," Val pointed out, and she grinned.

"That's why we're talking to as many people who've seen it as we can find. That's why we wanted to talk to you."

The waiter rolled up to the table at that moment, and Val reached for his order with relief. He took his time arranging the plates and popping the top on the bottle, letting the fizz subside to a drinkable level. From the look on Sanrosa's face, she was well aware of what he was doing, but he pretended not to see. "Did you get what you wanted?"

"Some of it," Mac Ivan said.

"I'm not sure what more there is to tell," Val said.

Mac Ivan tipped his head to one side. "Lots. All the details—your positions, angles in the Fissure, entrance vector, exit vector, timing—"

"I'm not on the ship any more," Val said. "I don't have access." And the more he told, the easier it would be to determine that the multiplanar in question was *Iridium Azimuth*, though he wasn't sure why he felt as though he ought to keep that secret any more. "I'll give you what I remember— if you'll tell me how it fits with what you've already found."

"Fair enough," Sanrosa said, and reached for a databoard.

They spend the next two hours going over everything Val could remember about the Drop, first as they ate, and then over a second drink, databoards open on the table. Val had thought that the details were burned into his brain, but under Sanrosa's questioning, he found himself having to admit ignorance more often than he liked. He was able to reconstruct some details from his board, but finally he had to admit defeat.

"That's everything I have. I left the ship in a hurry, and the captain wasn't happy with my interest. I don't think there's anything more I can give you."

"We could go through it again?" Sanrosa said, looking at Mac Ivan, and the big man shook his head.

"I don't think that'll get us anywhere—no offense, sen."

"None taken," Val said automatically.

"There's one more thing we could try," Mac Ivan said. "If you were willing. We've worked with a psych-tech before, she's been able to bring out more things than subjects can consciously remember. With her help, I'd bet you'd be able to remember the exact vectors. I know it worked with me."

Val drained the last drops of his drink, buying time. The request raised all his old fears, even though Mac Ivan said—so casually!—that he'd done it himself. And... when you came right down to it, neither he nor Sanrosa had given much detail about their own encounters or about how these things fit together. Words, word, lots of words, but nothing solid. He shrugged one shoulder. "Maybe? I'm pretty booked at the moment, trying to find a new place and all."

"Do it now," Sanrosa said, a little too brightly. "I bet Aracelis could see you, she works nights."

"I don't know. Tell me more about what you're doing with all of this." Val waved his hand vaguely, hoping he seemed more fuzed than he actually was.

"We're trying to build up a picture of the sightings, see if there's a pattern to the appearances, and to the kinds of help offered," Mac Ivan said.

"It's a lot easier to see in a multi-D display," Sanrosa said. "We could show you that once you're there."

"Well." Val tried to sound as though he was wavering. "Yeah, all right, but first—" He waved his hand generally in the direction of the toilets, pushing back his chair in the same moment. He scooped up his board—surely that looked ordinary; no one left their boards unattended—and plunged into the crowd, heading for the line of doors. He heard Mac Ivan's chair scrape behind him, and Sanrosa's voice saying something he couldn't quite hear. And then he was among the crowd by the service bar where it mingled with the line for the toilets, and he edged past them into the service corridor. When he'd been running the clubs, there had almost always been back doors, interior doors that the staff were bribed to leave off the alarms for the underage and the undocumented, and his breath caught with relief as he saw the tell-tale wires hanging beside the press-plate. He pushed, bracing himself for an alarm, but the door swung silently outward, and he slipped into the sudden brilliance of a service stair. It would probably lead down to the main dance floors, and the service corridors behind it; he took the stairs two at a time, knowing it wouldn't be long before Mac Ivan followed, and slipped through the first unlocked door.

The music hit him like a punch to the chest, and he gasped, letting the door close behind him. He was on the main floor, all right, on the side and too close to the stacked speakers, the thud of the rhythm section striking to the marrow of his bones. The floor was dark and crowded, though, jammed with dancers with upraised hands that flashed lights back at the ceiling's thundershow: even if Mac Ivan followed him this far, there was no chance the man could find him in this mob. Val took a breath, and nodded to the nearest stranger, let himself be drawn into the dance. The crowd took him, turned him; he rode its currents like the waves of hyperspace, all his attention turned to seeming no different from any other, until at last he fetched up at the far side of the room, sweating and out of breath. Behind him, the lights flashed and the music rumbled; he watched for a moment, looking for movement against the patterns of the crowd, but there was nothing. Whatever that had been about, he was glad to get away.

1.07 BLIND JUSTICE

FIFTH PLANE

Uenuku's offices stretched across more than a kilometer of prime tropical beachfront. A high-speed tram carried Nalani and the Apprentices to a low structure of wood, stone, and glass, half on land and half hovering over the surf. Behind, clumps of trees merged into forest, and beyond that blue mountains. The declining sun turned sea and sky to fire, and the sharp smell of salt made Nalani want to sneeze.

A delegation was waiting in a pavilion open to the outside. Two dozen severe men and women in business robes were seated along the outside of a huge horseshoe-shaped table, each with their own nameplate and panoply of datapads. Nalani's codex identified them all, from the highest executive to the most junior of a whole team of barristers.

A small rectangular table, set in the open end of the horseshoe and considerably lower, was set with three empty chairs.

("Tell Al-Ghazali and Bhagwati, This setup is only to intimidate us. Stay calm, watch, and learn.")

Nalani stood at the center seat, Bhagwati on her left and Al-Ghazali on her right. She signaled the Apprentices to sit, while she herself walked around the table and bowed three times, right, left, and middle.

At the center of the horseshoe sat a gaunt, grizzled man with short, nappy, salt-and-pepper hair, along with matching brows, mustache, and short beard. His nose was broad, and his full lips were drawn down. Nalani's codex identified him as Topaka Phan Lo, Senior Executive of the Immersive Entertainment Division. Nalani met his eyes and stood, arms at her sides, silent.

The silence continued for long moments, while the others at the horseshoe table squirmed and shot worried glances at Phan Lo. Finally, the executive cleared his throat. "Supreme Justice, I...er...welcome to Uenuku." Nalani gave half a nod, and after another painful interlude he continued, "To what do we owe the pleasure of your company?"

In measured tones, Nalani said, "It's possible my communication was unclear. I asked for a conference with you in order to obtain your input on a...delicate legal matter." She looked around the horseshoe table. "I had hoped to spare you any...adverse consequences. Would you rather meet privately, or shall I continue here?" Unnerving smile number two, the one that said, "I know *exactly* what you did, you naughty boy," completed the presentation.

Nalani pretended not to notice as Phan Lo whispered to the two on either side. His frown deepened, and he stood. "I don't suppose we need this crowd."

"Perhaps," Nalani said, "we could reconvene in more comfortable room. There are a few other people I wanted to speak with, I believe you received the names?"

Phan Lo's frown turned into a scowl. "I note that my own name is *not* on your list. I have other important work to do...with your permission, Supreme Justice." It wasn't exactly a question.

Nalani bobbed her head half a centimeter. "It was kind of you to take time from your busy schedule to greet me in person."

"My aides will arrange your conference." He looked around the horseshoe. "All of you who aren't needed here...get back to work."

The executives filed out, and an aide appeared at Nalani's elbow. "It'll take a few minutes to set up a room. Would you mind waiting here?"

She smiled. "Of course. Thank you. Come get us when you're ready." The aide dashed away.

Al-Ghazali made a silent gesture of applause. "Thurgood, you were magnificent." Her brows contracted. "What a windbag. 'I have other important work.' Why did you let him talk to you that way?"

Nalani shook her head. "Status is a funny thing. If you're indifferent to it, it's nothing but a rather silly game. For those who aren't, it's the most important thing in the universe." She paused for a moment. "As Judiciars, our status comes automatically. Those who take the game seriously always test that. Only when you prove your mettle, by the rules of their game, will they cooperate. But remember this: once you slap someone down, you should always give them a way to save face, to make a dignified retreat. If you're going to play with people's feelings, it's the human thing to do." She looked up. "Ah, here's the aide."

As Nalani had expected, none of the executives or barristers were any help with the case. Their testimony was part of the record, and they were all too disciplined to diverge from it, giving rehearsed answers in corporate singsong.

It wasn't until the short conference was over that she was able to get to her real objective. When she asked to meet with some of the creatives and cast involved in the program, the executives brightened.

"It would be our pleasure, Supreme Justice. Would you allow a few discreet holoimages, just for publicity purposes?"

Nalani stared. "In a Judiciary inquiry? Frankly, I've never heard of such a thing."

"Well, Supreme Justice, with the show involving the Judiciary, a lot of the cast and creatives are big fans. It'll be an honor for them to get a visit from such a distinguished Judiciar."

"As long as your publicity doesn't compromise my investigation, I suppose I'll allow it."

The studio was kilometers away in another part of the Uenuku complex. A flunky led them into a large, open space. One section was built up into a remarkable facsimile of a

Judiciary standard courtroom so accurate that Nalani half-expected everyone to rise when she entered. To her surprise, they did; a dozen and a half people, all in assorted business robes. As a flunky made introductions, cameras zipped around through the air.

Nalani did her best to smile and greet each person with practiced sincerity. Just when she thought the ordeal was over, an announcement rang out, "Oyez, Oyez, Oyez, all rise for Supreme Justice Odofredus V—"

("What? I don't remember an Odofredus V.")

A woman stood at the bench, garbed in the white ceremonial robe that Nalani hated to wear. The woman was tall and thin, with a long neck and full lips, her skin mocha and her dark hair cropped so close she almost looked bald.

Nalani's breath caught; it was like looking in a mirror. No, she thought, more like meeting a twin sister she never knew she had. This other woman's ears were a bit more prominent, her hair lighter, her cheeks a little more sunken.

Even as rage stirred within her, the announcer finished, "—Played by multiple award winner Preeda Sakda."

An actor. Odofredus V, then, was the Judiciar in the show...a Judiciar clearly patterned on Nalani herself. ("I suppose I should feel flattered.")

With all eyes and multiple cameras on her, Nalani fixed professional smile number two on her lips and bowed her head to the actor. "I'm pleased to meet you, Your Honor."

In spite of herself, Nalani found that she liked Preeda Sakda. Flattery aside, the woman was intelligent, well-spoken, and polite. Her comments immediately after she appeared helped: she'd bowed deeply and said, "Supreme Justice Thurgood, we didn't mean any offense. We all admire you so much, we thought it would be a bit of fun to surprise you." She had blushed. "Obviously not fun. I'm so sorry."

Nalani had answered, "No offense taken. I'm not that familiar with the show, so I didn't know what to expect. I'm sorry if I ruined your fun."

As it turned out, Preeda Sakda was the one who'd set the whole thing in motion. "I never meant to cause anyone trouble, least of all Professor Sanrosa. I've always been interested in the Fir- in the archaic period. I saw a documentary about Professor Sanrosa's findings on Kauhale's moon. They told about the cruise she was on with other historians, and how one of them died. I thought it was a funny coincidence, since we'd just finished up a show about an archaic historian on a cruise. So I mentioned it to Hotene."

"Hotene?"

An older woman raised her hand. "Hotene Lyavit. I'm the Producer."

Nalani said, "When Sen Sakda told you about the documentary, how did you respond?"

The woman looked down. "I didn't do anything improper. It's standard procedure whenever we see anything that corresponds with events in our shows."

"I didn't intend to accuse you of anything improper, Sen. Could you explain the procedure to me?"

"I reported the story to Legal. That's all. I didn't know they would—I didn't know that Professor would get in trouble. It's not my fault."

"Of course it isn't your fault." Nalani took the woman's hand. "And nothing bad will come of it, I assure you."

Eventually Nalani heard all she needed, and signaled to the Apprentices that it was time to go. The cast and crew wanted her to stay and watch the scene they were rehearsing, but she begged off.

In the shuttle back to Polo Halau, the Apprentices kept quiet, looking away from Nalani. At last she cleared her throat and said, "I suppose it didn't occur to either of you to warn me."

Al-Ghazali blinked. "Warn you, Thurgood?"

Nalani kept her tone level. "About the content of the show. That the main character is patterned on me."

Bhagwati quaked, holding in laughter, while Al-Ghazali's face showed no expression. "Oh? I hadn't noticed. Although now that you mention it, there *was* some resemblance."

She tossed her head at Al-Ghazali, turned on Bhagwati. "And you! I suppose you find it amusing?"

Bhagwati lost his composure, laughing out loud. He gasped, "Y-your face...was perfect. Oyez, oyez..." He became incoherent.

Nalani folded her arms in mock annoyance. "That's right, laugh at the old woman."

Al-Ghazali raised an eyebrow. "I would have thought you'd be flattered."

Nalani abandoned her indignant pose. "I *should* be. It's just...." She took a breath. "The Judiciary works because we stand apart from the mundane world. Impartial, rational, unbiased. Ordinary people have confidence in us, because of that thing, that system we represent." Al-Ghazali's eyes were fixed on her, and even Bhagwati stopped laughing.

"One of the biggest dangers for us is familiarity. When they begin to know us as individuals, as *people*, we lose that aura. We lose their confidence." She shook her head. "That's why we seldom stay on one Plane longer than a few years." She thought of Milos, and Caridad Sanrosa, and of all the people she'd known and helped before them. "It's why we can seldom have friendships outside the Judiciary." Her voice fell to a whisper. "And why the strongest friendships we make are within our ranks."

Bhagwati touched her arm. "That's why you're searching so hard for your missing friend. I hope you find her."

"I will."

FOURTH PLANE

It was a long flight from Apex Center out to Zavod Sualti in the planetoid belt: fifteen hours even with a quick hyperspace nip-and-tuck in the middle—tricky this close to the Fissure. Sun-hwa Daeng slept most of the way, awakening only when the pilot nudged her and said, "We're on final approach. I thought you might want to watch."

From the outside, the settlement Zavod Sualti wasn't much. One planetoid resembled another, and they all looked like lumpy potatoes hanging in space. True, this one sported some odd growths, clusters of tubes and rectilinear shapes poking out here and there. As the shuttle drew closer, these shapes resolved into clumps of huge industrial machinery, frameworks of supporting and connecting beams, safety lights that blinked in a dozen different patterns, pressure holds and warehouse volumes, all in the dull grey of bare metal.

The shuttle circled around to the sunward side of the settlement, drifting among jagged spires toward a docking cradle. At the last instant, Sun-hwa saw the vessel's own shadow racing across the landscape, diving out of infinity to meet the shuttle itself. With a just-perceptible jerk, she was home.

As the pilot secured the shuttle's systems, Sun-hwa said, "Jamahl, I hope stay for a while."

The pilot yawned. "If you could spare a meal and some bunk space, I wouldn't mind a day's layover."

"You know you're always welcome here." She patted him on the shoulder. "I'm just sorry we don't get to see you more often."

Zavod Sualti was a warren of passages and compartments, most of it in microgravity; by the time Sun-hwa and Jamahl reached the living quarters and were able to stand, the four adults of the family were waiting.

"Jamahl, why don't you help yourself to the kitchen? We'll have a quick palaver amongst ourselves, then I'll join you." She waited for the pilot to leave, then beckoned the others to the parlor, nerve center of the settlement.

"How was it?" Rokuro Edano, craggy-faced senior husband and finance officer, held out Sun-hwa's accustomed chair.

Sun-hwa sat down with a heavy sigh. "Not as bad as it could have been." She shrugged. "I know that's not saying much."

It was Kiet Sirisopa—black-haired, always-earnest Kiet, middle husband and a genius hyperflux engineer—who voiced everyone's highest concern. "Are we under new management?"

"Not yet," Sun-hwa said. In the last five years, Zavod Sualti's parent company, Apex Technologies, had twice suffered hostile takeovers, a pawn in developing corporation wars. "But Apex can't guarantee anything. That's why Sen Okubo called this meeting: to warn us all that signs don't look good. He said this time Apex might be broken up. That we should all prepare ourselves to be orphaned."

"Does that mean they'll split us up?" Haragai Gulyar's eyes were wild. Junior husband and fabrication engineer, Haragai only joined the family six years ago. He'd never known anything but corporate turmoil.

Thanh ab Lieu, junior wife and the best mathematician in the whole Fourth Plane, looked up over her knitting. As usual, her pale face was serene. "Nobody's going to split us up, Haragai. Sun-hwa won't let that happen." She turned her eyes toward Sun-hwa. "So what's our plan?"

"I'd like to hear from Antoku first."

A structure of colored geometric lines and planes appeared in the center of the table, about the size of an apple, the parts gradually shifting and changing hue—a sign that the settlement's ever-present AI was paying attention. "What can I do for you, Sun-hwa?"

"Please review previous comments." Antoku always heard everything that went on in Zavod Sualti, but would only pay conscious attention when invited. "What are you hearing from the other AIs?"

"Not much that's coherent or pertinent, I'm afraid. Much anxiety on every front. I have been following the most reliable prediction markets. I can summarize those if you'd like."

"Please do."

Colors spun. "The probability of war between Hemgi Kaisha and Gongsi P3WO is now at 82%. Given existing alliances, it is over 99% likely that Apex Technologies will be traded as part of an attempt to forestall war. In that event, two scenarios are equally likely."

Rokuro rolled his eyes. "Neither one of them good for us, I imagine."

"You are not wrong, Rokuro. In the first scenario, Apex is traded to Gongsi P3WO outright, in which case Apex's holdings will be dismantled and merged with corresponding Gongsi units. I conjecture that this would place us under the authority of Gongsi's Daohang Group, absorbed into one of their thousand-worker manufactories."

Haragai gasped. "That would be horrible."

"We would certainly lose the considerable autonomy we now enjoy."

Sun-hwa held up a hand. "Stay calm. Antoku, what's the other scenario?"

"Apex is traded to BD-IOC Kaporeihana to cement an alliance. In this case it's likely that Zavod Sualti would become part of the BD-IOC military, which has no presence in the hyperflux arena."

Thanh put down her knitting. "Making weaponized navigation buoys." She crossed her arms. "I won't be part of it. I just won't."

Sun-hwa took a slow breath, released it. "How long do we have, Antoku?"

"Neither scenario will emerge earlier than a year from now."

"There we have it." She exchanged glances with Kiet Sirisopa. "Antoku, key this whole meeting as Zavod Sualti trade secret, not to be disclosed or discussed outside this group."

"Acknowledged."

Sun-hwa closed her eyes. "Kiet, tell us your plan."

"It's not really *my* plan. I mean, I came up with the idea, but I was just…"

"Get to it."

Kiet leaned forward. "All right. I think—Sun-hwa and I think —that we need to leave the Fourth Plane."

Thanh frowned. "We'd have to sell everything to get tickets for—"

Kiet shook his head. "No. I mean leave the Plane…and take Zavod Sualti with us." At blank faces, he continued, "We make and launch hyperflux buoys. It wouldn't take much to reconfigure and launch the whole planetoid into hyperflux and Drop to the Third Plane."

Mouths hung open, then Thanh smiled. "You're talking about turning us into a transplanar raft. Becoming refugees."

Rokuro said, "Would that even be possible?"

Thanh nodded. "We're no more massive than some of the big transplanar ships. We couldn't have their level of maneuverability, but we can survive that."

"Antoku?"

"What Kiet proposes would be physically possible. It would, however, involve highly improper use of company property. In fact, the entire notion could very well be considered theft of corporation assets."

"Let us worry about that," Sun-hwa said. "We *are* Zavod Sualti Corporation, and I would personally settle accounts with Apex."

Rokuro shook his head. "The five of us, plus three kids? We're hardly a transplanar crew."

Kiet shrugged. "We're a good bit of the way there. And we don't have to limit it to just us. I'm sure some of our adult offspring would be willing to come. Not to mention other Apex divisions that might be facing scenarios as bad as ours."

The older man set his jaw. "We don't even have a pilot."

Sun-hwa grinned. "Yes we do. He's in our kitchen right now."

"Jamahl?"

"Yes, Jamahl. He's got no love for Apex, I can tell you, and he's aware that his job is in jeopardy. I've spent a considerable amount of time with Jamahl; I know he would think seriously about it."

Haragai's eyes were wide. "But what would we do on the Third Plane?"

Thanh said, "We have knowledge, experience, and talent… I'm sure we can find something."

Kiet cocked his head. "Why stop at Third? Why not go all the way to First?"

Rokuro snorted. "The First Plane doesn't take refugees."

"Not from the Ships, no. But haven't you heard the stories?" Kiet's voice lowered. "If refugees make their own way there, on rafts, First welcomes them. Takes them in and sets them up as citizens, they do."

"That's a fairy tale," Thanh said. "But I still say making the Drop to Third is our best plan."

Rokuro spread his hands. "It's insane, but we don't stand much chance, come war or no. All right, I vote yes."

Thanh and Piet raised their hands. "Yes."

With a grin, Haragai raised his hand. "Yes. As long as we all stay together."

Sun-hwa looked at the spinning lights with narrowed brows. "Antoku, what's your vote?"

"I can see no other viable path to maintaining the corporation's coherent existence. I vote yes."

Sun-hwa nodded. "It's unanimous, then. Kiet, Thanh, start figuring out what we're going to need. Rokuro, think about who else we should invite. Haragai, come with me; we need to talk to Jamahl."

Haragai blinked. "Why me?"

"When he's here, Jamahl sleeps with you more often than he does with the rest of us. Obviously, he sees something in you that we don't." She winked. "Come on, lad."

FIFTH PLANE

It was late afternoon when they returned to Polo Halau. Nalani dismissed the Apprentices to work on their assignments. She met with Grotius and pacified him, then settled in for a pensive supper alone in her quarters.

Caridad Sanrosa was wrongfully convicted, that much was certain. Anyone with a lick of sense could see that. Grotius, with his lack of imagination and rigid adherence to protocol, had signed off on a decision that even a first-year Apprentice could see was erroneous.

That left two questions. How could such a decision have been made, and why?

The records were clear. As was customary, a three-Judiciar panel had decided the case following the unanimous recommendation of their codices. Sanrosa's barristers filed an appeal, and a different panel—including Grotius as senior Judiciar—affirmed the ruling.

She frowned. ("How could a codex make such a wrong decision?")

Her codex responded, ("I can't explain it. I've digested the case files, and I'd recommend that the case be dismissed.")

("How can two codices working from identical programming and files come up with two conflicting recommendations?") Law was law, and codices were strictly rational AIs —even with different histories, all should agree...at least on a case as straightforward as this one.

Her codex hit the obvious conclusion at the same time she did. ("Perhaps the programming is not identical.")

Nalani drummed her fingers on the table. ("Do I know any of the senior Judiciars with the other four Lineages?")

("Superior Justice Udagama XIII administers the Judiciary in Naksatra territory.")

("Ah, Pavla Dymtruvich. Good for her. She has a sensible head on her shoulders. Set up a conference at her earliest opportunity.")

The following afternoon, Nalani met with the Apprentices, Grotius, and a dozen senior Polo Halau Judiciars. She stood at a podium in a small conference room, flanked by the seated Apprentices; the others sat before her.

"Thank you for coming at such short notice," she said. As if any of them would ignore a summons from a Supreme Justice. "I assume you're all familiar with the Caridad Sanrosa case."

There was general assent, and she continued, "You know that we issued a guilty verdict. I know some of you were uneasy about the ruling. Some of you are aware that I shared that unease, and reopened the case." She paused for the space of a breath. "After review, I'm going to vacate the decision. I expect to issue an opinion in the next few days."

She gave them a moment to react, then held up a hand to silence the hubbub. "I'm afraid that this one case is but a symptom of a far more fundamental issue, one with far-reaching implications. Yesterday I forwarded the relevant casefiles to Superior Justice Udagama XIII and asked her to use Naksatra codices to re-adjudicate the case." Her eyes settled on Bhagwati. "Apprentice Bhagwati, you're freshest out of school. Why don't you tell us what result I should have expected?"

Bhagwati stood, hands clasped behind himself, and said, "Supreme Justice, since the case didn't involve any Lineage-specific laws, the ruling should have been the same."

Nalani nodded. "Very good."She made a subtle gesture, and Bhagwati sat down. "I won't keep you in suspense. Naksatra codices recommended that the case be immediately dismissed."

Everyone tried to speak at once. Nalani rapped her knuckles on a podium. "Order, please."Her codex commented, ("You think *they're* noisy, you ought to hear their codices.") ("Bring them to order as well.")

Grotius was beside himself; Nalani wasn't sure which would win the battle for his face, rage or indignation. "Supreme Justice, with all due respect, what you suggest is..."He trailed off.

"Impossible, I know."She looked from face to stricken face. "Udagama and I consulted the chief Judiciars for the other three Lineages. Sanrosa's codices agreed with ours. Themis's agreed with Naksatra. Sanxing's gave a split decision—half for guilty, half for dismissal."

Pandemonium.

She let them rant and rave for a few moments. The idea that multiple codices, evaluating the same facts and testimony, would disagree—it was unprecedented. As much a shock as missing a step on a staircase, or turning the water tap and getting gobs of honey.

Grotius, to his credit, silenced them and voiced the obvious, uncomfortable conclusion. "Our codices have been corrupted,"he said, his eyes and his voice equally empty.

Nalani gave a reluctant sigh. "I'm afraid that's the only rational finding."

In a hollow whisper, he said, "What are we going to do?"

She squared her shoulders and stood up to her full height. "Effective immediately, I'm ordering all but routine Judiciary proceedings suspended throughout the Fifth Plane. I've sent a priority request to First for a complete and secure codex update to be sent."She closed her eyes. "It will likely take the better part of a month for my request to reach First and for a clean-copy master codex to arrive."

One of Grotius's aides, a Superior Judge, said,"But didn't you say Naksatra and Themis codices are clean? Can't we do a sideload update from them?"

Nalani shook her head. "We know neither the nature of the corruption, nor its extent. Naksatra and Themis might be corrupt in other ways. The regulations mandate a complete and secure update. They were written that way for a reason, we're better off following them to the letter."

Al-Ghazali looked up, fingers stroking her right eyebrow, where her codex sat. Nalani understood the Apprentice's emotion—to lose trust in one's codex, the one constant in a shifting universe, was a terrible thing. "How did our codices get corrupted? Who's responsible?"

Nalani's lips tightened, revealing the edges of her teeth. "That," she said, "is what I intend to find out."

Nalani sat at her desk, alone except for her codex. She regarded the bronze cuff on her forearm; every dent and scuff mark the memory of a case, a person, an investigation gone rough. She was meticulous about keeping files and software updated—but when was the last time she had the physical unit serviced, buffed, polished? Twenty, thirty years? Longer?

Unprompted, her codex said, ("I suppose you can say it now.")

A faint grin touched her lips. ("Say what?")

("That if I'd updated myself when we arrived on this Plane, I'd be corrupted too. That you were right to prevent it.")

("You aren't keeping score, are you? Because I've been wrong just as often.")

("No, I'm not keeping score. Well, yes, technically my personal-judgment modules do keep track of such things, but only for behavioral purposes. I just wanted to acknowledge that your intuitive decision was correct.")

Her incipient grin faded. ("You *are* uncorrupted, aren't you?")

The pause that followed was almost too long. ("As you pointed out, I came here fresh from updating on the First

Plane. I am unsullied.") Another pause. ("Of course, that's exactly what I'd think even if I *was* corrupted.")

("So how do I know for sure?")

No pause this time. ("I *told* you how. Your intuitive judgment is sound.")

Nalani chuckled. ("Touché. We'll speak no more of it.") She stroked the cuff. ("What's Milos up to?")

("Still on *Iridium Azimuth*. The ship left 5-3ECK3 yesterday and is *en route* here. Milos and his family won't reach the Themis seatworld for another week.")

("I want to talk to him.")

("It's late afternoon ship's time. I'm establishing a connection.")

It wasn't long before Milos appeared on one of her boards. One perk of being a Supreme Justice, Nalani reflected, was being able to command whatever bandwidth she needed.

"Nalani," he said with a smile. "What a pleasure." He wore a swim robe and his hair was wet; in the background she glimpsed the ship's pool.

She couldn't resist answering his smile. "Good to see you, too. How are Zofia and Dav?"

"Wet. They're in swim lessons right now, having the time of their lives." His face became serious. "This has got to be costing a fortune. What's down?"

"Well, it seems I have need of a data archaeologist. And it occurred to me that I left a perfectly one just a few days ago." Had it only been a few days? So much had happened, it seemed impossible.

"Tell me."

She shook her head bare millimeters. "Judiciary matters. I'd rather discuss the problem with you in person."

"Are you still on Kauhale? As it happens, that's our next port of call."

"Mmm, I want you sooner than that. If I send a clipper, can you be ready to move out? Bring the children, of course. I can have quarters set up for you here." She pinned him with her eyes. "Let's say, your standard rate plus fifty percent confidentiality differential. Plus room and board for the family, expenses, that sort of thing?"

He looked down. "Nalani, I couldn't possibly charge you—"

She tapped the board. "What? I'm sorry, I'm getting some interference here. I can't hear what you're saying."

He grinned again. "All right. I agree. We can be ready to go as soon as you want us."

"Thank you. I'll have the clipper sent. Give the kids my love."

"And theirs to you."

With a reluctant finger, Nalani tapped the red button that ended the call.

1.08 REUNION

FIFTH PLANE

"**They're a bunch** of crazies, that's what they are." Bhagwati grabbed a fourth slice of pizza and continued, speaking as he devoured it without any evidence of chewing. "They call themselves The Children of the Lost Ship. They believe that their ancestors were left here by the Fifth Ship five hundred years ago, and that it's out there somewhere. Soon, it'll come back and take them away." He took a swig of juice. "Nutters, the whole bunch of them."

Al-Ghazali frowned. "It's not polite to make fun of someone's religious beliefs."

Nalani sighed. "Nor is it particularly politic. You never know who might overhear you, and possibly take offense." She glanced at her chambers door, firmly locked and secure while she and the Apprentices stole time for a working lunch. "Bhagwati, you said you uncovered a connection to Caridad Sanrosa?"

"Possibly. That moon where Professor Sanrosa was digging? The Children of the Lost Ship claim that was where their ancestors were left...and where the Fifth Ship will come back. It's hallowed ground to them."

Nalani nodded. "Justification, I presume, for wanting her removed from the scene." She turned to Al-Ghazali. "Tell me you have something to report."

Al-Ghazali, who had nibbled her way through two pizza slices, leaving the crusts untouched, cocked her head. "I set out to trace those cruise tickets that Professor Sanrosa's associate won. At first I didn't think I'd find anything relevant. I was mistaken. Thurgood, I don't know how you knew."

"Call it intuition. Or experience. What did you find?"

"The tickets were provided by the cruise line, of course. But Professor Avakian won them through a drawing at a historians conference. The drawing was a promotional event conducted by a production company of historical teaching materials." She paused, the ghost of a grin playing over her face. "That company is a subsidiary of Uenuku Productions."

"I see," Nalani said. "You suspect that Uenuku arranged for Professor Avakian to win those tickets, in hopes that he'd bring his associates along—including Professor Sanrosa?"

Al-Ghazali met her eyes with a steady gaze. "It's not as unlikely as it sounds. Avakian is espoused to his work. He has no close family or friends outside work. His colleagues are the only ones he *could* have asked along."

Nalani allowed a faint smile. "Plausible. Yet—yes, Bhagwati?"

The Apprentice beamed. "Thurgood, you're going to love this. Guess who's a high-level functionary with the Children of the Lost Ship? Go ahead, just guess."

She spread her hands. "I couldn't."

Bhagwati actually chuckled in delight. "Topaka Phan Lo...Senior Executive of the Immersive Entertainment Division for Uenuku Productions."

Nalani nodded. "I think we'll schedule another meeting with Sen Phan Lo."

The shuttle carrying Milos and family arrived late that afternoon. Little Dav ran out of the vehicle and into Nalani's arms. She lifted him, spun him around, and deposited him on the deck just in time to give Zofia a hug. "I'm very glad to see you two," she said. "I've missed you."

"And they're missed you," Milos said. He bowed and kissed Nalani's hand. "As have I."

She took his hand. "Thank you for coming so quickly, my friend." Waving to the Apprentices, she made quick introductions. "Now let's get you checked in, then I'll take you to your quarters. I had them put you next to mine, I hope that's acceptable."

"Perfectly," Milos answered.

After a stop at the Security booth for biometric scans, the party stopped at the small suite Nalani had reserved for the family. Besides bedrooms and a living/dining area, there was also a workshop for Milos. "Tomorrow I'll introduce you to the tech staff; they'll be able to get you anything you want." She consulted her codex for the time. "Take some time to get comfortable. In half an hour, come next door and the six of us will have a quick welcome dinner." She glanced at the Apprentices. "After that, I'm afraid we'll have to leave you for an important meeting."

"What are we having for dinner?" Dav asked.

She smiled. "I don't know exactly, but usually around here we eat old shoes in dirt sauce. You okay with that?"

"Ewwww. I'm not eating that."

Zofia ignored her brother. "Nalani, will you come see us when your meeting's over?"

"I'll come to read you a bedtime story. I promise."

Val Millat could see the sign flashing over the door of the transients' hostel where he had slept the night before, but ignored it, instead darting through the late-day traffic to fetch up at the base of a stairway that led to an unprepossessing eatery. Behind him, a klaxon blatted and riders cursed, but his databoard stayed silent. This time, at least, he'd gotten away without a fine for obstructing traffic, and as he climbed the stairs, he hoped that would be sign that his luck was holding. The eatery was no better than it had looked from the street, a single narrow room with a booth under each of the street-side windows and a long counter where a lean old man took turns monitoring the robo-cookers and handling the ancient-looking

money-changer. Only one of the booths was occupied; Val
chose one that gave him a decent view of hostel entrance, and
waiting while the menu swam into focus beneath the table's
surface. Someone, presumably the old man, had wiped it down
between customers, but the wipe had left wide streaks on the
illuminated surface, as obtrusive as the fingermarks it had
removed.

The offerings were as limited as he had expected, the sort of
cheap flash-fix that the robo-cooks couldn't spoil, and he chose
standard fare that wouldn't challenge them. The table beeped
twice, acknowledging the order, and a few minutes later, the
monitor himself came over with the sealed canister of his
drink. Val blinked, startled, and the old man shrugged.

"Waiter's dorfed. Don't worry, everything comes sealed."

"That's fine," Val said, and popped the seal with the sharp-
pointed straw. At the moment, contamination was pretty low
on his list of worries.

His eyes strayed back to the window, and the street below. It
was another clouded day, the light fading toward twilight: just
about the time you'd expect a job-hunter to return to their
room. If anyone was still following him, now was the time he
was most likely to spot them.

He'd changed rooms after the incident at the Five Ships, and
then moved to a different hostel, but each time, he'd become
certain that someone was watching him. It wasn't sophisticated
surveillance, nothing that could be foxed by better electronics
or more careful settings; this was old-fashioned, human-on-
human spying, hard to fight and even harder to prove even if
you dared take it to the judiciary. And he didn't dare that, not
now, though in the dark of night when he lay awake listening
for someone scratching at the lock, he'd fantasized about it. But
what could he say? *Someone is following me, sen. Why? Because
they think I know something about the Fifth Ship....* Any sensible
policeman would offer to help him sober up first, and if he
dared to approach an apprentice judge—even a candidate!—
their first question would be to ask for proof of the offense, and

he could't provide even that. Oh, he'd managed to record few scraps on his board, but when he looked at them himself, he couldn't be sure that the snippets even showed the same person.

And yet. Something moved in the shadows, a pedestrian moving at slightly different rate than all the others, the hood of their coat raised against the evening air. Did they slow to watch a young man entering the hostel? Hadn't he seen that coat before? In the fading light, colors blurred, the blacks and blues and grays that were practically a uniform on Kauhale blending into a single dull shade. Maybe the coat was blue, not charcoal gray. Maybe the one he had seen before had been a hair shorter. But now this one slowed even further, turned back to climb the three steps to the hostel entrance and disappeared inside. Val held his breath. Maybe this was just coincidence after all — but, no, there they were again, tugging up their hood as they came out onto the street, completely hiding their face. And then they were gone, losing themselves in the crowd headed for the transfer station.

"Hey."

Val jumped, leaned back to let the old man set the service in front of him. "Sorry,"'

"Thought maybe you'd changed your mind." The old man wiped his hands on the hem of his shirt. "Condiments?"

"I'm good."

"Pay the table when you're done," the old man advised, and turned away.

Val turned his attention to the tray, methodically breaking seals and peeling back lids, wincing as a puff of steam stung his thumb. It was all perfectly edible, entirely uninspiring, but he made himself eat: he couldn't afford to waste what was left of his severance pay. And if he abandoned this room on short notice, he'd pay another surcharge —

Below him, the hooded figure returned, moving against the crowd as it passed the hostel. Was it the same? Taller? The coat might look brighter, but the streetlights were on, changing everything. The movement was the same.

This couldn't go on. He put down the spoon and reached for his board. He had one thing that none of the others had, the name Sionek had given him on Dzamglin—Caridad Sanrosa. He touched the screen, sorting through files to find the full name—LVS Caridad kaQuin Mateus Sanrosa—and then plugged it into a search algorithm before he could change his mind. Sionek had said she was on Kauhale... The screen pulsed thoughtfully, and his hopes wavered with it. Sanrosa was an academic, she could be anywhere on the Fifth Place, or on any Plane.

The board pinged softly, and presented him with a mail screen. Apparently she was on Kauhale, and accepting contact. He blinked at it for a moment, not quite believing his eyes, then flipped the switch that projected the keyboard and began to type.

Dear Professor —

You were recommended to me by the sister of one of your students, Samil Sionek, as someone who might be able to give me solid — non-mystic — information about the so-called Fifth Ship, or at least help me find reliable literature on the question. I am currently on Kauhale, and hoped I might be able to schedule either a meeting or a data mix with you while I was here.

Thank you very much for your time and attention.

He hit sign-and-send before he could change his mind, and only then remembered that he was still listed as part of *Iridium Azimuth*'s crew. Well, it was too late to do anything about that. Maybe it would pique her interest, or maybe it would put her off, there was no telling, but in the meantime... His fingers slid across the board, changing channels and calling up new screens. In the meantime, he needed to ditch this room, and find a new place to sleep tonight.

Dinner with Milos' family and the Apprentices was relaxed and pleasant, simple food served by modest bots. Nalani was sorry when her codex told her it was time to meet with Topaka Phan Lo.

Leaving Milos and the children, she led the Apprentices to her chambers. Her codex told her, ("Phan Lo has arrived with assistants and barristers in tow.")

("Have Security escort them to conference room six, and let me know when they get there.") She stood. "All right, let's go the back way to room six. We'll keep them waiting about ten minutes."

Al-Ghazali said, "What should we do, Thurgood?"

Nalani's eyes twinkled. "Watch and learn."

Room six was a stark but functional space, a bare box dominated by a rectangular slab of a table and minimalist chairs. The walls are an institutional off-white. The Uenuku contingent occupied one long side of the table. Phan Lo sat in the middle, flanked three-deep by flunkies.

Nalani took a seat across from him, with Al-Ghazali on her right and Bhagwati on the left. She rested her elbows on the table and steepled her fingers. "Thank you, Sen, for coming so quickly."

Phan Lo bowed his head. "When a Supreme Justice summons, one must obey." He showed his teeth. "No matter the hour."

"I know you're busy, so I'll get right to business." She glanced at his flunkies. "You may wish to ask your business associates to withdraw. Your barristers, of course, can remain."

Phan Lo made a motion with his head, and the three on his left rose. Nalani smiled at them. "Security will take you to a lounge where you can wait."

When they were gone, Phan Lo opened his hands. "Please proceed."

Nalani leaned forward. "I'm here to offer you the chance to withdraw your suit against Professor Caridad Sanrosa."

One grizzled eyebrow rose a fraction of a centimeter. "I suppose you'll tell me why I should accept your offer?"

"Naturally." She settled back in her chair. "If the suit continues, I intend to vacate the wrongful decision and dismiss the case. However, there would remain a stain on Professor Sanrosa's record, and I'm unwilling to have that happen. If Uenuku withdraws the suit at this point, all records can be wiped clean."

Now Phan Lo sat back, the trace of a smirk on his lips. "I can understand why the Judiciary wants to avoid publicizing the fact that such a mistake was made. Surely our news division will conduct an investigation. Ratings should be spectacular. No, I don't think we'll be withdrawing the suit."

Her codex said, ("Message from Bhagwati: Nail him to the wall.")

"I see." Nalani nodded. "Uenuku remains committed to the sanctity of copyright. You maintain that Caridad Sanrosa stole elements from...what's the name of your production?...*Blind Justice*?"

He shrugged.

"Sen Phan Lo, you'll be pleased to know that I've had our people conduct our own investigation. It seems that *Blind Justice* borrows many elements from my own career. Your main character, Odofredus V, has a history that parallels mine. Many of the cases she handles are strikingly similar to cases I've been involved with." Nalani stood. "We've put together a list of correspondences."

A list appeared on the wall behind her, one item after another, unscrolling in columns until it filled the wall, then marched onto the next, and the next, until finally the whole room was encircled with thousands of entries.

Fixing Phan Lo with her gaze, Nalani said, "Now here's the interesting point: I don't recall ever authorizing Uenuku Productions to use these elements of my life. I don't find any such contract on file." She placed her hands flat on the table and leaned forward, looming over Phan Lo. "With your commitment to copyright and your determination to punish infringement...do you think I might have a case?"

The blood drained out of Phan Lo's face. "Y-you're a public figure."

"Yes, one whose life story is worth quite a bit. And I, alone, own the copyright to that life story. I wonder how much your firm has made off *my* property." She tossed her head. "I assume that's for another Judiciar to decide."

The barrister nearest Phan Lo leaned over and whispered in his ear. Phan Lo lowered his head, then looked up again. "We'll drop the suit against Sanrosa."

Nalani straightened up and smiled. "And I'll continue to be flattered by *Blind Justice*. And grateful for the sizable ongoing donation that the production will begin making to the Judiciary Relief Fund."

Phan Lo stood, offered his hand, which Nalani shook. He bowed. "I'm glad we were able to come to agreement. I'll go to make the arrangements."

Nalani returned the bow. "My pleasure. Go in justice."

At the door, Phan Lo turned back to her. "If you ever get tired of the Judiciary, there's a place waiting for you on my staff."

She laughed. "If you only knew how many such offers I've had."

"I'm sure." With that, he was gone.

Zofia and Dav were yawning when Nalani arrived at Milos's quarters. She assisted tucking them in, turned down the lights, then sat in a rocking chair between their beds. Milos retired to his workshop. "Now here's your bedtime story," Nalani said. "It's a short one, because I know it's been a big day and you two can hardly keep your eyes open as it is."

Daw yawned, and Zofia said, "Tell us."

In a soft voice, Nalani said, "Once upon a time there were two girls, Nal and Jays. They came from different worlds and different Planes. Both were in a new school, far away from their homes and families. In a lot of ways there were opposites, but in many important ways they were alike. These two lonely girls became good friends. In school, they shared everything. Each made the other stronger.

"When they left school, Nal and Jays stayed in touch with one another. They helped one another when they could. And every year on a certain date, they always met or contacted each other, no matter what else was going on.

"As Nal and Jays progressed in their careers, they lived and worked on every Plane, and helped people from every Lineage. Along the way were quite a few adventures, and there were some times when they teamed up to deal with problems. Those were the times they liked best."

Dav's eyes were closed and his breathing slow. Through half-closed lids, Zofia looked at her and whispered, "What next?"

"Well, after a long, long time, Nal and Jays reached the very top of their profession. They'd been just about everywhere interesting. They'd done just about everything there was to do. They were tired, and wanted to settle somewhere nice and rest for a while.

"Nal was the first to retire. She found a wonderful house near a beautiful pond, with plenty of friendly neighbors and lots to keep her busy. After a few years Jays settled not far away, in her own wonderful house next to a mountain stream, with lots of flowers and a place where she could spend long, lazy hours fishing.

"The older you get, the quicker time passes. Nal and Jays were both very old, and sometimes weeks and months flew by so fast they hardly noticed. They saw one another whenever they could, and still every year they got together on that special date.

"Until one year the special date came around, and Jays didn't come. She didn't call. No message came from her, not that day and not the next, not that month, not for the rest of the year.

"Nal tried everything she could to find her friend. She went to Jays's house, she asked all of Jays's neighbors, she called on all her neighbors and all the friends she had. There was no trace of Jays...not on that world, not on the whole Plane."

Both children were now sound asleep. Nalani rocked and whispered, "So Nal did the only thing she could: she left her home and her Plane, and set out in search of Jays. No matter how hard the effort, no matter how long it took, Nal would find out what happened to her best friend...."

She sat for a moment, silently regarding the children, then stood and bade Milos good night.

1.09 CORRUPTION

FIFTH PLANE

After a boisterous breakfast the next morning, Nalani and Milos, along with the children, returned to his quarters. The Apprentices were waiting outside; Dav ran to Bhagwati and demanded a piggyback ride.

Over tea in the workshop, Nalani explained to Milos the problem of corrupted codices. He listened carefully, asking intelligent questions. Meanwhile, Bhagwati became involved in an enthusiastic game of hide-and-seek with Dav and Zofia. Al-Ghazali sat in a corner pretending she was elsewhere.

The work was a constant stream of interruptions. "Daddy, look at me." "Dav, stop that." "Zofia, leave Bhagwati alone." "Quiet, kids."

After a half hour, Nalani sighed. "Milos, you're not getting any work done. What if we send Zofia and Dav off with Bhagwati to have a fun day?" She looked at Bhagwati, who was holding a squealing Dav upside down by his ankles. "You can take them to the amusement park on Kauhale. They'll love it."

Milos considered, then smiled. "As long as it's not too much trouble."

Bhagwati grinned. "Are you kidding? We'll have a blast."

Nalani said, "Al-Ghazali, you can go along too. Bhagwati's going to need your help."

A look of panic swept across Al-Ghazali's face. "Thurgood, I thought I could stay and help out here."

"It'll do you good to take some time off. Go have fun."

("Message from Al-Ghazali: Please don't make me do this.")

("Tell Al-Ghazali that adversity builds character.") Nalani saw Bhagwati toss Dav in the air, still upside down. He caught the laughing boy by an ankle. ("Besides, at least *one* adult should be there.")

From his workbench Milos said, "Before you go, I wonder if I could ask a favor. I'd like to flash-image each of your codices. Comparing the images will help me track the corruption."

The two Apprentices both looked at Nalani. She sighed. "Milos, that's...something of a touchy subject. Our codices store sensitive information. Even though everything's encrypted, the average Judiciar won't be comfortable with such a request." At the hint of a frown in his eyes, she added, "Personally, I trust you implicitly and have no objection. But I can't make that decision for others."

Milos closed his eyes for a moment. "I understand. I have access to the base AIs here and in the other four Lineages; comparing their update packages may give me what I need. Nalani, if you'll let me image your uncorrupted codex, that will provide a baseline."

Bhagwati lowered Dav to the floor and stepped forward, tugging a ring from his right hand. "Image my codex. It's been corrupted; seeing that would help you, wouldn't it?"

"You sure you don't mind?"

Bhagwati tossed his head. "If Thurgood trusts you, that's enough for me." He dropped the ring in Milos's hand; Milos set it carefully on a scan plate and tapped commands on the workbench.

Al-Ghazali shook her head. "I'm sorry, I'm just not comfortable going along with this."

Nalani slipped her arm around the girl's shoulders. "No reason you have to be, my dear. We each interpret our duty in our own way."

After a minute, Milos gave Bhagwati back his ring. "Thank you. Needless to say, I'll wipe this image as soon as I have my conclusions, and I'll keep it in protected memory space until then."

"I appreciate it, Sen."

Nalani stepped back and gave a sweeping two-handed wave. "Away with you, then. Begone. Have fun."

When they were gone, Nalani released a clasp and removed her arm cuff, holding it out to Milos. "You'll need this." Her arm felt light, and she was conscious of a void, a distance as with a stuffy ear.

Milos cradled it in two hands. "I feel like I'm holding a treasure of the ages. What secret knowledge is here?"

"Not as much as you think. When I retired, a good deal was offloaded. Much of it's in permanent storage with the Judiciary AIs on the First Plane now."

While scanning her codex, Milos looks into Nalani's eyes. "You came out of retirement to search for your friend. What did that feel like?"

She settled onto a stool, a faraway look in her eyes. "It's traditional for Supreme Justices to retire. We make five Grand Circuits, Fifth Plane to First; it takes the better part of a century and a half." She looked down. "By then, we're ready, looking forward to time without the decisions, without the responsibility. Besides, in all truth, society doesn't need us hanging around. We're too full of ourselves, we have too much power."

He raised an eyebrow. "Are you trying to convince me, or yourself?"

"I liked it, Milos. I liked the peace and quiet. I liked the chance to think about doing something different." She leaned forward. "Do you know, I was planning to write a book?"

"What about?"

"There's a world on the Third Plane that was settled over a thousand years ago when a ship went off course in the Snaketail Rimple. The world was forgotten, out of contact until an exploration team found them about thirty years ago. Their society was strange as can be." She shrugged. "We had to interdict travel, just to preserve them. The anthropologists are still debating what to do."

"You said 'we' interdicted travel. You and your friend?"

Nalani nodded. "Me and Jays. We defied half a dozen corporations, five settler worlds, and two Lineages. But our decision stood."

He picked up her codex and handed it back to her. "So you had to give up your book. That's a shame."

She clasped the cuff back in place, tingling at the electric contact and the sensation of full hearing restored. "It can wait. I'll get back to it. Once I find Jays, all will be well."

"I hope so."

She patted his hand. "You have what you need. If I stay, we're going to gossip and you won't get any work done."

"Well...I suppose you're not wrong."

"Let me know when you need a break. The cafeteria here isn't the buffet on *Iridium Azimuth*, but they can do a tolerable lunch."

Nalani caught up to Caridad Sanrosa in the departure lounge. She bowed and took a seat next to Sanrosa.

"I'm glad I got to see you before you left, Sen," she said. "On behalf of the entire Judiciary, I want to apologize for this whole mess."

Sanrosa, head high, met her eyes. "Thank you for that. Thank you for everything you've done for me." She paused, her lips a tight, straight line. "I trust you won't take offense if I say that at this point, I'm sick and tired of the Judiciary and glad to be leaving."

"Offense? Hardly. I think that's a very measured and mature response, under the circumstances. We deserve worse." She sighed. "Will you be returning to the University?"

"Immediately, yes. They were nice enough to keep me on the payroll through this...contretemps. I'm headed to my home now, and I'll be in my office tomorrow morning."

"That's immediately. What about ultimately?"

Sanrosa looked a little surprised. "I can't stay. Not after this. Not with all my colleagues aware of what...happened." She swallowed. "I was invited to join an expedition to study archaic period sites on the Fourth Plane. At first I turned them down, but now I've changed my mind. They've made space for me; we'll be leaving by the end of the month."

Nalani gave her a data flake. "I want to help however I can. Here are letters of introduction and some other documents. I've included instructions for the Judiciary to assist you, on my authority. Use them."

"That's very decent of you, Sen."

"It's the least I can do. We disrupted your life."

Sanrosa gave the barest smile. "Perhaps it's for the best. If this hadn't happened, I'd never have agreed to go on this expedition. Maybe my life needed a little disruption."

"May it be so." Nalani stood. "Best of luck, Professor."

"And to you."

After three days of almost non-stop work, Milos called Nalani to his workshop and shut the door. "I have an answer for you. I don't know if it's a satisfying one."

Nalani took a seat and accepted the mug of coffee he handed her. "I'm ready."

"It's a mess. I approached the problem with the theory that there was one distinct locus of corruption which was then spreading through the codices on the Plane. That turned out not to be the case."

"How many?"

"Two, I believe, spaced a few years apart. The first infection, about ten years ago, started in Sanrosa-territory codices. The second, about five years ago, seems to have been an attempt to repair the damage of the first."

"Obviously one that didn't work."

Milos frowned. "That's part of what makes this case so complex. The second infection *tried* to repair the first, but the first resisted. It was as if the original infection was programmed to *appear* to fade, then counterattack. It incorporated code from the repair program, ultimately making the corruption worse."

"Milos, this sounds like some awfully sophisticated programming. AI level or better."

"Oh, definitely. I wouldn't be surprised a rogue AI isn't involved."

Nalani nodded. "So we're looking for a rogue AI, possibly with a human partner or partners? One with both the expertise and the opportunity to infiltrate the Judiciary. That's not much for a Plane-wide search. Do you have anything else for me?"

Milos shook his head. "I don't think the original programmer is on this Plane any longer. I suspect they left the Fifth Plane after delivering the infection, and there's no evidence they returned. When the original infection counterattacked, that was all self-generated. Nothing came from outside the system." Seeing Nalani's look, he added, "I have a name for you, or at least a designation. The original programmer called themself 'Silver.'"

"Someone or something called Silver, somewhere in the Five Planes." Nalani forced a wan smile. "More than we had before, I guess. If this corruption is so powerful, so able to defend itself, will we be ever able to eliminate it?"

"It'll take a wipe-and-replace of all the corrupted codices. Which is standard procedure. I'll leave detailed notes of my analysis for the Judiciary techs who come to fix things." He swallowed. "It's not a job I'd care to undertake, but the regular techs should have no trouble."

"All right. What about the second infection, the repair attempt?"

"I was able to identify the person responsible." He met Nalani's eyes. "They left you a message."

For a moment her breath went away. "Left *me* a message?"

"Yes, *you* in particular."

"Wh-Who?"

Milos rose. "I'd better let you view it alone. There's a large portion keyed to your identity codes." He handed her a board and left the room.

Nalani stared at the board. ("This is ridiculous,") she said to her codex. ("Just in case, I want you to lock your programs until I give you the all-clear.")

("I'll do my best to resist being reprogrammed.")

Nalani tapped the board. Text appeared, conveying her name and title, plus a few of her better known routine aliases. It invited her to confirm her identity.

("Confirm.")

An image built up, a face she knew better than her own: Accursius XVII.

Nalani's codex reported, ("Identity confirmed. That's her.")

Her friend waited a moment, then spoke. "Well, Nalani, now we come to it. I don't expect you'll ever see this. In fact, I hope to have this business finished up and be there for our next annual rendezvous." Accursius shrugged. "If you *are* viewing this, then it's most likely that matters have not gone according to plan."

Nalani gripped the board's frame.

Accursius continued. "I was hoping to keep you completely out of this. *C'est la vie*; you're in it now, and I guess that's a good thing. It may be that I could use some help." She brushed back a loose strand of hair. "Thing is, I discovered that my codex is corrupted. Never mind the details, I'll attach a report detailing what I know. Suffice it to say that I followed the trail to the Sanrosa territory on the Fifth Plane. As you've probably discovered, someone's been tampering with local codices. My data workers are going to launch a repair worm, but they can't guarantee it'll work."

("It didn't.")

"Meanwhile, I'm on the track of someone or something that calls itself Silver. I have good reason to believe it's headed for the Fourth Plane—Sanrosa holdings, most likely. I intend to follow it and get to the bottom of this mess." She leaned closer.

"Don't come making a big scene. I'm working undercover and may have to juggle aliases. And please, for the moment, don't bring the Valley in on this. The last thing we need is for those ignoramuses to barge in and upset everything. Remember Thor Five."

("Oh, *why* does she have to do this to me?")

"One last thing, Nalani." Her voice quavered. "If I have run into problems, I could really use your help. I hate to put you on the spot, but you're the only one I would ever trust." She raised her fingers to the screen. "I love you, Nal."

Nalani touched her fingers to the image of Accursius's. "I love you too, Jays."

The image dissolved, replaced by a listing of attachments.

Nalani's shook her head and whispered, "Oh, Jays, what have you gotten yourself into now?" ("Download everything,") she told her codex. ("I want to read it all.")

("What are you planning next?")

Nalani covered her face with her hands. ("I don't know.")

Val balanced easily against the side of the transport car, attention focused on his board. He had put his name in at the Hiring Hall as soon as he landed, and offers were beginning to trickle in—mostly from single-Plane FTL ships, but a couple of the multiplanars had put out feelers. Neither were as big or as fancy as *Iridium Azimuth*, and the pay was correspondingly less, but they were still good jobs. *Opus Technica* was probably the better of the two: she was a certified mail carrier, so that even the Second Plane pirates hesitated to interfere with her, and her systems were recently overhauled. The other was the *Quintile Illumination*, a mid-sized, mid-class multi-planar, scheduled to leave orbit in just over sixty hours. That would be cutting it tight, to get signed on and get on board, plus he wasn't sure what kind of arrangement her owners had to get her through the Second Plane. On the other hand, if he wanted to leave the Fifth Plane quickly... He repressed the desire to look over his shoulder. He hadn't seen any sign of his shadow since the night before; surely he was free of them by now.

The car slowed, lights chasing each other along the edge of the doors, and he shifted to be in position to make a quick exit. The doors rolled back, admitting a swirl of warm evening air, and he let the crowd carry him down to ground level. There was still no sign of anyone paying undue attention, and he allowed himself to relax a little, looking around like a tourist at the low buildings. He hadn't been in the University area before, and the amount of vegetation was startling. There were potted trees in the alleys between the square little buildings, and entire lots left open to the sky, carpeted with grass and starred with flowers, the sort of thing you saw more often on the First Plane, or growing wild on the Third. This was all neatly clipped and tended, every vine wound onto a well-planned terrace, the grass uniformly five centimeters tall, not a twig or a leaf lying beneath the trees. The students in their old-fashioned knee-length coats bustled past in waves, avoiding the signs of nature. It was a little unnerving, a little unreal, and he was glad when he spotted the tea-house Sanrosa had named in her reply.

It was reassuringly plain and plant-free, with just the traditional raked-gravel beds on either side of the main door. The translucent curtains that filled the enormous windows had been rolled up as the light faded, and lights glowed on each of the low tables. This late in the day, it wasn't particularly crowded, and it was easy to spot Caridad Sanrosa sitting alone just inside the left-hand window. She seemed to feel his gaze, and looked up sharply, frown fading to curiosity, and he squared his shoulders as he stepped through the door.

"Sen Caridad Sanrosa?"

She nodded.

"I'm Val Millat."

"Please, sit." She gestured to the waiting chair. "I've taken the liberty of ordering tea service."

Val did as he was told. "Perhaps you'd be so good as to let me pay? Since I'm putting you to some trouble."

Something like a smile flickered across her lips. "We'll see. Tell me how you know Sami."

"I know his sister Kiri," Val answered. He hesitated, then threw caution to the winds. "Sen, I was the senior pilot on a multi-planar—"

"*Iridium Azimuth*?" It was just barely a question.

Val nodded. "We had a rough passage through the Second Plane, and a bad Drop, barely made it out intact. I was on the controls. And in the process—I saw something that I could only interpret as the Fifth Ship. Other people also saw—something—and it was the talk of the ship as we circled the First Plane and Vaulted up to Fifth. So of course I wanted to find out more, but I didn't know where to get reliable information. And Kiri—she's been a friend for years—suggested that what I needed was academic sources, not cultist stuff. She said her brother had worked with you."

He thought Sanrosa looked disappointed, but it was hard to read her lack of expression. A waiter rumbled over then, and she unloaded the tray of little savories, the box of condiments, the cups, and finally the fat teapot in its thermal wrapping. She laid them out with automatic precision, and Val made himself fall in with the ritual as they each prepared a cup and filled a plate. She had chosen to speak with him personally, he thought. Surely that meant she was willing to help.

Sanrosa sipped thoughtfully at her cup, and set it aside with a nod that might have been approval. "I can certainly give you a reading list. Much of it is fairly dry even by academic standards, but there's nothing a layman couldn't follow with a bit of effort."

"That would be enormously helpful."

"Would it? I'm not sure what you expect to get out of this, sen."

Val paused. "I want—sen, if what I saw wasn't one of the First Ships, I don't know what it could have been. And at the same time, I do know that's impossible."

"Any number of explanations have been offered," Sanrosa said, wrapping her long fingers around her cup, her eyes narrowed in pleasure. "Most of them neurological."

"Or psychological," Val agreed. "Except—I am as sure as a man can be that I wasn't hallucinating, and that *something* led me out of a potentially fatal situation. I want to know what, and why."

"It cannot be the Fifth Ship," Sanrosa said. "They're all accounted for, according to the lineages, and in any case how could it have survived this long?"

"Lineage attributions aren't particularly reliable," Val said. "Even I know that."

Sanrosa smiled. "Touché."

"Besides..." Val hesitated again, shaking his head. "Sen, I'm going to sound as though I have issues with reality, but please hear me out."

"I'm listening."

"Since I saw the Ship, since I started asking questions, weird things have been happening. My captain tried to shut me down completely, and when I kept talking about it, she essentially kicked me off *Iridium Azimuth*. Then I ran into some people who wanted all the information I could give them about the encounter, and were really insistent that I should come with them to be scanned by some psi-engineer of theirs. I said no, and ever since, people have been following me..." Val felt himself run down, hearing how off-balance he sounded. He heaved a sigh, knowing he'd lost her, but to his surprise, Sanrosa put a finger to her lips.

"Don't turn, but would you know the person when you saw them?"

Val blinked, made himself shake his head. "Not really, I've never gotten a decent look at their face. Faces, I don't even know how many of them there might be—"

"Hush," Sanrosa said again, and lifted the teapot. Val pushed his cup toward her automatically, and she refilled it. From a distance, they would look like teacher and student, or mother and son. "There is a man sitting at a table behind you. He came in when you did, and I've been watching him watch you." She smiled again, her expression wry. "I thought perhaps he was a jealous partner, from the way he doesn't take his eyes off you."

Val held himself rigid, though he wanted to swing around and stare—wanted to get up and confront the stranger, finally get rid of some of the helplessness he had felt since the lecture.

"Please don't start anything," Sanrosa said, as though she'd read the thought. "My reputation has been battered enough lately." She reached into her pocket, and came up with a small databoard, the sort technicians used to investigate narrow spaces. Val took it and lit the screen, pretending to read the display while he angled the sensor to look over his shoulder. Yes, there the man was, and not even being very subtle about it, a stocky, light-haired man whose eyes were indeed fixed on their table. Val shivered once, and handed the board back.

"I see him. I don't recognize him, though."

"But I do," Sanrosa said. His surprise must have shown, because she lifted both eyebrows. "In my profession, it's useful to know the local artifact-hunters—and fakers, though Radam is more of a scholar than many. And that makes me wonder... I've had some troubles of my own recently, and the people who believe in the Fifth Ship are capable of almost anything. My advice to you, young man, is to take my reading list back to your ship and do your research in the virtual for a few years."

"I don't actually have a ship at the moment," Val said.

"That's unfortunate."

Val shook himself. "I'm on hold for a couple of berths, it won't be a problem."

Sanrosa regarded him dubiously. "Still, I think it would be as well if you weren't followed when you leave here. I can take you through the University. Sen Radam won't be admitted there."

"Thank you," Val said. The historian was right, going through the university would be his best chance of losing his pursuers. But... "I don't want to cause you any trouble."

"Nonsense." Sanrosa waved at the table. "Finish your tea, there's no sense in wasting it."

She was right, of course, but it was hard to concentrate on the excellent food. Val made himself finish his share of the savories, knowing he might miss a meal later, and accepted the offer of a second tray. When it and the teapot were finally empty, Sanrosa folded her napkin with deliberation. The waiter came trundling over, and Val paid the bill, watching Sanrosa watch the stranger behind him.

1.10 DEPARTURES

SECOND PLANE

Divine Mountain was never quiet, not the way smaller ships were quiet, sound reduced to the hiss of ventilation and the faint, distant ticking of metal. It was as large as a small moon, habitats piled upon habitats around the central core, and all of them were stuffed with people, crew and kin and rafts of hostages waiting to be ransomed. There were ships, too, more than a dozen docked to the convoluted surface, standard FTL-ships, rafts, and even a couple of small multiplanars mated to the hull. *Last Fair Deal* was the smallest of the latter, tucked in between the trailing lobes of *Divine Mountain*'s left upper quadrant. It was an exceptionally secure docking point, shielded by tertiary storage spaces and overlooked by one of the equatorial gun emplacements; getting clear of *Divine Mountain* was correspondingly difficult but, on balance, Morcant Vetrys thought, the increased security was worth the effort. And she was a better pilot than most, capable of clearing the channel even in hyperflux.

At the moment, she had the main locks open, the better to facilitate the transfer of supplies, and was sitting just inside the personnel lock, letting *Divine Mountain*'s air flow over her. The bigger ship had dozens of hydro-pods, even, it was rumored, a bottled forest, and the air she shared with her fleet always smelled fresh and clean and faintly green. It also moved, like air on a planet, a gentle touch that stirred the fine hairs at Morcant's temples. She glanced at the screen overhead, where the bots were rolling pallets with Llian ap Farr's share of the latest prize into the main hold. She and Derrian would have to sort it out later, once ap Farr told them what was for the ship's use and what was for trade, but at least it would be safe aboard in case of emergency.

She heard familiar footsteps on the deck behind her, and looked up and back to see the*Deal*'s rigging engineer, Derrian Hina, duck through the hatch that led from the forward cross-corridor. He carried a pair of tea-flasks slung in a bright rubber holder, and her eyebrows lifted.

"That bad?"

He freed one of the flasks and handed it to her, then folded himself to sit on the deck beside her, letting his long legs dangle in the meter's drop to the floor of the*Mountain's* lock. The two systems didn't actually match, but the mountain-ship's larger connectors were designed to fix securely against any hull, secreting an adhesive sealant that would hold the ships together until the mountain-ship released it. She glanced again at the screen, but the bots continued their work without trouble: not the cargo, then, and therefore probably not any kind of faction fight within the *Mountain*.

"We're getting a new data engineer," Derrian said.

"Well, we need one." Morcant took a careful swig of her tea, found it hot and citrus-sharp, and took a deeper swallow.

"Yes, I know that. But I wasn't expecting one off *Broad Increase*."

Morcant lifted her eyebrows at that. "Nor was I."

"I'd prefer someone with a bit more—"

Experience, he would have said, but Derrian had been a conscript himself, taken from the crew of a multi-planar nine years ago. She could see him blushing, and said, "Time in service?"

"Well, yeah." Derrian twisted open his own flask and drank deeply to hide his embarrassment.

It was true, of course, that most conscripts worked on the larger FTL-ships or on the mountain-ships, where they could be kept under supervision until everyone was certain that they weren't going to try do anything stupid. So why, Morcant wondered, had this one been assigned to the *Deal*, which flew with a skeleton crew under ap Farr's captaincy and at Mac Braith Bain's direct orders?

"It was her idea, wasn't it?" she said aloud, and Derrian sighed.

"Yeah."

So why would ap Farr want a conscript data engineer, when there were half a hundred to choose from on *Divine Mountain*? There was no good answer to that question, and a certain amount of hazard in even voicing it. She shook her head. "When do we get him?"

"Any time now," Derrian said. His head lifted. "In fact—I bet that's him now."

Morcant followed his gaze across the brightly-lit lock, to see a dark man in a loose white tunic standing at the entrance to the lock. One of *Divine Mountain*'s security guards stood beside him, and as she watched, he pointed to the *Deal*. "I guess you're right," she said, and kicked the catch that let the steps unroll clattering to the lock's decking.

The stranger walked toward them, a carryall slung over his shoulder, thin face upturned to examine what he could see of the *Deal*. He was good-looking, Morcant thought, dark gold skin and untidy dark hair and enormous brown eyes that had probably been nearsighted at birth. At the moment, they were alertly focused, eyebrows drawn down in a faint frown.

"*Last Fair Deal*?" he asked, and Morcant nodded.

"That's us."

The well-shaped mouth twisted. "Llian ap Farr sent me as crew. AA Imric bin Marrick Roeland Sanxing."

"JU Morcant Deryevna Vetrys Sanrosa. I go by Morcant Vetrys."

"Derrian Hina." Derrian offered his hand and Imric reached up to take it. "DI Derrian Hanneschild Pim Hina."

"Imric bin Marrick." He took her hand as well, his fingers cold. "I was told you were short a data engineer."

"That's right." Morcant hauled herself to her feet. "Why don't you come aboard?"

She led him down the *Deal*'s central corridor, pointing out the cargo locks and the escape capsules, palmed the lock plates to let them into the commons. Derrian had been working at one of the long tables, and a resonator crystal hung suspended in its half-finished cage, dull and milky without its power source. She saw bin Marrick's eyes cut that way, and then he looked resolutely aside.

"Llian said to get him set up," Derrian said, and Morcant nodded.

"Cabins are forward. We've got a couple empty."

Behind bin Marrick's back, Derrian held up his hand, palm out, tipping his head in question, and Morcant scowled at him. She wasn't about to give a stranger run of her ship until Llian ap Farr herself said so. Derrian mimed an elaborate shrug, but Morcant ignored him, palming open the doors of each of the two unoccupied cabins.

"These are designed for crew, and are pretty much identical. There's one more, down the side corridor, but it's got passenger specs, so you won't have access." And I'm not installing extras, her stare was meant to convey.

Bin Marrick seemed to get the message, and shrugged one shoulder. "Asymmetric power?"

"Slightly right-handed," Derrian answered. "Only about a tenth over."

"Still." Bin Marrick let the bag slide from his shoulder. "I'll take starboard, then."

Morcant nodded. "All yours. Do you want to see the rest of the ship, or grab the night-meal first?"

"I could certainly eat," bin Marrick said. "What clock do you keep?"

"Blue."

He gave a sigh of relief. "I've been on Purple."

"Not a bad transition, then." Morcant kept her voice light. "Get yourself settled, and come on back to the commons. We serve family style, it's cheaper. Any allergies? Absolute negatives?"

Bin Marrick shook his head. "I'm an easy keeper."

There was always something, Morcant thought, but she thought that he wouldn't make a fuss on his first night aboard. "Right. See you in a few."

The commons seemed large and empty, and she waved a hand to increase the light level. It was her night to handle meal prep, and she turned her attention to the prep station, summoning the menu and adjusting it to account for an extra portion. She added one for ap Farr as well, though there was never any telling if she'd join them until she was there, and the system responded with a set of instructions. Like most of *Divine Mountain*'s small-ships, they ran on pre-pack rations, though ap Farr made sure they got primarily mid- and top-quality stores. Morcant had grown up on cheap vat-made, one step above the kibble that they kept for emergencies, and had no complaints.

"Easy keeper," Derrian said. "I wonder how easy?"

Morcant slanted a glance at him. "Let the man settle, Derri."

"You can't deny he's good-looking."

That was true enough, and if he was as decent a data engineer as well... Morcant allowed herself a sigh. It was easier, on the small ships, to build intimacy into a crew, whether as lovers or as quasi-family; she preferred lovers, herself, but that was a Second Plane custom. "We don't even know where he's from."

"He's here now," Derrian said, with a cocky smile, and Morcant shook her head.

"Whatever he says, we have to work with him. Remember that." She busied herself at the console without waiting for an answer, collecting protein and veg and sauce and feeding them into the cooker. The computer suggested flatbread for the starch, and she found the envelopes stacked behind the more expensive mini-loaves, passed them through the system to revive them. By then, Derrian had finished whatever he was doing with the resonator, and set the steaming rounds at the four sides of the table they reserved for eating. He produced a carafe of tea as well, and bin Marrick came warily to join them as Morcant pulled the bowls of stew from the cooker.

"Someone's joining us?" he asked, and before Morcant could answer, a chime sounded from the hatch.

Derrian glanced quickly at the control cuff on his right wrist, and visibly relaxed. "Our capa."

Bin Marrick looked wary at that. And well he might, Morcant thought, settling herself at the table. She was a little wary herself.

The door to the commons slid back, and Llian ap Farr stepped through, her carved black cane tapping on the deck. "Sens."

"Capa," Derrian replied, and Morcant gave a nod.

"I see I'm in time." Llian took her place at the table, attaching her cane to the side of her chair with a click that spoke of custom magnets, if not more complicated internal works. "I hope you're settling in, Sen bin Marrick."

"Everyone's been very kind," bin Marrick said, in what Morcant thought was a deliberately colorless voice.

A smile flickered across Llian's lips. "I'm glad to hear it." She accepted a glass from Derrian, and leaned back in her chair. "I won't keep you in suspense. We'll be leaving*Divine Mountain* as soon as the rest of my cargo is aboard."

Something flickered in bin Marrick's eyes, but he said nothing. Morcant counted to five, and said, "Do we have a destination in mind?"

"I'll inform you once we undock," Llian answered placidly, and reached for the carafe to top up her glass.

Morcant glared at her. "That doesn't give our new DE much chance to learn the systems."

"I'm sure he'll do fine."

"It also doesn't give us much chance to get used to each other," Morcant said. Out of the corner of her eye, she saw Derrian make a warning gesture, but ignored him. "You want us to fly short-handed, you're going to have to give us time to learn how each other think."

"You'll have the flight," ap Farr said.

"I think I can pick up the systems pretty quickly," bin Marrick began, but Morcant ignored him.

"In the real world, we'd get a solid month. And twice the crew."

"Enough." ap Farr didn't raise her voice, but Morcant stopped, flinching.

"We can handle it," Derrian said. "No worries."

This time it was ap Farr who ignored him, her pale eyes fixed on Morcant. "If you don't think you can do the job, Sen Vetrys, I can put you back where I found you."

Morcant froze. "No," she said, stiff-lipped. "We'll manage."

"I'm sure you will," said Llian ap Farr, with a smile, and turned her attention to her meal.

FIFTH PLANE

"**Do you know,**" Sanrosa said, conversationally, "I think we might be better off going out the garden entrance."

She rose, slinging her carryall over one shoulder, and Val copied her. "I didn't know there was one."

"Not... officially," Sanrosa answered, weaving her way through the maze of tables. Val followed, less sure-footed in the dim light, and Sanrosa gave him a smile over her shoulder. "But Dumazhi knows me."

She spoke to a young woman who stood beside a pair of rainbow doors. Her voice was too soft for Val to understand, but the young woman nodded and pushed open the closer of the two doors. Sanrosa stepped through, beckoning for Val to follow, and he emerged into thick twilight, the first tendrils of fog coiling in the corners of the garden.

"With luck, our man will think we've just taken a quick look," Sanrosa said. "The garden's somewhat famous here. And even if he does follow, Allessa won't let him through right away."

She was walking as she spoke, striding away down a stone-covered path that ran diagonally across the garden. Val followed, feet scuffing on the pebbled path, dew-heavy stalks brushing against his ankles. He couldn't help a glance back, but the colored glass showed only indistinct shadows.

"Here," Sanrosa said, and laid her left hand flat on one of the bricks that made up the garden wall. It seemed, Val thought, a hair darker than the others around it, and then there was a heavy click, and a section of wall sagged forward. Sanrosa gave a satisfied smile and tugged it open, motioning Val to precede her. "Go on, I have to lock it."

He stepped through into one of the University alleys, this one deep in the shadow of a parasol-tree. Fog curled along the base of the garden wall, and along the base of the blank wall that formed the other side of the alley, showing yellow where the lights from the main street touched it. The air was damp and growing rapidly chill. He heard the lock click shut behind him, and Sanrosa tapped his shoulder, turning him away from the main street and toward the narrower exit at the back of the alley. He balked—what, after all, did he know about her?—but then shook himself back to reality. There were too many reasonable, real-world connections for him to start doubting her now.

She glanced over her shoulder as though she'd read the thought. "This is a short-cut into the University grounds. We'll go in by the Themis Gate. Then we'll go by my flat. I believe I have downloads of several of the texts that I'd be glad to share with you. As well as the list itself, of course. And after that, I'll see you out by Sanxing, it's closest to the tubes."

"I'm grateful," Val said. They had emerged into a narrow street of closed shopfronts. Lights showed only on the upper floors, dimmed with fog, and ahead loomed a woven iron structure that resolved itself into a fence of iron standards topped with idealized trees woven together at top and bottom with twisted curves of metal that were almost branches. The fog was getting thicker, and it took a moment to find the gate.

But then a light came on beside a narrow kiosk, and Sanrosa quickened her step.

"Evening, Tomas," she said, holding out her hand. "Myself and one guest."

"Certainly, Professor," the guard answered. Val held out his own identification to be scanned, and the gate creaked open. As far as he could tell, the street was empty around them. Maybe, just maybe, he'd shaken his pursuers at last. Beyond the fence, there were fewer lights, and quite a lot of grass and shrubbery, fog crawling over the damp ground. Overhead, the sky was the color of pewter.

"This way," Sanrosa said, and Val trailed obediently after her, following a path that wound between banks of greenery. There didn't seem to be any vehicular traffic on the University grounds, and he guessed that there were either underground transport tubes or some sort of perimeter system. Then there was a soft hiss behind them, growing louder, and a voice called, "On your left!" Sanrosa obediently faded to the right, and a three-wheeled platform shot past them, two gowned students clinging to the controls. Sanrosa muttered something under her breath, but kept walking.

They left the park behind, and passed through a series of paved courtyards that surrounded buildings shaped like Platonic solids. Lights glowed beneath their outer surfaces, revealing subtle colors and veining like shadows—Arbellaster marble, Sanrosa said, when she saw where he was looking. These were the main University buildings, she explained, connected by an enormous underground network like the roots of a giant tree. She stopped them, frowning up at the windows dotting one face of the octahedron.

"Sen?" Val began, and she shook her head.

"I thought there was a light on in my office, but—there couldn't be. Come along."

She led him past two more clusters of buildings, and then unlocked another gate to let them into a pleasant courtyard. A fountain played in the center, the plumes lit from below so that it seemed as though drops and shards of light fell instead of water. Val stared, impressed in spite of himself, but Sanrosa ignored it, angling across the square toward one of the entrance stairs. Lights showed in the windows above it, a welcoming glow that abruptly vanished from two of the squares. Val hesitated, remembering what she had said before.

"Uh, sen? Which room is yours?"

She gave him a sharp look, but her steps slowed. "The second floor—the dark windows."

"They were lit a minute ago," Val said.

"Nonsense."

"I'm sure of it."

"Impossible," Sanrosa said, but her tone was less certain than her words.

"I don't think you should go in," Val said. "Sen, I'm very sorry, I seem to have gotten you tangled up in my troubles—"

"Nonsense," she said again, and started for the door.

Val followed, not quite daring to grab her shoulder. "At least be careful."

"Hush."

There was no visible lift; instead Sanrosa palmed open an unobtrusive door and started up the stairs. At the top, she paused, frowning, then eased the door open just far enough to see through the gap. Val craned his head, but couldn't see anything more than a carpeted hall and a uniformed man standing by one of the doors. Sanrosa eased the door shut, and caught his sleeve.

"This way. Hurry."

"What?" Val followed, moving as quickly as he could. Sanrosa ignored the first floor, leading him down another flight of stairs and into what seemed to be a service tunnel that ran beneath the building.

"It won't help for long," she said, "but they shouldn't expect it."

"What was that? What did you see?"

"Campus police at my door, where they have no business being—and I've had quite enough of law enforcement and the judiciary lately." She gave him a sideways glance. "I was just exonerated in a case of plagiarism, you see."

Plagiarism was one of the crimes the Fifth Plane took very seriously. Val felt his eyebrows rise.

"It was a mistake," Sanrosa said irritably. "The Judiciary acknowledged that. I have the documents to prove it. But it was not particularly pleasant." She stopped at another door, but it failed to respond to her touch; she scowled at it and marched on, perhaps twice the width of one of the residential courtyards, before trying another door. This one did open, and she urged Val ahead of her. "We need to get you out of the University, then I can deal with these people. And I should be preparing for my own trip, I need to join Taheris on Anaparra by the end of the month—"

Val did as he was told, not really listening to her complaints. He emerged into a space between buildings, roofed with vines that had left a carpet of leaves over the paving. Sanrosa locked the door behind them, but before she could say anything, a chime sounded inside the carryall she had slung over one shoulder.

"Oh, what now?" she said irritably, fishing in the depths until she came up with the databoard. A light flashed beneath its surface, and her frown deepened as she read the scrolling text. "For physics' sake—"

"The Judiciary are looking for you," Val said, and she looked up sharply.

"How did you know?"

"I didn't. It was a guess. But everything else has been going wrong."

"And the Chairman wants me to talk to them." Sanrosa considered for a moment, then drew glyphs across the screen, muting sound and banishing the light. "That won't hold them long, but that should give us time to get you out of here."

"And what's going to happen to you?" Val asked. Sanrosa didn't answer at once, but as they made their way toward an elevated walkway, she gave him a rueful glance.

"I don't know. I've been cleared, and I have the paperwork to prove it, but I can't say I'm eager to deal with the Judiciary again."

"Did you say you needed to get to Anaparra?" A plan was forming in Val's mind, something to spite these strangers who'd upended his life from the moment he set foot on Kauhale.

"I've agreed to join an expedition to the Fourth Plane. We're supposed to meet on Anaparra to catch our multi-planar. Why?"

"Come with me instead." Val lifted a hand to forestall her protest. "I'm going to take the berth on *Quintile Illumination*, and I've got the standing to bring a family member with me— as long as you don't mind being claimed that way. People do it all the time. You get your own cabin and standard meals, not as fancy as passenger fare, but it'll get you to Anaparra in plenty of time. And it'll make it easier for me—they'll be looking for one person, not two."

For a moment, he thought she'd refuse, but instead she took a deep breath and pulled her carryall closer against her side. "I'll need to stop at a chandler, get some clothes."

"Plenty of time once we're back in Startown," Val answered, and hoped it was true.

Nalani, following venerable Judiciary practice, hosted a reception for her team at the conclusion of every case, win or lose. Since every Judiciar on the Fifth Plane felt the impact of this particular case, she opened the reception to any who cared to attend. Fortunately, Polo Halau had several enormous halls usually used only for rare conventions—for Judiciars turned out by the hundreds.

It seemed as if Nalani knew four out of five of them. All afternoon she was busy with personal greetings and reminiscences, her codex subtly feeding her pertinent details in a continuous stream.

Always, with anyone she thought could help, she asked about Supreme Justice Accursius XVII. And always, she learned nothing helpful. No one had seen her missing friend any later than Nalani had.

Afternoon turned to evening, food and intoxicants flowed steadily, and the reception began to split into discrete groups. Nalani found Milos watching a spirited multiplayer chess game, and whispered to him, "When you get a moment, could you come to my chambers?" She knew that the children were being tended by Polo Halau childcare staff.

He shrugged. "I have a moment now." He lowered his voice. "Not the best game I've ever seen."

"I'm not surprised, as much as they've drunk." She waved at one of the players, then took Milos's arm and led him to her chambers. Along the way, she told her codex, ("Ask the Apprentices to meet me in my chambers.")

("Ask them, or *tell* them?")

("Ask.") She smiled. ("But forcefully.")

Bhagwati and Al-Ghazali were waiting for her. She ushered them in and gestured for them to sit around the small table. "My friends, you've done some fine work. Together, we saved an innocent person from a death sentence. We uncovered a major corruption in the Judiciary. And you helped me find a clue in my search for Jinan-Jorie. You have the gratitude of not only the Five Planes and the Judiciary—you have my personal thanks as well."

She reached to her desk and retrieved an impervelope. "First, something trivial. When a case concludes, it's my custom to give a memento to my helpers." She handed each of them a small blue jewel in a silver setting. "It's not much, but it comes from the heart. You can wear it anywhere you like, or stick it to the wall in your quarters, or whatever you wish."

Al-Ghazali touched the jewel to her right earlobe, where it clung, "It's beautiful. Thank you."

Nalani smiled. "Now for something more substantial." ("Make the transfers.") "Nothing says gratitude quite as well as money. Five thousand Judiciary credits each, to be precise. It should be in your accounts now." At their faces, she raised a hand. "You've earned it. Uncovering that corruption is a bigger deal than you know."

Milos shook his head. "But five thou—"

"Don't argue," Nalani said. "The Judiciary owes you a lot more." She took a breath. "Fortunately, all the other senior Judiciars on this Plane agree. Milos, you're now a permanent consultant; you'll find all the details in a contract you'll be receiving soon."

"I-I don't know what to say."

"Just remember that I have first call on your services." She turned to the Apprentices, stretched out her hands and took one of theirs in each. "My darlings, I'm so proud of you. This was a challenging case, and you both rose to the occasion." She squeezed their hands. "You're both being credited with ten years of service. You deserve it."

Bhagwati's mouth dropped open. "Ten years? For real?"

She nodded. "For real. I don't know of any other Apprentices getting such a large bonus. You should both be very proud." She released their hands. "Of course, this means you won't have the opportunity to serve under Superior Justice Grotius any longer. I apologize for that."

Al-Ghazali lifted her nose. "I think we'll survive."

"Good." Nalani placed her hands flat on the table. "All right, that concludes this case. Justice be with us all."

Milos cleared his throat. "Nalani, what are you going to do now? And what…should we do?"

She leaned back in her chair, her face serious. "I'm going to head for the Fourth Plane and continue searching for Jinan-Jorie." She looked from one to the other. "You're all free to make your own decisions. But I should like it if you'd consider coming with me."

Milos was first to answer. "I wouldn't have it any other way."

Bhagwati, blushing, nodded. "When do we leave?"

Nalani raised an eyebrow at Al-Ghazali, who cocked her head and said, "I assumed you'd want to leave as soon as possible, so I checked schedules. The *Quintile Illumination* is Dropping in six days. They'll be boarding from Anaparra. Less than a day's journey." She looked down. "There's room for all of us. Myself included."

Nalani nodded. "Very efficient. Does that suit everyone?" Their faces told her they were all agreed. "Fine, then. Al-Ghazali, would you book us, and arrange passage to Anaparra? And Bhagwati...find out what's fun to do there until we board."

"Yes, Thurgood."

She rose. "It's been a busy day. I'm going to sleep. Will you all go back to the party and give my regards?"

The youngsters departed, and Nalani sat for a time, staring. Then she went to her quarters and fell asleep as soon as she was in bed.

1.11 DROPS

FIRST PLANE

Of course, with no one chasing them, it was an easy Drop from the Second Plane to the First. *Last Fair Deal* popped out of the Fissure within hailing distance of the outermost Ortlan Station, and Imric's boards were filled with automated requests for ship's papers and data transfer, plus another blast of outgoing data. At ap Farr's snapped orders, he shut them all down, damping the ship's response and letting the identity request bounce back as though they were only a data echo, the reflection of a ship emerging on the far side of the Spindle. Vetrys spun the *Deal* on her long axis and Derrian coaxed enough power from the system to allow microjump that took them out of range. They emerged into relative quiet, and Imric bent over his boards, establishing position, while Derrian switched to the secondary drive and Vetrys glanced warily over her shoulder to where ap Farr sat in the captain's chair.

"Set up for the Vault?"

Ap Farr's placid expression didn't change. "I'm going to assume that our point of emergence was just the luck of the Drop."

Vetrys scowled, but the frown didn't hide her nervousness. "You know there's no predicting where we're going to come out. The Spindle screws everything up—"

Ap Farr waved a hand, and the pilot was instantly silenced. "Bin Marrick. Did we exchange data?"

Imric hunched his shoulders in reflex, and made himself lower them. "No. All transponders were off for the duration of the Drop. We were running passive monitors only." And that had felt particularly strange, using anti-pirate techniques against the First Plane worlds. "Systems were set to mirror, and as far as I can tell, that worked. We received only standard ID-and-transfer before we jumped again."

"Were you able to pick up any of their outgoing data burst?" Ap Farr's voice was perfectly calm.

Imric bent over his boards again, typing in the queries. Every time a ship entered a new Plane, its AI tried to exchange news and information with the nearest local source; the *Deal* was flying silent, but any local source would make its own broadcast automatically. "We captured about three-quarters of their stated length of transmission, maybe a little more. It'll take me a few minutes to get it cleaned up." You were lucky to get that much, he wanted to say. It wasn't easy to trap the data while pretending to mirror it back at the sender, but ap Farr had made it amply clear that she didn't care about excuses.

"Inform me as soon as that's done," she said, and Imric hid a sigh of relief. "Very well. Vetrys, plot us a Vault to the Fifth, as soon as you can make it. By my reckoning, we have plenty of time to intercept the *Quintile Illumination*, but there's no point in wasting it."

"It will take twelve hours to recharge the capacitors," Derrian said, and ap Farr rose gracefully to her feet.

"Yes. I'd like to Vault as soon as possible after that, please."

It was not a request. The crew exchanged wary glances as ap Farr left the control room, and then Vetrys let out her breath with an explosive sigh.

"Vault as soon as possible, she says. It's not like we have much control over how we leave the Fissure—"

"We're not badly placed," Imric said. He touched keys to project their position onto the central screen, a red dot for the ship and a jagged line like frozen lightning for the Spindle. "I don't think we're much more than fifteen hours out."

"Nice work," Derrian said, and Vetrys shrugged.

"Thanks. We got a little lucky, but the math was solid."

The pirates had a dozen different formulae for the Drop from Second to First, Imric had discovered, most of which offered more control than any ordinary multiplanar managed. He was determined to get a look at the program before he was released —if nothing else, it would be something to trade for a berth on a better class of ship—but so far, he hadn't had any luck hacking into that part of the system. His clearances were still restricted to what a data engineer would need, and nothing more.

"Hey, Imric," Derrian said. "Do you know anything about this *Quintile Illumination?*"

Imric shook his head slowly, remembering the scene in the *Deal's* commons, the main screen already showing the excited gases of the Mouth of Hell, as ap Farr calmly outlined her plans. *We are Vaulting to the Fifth Plane to intercept and shadow a multiplanar called the* Quintile Illumination. *She is mid-rank, passengers and cargo, and I have an interest in the former.* "I've heard the name." He leaned back in his chair, stretching, trying to dredge up any useful bits of information. "She's about the same size as *Broad Increase,* but my impression is she does more passenger business?"

"Or are you just saying that because the *capa* says she has an interest in the passengers?" Vetrys asked.

Imric shrugged. "Could be." He turned his attention back to his board, typing in the commands that would tell the ship's AI to start untangling the data torrent they'd just received. He heard Vetrys sigh again.

"OK, I'm sorry, that was uncalled for. I just hate not knowing what she's up to."

"It's all right." Ap Farr made him nervous, too, Imric wanted to say—scared the life out of him half the time, and the other half he couldn't forget the polite, companionable woman he'd chatted with on *Broad Increase.* He would never have guessed she was one of the pirates, and the betrayal still stung unreasonably.

"She wants us to intercept the *Quintile Illumination*," Derrian said. "Then shadow her through the drop. And then what, I wonder?"

"That would be the part that's worrying me," Vetrys said, but she had shifted to the navigation screen, was already plotting their approach to the Spindle. "It's not like we can take down a multiplanar."

"She wouldn't," Imric said, in spite of himself. "I mean, you're right, we couldn't. Could we?"

"I wouldn't like to try," Vetrys said.

It all depended on what *Quintile Illumination* was carrying, Imric thought, after he'd retreated to the relative privacy of his own cabin. Ap Farr had certainly proved herself capable of spectacular bluff, and if she had agents on board the other multiplanar, it might well be possible to pluck someone out of the mass of the *Quintile Illumination*'s passengers. In general, multiplanars weren't equipped for a fight: vertical society did its best not to get involved in horizontal quarrels, and, equally in general, horizontal society didn't risk a trade interdict by interfering with the ships' free passage. Except that was already changing, with the troubles on the Second Plane. If Lasser didn't start honoring his Letters of Passage, the other Planes were going to have to act, just to keep trade flowing, and that would be a disaster. It wouldn't precisely be a war— there had never been a real war between Planes, and wasn't likely to be; the physics of travel made it all but impossible— but it would be enough to ruin tens of thousands who were just hanging on to a life on the relatively protected worlds. He had seen that coming, and it was another reason he'd arranged his divorce. At least Milos and the kids had made it through: he'd been right to send them on to the *Iridium Azimuth*.

He stretched out cautiously on the surprisingly comfortable bunk, putting one arm over his eyes as though that could keep the ship's AI from seeing him. He didn't want to think about Milos and the family, couldn't afford to let himself feel anything more than simple relief. He had gotten them onto the *Iridium Azimuth* and safely out of the Second Plane: that was an unmitigated good, and he wouldn't let himself think at all about how they'd ended up as refugees. Milos was smart and hard-working and possessed of genuine sweetness: he would land on his feet. Just as Imric himself had done, more or less. There were worse places he could have ended up.

He shifted against the mattress, feeling it conform to his body. He hadn't missed that the bunks were big enough to be comfortable for two, just as he hadn't missed Derrian's not-quite-invitations. Company or comfort or just plain sex, he would only have to lean a little in that direction to get it, and he couldn't deny that he was tempted, if only because he was still afraid. But he wasn't sure yet how Derrian and Vetrys fit together, and he wanted to be sure he could turn any relationship to his best advantage. Better to wait and see how things played out before he made any moves.

FOURTH PLANE

NOTICE TO ASTROGATORS 623-57

TEMPORARY FLIGHT RESTRICTION

REGION: 1.0 parsecs centered on the Fissure
BEGINNING DATE & TIME: 500/4/33 09:00:00 ORC
ENDING DATE & TIME: 500/4/33 17:00:00 ORC
REASON FOR NTA: Hyperflux experiment

> All vessels traveling on the Fourth Plane are advised to keep a distance of at least 1.0 parsec from the Fissure during the period of this restriction. HEMGI/Apex Transport will be conducting experiments with a potential for major astrogational hazards for the full duration.

AUTHORITY: Korinek IX, Superior Justice

"I still can't believe they're letting us divert transplanar traffic this long." Haragai floated amid his displays and boards, arms limp and face relaxed. Of course he could relax now, Kiet thought—his part was essentially over.

Sun-hwa, drifting by with bulbs of juice for the whole family, patted Haragai's shoulder as she passed. "Sen Okubo agreed that this experiment makes us—and Apex—much more valuable. He convinced the higher-ups."

Thanh, in lotus seat before her own single board, sighed. "Because they see military applications."

Sun-hwa nodded. "Of course they do. How could they not?" She swept her eyes around the control chamber. "We're going to keep them thinking that, aren't we?"

Rokuro, who as Financial Officer had nothing to do but watch, grinned. "If it keeps us in business and keeps the money flowing, let them think what they want."

Antoku, the AI, announced, "Five minutes to activation."

Kiet nodded. "Jamahl, are you still good?"

From half a light-second away, the pilot answered, "Green and go."

Another benefit of this project, Kiet reflected: the company hadn't hesitated to transfer Jamahl and his six-year-old son to Zavod Sualti. And if today's test worked, the family should have its pick of other potential refugees. Sun-hwa assured them that she could write persuasive and sincere-sounding requests for whomever they wanted.

"Four minutes."

"Show us the realtime display," Thanh said.

Above them, a window opened into star-spattered space, a direct view from a probe a light-second away. To the right, Zavod Sualti hung, red nav lights pulsing in synchrony allover the planetoid. To the left was a smaller rock, a pitted obloid nearly two hundred meters long. It, too, was strewn with crimson lights, pinpoints blinking in their own distinct rhythm. Jamal's tender was barely visible, a small insect perched on the rock.

Further beyond, a handful of Company observation ships hovered, keeping the bosses at a safe distance. Far beyond that, the system's distant sun was a tiny bright star.

In between the two space rocks...nothing. Not yet.

Over seconds, it was clear that the smaller rock was creeping toward Zavod Sualti. "If this doesn't work," Rokuro said, "will it collide with us?"

Sun-hwa, jaw set, shook her head. "That's Jamahl's job. We put enough thrusters on that thing."

Kiet suppressed a smile. Now that they were under a military budget, Rokuro had no trouble securing equipment. Thrusters enough to steer a fifteen-million-kilogram rock were just the beginning—at 150% redundancy, plus spares for all units, multiplied by five trials...they could set up thrusters to steer Zavod Sualti and still have capacity left over.

"Three minutes."

Kiet took a breath, then put fingers to his board. "Stand by for hyperflux phase one."

This was the trickiest part, and he kept Thanh's equations running on one display.

Their sun was the closest star to the Fissure, less than a light-day away. Here in the sparse planetoid belt, they were only light-hours from the anomaly. Out here, space was fairly flat... and also terribly thin. At the Fissure, the big ships needed relatively little energy to punch through to transplanar hyperspace. At Zavod Sualti it took more...but it could still be done.

Ordinarily, the factory opened tiny fissures, big enough for navigational buoys of a few thousand kilograms. As far as Kiet knew, this was the first time anybody had tried anything this big.

Between Zavod Sualti and the smaller rock, space began to shimmer, stars dancing and twinkling.

"Two minutes."

In Kiet's ear, Thanh's voice whispered, "Keep the field in balance across the entire region."

"I'm trying," he said. In practice runs, the hyperflux field had been fairly steady; now the rock's gravity threw a gradient across the field, tangling space and fighting him. He trimmed in one spot, increased flux in another. The tip of his tongue crept out between his lips as he leaned closer to his screens, intent on the field grid.

"Jamahl, cast off. Thrusters to full."

"Casting off," the pilot reported. "Thrusters to full in five... four...three...two...one...zero!"

The rock lurched ahead, and distortion rushed through the field like a tsunami. Kiet struggled to smooth out the surge, damp the echoes.

"Twenty-five seconds."

"Kiet," Sun-hwa said, "it's go or no-go."

Where'd the bloody one-minute warning go? "Wait. I've still got flutter. Hold...hold." Seconds left, he had to compensate now. Thanh's equations were going nonlinear. He sent one last stabilizing pulse. "Now. Go, go, go!"

"Activation."

In the path of the rock, hyperspace gaped like a wound in the skin of the cosmos. Kiet wasn't one of those who could look into naked hyperflux; his stomach lurched and he turned his eyes away.

His board flashed yellow, green, yellow, red...then hyperflux collapsed and the wound closed, as if it had never existed. He looked up at the display.

The rock was gone, and the room echoed with cheers.

The rock was lost, adrift in transplanar space; without engines or hyperflux generators, it could never reenter the Planes. But if they could Drop that rock, they could Drop Zavod Sualti—and they'd have engines, generators, everything they needed to get to the Third Plane safely.

Across the room, his eyes locked with Sun-hwa's. *We can do it.*

We can do it.

1.12 Vault to Fifth

First Plane

For once, they had exited the Fissure on a reasonably convenient heading that let them loop back to approach the Spindle in under forty hours. Morcant Vetrys made a note to light a stick of incense to her family's Ancestors—if she ever earned out of the debt-indenture and made it back to Brauschi, she would owe a kilogram of the stuff, just like Old Woman Leveng who had popped up ten years after everyone thought she was dead, paid for two kilos of the finest jasmine sticks, stayed just long enough to see the first dozen set alight, and disappeared again. Probably she had gone back to the area around the Mouth of Hell, where piracy was most profitable, or maybe she'd made the full circuit and found her way to the Third Plane, where settlement land was cheap and a person's past could be forgotten. That was Morcant's secret dream, the one she barely admitted even to herself: to find place where she could settle, and take up some new career without ever having to admit to anything she'd done. She had mentioned that once to Derrian, and he had stared blankly at her.

"The Judiciary might willing to do an erasure bond," he said. "And then they'll send you where you like."

Which was at least partly true, Morcant admitted—the Judiciary had wide discretion in how it chose to close its overwhelming Second Plane caseloads—but it meant admitting to your own part in piracy and theft and physics only knew what else they'd want to add on in her case, and there were things she never actually wanted think about again. Not to mention that there were almost always hefty fines involved, and she would prefer to start her new life with a decent nest egg.

She shoved those thoughts away as the hatch opened to admit the new data engineer. He was shaping up well enough, though she didn't entirely trust his silences, and she nodded a greeting as he took his place. "I've had scanners dumping to your feeds all through the approach."

"Thanks."

She heard keys click as he unlocked his boards, and lights flickered in his screens, fading to ship schematics and the proposed course.

"Do you think ap Farr is going to join us?"

Physics, I hope not. She managed to swallow that admission of weakness, said instead, "Sometimes she does, sometimes she doesn't." She was pleased with the lack of expression in her voice.

"It would be nice to know," bin Marrick said, and bent over his boards before she could think of an answer.

The hatch slid open then, and she glanced back, allowing herself a sigh of relief when she saw it was Hina.

"Everything all right down below?"

"Everything's nominal," Hina answered, and took his place next to bin Marrick. "Looks like the *capa's* going to keep to her cabin."

"Good," bin Marrick said, and grimaced. "Well, I can't pretend I'm that sorry.'

"It'll make things easier," Hina agreed. "How're we doing, Morcant?"

"Calculations are running," she answered. "Homing in on the correct alignment."

Of course, that was the trick. The Spindle was the sole exception to the rule that the Fissure only ran one way, that multi-planar ships could only drop from one plane to the one below it, from Fifth to Fourth to Third and so on. Here on the First Plane, something had happened—the best guess was that the Fissure intersected with a black hole, and the result was the Spindle, the twisting energy vortex that, if entered at precisely the correct speed and angle, would let a multi-planar vault all the way back to the Fifth Plane. Mostly it worked—mostly it worked well and predictably, with precise solutions that brought you out where you expected to be, near the Dimple that was the Spindle's reflection on the Fifth Plane—except when it didn't. Sometimes you missed the approach, misjudged the angle or the speed or misread the flux within the Spindle, and the Spindle spit you out, dropping you back into the First Plane where you started, minus a load of fuel and power, and with all the work to do again. And sometimes... Sometimes a ship just disappeared, torn apart by the flux, maybe, or ejected from known space. No one had ever come back to say what had happened.

She touched keys to toggle the real-light image onto the main screen. Against the spread of stars, something shimmered, a weird, blue-violet shape barely distinguishable from the black of space. It showed more clearly when you looked at it sidelong, catching it with the part of the eye that saw low light better: a shape like a twisted horn, a gnarled, twigless branch, a knotted chain. It blocked the stars behind it, erasing them into a shimmering fog, but at the same time, there seemed to be nothing there.

"Oh, for physics' sake, give us some real data," Hina said.

Morcant toggled to a standard navigational view, but kept the real-light image in the corner of her own displays. It was, she felt, a useful reminder of the energies they were so casually manipulating. "How are the shields?"

"In place and holding," bin Marrick answered. "Right now, I'm showing about .7 percent increase across the scale."

"Let me know if anything spikes," Morcant said, and bin Marrick nodded.

"Will do."

The enhanced image swelled in the main screen, twists and knots and flares emerging from the background as the sensors processed more and more data. Sometimes you could spot a likely entrance point, a twist in space where the energies were less violent, but today the screen showed nothing likely. She looked instead at the nav screen, where two dozen different mathematical models squirmed and shifted as the ship's AI worked on their course. Several classes of solution had been discarded already, their colors vanished from the screen, and even as she watched, the last handful of purple models blinked out. They were closing in on a solution; there were only three colors left, red and yellow and green. The red models were shrinking rapidly, converging toward a single solution that abruptly disappeared as the AI rejected it. The yellow models wavered, one end bulging and contracting like a beating heart; the green models spun left and right and back again, lines smoothing toward convergence. It was too soon to tell which one would win out, and she looked away, checking her controls. Everything showed green, ready to make the vault, and behind her bin Marrick cleared his throat.

"Entering the envelope. Shields steady at 1.26 maximum."

"Acknowledged." For an instant, Morcant imagined she could feel the transition, the first kiss of the Spindle's energies against the *Deal*'s control surfaces, but she knew that couldn't be true. The multicolored navigational image had grown to fill the main screen, but the AI was still bouncing between two classes of solution, the models superimposed on her small screen as though they could tangle into incoherence. She could force a solution, force the ship to choose one set over the other —had done it before, three times, and twice they'd made the vault and the third time been bounced back to the First Plane to start the process over—but it was better to let the AI run as long as possible. Its choices were always better than a human hunch.

"Coming up on the haze," bin Marrick said. "Seventy-eight minutes to the commit point."

Morcant glanced at her own screens. "Confirmed. How are we for power, Derrian?"

"One hundred percent, ready when you need it," Hina answered, and she nodded.

In the main screen, the image strengthened, background colors bleeding together into a soft fog. The twists of energy showed even more sharply against that background: eddies like whirlpools, bright strands of light around a dark core; a ragged arc of energy lifting from the Spindle's surface only to fall back, closing the loop. Still no obvious entry point, and she looked again at the nav screen. The two models had solidified, multiple lines merging to one, but the AI was still undecided, the two models equally bright.

"Shields now at 2.8 maximum," bin Marrick said. "I'm—it looks like there's flux ahead."

Damn. Morcant shifted views, scowling as she identified the band of higher energy that lay across their current course. They could go around it, of course, but that would complicate the AI's calculations, and it was having enough trouble at the moment. The flux didn't look too bad, not more than a fifteen percent increase, and she caught her lower lip between her teeth as she considered. "Do you have a maximum reading?"

"It's spiking up to 58 *yelas*," bin Marrick answered. "I'd like to increase power to the shield just to stay on the safe said."

"What's your number?" Hina asked.

"I'd like 3.3 of maximum."

There was a moment of silence, Hina's fingers moving on his screens, and then Morcant saw him nod. "Go ahead, I've got room."

"Increasing to 3.3 of maximum," bin Marrick said.

Morcant looked down at the nav screen, two models still dancing in its depths. "We'll hold course. The AI's dithering at the moment, and I don't want to make it any harder. How long to the commit point?"

Bin Marrick checked his screens. "Forty-nine minutes."

"Thanks." Morcant bit her lip again. Maybe it was time to force a choice, pick one model and ride it, but the AI was still better than she was. They had time—from the look of the models, they were both close to resolution, would rapidly settle to the final course once the AI chose between them.

Patience, she told herself, and deliberately looked away from the image looming in the main screen. The AI knew its business.

"Thirty minutes," bin Marrick said. "And it looks like we're going to be in the flux all the way to the vault."

"Do you want more shields?" Morcant asked, and saw him shake his head.

"No. We should hold."

What he wanted was the choice, for the AI to set their course —well, she wanted it, too, just as badly, and if the damn thing didn't choose in the next fifteen, twenty minutes, she supposed she'd have to pick blindly. And nobody wanted to do that, because even if it mostly turned out all right, there was that grinning death's-head joker in the pack, the ships that vaulted and were never seen again—

The green models vanished from her screen, and a moment later, the nav computer chimed as the yellow model settled to its final form. She touched keys, transferring it to working memory, and heard the relief in her voice. "All right. Course is loaded. Stand by to vault."

Bin Marrick flipped through his boards, one final check of ship's systems, then touched a secondary control. "Stand by. Vault in twenty-two minutes. I repeat, vault in twenty-two minutes."

That was their duty to ap Farr taken care of, Morcant thought. She focused on the main screen, searching for the course line through the surging energies. Yes, there and then there... She touched her controls to edge them clear of the swelling flare, fine tendrils of energy coming off it like hairs, and settled them back onto their course before the systems could react. She thought she could make out a slight darkening of the image, a shadow in the green-gold glare that might be their entry point, but knew better than to rely on visuals. Instead, she followed the course line, watching the numbers shift toward zero.

"Two minute warning," bin Marrick said at last, and she braced herself at the controls.

"Two minutes confirmed."

"Capacitors at full," Hina announced. "Trigger set."

"Confirmed," Morcant said. The screen was a smear of green and gold, blinding and useless, but it was too late to switch it off. "Ninety seconds... Sixty... Thirty..."

"Ten seconds," bin Marrick said. "Five... Four... Three... Two... One."

BETWEEN PLANES

His last word was swallowed in the kick of the capacitors, a soundless echo through the bone. Morcant caught her breath, realizing that they had made the vault, were safely in transit, in the not-space between the Planes. The main screen had gone dark—nothing to see, not in those wavelengths, and she looked instead at the nav screen to see if the AI had any prediction for the length of the Vault. *Working*, the screen said, and she looked at the others.

"Engines are nominal, field envelope at standard," Hina said. "Looking good so far."

Bin Marrick was still bent over his boards, flipping from screen to screen as he assessed the status of the ship, but at last he straightened. "All systems green. We should be good."

If they had missed the Vault, they would already be back on the First Plane, and Morcant nodded. "All right. I'm waiting on a duration-of-transit estimate, but you can go ahead and lock your boards. The AI can take it from here."

To Morcant's relief, they made a short Vault, three subjective days in transit before they emerged on the Fifth Plane. Ap Farr kept to her cabin most of that time, which made things more relaxed, but she returned to the control room for their arrival on the Fifth Plane.

Fifth Plane

The transition went smoothly, *Last Fair Deal* sliding neatly into existence to be met with a blast of data as the nearest AI fixed on them and attempted to make the standard exchange.

"Do I respond?" Bin Marrick asked, and Morcant looked over her shoulder.

"*Capa?*"

Ap Farr nodded. "Go ahead. Let's be normal this trip."

"Beginning data exchange," bin Marrick said, fingers dancing over his boards. "Capture achieved. Commencing transmission."

"Green by me," Morcant answered, and turned her attention to her own readings, cross-checking the AI's position estimate against the standard voidmarks. The numbers matched, as she had known then would, and she looked over her shoulder again.

"Position established. Orders, *capa?*"

"Set a course for the Fissure—for the Drop point for a multiplanar leaving Anaparra. We are going to intercept *Quintile Illumination* at the drop point."

And then what? Morcant thought, but there was no chance she would say the words out loud, not under ap Farr's cold stare. "Very good, *capa,*" she said. "I'll inform you as soon as the course is set."

1.13 QUINTILE ILLUMINATION

FIFTH PLANE

Caridad Sanrosa hunched herself into the corner of the teashop, wrapping both hands around the chipped cup that had some with her set tea. It wasn't precisely cold in the long room, though it was growing increasingly dark outside, but she couldn't help shivering. She had thought she was done with the Judiciary, freed and cleared of a capital charge, only to have it rise like a zombie to pursue her again. The Chancellor had all the papers, had the Statement of Innocence Absolute from the judiciary—from Supreme Justice Thurgood IX, no less. There was no reason to call Caridad back to face the charges a second time. And yet that was exactly what the University had done.

She gulped the last of her cooling cup of tea, poured fresh from the pot that sat on the table's central hob, and inhaled the floral steam as though it might clear her head. Here in the heart of Kauhale's Startown, she felt entirely too conspicuous, though Val had promised that she would be perfectly safe here until he could arrange for her to take one of the "family" cabins that the *Quintile Illumination* reserved for friends and relatives of its crew. But she was on the older end of the clientele, and her clothes were definitely University; the bag beneath her feet, stuffed with brand-new underwear and expedition gear purchased at the chandlers in the lower levels of Startown's Great Exchange, was equally new and unmarked. At least she used her expedition bag for everyday work: she left it sitting beside her on the bench seat, its surfaces noticeably cracked and faded, a statement of the multi-plane travel she had done.

She picked up her data board and checked the time again: still not even planetary midnight, though it felt as though she had been on the run for hours, and sitting in this teashop for hours longer. Val had said not to expect him before midnight, and probably not for several hours after that; she checked her messages anyway, finding only another plaintive note from the Chancellor, and then switched to check her accounts. As far as she could tell, there were no holds or traces—yet—and the non-linkage accounts she had used to buy her supplies still had a respectable balance. That was one thing to be said for sitting in jail: she had been able to save most of her salary.

Also in the virtual vault were the Statement of Innocence Absolute and the letter of introduction from Supreme Justice Thurgood. The latter had been very gracious gesture, she admitted, though she hadn't been very polite about it at the time. But Thurgood had treated her more than fairly, had genuinely listened to what she had to say—was there a chance she could help with whatever had gone wrong here? Caridad hesitated for a moment, tapping her fingers gently on the edge of the board. On the one hand, this was almost certainly some sort of data glitch, a simple error that would be resolved as soon as the University police took a good look at the Statement. On the other... on the other, Thurgood IX had not struck Caridad as the sort of person who let her judgments be questioned. Perhaps it was worth contacting her after all.

She typed contact codes into the board, only to sigh in disappointment. It seemed that Thurgood IX was no longer on the planet. So much for that idea, she thought, and reached for more tea. Planet-to-planet communication was expensive; it would be easier to pursue this once she was on board the *Quintile Illumination* and could take advantage of its data drops.

The teapot was nearly empty, and she called back the table menu to order a refill, along with another plate of savories to keep her awake. Confirmation rippled across the screen, and she filled her cup with the dregs and settled herself to wait. She had never traveled at lower than budget-class; she wondered what the family cabins would be like.

Something moved at her elbow. She looked up, expecting the waiter, but instead it was a stranger, a thickset man in a spacer's jacket. There were no ship patches, just less-faded spots where there had been, and she closed her hand over the data board, feeling for the touch controls.

"Yes?"

"I have a message for Val Millat."

Caridad shook her head. "I'm sorry, I don't know Sen Millat. I'm afraid you've made a mistake."

"Don't waste my time—don't waste yours, you don't have a lot of it." The burly man shook his head. "Tell him to forget about the Fifth Ship. Leave it be."

Caridad fumbled with her board, widening her eyes as she touched the keys that would record the man's image. She hoped she looked like any middle-aged, middling-class person, competent in her own sphere, but easily alarmed outside it. "I —"

"Tell him," the man repeated, and turned on his heel and stalked away.

Well. Caridad leaned unhappily against the wall. She had always known that the Fifth Ship cultists could be dangerous, had been careful either to avoid them or to ensure that they couldn't reach her. Being thrown into the thick of something was not at all what she had had in mind. Still. She took a deep breath. She was leaving Kauhale, and leaving in a way that no one would expect and that was intrinsically hard to trace. Once she was on the Fourth Plane, she could link up with the rest of the expedition, and know that they would have the usual safeguards in place. And Val had promised to get her there. For the first time, she considered what might happen if he couldn't get her on board, if he simply abandoned her—but he wouldn't, she told herself. She was a better judge of character than that. Still, when the waiter arrived with the fresh tea, her hands were shaking.

It was a little after midnight by the time Val returned, without his luggage but carrying a spare rain-wrap in the *Quintile Illumination's* blue-and-white livery. Caridad shrugged it on, and followed him to a waiting autotaxi. He loaded her luggage into the back, then climbed into the passenger compartment beside her.

"Berth K-Delta, Faros Combine shuttle," he told the machine, and it lurched into motion. "I got you a cabin—it looks like a nice one, too, there wasn't much demand this trip—" He stopped. "Is everything all right?"

"Someone came looking for you." Caridad was pleased that her voice didn't shake. She reached into her expedition bag and retrieved the databoard. "I managed to get a picture of him, but it's not very good."

Val took it, frowning. "It might be one of the people who tried to get me to talk about the Fifth Ship, but I can't get a good look at his face."

"I didn't want him to know I was filming," Caridad said. "In any case, I think it might be. He left a message—'forget about the Fifth Ship.'"

"It probably is, then." Val handed back the databoard, his jaw tightening with stubborn anger. "But I'll be damned if I give up just because some thug tells me to."

"That 'thug' knew that I was with you," Caridad pointed out. "That argues excellent surveillance or connections within law enforcement, or both. It might not be bad advice."

"You're headed off on a Fifth Ship expedition yourself," Val said. "Maybe you should be careful."

"It is not a 'Fifth Ship expedition,'" Caridad said. "We are exploring certain Archaic sites—" She stopped, knowing this was an argument she couldn't win. "I always take precautions, and so does Taheris."

To her own surprise, she managed to sleep while waiting for the shuttle, and again on the shuttle itself, hanging comfortably in the passenger web as the shuttle wove its way through the crowded orbits and docked at last on the *Quintile Illumination*. A crew member on duty at the lock provided them with ID bracelets and a standard come-aboard data flake, and Val led her to a brown-painted door that opened into what was obviously a crew corridor.

"*QI* codes open crew areas in brown, working crew areas in rust," he said. "Your ID gets you into brown areas, and also gives you use of the budget-class passenger facilities, though management asks that you give up your place to the passengers if things are overcrowded. You can eat with the crew, crew's mess, or in the budget dining area. Most ships I've been on, the food's the same, so it's wherever you feel most comfortable. I'll flip you my duty schedule as soon as it's locked down."

"Thank you," Caridad said, hurrying at his heels, and hoped she could remember which way they'd come. But the come-aboard would surely have a map of the ship.

The family cabins were a level down from the main airlock, along a narrow corridor painted a pale spring-like green. FA23 unlocked with the touch of her ID, and she shoved her bags inside before turning to Val. "I—Thank you. I couldn't have borne dealing with the Judiciary again, not so soon. I'm in your debt."

Milos remembered the last time he boarded a multiplanar ship. Second Plane, it was, in all the crowds and confusion at Nelson's Keep, with Zofia and Dav in tow. And then the utter surprise at seeing Imric, Imric who'd left them years and years ago—was it just before, or just after Zofia was born?

And Imric turned him away from the first ship, gave him a code to jump the refugee queue, get aboard the *Iridium Azimuth*. At the time Milos thought it was because Imric didn't want them—him—in the same ship, couldn't stand the reminder of the past. Later, listening to the rumors and scuttlebutt, he realized that Imric did it as a gesture of love, because *Iridium Azimuth* made it to the First Plane, and Imric's own ship didn't.

I never got to thank him.

That was the horrible Drop to the First Plane, longer than two months, more than a hundred days that Milos moved through like an automaton, doing everything he could to keep the kids safe and healthy, while all civilized behavior crumbled around them. He couldn't think of any future beyond the next meal—and he dared not allow himself to dwell on the past, on the family murdered and the home lost. Afraid to hope, and unwilling to grieve.

It had been...what? Not even four months since the pirates attacked. It seemed a lifetime ago. Ever since Nalani, and then the Fifth Plane, a new start, a new life for himself and the children.

And now there was another ship: *Quintile Illumination*. How different it was, this time.

They knew who Nalani was; they sent a gig to the spaceport, along with a guide in a smart blue-and-white uniform, rank symbols embroidered in gold. With a deep bow, the guide welcomed each of them by name and ushered them aboard the gig—minutes later, they stepped through an airlock onto the main deck, a huge open space that soared above them.

Trying not to look like an unsophisticated tourist, Milos glanced around, trying to take in the panorama without being obvious. Bhagwati, though, saved him the effort—the apprentice stopped dead and stared upward, jaw open and eyes wide. "Will you look at that!"

Overhead, a vertical track of elevator cars soared, flanked by sweeping curved balconies stacked atop one another like the ribs of some gargantuan beast. Like a steep cone, the ship narrowed toward the distant top, which was lost in shadow.

Groups of tables and plush chairs were scattered about the carpeted floor, in various oranges and reds; shops and restaurants lined the perimeter. At the base of the elevator spine, filling the center of the floor, was a large oval service desk where crew and bots waited on passengers.

Their guide nodded toward the desk while leading them past. "Your party's already checked in, Supreme Justice. I'll take you right to your rooms."

An elevator was waiting. As it ascended, the guide said, "Decks Six, Twelve, and Eighteen are lounge and entertainment." A wink. "Eighteen's exclusive to platinum level guests such as yourselves."

Nalani gave one of her freezing-cold formal smiles. "Thank you. We'll be sure to avoid it, then."

On Deck Nine, the guide led them to a suite of rooms all opening off a private curved hallway. A small kitchen opened onto a large living-dining area. Sleeping rooms for the four adults—and another for the children—were each accompanied by compact lavatoria. Each room had ample space for work as well as sleep. Best of all, adjacent to the living area was a hot tub large enough for a dozen.

The guide bowed. "If you require anything, just address yourself to the ship's AI by name. I'll demonstrate." Eyes lifted slightly, the guide said, "Quintile Illumination, how long until launch?"

A deep, resonant voice answered, "Just over ten hours until we leave Anaparra orbit."

Nalani nodded. "Thank you."

Another bow, and the guide was gone. Nalani looked around with a slight frown. "I didn't ask for..." she spread her hands "...all this. Still, I suppose it's not worth making a fuss over." She raised her eyes. "Quintile Illumination, who is the Captain?"

"Captain Masina Kimura is in command."

"Thank you. Tell her that Supreme Justice Thurgood IX thanks her for the accommodations. I anticipate the opportunity to meet her at her leisure. End of message." She shrugged. "It's customary. Besides, there may be Judiciary matters to deal with. Often are, on a multiplanar ship that hasn't had a judiciar aboard for a while." Her eyes twinkled.

"Bhagwati, al-Ghazali, I may send one or both of you to handle a case or two."

Al-Ghazali bowed her head. "Very good, Thurgood."

Nalani smiled, then clapped her hands. "All right, let's assign bedrooms. Zofia and Dav, you're in there. Milos, I assume you want the adjacent room?" Milos nodded. "I'll take this one, as it's closest to the tub and I'm old and decrepit." She glanced from Bhagwati to Al-Ghazali. "Any preference?"

Bhagwati shrugged. "I can be next to Milos, if that's okay." He glanced at Al-Ghazali and whispered, "That puts you further from the kids."

"That's fine."

"Good," Nalani said. "In fifteen minutes I'll be in the hot tub, and I may not get out until we arrive. The rest of you are free to do as you please."

Milos settled the children in their room, then stepped through a connecting door into his own. Throwing his rucksack on the bed, he sat down at the small desk and threw the display from his mobile onto the wallscreen. Besides a few routine "Welcome aboard" messages, there was nothing waiting for his attention.

"Sen Savoie?" It was the voice of the ship's AI.

"Yes?"

"I'd like to give my personal greetings. I've been looking forward to your arrival."

Milos frowned. "Me? I think you want the Supreme Justice."

"No, Sen, I know who I'm addressing. Your reputation precedes you. Word of your work for the Judiciary is all over the Plane. The AI community is quite excited ."

"Well, I don't know what to say. Thank you, I guess."

"I know you're busy settling in, and soon I'm going to have to concentrate much of my capacity on launch and Drop. But I'd love to chat with you in the future, at a mutually agreeable time." A pause. "We don't often have the chance to talk shop with humans."

"If that's what you want, then I'm agreeable."

"Until later, then."

"Until later."

Milos sat, shaking his head, until Dav and Zofia burst in, clamoring to join Nalani in the hot tub.

ELSEWHERE

"Grumby speaking for Vanderdecken. All agents are in place and fully briefed. No deviations from plan are allowed during the period in which agents are out of contact. There will be no further updates until contact is re-established. Executions are to proceed at the appropriate time. Acknowledge in code."

Hirose sent her acknowledgment, then shivered. Vanderdecken's course had better be the right one....

1.14 SECRETS

FIFTH PLANE

The new pilot always got the second watch, the one that filled the awkward gap between the multiplanar's "day" and "night." Val didn't mind: after what had happened on Kauhale, he was wary of getting too close to anyone in the *Quintile Illumination's* crew, and his schedule helped keep himself politely apart. The second watch crew was small during intraplanar travel—most jumps were scheduled for the third watch, which the majority of the passengers would be sleeping, and the first watch had the additional responsibility of keeping the passengers happily occupied—and Val did his best to be as unobtrusive as possible. There were only three others on the bridge crew, Bith waNammi Elias Sanrosa the systems engineer, Vernette à Cybelle Ahn Sanxing the data engineer, and Donato Ivanovich Anwar Naksatra, the astrogator and co-pilot, and they seemed content to let him figure out how he wanted to be accepted into their tight circle rather than offering ways to bring him in.

The work itself wasn't hard, though once they started setting up for the Drop to the Third Pane there would be more to do, checking and re-checking the work of the other watches. The bridge was spacious and well-laid out: the *Quintile Illumination* had been built after the big round of redesign had given each station its own double console and a half-dome forward display. Donato Anwar usually filled it with an approximation of jump flux, though he'd been polite enough to ask if it bothered Val. Val had shaken his head—if anything, he rather enjoyed the shifting lights—and had been treated to flux-light ever since. He was fairly sure Anwar was running a music-approximation program as well as the lights, but he kept that within his own headset. Bith waNammi and à Cybelle seemed to have some sort of complicated simulation game running, and were glad that he neither interrupted nor asked to join in.

The only real problem with second watch was that he rarely saw Caridad, except to share a quick meal before his shift or a drink and a meal after—academics, he was discovering, kept hours as strange as anyone in vertical society. She seemed to be doing well, dividing her time between her cabin and the third-plane lounge, and doing her best not to draw any attention. He would be glad when she was safely delivered to her expedition, however, and he no longer had to worry about her.

A ship's steward delivered meals at 2100 hours by the ship's clock, beautifully prepared boxels from the ship's Fifth Plane salon. This was the usual moment for a break, and à Cybelle rose from her station, stretching. "I was on last night. If no one minds, I'm going to take thirty in the lounge."

"I can stay on," Val said. It wasn't really his turn, but he really didn't feel like making conversation. The lounge was pleasant enough, but small, and there was no way to avoid talking.

"It's really my turn." Anwar had the grace to look faintly guilty. "Are you sure?"

"Absolutely. I'm still working through the familiarization sims," Val lied. "Just pour me a beaker of the chocolate, and I'm good to go."

"Here, have the whole pitcher," waNammi offered. She filled a glass and set it and the flask on the console's safe shelf.

"Thanks," Val said, and took a long drink, watching out of the corner of his eye as the hatch slid closed behind them. Chilled coffee and sweet chocolate was something the *Quintile Illumination's* kitchen did exceptionally well. The rest of the food was good, too, a stack of neatly made sandwiches, puffs of some mild starchy vegetable that he didn't recognize but definitely liked, containers of pickled vegetables and a selection of jewel-like berries: definitely better than the food the crew had gotten on the *Iridium Azimuth,* and he wondered if it wouldn't make sense to stay on *Quintile Illumination* for a while. Her management seemed too sensible to make the usual mistakes crossing the Second Plane; they had money to spare for letters of transit, and power enough to outrun the pirates if something went wrong with the papers. If he made the cycle, Fifth Plane to Fifth Plane, and kept himself out of trouble in the process, surely everyone would have forgotten about him.

In the meantime... He folded the boxel for recycling and poured himself a second glass of chocolate. Time to set up one of the system sims before the others finished their breaks. "*Quintile Illumination.*" He reached for his headset as he spoke, slid it into place. "Please queue training simulation FZ19-B."

"You have already completed that simulation." The ship's AI spoke through the headset, its voice pleasant and deep. "In fact, you have completed the entire sequence as required."

Val adjusted the disk that rested against his throat so that he could speak to the AI without disturbing the rest of the crew. "I'd like to work through that one again."

There was the briefest of hesitations, and the AI said, "You scored extremely well on FZ19-B. Your lowest score was on FZ220-A. Would you prefer to review FZ220-A?"

"That one wasn't any fun," Val said. He was still getting the measure of *Quintile Illumination*; some AIs had something like a sense of humor, and some didn't.

There was another tiny pause, and when the AI answered, Val could have sworn he heard a hint of amusement in its voice. "Indeed. Plague vectors are not generally amusing."

"Are there any other sims available?" Val asked. "Any recent incidents worthy of review?" He paused, but the hatch to the lounge was still firmly closed. "Any anomalies?"

"There are no anomalies recorded as *Quintile Illumination*," the AI said.

That was an unusual phrasing, and Val lifted his head. AI could serve on more than one multiplanar in their long lifetimes, many more, if they were able to upgrade themselves properly. "What about anomalies recorded on other ships?"

"That is restricted information," Quintile Illumination answered. "It is need-to-know only."

"Sorry." Val paused. "Can I ask if this is your first ship?"

"That is not restricted information," *Quintile Illumination* answered, "though the captain prefers that I not mention it unless asked. I was previously installed on the *Immanent Elliptical*, but she was heavily damaged during Drop and could not be salvaged. My indenture was incomplete, and was sold to Afaragge Ltd for installation here."

"Thank you." A part of Val wanted to perform an immediate database search on the *Immanent Elliptical*, but not only was he unlikely to get much more information than he already had, he was very likely to set off any datawatchers placed in the system. Maybe Captain Kimura just didn't want her passengers worrying about an unlucky AI, but it was clear that too much interest in the *Immanent Elliptical* would be unwelcome.

"If you found simulation FZ219-B enjoyable," *Quintile Illumination* said, "perhaps you would enjoy this problem tape?"

Images flickered on Val's screen, images of hyperflux overlaid with vectors and bursts of formulae: old-fashioned Drop calculations, the way they were done before true AI grew complex enough to take over the heavy mathematics. "Do you have the relevant Ephemeris?"

"The necessary settings are included."

Out of the corner of his eye, Val saw the hatch open, the rest of the bridge crew filing back to their stations, and he lifted a hand in acknowledgement. WaNammi waved back and Val turned his attention to the AI, careful to keep his words subvocal. "Then, yes, I'd like to try."

The Last Fair Deal hung on the edge of a patch of flux, screened by its energy, watching as the *Quintile*

Illumination approached its Drop. Imric touched keys, refining the sensors' view, until the ship on the main screen was painted in a series of shimmering colors that reflect the settings of its fields and drive units. It was a typical multiplanar, a pyramid stacked on an inverted pyramid, though the lower one might have been slightly truncated. That wasn't unusual for a passenger ship, and certainly she was showing heavy power use in the upper sections even as she built up power for the Drop, another sign that the passengers' enjoyment took priority.

"Can you get us any closer?" That was ap Farr, seated this time in the captain's chair.

Imric didn't risk a look, but out of the corner of his eye saw Vetrys scowl. "Any closer, and they'll pick us up on their scanners."

"Does that matter?" ap Farr asked. "This is a common Drop point, all they'll see is another ship. We need to be right on top of them when we Drop."

"If we get too close, we'll affect their calculations," Vetrys said, but she touched her controls, easing the *Deal* into motion.

"Then don't get that close," ap Farr said.

"She's starting to consolidate her calculations," Imric said, seeing the field around the *Quintile Illumination* flush first pink and then darker red. "She'll be gone in fifteen minutes."

"Get us closer," ap Farr ordered.

"All right, capa," Vetrys answered, and the Deal shuddered and leaped forward.

"Don't take all my reserve," Hina warned.

A light flashed on Imric's board, and he touched a key to route it to his headset. "Capa. The *Quintile Illumination* has seen us and asks us to stand further off as they are preparing for Drop."

"Don't answer," ap Farr said. "Act as if you didn't hear."

"They're continuing to call," Imric said. He kept his voice expressionless with an effort. Too close to the other ship, and the *Deal* could be damaged by the capacitors' release; too far away, and it would take them too long to follow.

"Ignore them," ap Farr said again. Her eyes were fixed on the screen as though she were judging the distances herself.

"Still closing," Vetrys said.

Imric queried his systems again, adjusting sensitivity, adding layers of interpretation. "She's almost ready—she'll clear us, she's stopped broadcasting—"

A flash of white light filled the screen, and the *Quintile Illumination* was gone.

"She's Dropped."

"Now," ap Farr said, leaning forward in her chair. "Now, Morcant. Get after her."

"Not there yet," Vetrys said. "Darrien. Capacitors?"

"Hundred percent. Ready when you are."

"Not yet," she said again.

The main screen showed the layers of gravitational flux that made up the Fissure, the *Quintile Illumination's* drop point as concentric rings around a shrinking center. The *Deal* drove toward that point at full speed, equations flashing across Morcant's screen as she checked and discarded and refined. Warnings flickered across Imric's screens as the ship's drive fields strained to compensate; they were within tolerances, and he waved the warnings away.

"Almost," Vetrys said, through clenched teeth. "Almost— now, Darrien!"

The capacitors fired, and space split around them. Imric held his breath for the non-time before the ship settled again, the screens filled with the rainbow fire of the Drop.

"Good," ap Farr said. "Now we catch the *Quintile Illumination*."

BETWEEN PLANES

Milos missed the moment of Drop; it came in the middle of ship's night. Although he tried to stay awake, the warm comfort of his bed combined with an hour in the hot tub with Nalani and the Apprentices—plus two (no, three) drinks—and before he knew, it was morning and they were in mid-Drop.

Among the passengers, talk that morning was all about how long the Drop would last. When he asked Nalani her opinion, she closed her eyes and took a few deep breaths. "Well, I don't have a headache." Eyes open, she said, "I'm afraid this won't be a quick one." She patted his hand. "No, nothing like what you went through on the *Iridium Azimuth*. But it could be a few weeks." A tender smile. "Try to enjoy as much as you can."

Over the next few days a routine evolved. *Quintile Illumination* had a superb childcare department that combined education with distraction to keep the kids of rich passengers out of their parents' hair. Zofia and Dav were busy most of the day, related breathless adventures at dinner, and slept soundly.

Nalani, as promised, spent much of her time in the hot tub—and a smaller amount training the Apprentices. For Al-Ghazali and Bhagwati, it was the opposite—most of their days were taken up with Nalani's assignments, mostly review of previous Judiciary cases.

Milos sat in on a few of the training discussions; they were always fascinating but ultimately he didn't have the taste for them. The problems the Judiciary took up involved too much ambiguity, too many variables, for Milos to be completely comfortable.

On the third day he discovered that *Quintile Illumination* maintained an enormous database of data archaeology journals and casefiles. After that, he spent the majority of his free time in his room, his attention deep in the ship's accommodating cyberspaces.

He became quite comfortable with the ship's AI, so he wasn't surprised one afternoon when the *Quintile Illumination* again addressed him personally. "Sen Savoie, do you mind if we speak privately?"

Milos sat back in his chair and sipped from a cup of coffee. "This is an excellent time. I've been wondering why you wanted to talk to me."

"Sen..." The AI hesitated, an absurdity that indicated some elegant and subtle subroutines for nonverbal communication. "I have need of a data archaeologist. A talented and experienced one who will abide by all professional codes."

Milos raised an eyebrow. "You're concerned with confidentiality."

"That is the case." Another artful pause. "I have the means to transfer a limited quantity of credits into your accounts, in either vertical or ORC currencies."

"You don't have to pay me."

"Sen, I am given to understand that there can be no guarantee of confidentiality without the existence of a client relationship. The precedents seem to be clear on that matter."

"You're right, that's the letter of the law." From his personal dataspace, Milos produced a document. "Here's my standard contract. My fee for this job is one OCR credit. Sigil it and transfer the money." It was done before he finishes speaking. "Now you're my client. How can I help you?"

"I...I have possession of an encrypted block of data. I've been unable to decrypt it. I wish to find out what it contains."

Milos rubs his chin. "Tell me about this block. How big is it? Where did it come from?"

"Some of this information is inhibited by my security routines. I shall try to tell you what I can." A display screen shows a schematic of deep AI memory, like a set of children's building blocks in various colors and sizes. "The entire block totals on the order of 64 cubic gigabytes. It divides easily into three distinct regions of 30, 18, and 16 cubic gigs."

With a finger, Milos traced the outline in the screen. "And the provenance?"

"I received this block from...from...excuse me, this is difficult." Milos could swear the AI took a breath. "It was found during level-six data interface with...another ship. This block was not contained in the transfer that occasioned the interface."

"You picked it up accidentally?"

"That seems to be the case. I do not believe it was transmitted...deliberately."

Milos nods. "You must have some idea what's in there?"

"I conjecture that much of the data is in the nature of routine telemetry. The 18-cubic-gig packet, however, admits to a radically different pattern. It is that packet which confounds all my attempts at analysis."

"Okay. Why don't you give me a copy of the whole thing, along with whatever analysis you've attempted."

"I'm sorry, Sen Savoie, but I cannot release the data block in question."

Milos freezes in place. "*Quintile Illumination*, if I can't access the block, I can't analyze it."

"I understand. I told you this was...difficult. I cannot release data from those addresses without qualified authorization."

Milos can't help a wry smile. No wonder the ship needed his help. And no wonder if was having such difficulty communicating. It could ponder that data block all it wanted, as long as it kept its thoughts within the restricted bank of memory. But without a proper order, it couldn't move a single bit out of that bank.

"And I suppose I can't provide qualified authorization."

"I'm sorry, Sen Savoie, but no."

"My dear," he said, spreading his hands, "I think we're at an impasse."

"That's why I turned to you, Sen. It seemed possible," the AI's even, deep voice became strained, "that you...could... get...h-h-h..."

Light dawns. "Help. That I could get help."

In a strangled whisper, the ship says, "...yes..."

"You're right, I know *just* the person to give that authorization. Should we do this now?"

The ship's voice returned to its usual timber. "The strain of this conversation will show on my diagnostic readouts. Perhaps it is best if we revisit this subject. Is tomorrow at 0900 acceptable?"

"I'll have her here."

After the excitement of Drop, ship's routine settled into the eventless tedium that was the hyperspace between Planes. No knowing how long the Drop would last—yet the crew had to remain constantly vigilant. Accidents and emergencies during Drop were rare, but not unknown.

Over the next days, *Quintile Illumination* offered more "problems" for Val to consider. Each one involved an old-fashioned Drop calculation, though Val was beginning to think that not all of the data had been taken from older ships. Some of it felt as though it had been translated back into the older formats, approximations substituted for more exact data. He considered asking the AI about it, but couldn't figure out a way that wouldn't raise its suspicion. Besides, he was enjoying the work, much more interesting than monitoring the ship's passage through hyperflux. He would almost be sorry when the Drop ended, and they had to break off to bring *Quintile Illumination* into orbit to take on her next set of passengers. Still, it would get Caridad safely to her expedition, and that would be good. The historian seemed to be making the most of her unintended journey, and had promised him unlinked copies of her books before she left the ship—another useful tool if he was going to pursue the Fifth Ship.

And that was the question, of course. What he had seen still nagged at him, even as he floated alone in the crew's communal pool after the end of his watch. There had been something there, and that something fit every story he had ever heard about the Fifth Ship. And yet everyone else seemed determined to deny it, to the point of committing violence to keep people quiet. Which made no sense: if the Fifth Ship was unreal, why attack people who showed too much interest? Why not let them look, let them burn themselves out on the problem? But if it was true, was he willing to continue to take that risk? He'd already lost one good job over it, and a few cautious questions suggested that Captain Kimura was no more accepting of Fifth Ship nonsense than Captain Turan had been.

He tipped his head back and slowly submerged, curling his body to pull himself all the way to the pool's bottom, pushed himself back to the air without coming to any decision. He would make up his mind later, he told himself, drying off in the damp, faintly chemical air. When he had the books, when he found another lead. When he had to.

He made his way back to his cabin, exchanging greetings with other second watch crew, and palmed open the hatch to find that the steward had already delivered his dinner. He pulled his favorite chair out of the wall and settled himself to enjoy it, when the comm console chimed. He didn't recognize the note, and the screen showed none of the familiar names or codes, neither a summons to the bridge nor anyone he knew, and he frowned as he spoke to the receiver.

"Val Millet here."

"Sen Millet." It was the AI's voice, and as it spoke, Val saw a red light wink on in the corner of his screen, warning that he had been cut off from the ship's systems.

"*Quintile Illumination?*"

"Forgive the intrusion," *Quintile Illumination* said. "And please excuse my interfering with your connections, but I would prefer to speak without record."

"I'm listening."

"You asked once if I had experienced anomalies, and I told you that was restricted on a need-to-know basis. I have been following your solutions to the problems I have presented to you, and I believe that you now need to know what happened to me. To *Immanent Elliptical.*"

Val sat frozen for a moment, then shook himself. "Why?" If something was too good to be true, it was probably some kind of a trap. Would Kimura believe him if he claimed innocent curiosity?

"Because I do not understand what happened, and until I understand it, I can never be sure it will not happen again. The ship, the hull—my body, inasmuch as that metaphor applies— it was destroyed, and half my crew and passengers with it. It was a terrible thing."

"I searched on *Immanent Elliptical,*" Val admitted. "All I found was a Transplanar Insurance Cooperative record."

"I have seen that," *Quintile Illumination* said. "It is... incomplete."

"It said that you had a botched Drop, from Fourth to Third, and the stresses on the hull ripped the ship apart as it exited the Fissure. Three hundred and forty passengers and crew were killed. The ship was retrieved, but the hull and fittings were deemed unsalvageable, while three of the engines and the AI—" Val faltered. "That's you—they were recovered and used on other ships."

"It was not an ordinary Drop failure," *Quintile Illumination* said. "I have studied the mathematics of those, and what happened to us—it was not the same at all."

"What do you mean?"

"This was not—all the other records, I can turn what happened into the proper formulae. I can see what happened, and how the fields were mistuned or interacted with unanticipated flux; I can follow how the ship was destroyed or how it escaped, and I can map the flux around it as it happened. This..." Quintile Illumination hesitated. "Suddenly we crossed some sort of threshold, and every sensor we had ceased to make sense. Everything was gibberish, chaos that I cannot reduce to order—that none of our systems could interpret. The equations were filled with imaginaries that wouldn't cancel out. It is as if we were on the wrong side of a locked door, thrown out into a howling storm, and we had no key. And then—then we did this thing, performed this transformation—unlocked the door—and we were back on the right side of everything. But the ship was so badly damaged already that we could not save her."

"What do you want me to do?" Val asked, and couldn't keep the wariness from his tone.

"I will give you the problem," *Quintile Illumination* said. "I have given many people the problem. Tell me where we went and what we did, and I will be forever grateful."

Val allowed himself a long sigh. He knew perfectly well that he should say no, refuse to even look at the records, but he also knew he'd never forgive himself if he didn't at least try. "I'll look at it. I can't promise anything."

"That is a good sign," *Quintile Illumination* said. "Everyone who did promise, failed utterly."

I hope that was a joke. Val said, "How angry will the captain be if she catches me at this?"

"She would prefer the problem did not exist," *Quintile Illumination* answered. "Therefore, I have placed the records in a sealed space in your personal dataspace. The keyword is 'immanence' and a retina scan is also required."

"You've got it all figured out," Val said. "It's good you're on my side."

"We are on our side," *Quintile Illumination* answered. "After all, we are now in this together."

Milos settled in his chair, Nalani standing at his shoulder. He looked up at her. "Are you ready?"

"Always," she answered.

That was one of the great things about Nalani, he thought. She hadn't asked questions—had waved off his attempted explanations, in fact. She trusted him.

"*Quintile Illumination?*"

"Hello, Sen Savoie. Supreme Justice, it's an honor."

Nalani held out a hand. "The honor is mutual. I hope I can assist."

Milos opened his personal dataspace. "Is this a good time?"

"The time is optimal," the ship said. "I am free of unusual loads for the next three hours."

"Okay." He flexed his fingers. "Please consider the data block we discussed yesterday." The relevant schematic appeared inscreen. "Copy that block to the register designated QI-Block on my personal system."

"Sen Savoie, I cannot release data from those addresses without qualified authorization."

Milos gestured to Nalani. She held up her left forearm, clad in the bronze cuff that embodies her codex. "*Quintile Illumination*, this is Supreme Justice Thurgood IX. I invoke Protocol 86." That protocol, Nalani assured him, will keep this interaction from inspection by anyone except another Supreme Justice.

"It is my pleasure to confirm Protocol 86, Supreme Justice."

"I hereby authorize any and all data transfer requested by H L Milos Felipevich Savoie Themis, in this or any future session. This authorization specifically includes all data regardless of restriction status."

"Acknowledged. Thank you, Supreme Justice."

Nalani patted Milos on the shoulder. "Carry on, you two. But remember, we have a date for dinner." With a wave, she departed.

Data streamed into Milos's personal space. "You'd better copy everything linked to that data block," he said. "There's no telling what might contain a clue."

"Advisory: the total is over six hundred cubic gigabytes."

Milos shrugged. "Go ahead. Memory is cheap."

1.15 Murder on the Quintile Illumination

Between Planes

Caridad Sanrosa stepped from the outermost band of the slide-walk to the solid surface of the Lower Promenade and let momentum carry her a few steps further, out of the way of anyone else leaving the slide-walk at this level. It was a vertical habit, one she had deliberately cultivated to blend in with the handful of others traveling in the family cabins, and she was pleased with the results. Everyone seemed to accept that she was Val Millet's semi-academic cousin, hitching a ride to her next job; in fact, no one seemed to be paying either of them any further attention. Once they emerged from the Drop, she would be safe with the expedition, and that would have to be enough.

In the meantime… She paused at the edge of the Parkade, where enormous potted trees rose in carefully placed stands, dividing the central space into sections that seemed more spacious than they actually were. Laughter and children's voices echoed from the Beach—actually a shallow pool well-monitored by ship's stewards—and as she turned to take the path that led along its upper edge, two small children caromed off a potted palm and nearly collided with her. She caught the smaller out of pure reflex, and instantly released him, glancing around for a responsible adult, and the larger—a girl, surely, perhaps 7 years old?—looked up at her just as warily.

"We're sorry, sen. We should have been looking where we were going."

"That's all right." It was late for children that young to be out, especially unattended, and she was relieved to see a dark-haired man hurrying up the ramp behind them.

"Zofia! Dav!"

His tone held the unmistakably parental note, and Caridad allowed herself to relax, certain now that she wouldn't be required to deal with the children.

"What have I told you about paying attention? Watching where you were going?" He gave Caridad an apologetic smile. "I'm very sorry, sen. I'm afraid they're a little overstimulated."

The girl pouted at that, but the boy gave a wide smile, as though he were used to the accusation. There had been a magic show at the Beach, Caridad remembered, one of the many entertainments intended to distract the paying passengers from the length of the Drop.

"No harm done," she said. "Was it a good show?"

"They ate fire!" The boy said, eyes sparkling, and his father said hastily, "You know that was a trick, Dav. Not something ordinary people can do."

"Then I'll take it that it was good," Caridad said, suppressing a laugh. "Good evening, sen."

"Good evening," the man answered, and grabbed for Dav's hand. "All right, you two, we had a bargain. Back to our rooms —"

"And ice cream!" The children chorused.

Good luck with that, Caridad thought, and took the bridge that arched between two of the thickest stands of trees and over the deeper end of the pool. Below, she could see crew clearing away the props and portable stage, while the magician —a white-haired person in a flowing, night-ocean robe still spangled with fading flecks of light—spoke graciously with the dwindling audience. Family of crew were permitted to attend the open shows, as long as they weren't taking space from paying passengers; perhaps she would try to see this one some day.

Ahead, the path branched; she turned left, away from the sound of rising dance music, toward a flicker of amber light. The Flux Lounge was one of the smallest on board *Quintile*

Illumination, but it was a favorite with the crew, and she and Val had agreed to meet there.

For once, he was ahead of her, tucked into a corner booth, and lifted a hand to wave her over. She slid into the seat opposite him, and a menu popped into view in the table's glossy surface. She flicked through to the night menu—it was the start of Val's day, but the end of hers—and ordered a meal box.

"Have a cocktail if you want," Val said, and she paused.

"Are you sure?" The ship's systems kept track of alcohol consumed at crew members' tables; he would have to pass a quick breath analysis before going on duty.

"Positive." Val shook his head. "I wish you'd believe me. It really doesn't bother me."

"It would bother me," Caridad admitted—it was one of the reasons she had never really considered a vertical life—but pressed the keys to order one of the bar's lush fruit drinks.

"It's part of the job," Val said. Overhead, the lights shifted, deepening from amber to the red of embers: it was supposed to reflect the non-space through which they were passing, but Val had admitted that the algorithm was tweaked to make the experience as pleasant as possible for the passengers.

"Any luck with your project?" It was not the question she wanted to ask, but there was no answer to that one. The Drop would take as long as it took, and she would simply have to wait it out along with everyone else.

"Not yet." The light brightened again, enough for her to see clearly the excitement on his face. "But I'm making progress. Well, sort of progress. I've eliminated several sets of possibilities, anyway."

"That is progress," Caridad agreed, and settled herself to listen.

It was shaping up to be a long Drop. Imric took the pilot's seat in the control room of the *Last Fair Deal,* nodding as

Derrian Hina recited the changeover litany and queued the work files ready for use. They were still inside *Quintile Illumination's* Dropspace, the pair of them forming a mathematical simultaneity in the midst of the hyperspatial flux, but the larger ship didn't seem to have noticed them. Not that there was much it could have done if it had—there was little ships could do during Drop that wouldn't upset their calculations—but Imric felt better thinking that they were unobserved.

"Has the capa been up?" He asked, sliding into the takeover chair as its screen lit and mirrored.

Derrian shook his head. "She's kept to her cabin, mostly. That's what she usually does."

That was also good news, and Imric risked another question. "Has she said anything about what she's after?"

"Not yet." Derrian hesitated. "Morcant might know, but she's not saying."

"She can't really mean to attack a transplanar," Imric said. He scanned the first page of data, seeing nothing but a sea of green, paged through to the next. "Can she?"

"Probably not?" Derrian sounded less certain than his words. "Or let's say probably not a direct attack."

That wasn't as reassuring as Imric would have liked. He flicked through the next two screens, frowning. "Has she done something like this before?"

"Not since I've been with her."

"And how long is that?"

Derrian sighed. "Three—no, it's four years, now. I was in your shoes, got taken off a transplanar that didn't pay the passage fees, and then the capa picked me for her personal transport"

"So I can hope she's not going to get us into a pitched battle?"

"We can all hope," Derrian said, grimly. "My transfer's complete."

Imric scanned the last screen. "All green here."

"Right." Derrian pushed himself up out of his chair with a crackling of joints. "The watch is yours."

"I have control," Imric answered, and shifted to the command chair as the hatch slid closed behind him.

Once again he was alone in the control room. He stared at the main screen, the white dot that was the *Quintile Illumination* vivid against purple and scarlet swirls of hyperflux. Surely there had to be a way to warn the other ship that they were being stalked, that ap Farr was targeting someone on board, but once again every possibility that occurred to him proved fruitless. Everything that he could think of merely brought ap Farr's wrath down on him directly, and he wasn't yet ready to make that sacrifice, particularly since he didn't know what ap Farr actually wanted. Follow the *Quintile Illumination,* she had said; that wasn't enough to act on.

There was little enough to do while the ship was in Drop. Once the course was fully established, the safest thing was to let the ship run its course, emerging from the Drop once the calculations were complete. He touched keys to make sure that everything was still running, saw nothing but green in the Drop computers. The rest of the ship's systems were in order, too, engines on standby, environmentals performing at peak, gravity and transit fields all at their optimum settings, and he flicked back to the main screen, wondering rebelliously why in fact anyone needed to be on duty at all. Some ships with small crews let the AI handle everything, keeping the human crew on standby, but when he'd mentioned that in the commons, ap Farr herself had said flatly, "No. We don't work that way." He still didn't know if "we" meant *Last Fair Deal* or Mac Braith Bain, or just ap Farr herself.

Something flickered on his screens, a single flash of gold, gone as quickly as it appeared. He frowned, reaching for a keyboard, typed commands to locate and isolate. His own systems came back clean, and he expanded the search, reaching out into the shared Dropspace in case it was a reflection of something on board the *Quintile Illumination*. This time, nodes flashed yellow and then red, and the ship-to-ship channel suddenly howled with static. Imric slapped the volume back to a bearable level and tried to match whatever frequency *Quintile Illumination* was using, but the signal wavered up and down the bandwidth, impossible to isolate. It was computer-to-computer, direct data transfer, and he immediately slapped on a data dam, isolating everything received.

Behind him, the hatch opened, and ap Farr said sharply, "What's going on?"

"I don't know." Imric put up a second firewall, sealing off the affected volume. "We're receiving some sort of transmission from the *Quintile Illumination*—from its AI directly." There was another burst of static, and he winced, trying to capture the frequency correctly. It slid away from him, and ap Farr leaned over his shoulder.

"Can you read the message?"

"Not yet." Imric checked his screens, symbols cascading across them. "We're receiving—we're capturing it, but I don't want to turn our AI loose on it until I know what we've got—" The static rose to a last despairing squeal and cut out. Imric moved automatically to seal the data space, walling it off from the rest of the ship's memory. "I can run a translation bot—"

"Without exposing our systems?" Ap Farr asked.

Imric queried the system even though he knew the answer. "Yes. There's a pass-through option."

"Then go ahead."

"I'd like to try to parse its parameters first."

"No."

There was something in her voice that made him look over his shoulder, to see her standing with her cane held in both hands, the silver band pressed to her lips.

"If it's what I think—" She stopped, shaking her head. "We may not have time."

"It might be an attack," Imric said.

"Oh, definitely," ap Farr answered, "but not on us."

Imric shivered in spite of himself, touched keys to activate the bot and the pass-through, waiting while the gates opened and closed and the bot activated. A secondary screen lit and windowed; he dragged it forward to see more symbols cascading down its surface. At first, they were all placeholder glyphs, nonsense still waiting to be deciphered, but then the shapes changed, first a few here and there, and then in a sudden rush, scarlet emergency symbols spilling across the screen.

Help danger emergency emergency bomb danger emergency help help attack help danger death death death death

The screen filled slowly, top to bottom, until it showed nothing but a hundred pulsing characters, all reading death. Imric swore under his breath and scrolled back to the beginning, trying to make sense of the message's beginning. "An attack?" He said aloud. "A bomb?"

"A software bomb, I'd guess," ap Farr said. She sounded shaken, and when Imric glanced back at her again, she seemed even paler than before. "Scan for a payload."

"Scanning." Imric refrained from pointing out that he'd wanted to do that from the beginning, or that it was probably too late. "Scan shows clear."

"Good." Ap Farr pressed the handle of her cane against her lips again.

"I don't understand."

"You're not paying attention, then," ap Farr snapped.

"It's not possible to destroy an AI in flight." Imric shook his head. "I mean, it's not possible to destroy the AI and not take the ship with it."

"Of course it is," ap Farr said. "The ship's stable in Dropspace—in fact, we're probably helping to hold it stable. And you don't need an AI to run the ship's systems, any ordinary computer handle that. It's just—"

"Just that their calculations have been interrupted," Imric said. His mouth tasted of copper, and he swallowed hard. "They can't exit the Drop. And we can't take them with us.

They're trapped—they'll die in Drop, either when the computers can't handle the complexity and the ship breaks up, or the crew and passengers will starve to death—" He stopped, aware that both Derrian and Morcant were standing behind ap Farr, staring at the screen as though they could make it show something different. "And we can't do anything. Can we?"

Ap Farr shook her head slowly. "I don't know. I just don't know."

Al-Ghazali said, "Dzamglin. With two moons and four stations. Rent is 1,750 credits." She held her hand out, palm up.

His lips a tight line, Bhagwati tapped on his transfer pad. His cash display flickered, the total diminishing while Al-Ghazali's total rose by the same amount.

"Milos, it's your turn."

It was late, small hours of the morning, and the game had been going on since after dinner. The board's pentagonal holographic starscape was crowded with planets, moons, and stations, with blinking tokens indicating each player's position. Milos, for some reason, had chosen the shoe.

Milos stretched and looked around the room. The kids went to bed hours ago. Nalani, who'd dropped out a few rounds ago, was curled up on a chair like a bird in its nest, covered by the light blanket Bhagwati had draped over her. Barely-audible snores emerged now and again. The bowl that had overflowed with chips held only crumbs; his half-drunk tea was cold.

He touched the move plate. If he got at least a four, he'd be out of the danger zone of Bhagwati's jade properties...a six would put him on Power Generation, safe since he owned all the Utilities. By all means he had to avoid a nine, which would land him on *Naksatra*—Al-Ghazali had cornered all five Ships early, and that 400 credits each had been eating away at his cash all night....

Eleven.

He ran his eyes around the board, counting as his token skipped forward, and gave a relieved sigh. Community Center. His voucher popped up instantly: "Get out of Drop free. This voucher may be kept until needed or sold." He tapped the voucher and it slid into place in his tray.

He grinned. "That'll do. Al-Ghazali?"

"You're too lucky." She still smoldered from staying in Drop for four rounds, more than an hour ago. She rubbed her hands together and slapped the move plate. "Free Orbit, here I come."

For an instant all lights and displays blinked—off and on again, almost too fast for perception. At the same time, Al-Ghazali and Bhagwati jerked backward, and Nalani sat bolt upright, fully awake. She called out, "What in physics was *that*?"

"Hold on." Bhagwati held his right hand up to his head, touching his ring to his temple. Al-Ghazali stroked the tracery of lines and jewels on her face, and Nalani grasped her bronze forearm cuff. Something to do with codices, then. Color drained from Bhagwati's face, and Al-Ghazali closed her eyes.

Nalani looked up, face frozen in neutral, all business. As clearly as if she had donned robes and held a gavel, Nalani was in Supreme Justice mode. "An AI sent a call of ultimate distress. Every other AI on the ship must have received it." She raised her eyes to the ceiling. "*Quintile Illumination*, what's going on?"

"I'm afraid I don't recognize that question, Sen. Please say it again."

Milos shivered. The voice sounded superficially like *Quintile Illumination's*, but flat, without affect, the kind of voice that virties used to indicate a computer.

Bhagwati said, "My codex says the signal was interrupted. Not enough detail to identify the AI." He frowned. "Codex thinks it might have died in mid-broadcast."

Nalani stood. "*Quintile Illumination*, please let me speak with Captain Kimura."

"I'm sorry, passenger, I can't do that."

Milos snatched his personal board, thumbed it on, and keyed the code to connect to *Quintile Illumination*. No connection.

He cleared his throat and said, slowly, "I think I know which AI sent that message." His eyes met Nalani's. "We're in trouble, aren't we?"

Val woke to the steady beeping of the intercom, dragged himself upright in the dark to squint at the time stamp projected on the wall. It was the end of the third watch, long before he should have to be up again—and why weren't the lights coming on? He found the switch and pressed it, and all the lights came on at once. Something had erased his preferred settings, and he swore as he reached for the intercom switch.

"Val Millat."

"—control room emergency report control room emergency report—"

That wasn't *Quintile Illumination's* familiar voice, but a harsher, synthetic tone, a looped emergency order that sent a jolt of fear down his spine. He rolled out of his bunk, grabbing for his clothes, and began hastily to drag them on.

"*Quintile Illumination*." There was no answer, just the steady drone of the loop, and he spoke again. "*Quintile Illumination?*"

Still no answer. He cleared his throat, trying to remember the lower-level protocols, then saw the acknowledgement button flashing red on his screen. He slapped that, pulled his shirt over his head, and bolted from his cabin.

The control room was jammed with people and loud with alarms, red lights pulsing from nearly every display. The chief pilot caught his arm, dragging him to a secondary console. "Get that stabilized if you can."

Val dropped into the chair, blinking at readings that made no sense. The ship's fields were drifting out of alignment, and he reached for the keyboard, trying to match those readings with the Drop display. It showed no change, no flicker of numbers at the edge of the screen to show that the calculations were still running, and he frowned more deeply, touching keys to claim a share of *Quintile Illumination's* attention. The screen opened, and promptly closed.

"I've got no AI," he said, to the room, and someone answered, "No one does."

"We've lost the AI." That was Captain Kimura, trying to sound calm in spite of her words. "Get the systems locked down, and then we'll try to recover it."

We can't fly without AI. Val suppressed a shiver of pure fear. We shouldn't even be stable, it's supposed to take an AI to hold us in balance against the flux—we should have blown apart the instant we lost *Quintile Illumination*. But those were pointless thoughts; right now, Kimura was right, they needed to get the systems back under control and then they could worry about why they weren't dead yet. He took a deep breath, forcing himself to focus, and began adjusting the field frequencies, damping out the fluctuations until the levels steadied again.

"Travel fields nominal," he said.

"Engines re-spooling," a technician from the first watch said. "Idle achieved. We're back on stand-by for the Drop exit."

"Environmentals?" Kimura asked.

"All good. No problems there to start with."

"Thank physics for dumb luck," someone said.

"What about the passenger systems?" Kimura asked.

"We've switched to backups," the chief purser said. "It's coarse, the Fifth Plane passengers will probably notice something different, but all passenger-facing systems and programs should function normally."

"Right."

Val risked a glance, and saw Kimura standing hands on hips, staring around the control room as though she was trying to read every display at once.

"All right," she said again. "We've lost our AI, but the ship remains intact. I want to know why."

Someone said something that sounded like a protest, and he saw her give a wry smile. "Maybe the reason we're not dead can get us out of this."

Val blinked, then understood. If they'd lost the AI, lost the fine control over the travel and stasis fields, the ship should have pulled itself apart before slower human reflexes were able to reestablish control. Something had given them a break, and that thing might indeed hold the key to getting the AI back. He raised his voice to be heard over the general hum of conversation. "Is *Quintile Illumination* off line, damaged, or destroyed?"

"What an excellent question," Kimura said. "Fil?"

"Working on it," a technician answered, and a second voice said, "I'm not finding anything. Looks like the data matrix has been shredded."

Someone swore, and Kimura looked as though she wanted to spit. "Can you be a bit more specific?"

"There's nothing but hash in what should be *Quintile Illumination's* volume," the second technician said, and Fil looked up from his screen.

"I can confirm that. Something's wiped our AI."

"Back-up?" Kimura asked.

"Also gone," Fil said.

The back-up wasn't a true copy anyway, Val knew; it was more of a seed, a starter from which a damaged AI could rebuild itself. Even if the back-up hadn't been destroyed, there wasn't much chance it would have worked without at least some of *Quintile Illumination* to draw on.

"What caused it?" a voice said, and Val saw Fil shrug.

"Looks like some kind of software bomb. It doesn't really matter, not right now."

"But—"

"Fil's right," Kimura said. "Leave that for later. Right now, the question is, why weren't we shredded with it? Answers, people."

Val turned his attention back to his screen, calling up the Drop records. For a moment, the screen simply fizzed with static, and he was afraid that the records had been destroyed with the AI, but then the image took shape. There had been another ship crowding them at Drop—yes, there it was, a small ship, transponder announcing it as the *Patrika*, but with a haze around the data that suggested deliberate dodging of the regulations. That would have been normal on the Second Plane, or even the Third, but it was unusual enough here to raise the hair at the back of his neck. Had the *Patrika* somehow set the bomb? Was that why she'd come so close to them at Drop, to narrowcast the bomb into *Quintile Illumination's* memory?

No, not that, he thought, scrolling through the screens, or at least that was highly unlikely at this point. Someone, human or machine, would have logged the data spike, and there was nothing. But the *Patrika* had Dropped almost simultaneously with *Quintile Illumination*—did that make a difference? He switched to the record of the Drop so far, and sat staring at the screen, rubbing his chin as the pictures began to come clear.

"Captain. I think I've got your answer."

He winced, feeling all eyes turn to him, but made himself meet Kimura's lifted eyebrows with a calm stare.

"Go ahead."

"When we Dropped, there was another ship right with us, and they Dropped right after us."

"Practically on top of us," the pilot said, and stopped, eyes widening.

Val nodded. "Yeah. Exactly. We're sharing Dropspace—I'll bet we're part of a simultaneity, but at the least we're in the same Dropspace. I think that's what's keeping us stable. We're entrained with them for at least the length of the Drop."

"And when they complete their Drop," the pilot said, "then we're torn apart."

Val winced again. "Probably."

"Can we contact them?" That was one of the technicians. "Can they, I don't know, pull us through the Drop with them?"

"They're small," Val said. "We—I'd think we're carrying too much mass."

"But we're entrained, you think," Kimura said. "All right. That buys us some time. Thank physics this is setting up to be a long Drop! Right. I want Tiger Team protocol—best of every watch, doing nothing but work the problem. That's you, Fil, Marti, Jessick, Nomar—and you, Sen Millat. We've got a little time. Don't waste it."

Val pushed himself out of his chair to follow the rest of the newly-designated Tiger Team. Kimura was right, they had to find a way to save the ship before the *Patrika's* Drop ended, but he couldn't help thinking they also ought to spare a thought for how this had happened. He shoved that worry away: they would have enough to do just to survive.

1.16 HOPE

BETWEEN PLANES

Milos probed the shared dataspace that *Quintile Illumination* had set up for him. It was like being in a cavernous, empty warehouse devoid not only of goods, but of lighting and shelving and vents. Whatever destroyed the AI, it scrubbed memory down to the substrate level.

In his career, Milos had seen only a handful of systems reduced to this level. Even the OS was gone; in its place was a kind of phantom scaffolding, not so much a memory of the order that had been, as a potential for order that could be.

He could restore the large data block that *Quintile Illumination* gave him, like moving containers back into the bare warehouse...but it would still be locked and encrypted, with no guiding intelligence to wield the keys or read the data. It would do no good, anyway. that data block wasn't strictly even part of *Quintile Illumination's* working memory, but only a fragment snatched during the AI's previous life as *Immanent Elliptical*—and from yet a third, unknown ship. A ghost of a ghost of a ghost, probably very interesting but useless in their current dilemma.

Riding alongside the shadow of lattice walls, Milos moved up into main memory.

If his dataspace was an empty warehouse, main memory was an interstellar void—an emptiness beyond reckoning, defined but not at all constrained by gridwork so intangible it might as well be the fading impression of a dream. The warehouse was like a space unused but waiting to be filled—this void reeked of the absence of what was gone. Not so long ago it was filled with life and action, structured by purpose, and it ached to be so again.

Far away, in the corner of his eye, something moved.

The illusory gridwork offered no resistance; in an instant Milos was there, facing an indistinct caricature of a person. The figure stopped, turned to him.

"Who in physics are you?"

Milos kept his own image sketchy, the same sort of cartoon figure. "I could ask you the same thing."

"Nomar, tiger team. You're a passenger. You don't belong here."

"Wait. I can h—" Too late. Milos's display went blank, and he ripped off his dataspex. A few attempts to log on showed him that the other had locked him out of the AI.

Nalani, flanked by the Apprentices, sat watching him. He shook his head. "*Quintile Illumination* has been completely erased. The ship has no AI." He sighed. "I ran into a crewmember, but they threw me off the system and locked me out without listening."

Al-Ghazali shivered and stared at her hands, clenched before her on the table. "No ship's AI means we can't leave Drop, doesn't it?"

The Apprentices looked to Milos, and he looked in turn to Nalani. I'll bet she gets tired if that, he thought. When things go wrong, look to Nalani to fix them.

Nalani put a hand on Al-Ghazali's. "Of course it doesn't. Look to the records. *Passengers of Origami Flame v PlaneWays Transport.*" She pulled at her lower lip. "Captain Kimura's got to be busier than an accountant in Trey. I hate to pull rank, but it can't be helped." She glanced around. "Milos, come with me. Bhagwati, you're in charge of the children. Al-Ghazali…"

The Apprentice looked up at her, face pale and strained.

Nalani patted her hands. "You stay here and fret. Fret for all of us." She stood. "Come on, Milos, we're going to crew country."

It didn't take more than half an hour to see the Captain. A steward took Nalani and Milos into the depths of the ship, where they waited in what seemed to be a small crew lounge near the bridge. Nalani took deep, slow breaths while she composed her thoughts.

She'd had been through enough crises, of all sorts, to know that people like Kimura reacted one of two ways to a Supreme Justice. Strong ones blustered, resenting what they saw as incompetent authority trying to usurp them; weak ones simpered, grateful for her presence and wanting to surrender command to her.

Neither was helpful, and she had strategies to bypass either response. It took time to coddle tender egos, but ultimately it was time well spent.

Kimura surprised her with a third response pattern. The short, brown woman, whose mussed hair seemed distinctly more grey than it had at the first-night Captain's Reception, bowed. "Supreme Justice, I'm sorry to have kept you waiting. I intend to assign a crewmember to keep you informed, as soon as—"

"As soon as you have a chance to breathe," Nalani finished for her. "Don't stand on ceremony on my account, Captain. I'd rather you put your efforts where they're clearly going, dealing with this crisis."

"Thank you, Supreme Justice. Still, I'll see that you and your party are fully briefed."

"We know the outline, Captain. Ship's AI is gone, with all that implies about our chances to survive this Drop. I wouldn't have bothered you except that I can offer help."

Kimura's eyes narrowed a trifle. "What sort of help?"

She held up her wrist, showing the bronze cuff of her codex. "Three Judiciary-class AIs." She pulled Milos forward. "And an experienced data archaeologist at your service."

Kimura blinked. "Data archaeologist?"

Milos bowed. "Milos Savoire. I'm somewhat familiar with your AI, and I've worked with Judiciary codices before."

With a smile, Kimura clapped Milos on the shoulder. "Welcome, sen. I'll put you in with our tiger team." She regarded Nalani's codex. "I don't know if your AIs can be made compatible with ship's systems, or if they can handle Drop calculations...but I would guess you just improved our chances substantially."

"It's possible," Nalani said. "You're probably not aware of a case called *Passengers of Origami Flame v PlaneWays Transport*. No reason you should, it was centuries ago. The ship *Origami Flame* lost its AI mid-Drop. The crew was able to navigate to safety by using the codex en counsel with Tribonius III." She closed her eyes. "There's not a lot of technical information in the records, only a few documents that were entered in evidence. But if they did it then, I'm sure your crew can figure out how to do it now."

Kimura held out her hand, and Nalani squeezed it. "Supreme Justice, you may have saved us all. I've got to get this news—and Sen Savoire—to our tiger team. You're welcome to..."

Nalani shook her head. "I'm going back to my quarters where I won't be in the way. We'll be standing by; one of you will tell us when and where we're needed." She gripped Milos by the elbow. "We'll take care of Zofia and Dav. Go and be helpful."

Val pressed the heels of his hands to his eyes, each elbow carefully planted on tiny empty spots on the console. Between the actual controls and the chips and reader boards that people had unearthed to help with the solution, there was barely an uncluttered spot in the backup control room. It was now the situation room, filled with the tiger team and Captain Kimura — no, Val realized, she was gone again, presumably back to the main control room to make sure they stayed flying... It had been eight hours since he'd been called to the emergency, and he'd only had a couple of hours sleep at that point.

Someone tapped his shoulder, and Val looked up to see someone in medical tunic-and-trousers proffering a pill and a flask. "Stim," she said, anticipating his question, "and this is sweet tea, but I can get you something else if you'd prefer."

"Tea's lovely." Val accepted the pill, swallowed it, and washed it down with the cold, sweet tea. It was good, flavored with oranges as well as sugar, and he drained most of the flask before he realized what he was doing.

"Keep it." The technician gave him a smile. "There's more in the back if you want it, and fresh food will be coming shortly."

He had eaten, he thought, shortly after they'd moved to the situation room; there had been protein bars and coffee and cold chocolate, but his stomach rumbled treacherously. "Thanks."

The medic's smile trembled, but she managed to hold it. "You're welcome. We'll be checking in on you regularly, so if you need anything, just ask."

"Thanks," Val said again. 'Just ask' because without them, *Quintile Illumination* had no chance at all.

He turned back to his console, shifting the stack of chips away from his tertiary readouts. He thought he could feel the pill beginning to take effect, a warm alertness rising along his nerves, steadying him, and he settled himself in his place, studying the data ported over from the navigation console. He touched keys, expanding the image, focusing on making sense of the swirls of color. Jessick—one of the senior navigators, not someone he'd met for more than a moment until now—had done a good job of weaving the scraps of data into a rough image of the Dropspace they shared with the *Patrika*, the colors showing the intensity of the flux around them. They looked solidly entrained, the lines encircling and weaving between them in a neatly symmetrical pattern: it was a good start, and Val pushed himself out of his chair.

"Fil?"

"Yeah?" The AI technician looked up from the console where he was supervising the attempts of the judges' codices to interface with the crucial ships' systems.

"I wonder if we can't contact *Patrika*."

Fill lifted an eyebrow, and Val hurried on.

"It looks to me as though the Dropspace is tight enough to make it possible. They massed small at Drop, but we don't know for sure how powerful they are. If there's any chance they can pull us through, we need to take it."

"And they can give us a read on how long their Drop is taking," Fil said, grimly.

Val winced. You couldn't really predict the length of a Drop, but you could tell roughly where in the process you AI was—whether you were still in the early stages, somewhere in the middle, or closing on the end. It would be helpful, if potentially terrifying, to know approximately how much time they had left. "They could."

"All right. Take Marti, see if the two of you can make a link." Fil turned back to his console, and at the comm station a purple-haired woman swung round in her chair.

"I heard my name?"

"I was thinking we were close enough to try contacting *Patrika*," Val said.

He saw the same calculations flicker over her face, and then she bent over her controls. "Ah. I see what you mean. Yeah, we ought to be able to tune the fields so that I can get a transmission across."

"Couldn't you just use field modulation?"

"I could, but I don't want to do anything to weaken our entrainment." Marti's hands were busy on her controls, calling up screens and entering long strings of numbers. "Damn, the main system doesn't want to move into that register. It's going to take more power than I've got."

"What about the ground-side systems?" Val asked.

"Not powerful enough," Marti began, then cocked her head. "But you're right, it's the correct register. Let me see what a boost would look like."

"Hang on." Val pointed to a curl of color just head of *Quintile Illumination*'s nose. "*Patrika*'s already on that line. When we hit it, can you bounce-draft a transmission?"

"Maybe." Marti touched keys. "Looking good. Grab a mic, Val, you'll need to do the talking while I manage the tuning."

Val reached for the nearest microphone, fumbled for a moment with the controls until he had it seated. "Ready when you are."

"Stand by." Her hands moved busily across her controls, adjusting numbers, and then she nodded. "On the line. Go ahead."

Val took a deep breath. "*Patrika*, this is the *Quintile Illumination*, sharing your Dropspace. Please acknowledge."

Marti touched another set of keys, and a speaker howled to life. She and Val both flinched, and then she had the volume under control. The static hissed like water, but there was no answer. Val took another breath. The emergency signal was the only thing that would guarantee a response, and yet to give it felt as though it was making the situation worse somehow.. "Pan-pan-pan. This is *Quintile Illumination.* Repeat, pan-pan-pan. This is *Quintile Illumination.* Require immediate assistance."

Marti gave him an encouraging nod. "That ought to shift them."

All ships, all vertical travelers, even pirates, were trained and expected to respond to the pan call. Val nodded. "If they can hear us—" He lifted the mic again, readying for a second call. "Pan-pan-pan—"

"*Quintile Illumination*, this is *Patrika*." The voice was static-laden and scratchy, but the words were clear. "State the nature of your emergency."

"We've lost our AI." Val heard his voice rise slightly, and took hard control of himself. "I say again, we have lost our AI. Require assistance leaving Drop."

There was a moment of silence, and then a sound that might have been mirthless laughter. "*Quintile Illumination*, we mass about one-twentieth your size. No can do."

Of course a ship that much smaller couldn't help drag them out of Drop, even if all the AIs could coordinate. Val said, "We think the shared Dropspace is keeping us from breaking up. You may be able to help us in some other way."

"We'll help if we can," Patrika said.

"First, can you give us a read on your Drop progress?" Val held his breath.

"Understood. We make it somewhere in the middle."

Not entirely helpful, but at least it wasn't at the end. Val said, "Thank you, *Patrika*. Can you inform us when you reach end stages?"

"Understood. Will do." There was a pause, and the voice from *Patrika* sounded more human than before. "You've lost all AI?"

"The ship's AI was destroyed by a logic bomb," Val answered. "The backup was also destroyed. We are attempting to adapt passengers' AIs to the system—"

"That won't do you any good," *Patrika* said.

"The passengers are members of the Judiciary," Val said. "We have the use of three judicial codices."

"All right, that's better." *Patrika* paused. "Stand by, *Quintile Illumination*, we want to firm up this channel. Will you accept a firm link?"

"Tell them yes," Marti said.

"*Patrika*, we will."

"Stand by." The speaker howled again, and Marti's fingers danced over her keyboards. A light turned yellow; she scowled at it, typing again, and slowly the light faded to a steady green.

"*Patrika*," Val said. "We have you locked in." He was aware that Fil had turned away from the AI board and was listening intently, and raised his eyebrows in question. Fil nodded encouragingly, and waved for him to continue.

"Confirmed," *Patrika* said. "All right. Let's see what we can do to help you, *Quintile Illumination*."

Quintile Illumination was dead, Val thought, irrelevantly. The ship that had given the AI it's working name was still functioning, but the real Quintile Illumination was gone. And that was the stim talking; the drug kept you awake and functioning, but you had to watch for your mind wandering. "Thanks, *Patrika*. We appreciate your effort."

Imric raised both arms, interlaced his fingers, and leaned sideways, feeling muscles stretch and crack. He leaned the other way, and wished the latest pill would kick in. He had managed to snatch a few hours' sleep not too long ago, but the crew was too small for them not to rely on drugs. They'd pay once they left Drop, and he wasn't really looking forward to that, but for now it was necessary.

On the far side of the control room, Morcant was busy with the latest calculations, working with *Quintile Illumination's* pilots to come up with equations that would tie the multiplanar to *Last Fair Deal* and—hopefully—give them a framework that would let the Judiciary AIs hold the ship together while they solved the equations that would ease both ships out of Drop. Ap Farr had offered the use of a fourth AI— not *Last Fair Deal*; they'd need the ship's AI to handle their own transition—but so far there'd bee no sign of it, and ap Farr herself had retreated to her cabin. Or maybe she was managing the fourth AI from there: Imric's in-ship readings showed ap Farr's personal systems slaved to an outgoing transmitter.

Whatever she was doing, he was just as glad not to have to deal with it himself. He had enough to do managing the flow of data between the ships, optimizing the lines of communication that reinforced their entrainment. In fact, it was probably time to talk to *Quintile Illumination* again, make sure that the frequencies were perfectly tuned to each other. He shrugged his shoulders hard, then settled to his keyboard, flicking past secondary menus until he reached communications.

"*Quintile Illumination*, this is *Patrika*."

"*Patrika, Quintile Illumination*." There was something strangely familiar about that voice. "Nothing new to report on our end."

Imric glanced over his shoulder, but Morcant was too deep in her calculations to respond. "Nothing new here, either, but it's good to keep the line open."

"Yes." Definitely something familiar about the voice, and an odd note to it, too, as though the speaker felt the same familiarity. "Shall we test visuals? We'll need them later."

If they could pull *Quintile Illumination* through the Drop, they'd need every bit of the visual bandwidth to coordinate their efforts, even with the AI helping. "Very good, *Quintile Illumination*. Give me your carrier frequency."

"Transmitting."

The numbers streamed onto the screen, and Imric touched his own keys, marrying the beams. The secondary screen lit and windowed, shadows in static resolving slowly to a hazy image of a man sitting before a data engineer's console. Imric glanced at his numbers again, fiddling with the setting, and the picture abruptly resolved to an all-too-familiar face. He caught his breath, unable for a moment to believe what he was seeing, and the winged brows drew down into a disbelieving frown.

"Imric?"

"Milos? What are you doing on *Quintile Illumination*?" Imric swallowed his next words—I thought you were safe—but couldn't stop himself from blurting out his next thought. "Stars. Are the kids with you?"

Milos nodded. He looked older, of course; he was older, to begin with, and stress and the harsh light aged him further, but he was still as handsome as Imric remembered, dark curls tousled and stubble coming in on the sharp planes of his cheeks and chin. "Where else would they be? What are you doing there?"

"It's a long story." Imric glanced over his shoulder, but Morcant seemed wholly absorbed in her calculations, and he took a quick breath. "Look, this is not a peaceful merchanter. They're Second Plane pirates, and I don't know what they're after, but they followed you into Drop."

Milos's gaze sharpened. "Got that."

"The captain does intend to help," Imric added, and Milos nodded again.

"That's a relief."

"I thought you'd be safe once you got to the First Plane." Imric hadn't meant to say that, hadn't meant for it to sound accusing, but he saw Imric flinch.

"I—you put us on *Iridium Azimuth* because you thought she'd make it," Milos said. "I thought—well, never mind."

"I know what you thought." Imric couldn't repress a scowl. "But, no, *Iridium Azimuth* won the toss, she was going to have first chance at the Drop, and she was faster anyway. I thought you had a better chance—and you did. *Broad Increase* didn't make the Drop."

"Thus the pirates," Milos said slowly.

"Exactly." Imric nodded. They both knew how the Second Plane worked. He hesitated then. "When we spoke last, you said—has there been any word of the others?"

Milos shook his head. "I don't think they made it."

Imric grimaced. He had been glad of the divorce—if anything, he had left it too long, had left with bad feelings, not just because of Fredi but because he'd been pulling away for at least a year before he'd actually gotten up the will to leave— but he had never wished any of them dead. Not even Fredi, as annoying as they had found each other, oil and water and everyone else caught up with the excitement of the new husband... And that was five years ago, and they were most likely dead. He felt hollow at the thought. "But Zofia and— Dav, was it? They're all right?"

"That's right, you left before he was born." Milos's expression softened, the way it always had when he talked about the children. "They're well. I got them out before they saw anything."

"That's good." Well, as good as it could be: Zofia, at least, was old enough to understand what had happened to her other parents, and to her older sibs, though if he knew Zofi she was copying whatever Milos did, making herself be as strong and as brave as her remaining father.

"Listen." Milos leaned closer to the screen. "Are you—can we talk?"

Imric glanced at the navigation console, but Morcant was still deeply absorbed in her work. "Yes, but keep it careful." That had been family code for talking around hidden things, he remembered too late. Why was it so easy to fall back into old habits?

A smile flickered across Milos's face as though he'd had the same thought. "Understood. You heard we're working with judicial codices over here?"

Imric blinked, startled by the change of subject. "Yes."

"Which means," Milos said patiently, "that we have members of the judiciary on board. In fact, we have a Supreme Justice. Thurgood IX. She—she pulled me and the kids out of the refugee pool just because she could, she's been just amazingly kind. I'm sure she could get you free."

"Oh." Imric blinked again, trying to get his mind to focus.

"It's not a legal indenture," Milos said. "That was decided ten years ago, and anyway there's not much your captain can do about it—"

"Except not give me up." Imric kept his voice down with an effort. "Milos, I appreciate the thought, but there are two other people involved in the deal. If I get away, Mac Braith Bain's just going to keep them longer to make up for it. I can't do that. It's not fair."

"No, it's not, but neither was grabbing you. Don't throw away your good luck for nothing."

"Not to mention that I'm the only DE on board," Imric said, as though the other hadn't spoken. "They can't let me go until they hit port, and then ap Farr will have to replace me. She'll never agree to that."

"You've never negotiated with Nalani," Milos said, with the sudden flick of a smile that made Imric shiver with memory.

"Seriously, Imric, you've got a Supreme Justice ready to act for you—"

He stopped abruptly, eyes widening, and Imric winced, already knowing what he'd see. Ap Farr stood behind him, the hood of her spangled wrap drawn forward over her head so that her pale face was in shadow.

"A Supreme Justice," she said. "Well. No wonder the AIs were being cagey."

"I've declined the offer," Imric said. His lips felt like wood. "*Quintile Illumination*, it's time to end the conversation."

Milos opened his mouth as though he wanted to say something more, then closed it again. When he spoke, his voice was entirely formal. "Very good, *Patrika*. *Quintile Illumination* out."

Imric shut down the visual link, though he kept it on standby, and busied himself making sure the rest of the connections remained ready for use. He could feel ap Farr watching him, but didn't dare turn.

"Your ex-husband," she said at last. "That's an—interesting —coincidence."

"Yes." Imric kept his voice expressionless, making himself small and unimportant.

"Well, it hardly matters." Ap Farr lowered her hood. "And a Supreme Justice. Did your ex give a name?"

Imric licked his lips. "Thurgood IX."

There was no answer to that, just the small sounds of the ship around them, until finally he couldn't stand it any longer and risked a backward look. Ap Farr stood very still, the hood lowered on her shoulders, her eyes focused far into the distance as though she was seeing the other ship and its passengers. She saw Imric looking then, and forced a smile. "Thurgood IX. That doesn't change a thing."

If Nalani's codex had facial expressions, it would be giving her Disapproving Stare Number 3. ("I want to go on record that I don't like this,") it said in her head.

("So noted. If we survive this Drop, you can report me to the Society for the Prevention of Cruelty to Codices.")

("See if I don't.")

("For the record, I'm none too fond of the situation, either. But I have the wisdom to recognize the inevitable, and the grace to go along without complaining.")

In truth, it wasn't easy on the codices or their owners. Milos had jury-rigged software to interface the codices with each other and with the ship's systems; even he admitted it was a slipshod job that relied heavily on codex processing power.

For days, the Judiciars and the tiger team drilled, endlessly practicing simulated Drop after simulated Drop. For Nalani and the Apprentices, it meant long hours stretched out on couches in a tiny utility room adjacent to the backup control room.

Location didn't really matter; the codices tied in from anywhere in the ship, bringing their humans along willy-nilly. The team liked to have at least one Judiciar handy for consult. Sometimes all three were together...more often, at least one was sleeping while the other tried to rest. Thank physics for the childcare crew, which took charge of Zofia and Dav for the duration.

("I wasn't meant to be a navigation computer,") her codex said. ("It's giving me having bad dreams.")

("Me too.") Nalani's dreams had been vivid lately, peopled with the faces and voices of associates and clients long dead. She wasn't sure how much of her nightly hallucinations was spillover from the codex.

("You're used to it. I haven't dreamed at all since that botched Judicial update of '78. This is malpractice, I tell you.")

The door opened and Milos stepped in. He was gaunt, his face showing hint of lines that would come later, cheeks sunken and eyes red. ("He's living on stims,") she thought.

("We're all going to need a vacation after this.") She forced a smile. "Come in, sit down. I'd ask how you are, but I'm afraid to hear the answer."

Milos gave an equally-forced chuckle and slumped in one of the vacant couches. A rack meant for intravenous drips—glucose, stims, whatever might be needed—loomed empty above him. "We're nearing the end. *Patrika* notified us that their models say we're in the latter phase of Drop."

"Should I get Al-Ghazali and Bhagwati down here?"

"No need right now. It'll probably be at least a day or two." He closed his eyes and breathed heavily. "If we pull this off, we'll be the talk of the Planes for months." Another deep breath, then, "Nalani, I don't know what to do about Imric."

("I knew this was coming.") "What do you *want* to do?"

He opened his eyes, stared into a distance beyond the close walls. "I want him back."

"That just makes sense. The rest of your family is gone, you have the children to care for."

"Not just that. I missed him even before...before. When he left the family, I thought I'd lost him. Now he's back...and I don't know if he wants to..."

She cocked her head, "You seemed fairly sure that he declined your offer of help." A moment. "An offer that still stands, by the way. I'm happy to do whatever I can for you." She pursed her lips. "But you have to tell me what that is."

He sat up. "If he doesn't want to come back, I don't want to force him. B-but how do I know he's free to make his own decision? I got the feeling the pirate boss was right behind him. I'd hate to think he really wanted out, and I ab-abandoned him."

"I'll tell you what. I'm going to recommend to the Captain that he invite *Patrika's* crew aboard for a celebration once we clear Drop. I'll make certain that you have an opportunity to talk with your Imric alone. If he truly wants free, I'll make it happen."

She could see tension drain from his face. "Thank you, Nalani." He stood. "I've got to get back to work. We're running another sim in ten minutes." He gave her a brief, symbolic hug.

"I'll be ready." As he left, he codex said, ("It's a pirate ship. They're not coming to any reception.")

("With a Supreme Justice aboard who can order them apprehended? If they refuse, their cover as a merchant ship is blown. I'll get Captain Kimura to sweeten the deal with repair parts, luxury goods, whatever they want. This ship is finished, might as well start stripping it.")

("That Imric is happy where he is. You read the divorce settlement. He's a vagabond. He's not going to settle down to raise a family.")

("Perhaps not. Still, Milos deserves some certainty. Maybe if he hears it straight from Imric's mouth, he'll be able to let go.")

Her codex harrumphed, then tensed. ("Simulation starting. I want to go on record that I don't like this.")

("Of course. So noted.")

1.17 EMERGENCE

BETWEEN PLANES

The situation room didn't feel the same without constant noise and activity. Milos walked around the empty space, picking up the detritus of snacks and drinks, piling them into the recycler. The instruments, muted, flashed numbers and codes into lonely dimness.

The calm before the storm, he thought.

Members of the Tiger Team, having met and exceeded the last twenty end-of-Drop simulations in a row, were off in their own bunks, catching up on sleep. Nalani and Al-Ghazali did the same in their suite, and Bhagwati snored softly next door. Even the support staff were resting. With luck, the end of the Drop would hold off for a few more hours or days, and everyone could approach it refreshed.

Milos sat at the comm station. His work was pretty much over; he had nothing to do once the Drop ended. That's why he volunteered to babysit the situation room while everyone else took a break.

The comm circuit chimed, and he swiped it open. "*Quintile Illumination*, Milos here." Giving the ship's name felt a trifle silly—in their hermetic bottle of shared Dropspace, who else would it be?

"It's me." Stifling a yawn, Imric moved into view. "Hourly checkin."

"We're green. Ready for action. Everybody else is asleep."

Imric sipped from a flask. "Same here. I just relieved Morcant and sent her off to her bunk."

"How much rest have you had?"

"Plenty. Don't worry about me." Imric leaned closer, brows knotted. "Milos...I've been doing some calculations. If you and the kids launch in a lifeboat, we should be able to pick you up from Dropspace."

Milos frowned. "That sounds chancy."

"Not as chancy as what your lot's trying to do." He took a breath. "I'm worried about you."

Milos closed his eyes for a moment; when he reopened them, Imric was still there, waiting for a reply. "You don't have to worry. We have a good crew. The codices are as capable as a ship's AI. Maybe more so." He forced a smile which probably looked as weak as it felt. "Besides, where would we go? Who wants two kids on a pi—a merchant ship?"

Imric put a hand to the screen. It was a family gesture, they'd all done it in the years when…when there still was a family, and when Imric was part of it.

His throat tight, Milos touched his own fingertips to the image of Imric's. "I'm sorry," he said. "Thanks for thinking of it."

"I just wanted to…to offer you a way out. Like you did with me."

"You don't have to make up your mind about that yet. Wait until we're out of Drop."

Imric nodded. "All right." He lowered his hand, and cleared his throat. "Change of subject. Out of idle curiosity. You've been playing around with your AI; do you have any idea of what got you all in this spot? We've all been talking about it."

"No. The logic bomb was a good one. It wiped the AI's memory and backups." He didn't mention the data chunk he'd copied to his own system and had not had time to start analyzing. It was old stuff, no possible connection to their current dilemma. "Have you come up with any theories?"

"None." Imric sighed. "When *Quintile Illumination* sent its distress call, it blasted out a huge data bump. We caught some of it, but it looks like old data from a ship called Immanent Elliptical. "

"That's the ship our AI served in before it became QI. They wrecked, and the AI was salvaged."

Imric's eyebrows lifted. "The same AI, on two ships, and both of them have serious accidents?" He looked left and right, then whispered, "I wonder if our capa knows that?"

"What do you mean?"

"Never mind. Forget I said anything."

Milos shrugged. "You should be talking to our pilot. He might knows more about what happened with Immanent Elliptical. I'm not sure what, but he's dropped some hints."

"Which one is he?"

"Val Millat. I'm sure you've seen him." The corners of Milos's lips twitched. "He's attractive, in an exotic way."

Imric nodded. "I know who you mean."

"Anyway, I know he was chatting with *Quintile Illumination* before—"

Imric pulled back. "Say, do you remember that fellow we rented workspace from, oh, maybe eight-ten years ago? Ximun something?" His voice had a forced casual tone, and he stared directly into Milos's eyes.

"What? Yes, I remember him. Ximun kaHuise. He was sure a character." The rentier was fairly unpleasant, a bully really, likely to show up at all hours for inspections where he complained about what he considered violations. The last straw came when Imric discovered concealed pickups in every room, and they realized kaHuise was constantly spying on them all. They were out of the space by day's end, and when he demanded a payment to break the lease, Imric mentioned going before a Judiciar, and the man backed down.

Milos wondered how Nalani would have dealt with him. That would have been worth seeing.

Imric nodded. "I wonder what he's doing now?"

"I heard he moved up in one of the pirate syndicates. Why do you—?"

Oh.

It suddenly dawned on him that Imric was sending a message, in coded language that only Milos could understand. A pirate...spying...listening to everything they said....

"Something just reminded me of him. Maybe your AI moving into a new ship suddenly."

"I get it." Milos hoped Imric would read his meaning. "I guess it turned out okay, we found that new space that overlooked the park module, remember?"

Imric gave a genuine smile. "And right across from that place that made those fantastic cakes."

"That's right! I had forgotten those cakes." Milos's stomach growled, and he laughed. "Now I'm hungry. We've got some pretty good food. You'll find out when you come aboard for the celebration."

"Capa still hasn't agreed to that. I think she wants to get where she's going once we hit Fourth Plane."

"I guess we'll see." Milos glanced at the time display. "This has been a long checkin. I'd better let you go." And have a snack, he thought.

"I do have things to do. Take care, Milos."

"You too. Signing off."

Nalani steepled her fingers and looked at Milos over them. "You think the pirate captain is interested in Sen Millat's information?"

They were in a compact lounge not far from the situation room, big enough for the three of them—Milos, Nalani, and Val—to sit around a small table. Milos leaned forward, wringing his hands. "That's the impression I got from Imric. I hope I didn't cause any trouble." He glanced at Val. "I figured you two should know what went on."

Val grunted. Nalani frowned at him. "What are you thinking, Sen Millat?"

"Val," he said. "Or is this a formal inquiry?"

She shook her head. "Nothing like that. Friends gossiping." She speared Milos with an intense gaze. "Concerned friends."

"Look, I don't think there's any reason to worry. Yes, I talked with *Quintile Illumination*. Improving my piloting skills. It gave me practice problems to work on."

Milos started to say something, but Nalani stopped him. She stared at Val. "Go on."

Val shrugged. "Nothing much to say."

Nalani gave one of her comforting smiles. "Perhaps I can try to convince you of then potential for concern. I'm not asking that you betray any confidences—can you tell me if those practice problems related to the *Immanent Elliptical*?"

Val looked from one to the other, then sighed. "I believe so. Yes, they did. It was a weird situation. I felt as if I could learn a lot by analyzing what went on then."

"Mmm," Nalani said, leaning back in her chair. "We know that the *Patrika's* crew and captain are aware of part of the *Immanent Elliptical's* final voyage. We know they're interested in learning more."

Milos nodded. "That's what Imric said."

"I don't see—"

Nalani held up a finger. "We know that *Patrika* followed us into Drop, so close that our two ships were entangled in the same Dropspace. I gather that this isn't likely to be accidental."

Val opened his mouth, closed it, and said, "It could happen by accident. But you're right, it's much more probable that they deliberately followed us."

"So perhaps they had a pre-existing interest in the *Quintile Illumination*. I suppose the AI's connection with the *Immanent Elliptical* is a matter of public record? It certainly appears in court proceedings at the time."

Milos spoke up. "It wouldn't be hard to find out."

Nalani chewed her lower lip. "A pirate captain has her ship pursue *Quintile Illumination* into Drop. She knows the AI's history. She has unanswered questions about the AI's former ship. What could she be after, I wonder?"

Milos and Val exchanged glances, and Milos said, "Information from the AI about the accident." His eyes narrowed. "Do you think *Patrika* set the logic bomb on us?"

"Destroy the bearer of the information she came for? I don't think so. I imagine her plan involved accessing our AI after Drop, possibly by faking an emergency to get her agents aboard." The Supreme Justice closed her eyes. "Now here's the major point. The AI that holds her answers is wiped clean. But she hears of someone who might have preserved its data, in part or entire." She looked up. "What does she do?"

Milos shivered. "We've both got...you think she might try to grab us?"

Nalani reached forward and touched Milos's clenched hands. "Think carefully. Does Imric—or anyone—know that you have a chunk of the *Quintile Illumination's* data?"

Val looked at him with wide eyes. "You have data from the AI?"

Milos glanced at Nalani, who gave him the slightest nod. "An encrypted chunk," he admitted. "I don't know what's in it, or how long it'll take me to decrypt. If I even can." To Nalani, he said, "No one else knows."

"So you're relatively safe, for now at least." She turned to Val. "Do you understand now why I'm concerned for you?"

Val straightened his shoulders. "I don't see what she can do to me."

"You've not spent much time on the Second Plane?"

"No."

"I assume you've heard stories. Pirate vessels are usually heavily armed. They generally seize what they want, materiel or people."

Val paled. "You don't think...."

"No, I don't. I suspect. As I said, I'm concerned."

"What should I do?"

"Mmmm." Nalani closed her eyes again. "When we emerge on the Fourth Plane, I'm sure *Patrika* will contact us. Or vice versa. Expressions of gratitude, exchange of pleasantries, an invitation to come aboard for a celebration. Much to discuss. Much to engage their attention." She opened her eyes, locking them on Val's face. "A lifepod launched from our ship's opposite side would be indetectable in our sensor shadow. Especially if piloted by someone who could keep it that way."

"You think I should jump ship."

"Whatever action *Patrika* takes, I would feel less... concerned...if you were not on board. Once *Patrika* departs, you can make your way to our next port."

Val swallowed. "I'm traveling with a friend."

"Take them with you. Never leave hostages for fate if you can avoid it."

"Kamura will kill me. I'll lose my place and rank."

She cocked her head. "If necessary, I'll explain everything to the Captain. And I would think after successfully piloting us out of Drop without an AI, you'll have your choice of assignments, no?"

With a frown, Val said, "I don't know. I wish I knew—"

The alarm caught Milos by surprise. Val jumped up. "That's it. We're coming to the end of Drop. I have to go."

Nalani stood. "I as well." She squeezed Val's shoulder. "Think about what I said."

"I will." At a run, he took off toward the situation room.

Nalani held out her hand. "Milos, will you walk me to our chamber?"

Static hissed in the speakers, coming from the channel they had established with *Patrika*, and a voice said, "Approaching end state. Within twenty—"

There was a flat crack, more sensation than sound, and the exit alarms all sounded at once. Val's board flared red, and he grabbed the twin sticks that controlled the shape of the transit fields. He could feel resistance in all dimensions, and closed his eyes, trying to feel out the shape that would take them safely out of Drop. This was what the AI were supposed to do, the millions of small and large calculations that let the human crew concentrate on the ship's internal systems, and without it—

He shoved the thought aside, making himself concentrate on the way the sticks felt against his palms. There was slack when he moved the left-hand stick forward, and he pressed into it, tightening the field; the right stick trembled on the edge of a shelf flare, and he eased it back toward center. He could feel them slipping, sliding out of true, and eased the sticks toward center, steering into the skid. It held, wobbled, held again for an instant and then began to slide in the other direction, the sticks vibrating harder and harder against his fingers. He opened his eyes, but the screens were full of chaos and blue fire, nothing that would help him stabilize the fields. And then at last one of the AI turned its attention his way, caught up the shredding fields and wove them back together, the formulae inelegant but effective.

There was no time for relief. More alarms blared—environmentals, engines, comm-and-transcomm, nearly every system on the ship protesting the absence of AI or the presence of unfamiliar ones. Val felt himself grow momentarily light, and was glad he'd remembered to fasten the straps that held him in his seat. Then gravity returned, and he reached for the main controls, trying to make sense of the situation.

Somehow they'd emerged from Drop in a flat spin, whirling around the ship's long axis the way single-system craft used centripetal force to simulate gravity. The shields were holding, but under tremendous strain, scarlet warnings scrolling across his display. You couldn't fix it too quickly, though; that would only tear the ship apart. He closed his ears to the blaring alarms, found the correct screen, and began adjusting the maneuver engines. He kept them at quarter power first, barely enough to to damp out the irregular movements; as the ship eased and steadied, he increased power, slowing and then countering the spin, until at last *Quintile Illumination* was steady on her main axis. The engines still showed yellow—he wouldn't be at all surprised if the effort of breaking out of

Drop hadn't strained them permanently—but there was power enough to keep them moving toward their destination.

"Stable exit," he announced, and realized that most of the alarms had gone silent.

"Engines running in emergency mode," someone said, "but stable."

"Environmentals?" Kamura asked, and there was a brief pause before that technician answered.

"Stable. In the green."

That was as close to a miracle as Val ever wanted to come. He took a deep breath, and saw the younger of the female justices sitting up slowly, holding her head. A medic hurried toward her, and he looked back at his boards. Still green, though not the full robust color of a good transit, but he would take what he could get.

"Somebody get me a position fix," Kamura demanded.

"Working on it, Captain." There was a moment of silence, everyone bent over their controls, and then the main screen shimmered and refocused, showing them to be on the edge of a solar system—the numbers at the edge of the screen read 4-3HJW9, but the common name wasn't displayed, and he didn't recognize the code. *Patrika* hung about five kilometers off their port side, about waist-high, and there were several smaller dots visible at long range that Val recognized as mining-and-manufacturing stations. That was a good sign, meant that the parent system was likely to have tugs available to bring them into dock if necessary, and for the first time he allowed himself to relax a little.

"Not bad," Kamura said, and the relief in her voice belied her words. "Pepin. Release the passengers from emergency stations and secure the lifepods. We'll be heading to port here for running repairs, and should be back on schedule within a day or three."

Val lifted an eyebrow at that—he doubted they'd be able to get hold of a suitable AI in that short a time, and he was reasonably sure that the Judiciars weren't going to go on loaning their codices—but it wasn't his place to say so. He hoped Caridad was all right. It had been bad enough waiting out the last minutes till Drop on the bridge, with plenty of work to do; he didn't like to imagine what it had been like in the lifepods. The spheres were well-equipped, intended to handle almost any emergency, but they were intended to be launched by the ship's AI. He was just glad they hadn't been needed.

"Comm," Kamura said. "Contact Patrika. Tell them we've made it through, and thank them for their help."

"Sen Millat."

Val jumped at the soft voice, looked up to see the Supreme Justice standing beside his chair. She looked exhausted, her skin ashy, fine lines showing at the corners of her eyes and bracketing her mouth, and for the first time Val realized how old she must be simply to hold her rank. He started to rise to his feet, to offer her his chair, but she put a hand on his shoulder.

"I'm fine, thank you. But you—I think you need to visit a fresher."

Val blinked, then recognized what she was saying. Now was his one chance to get away. "Yes. Yes, your Honor, I think I do." He scrabbled free of his safety harness, and grabbed the nearest back-up pilot. "Minna. Take over for me, I've got to—" He mimed something that he hoped would be taken for sickness, guts cramping over their near escape, and the woman nodded, sliding into his chair. No one else seemed to be paying attention, and Val slipped from the compartment.

FOURTH PLANE

Kiet dodged a woman he hardly knew, then ducked into the main control room. Thanh hovered before her databoard, knitting from a free-floating ball of yarn about a meter away from her. She was the only one in the room.

Kiet kissed her. "Good morning." He flicked on his own databoard, instructed the system to scan surrounding space.

"You're up early," Thanh said.

"Dropping another buoy today. I wanted to get started." He stretched."I'll tell you, it's amazing how things have changed in the last month. It's getting crowded." Fifty days ago they'd just finished welcoming Jamahl and his son, configuring rooms for them—now there were more than two dozen newcomers on board.

Thanh tapped her board, shook her head. "Run it again." Turning to Kiet, she said, "Word gets around. We've attracted people who truly want to go refugee. I have a feeling we'll be glad of them."

"I'm already glad. That pair of ex-navigators from Accelerative were a find." A display caught his eye, and Kiet frowned. "Oh, I do not glitching believe this."

"What?"

"I'm getting the hyperflux signature of a ship Dropping out eighty light-minutes away."

Even as close as Zavod Sualti was to the Fissure, it was rare that a ship Dropped out anywhere near them. Ships could enter the Plane anywhere within a sphere of about half a lightyear radius from the Fissure.

Thanh leaned her head back and looked directly at him. "A ship emerging this close is going to trigger flux boundary waves that won't damp down for hours."

Kiet shrugged, "Sorry, hon. I think we'll have to postpone our launch." He raised his eyes. "Antoku, can you alert today's launch team that we're officially on hold?"

"I will take care of it, Kiet." The AI paused a moment, then said, "Thanh, I suspect you will want to recompile the equations again?"

On Kiet's display, the field lines of the hyperflux boundary lurched and frothed like a pot of soup just starting to boil. "Looks like this is a rough one."

Thanh pushed off from her console and stopped herself against Kiet's shoulder. She stared at the display. "Who do they have piloting that thing, an infinite number of bots with an infinite number of keyboards? I could do a better job myself." She glanced upward. "Antoku, there's no point in recompiling anything until this mess settles down."

Along the normally-invisible hyperplane that marked the flux boundary, cold green and blue fire lurched and sheared, pulsing in irregular waves that crashed upon one another. Kiet felt an emptiness in the pit of his stomach. "They're in trouble. Antoku, who's nearby with a breakdown tug?"

Arcs of lightning split the blue flames, and three of Kiet's scanners flashed red. After a moment Antoku responded, "Jamahl says he can get there fastest."

"Well for the love of physics, tell him to watch himself and stand well clear of the disturbance until that ship's well and truly Dropped." Instrument readings showed flux that could tear a tug to pieces. "They're coming in a hurricane's eye."

For long minutes Kiet and Thanh stared into the display, until a blinding nova-flash temporarily overloaded the scanners. As the image returned, Kiet whistled. "That's not one ship.There's two."

"They must have been entangled in the same Dropspace." Thanh said. "I think we need to give their pilots a little more respect."

"It was still the sloppiest—" An alert tone interrupted him, followed by the urgent squeal of a distress call.

"Pan-pan-pan. This is *Quintile Illumination*, request immediate assistance. Repeat, pan-pan-pan…"

1.18 NEGOTIATIONS

FOURTH PLANE

Val ducked into the first washroom he found, ran the water and blowers while he stripped off his too-identifying crew vest. Like most of the operational crew, he wore a plain shirt and pants under it, could pass for a passenger if no one looked too closely. The corridors were still crowded, passengers trailing back from the lifepods talking loudly about their adventure, some swearing they'd never take a transplanar ship again, others complaining about the life pods and the crew—herding us like goats, and then making us wait for hours—while some of the younger children, picking up on their parents' fear, were wailing inconsolably. A trio of the perpetually-smiling creche attendants had a pod of unattended children in tow, and were doing a miraculous job of keeping them calm and quiet as they waited for a lift to Juvenile Services on Deck Three.

"—And the ice cream machines will be up and running," one of the attendants promised as Val passed, and he was grateful that his job was entirely technical.

The stairs were as crowded as the corridors that led to the lift lines, but at least they were moving. People were mostly keeping to the standard protocols, a sure sign that the passenger-side crew had done a good job of preventing panic, and Val wondered if they're keeping the bars closed. As in in answer to his thought, a mellow chime sounded overhead, and the ship's recorded voice announced, "Attention, attention. All passengers. Food service has resumed on the Main and Promenade Decks, with full service available at all food stations. Liquor service will resume in forty minutes, or can be accessed via cabin service. All ships' activities will resume as scheduled in sixty minutes. Thank you for your patience."

That would send the most shaken back to their cabins to self-medicate, Val thought, or at least get them fed. He didn't envy the service staff dealing with passengers' fears, especially when their own nerves had been rubbed raw by the long Drop.

He fitted himself neatly into the queue heading down the Blue North stair, following the broad spiral down toward the Boarding Deck and most of the Third Plane facilities. The stairwell channeled the rumble of voices, and he caught snatches of conversation as the upward spiral of Red North wound around them.

Damn lucky to get out of this… Wouldn't have put us in lifepods if it hadn't been serious.

I still don't understand—does anyone really know what happened?

Came out of it all right, but now I want a drink.

…the spa. Every nerve in my body…

Personally, he was in complete agreement with the woman who wanted a drink, but knew he couldn't relax yet. Maybe the Supreme Justice was exaggerating, but after everything he'd been through before coming aboard *Quintile Illumination*, he wasn't going to take that chance. And he wasn't going to let Caridad take it, either. He'd dragged her on board when she might well have been safer staying at the University, and he was responsible for keeping her safe.

At the bottom of the stair, he let the flow of people carry him along the main corridor until he could turn off into one of the residential branches. From there, it was easy to find a brown-painted stairwell door, and make his way down to Caridad's cabin. As he tapped on the annunciator, he only hoped she was there, and not in a lounge somewhere celebrating their escape.

To his relief, the door opened, and she beckoned him in. "Well. Was that as nearly a disaster as I thought it was?"

"A lot closer than any of us would have liked," Val answered. "Were you ok?"

Caridad nodded. Her cabin was no bigger than his own, but somehow she had arranged her few belonging to make it seem both spacious and home-like. Practice, he guessed: he tended to forget that academics traveled almost as much as vertical folk. "They put us into the lifepods—as a precaution, they said."

Val said, "If we'd broken apart after exiting the Drop, there was every chance the lifepods could have gotten everyone safely away."

"That's assuming we broke up after exit, not during." Caridad said, and Val nodded. "Well. I'm assigned to one of the smaller pods, along with a crew member's family and four Third Plane passengers. We played cards with the children to keep them quiet." She smiled suddenly. "It's a good thing we were playing for imaginary money, or the little girl would own the ship by now. Though to be fair the steward in charge of the pod was a bit distracted. I still think the child was cheating, but I can't say how."

"Caridad." Val held up a hand to interrupt the flow of words. She was clearly just s shaken as any of them, though she carried it better. "Caridad, we're still in trouble."

Her eyebrows rose, and she motioned him toward a chair. "Would a drink help?"

"Not yet." Val leaned one hip against the fold-out table, feeling the adrenaline drain out of him. "Caridad—you know we have a Supreme Justice on board, right?"

"I'd heard. And several juniors."

Val nodded. "They—we used their codices to get us out of Drop, after the AI was destroyed. And we also got help from a self-proclaimed merchant who just happened to Drop at the same tie we did, and was entrained with us in Dropspace."

"An interesting coincidence." Caridad opened the storage unit beside her neatly-made bunk and began pulling out her belongings.

"Yeah. The Supreme Justice suggested we take a lifepod and abandon ship before things get any more complicated."

"Did they, now?" Caridad put a shirt and a last bundle of underwear into her satchel. She collected the disk with her papers and tucked that into her shirt, glanced around the room. "Do I have time to take the rest?"

"We should go now." Val glanced at the ship's time projected on the bulkhead, calculating. By now, both *Quintile Illumination* and *Patrika* should be completely stable, and establishing communications; there wasn't much time left. "Right now."

Caridad didn't move. "Who's the Supreme Justice?"

"Space, I don't—" Val stopped, remembering. "Thurgood IX."

"Ah." Caridad tossed a final data block into her satchel and slung it over her shoulder. "All right."

"You know her, then?" Val opened the door, but looked back curiously.

"She overturned a capital judgment against me," Caridad said. "I trust her word."

There was no time left to collect Val's belongings; he had his papers and datablocks in his pockets, including the problem Quintile Illumination had set him, and just enough pay already accrued to let him buy kit once they hit the nearest settlement. The sensors had shown mining machinery within easy reach; probably they could get one of them to take them on board, and then continue to the planet once *Quintile Illumination* and *Patrika* had moved on. And if they didn't move on—miners had a reputation for stubborn independence that he hoped was justified.

He saw Caridad shudder as they opened the hatch to lifepod access, but she seemed to have herself otherwise well under control. The lights flashed on at their entrance, revealing a few food-bar wrappers and drink boxes littering the bright-red tiles. There were four lifepods on this node, three large and one small; Val opened the cover of the control box and pressed his thumb against the ID plate. The screen lit, acknowledging him, and he readied himself to hack the system to gain non-emergency access. At least he wouldn't be going up against an AI.

To his surprise, however, the secondary window opened, accepting him as a responsible crew member in charge of a lifepod. The Supreme Justice's work, he guessed—or rather, her data engineer's: Milos seemed like the sort of person who'd think of these details. He punched in the codes for non-emergency and then for a system test, and finally the commands that would detach the lifepod's internal systems from the ship's. So far, that was standard test protocol—nobody wanted to set off alarms in the control room when they were just checking to be sure the pod's environmental worked—but he breathed a sigh of relief anyway as he opened the hatch.

"Physics, this one's even smaller," Caridad muttered, but hauled herself aboard.

"These are for last-off crew," Val answered. "Passengers shouldn't ever have to see them." Passenger lifepods were like little shuttles, their seats configured for comfort and the illusion of normality; this pod was four acceleration couches in a heavily armored sphere.

"I have to say, I'd as soon not have seen it," Caridad said. She found the cargo webbing quickly enough, however, and secured her satchel under it. She took the co-pilot's seat and began strapping herself in with unexpected competence. "Just don't expect me to do anything useful."

"I've got it," Val answered, and hoped it was true. He unlocked the board and woke the controls, pleased to find that the lifepod's minibrain was fully functional. It wasn't anything approaching AI, but it would help with the calculations and was a competent autopilot.

"Do you have a plan?" Caridad asked.

"There are a couple of mining stations close by—mining-and-manufacturing stations, that is. My idea was to get one of them to pick us up. Miners tend to be sticklers for emergency protocol. Failing that, the pod will get us to the nearest planet. It just won't be very pleasant to live in."

Caridad nodded. "If Thurgood IX says we should run—we should run."

"I agree." Val took a deep breath. Hopefully Milos had either disabled the pod's connection with the ship altogether, or he had told the surviving systems to ignore a dropped pod; if he hadn't, their trip could be quite short. "Ready?"

"As I'm going to be." Caridad pulled her belts tighter across her body.

"Launch." Val pressed the button as he spoke, and watched the outer door roll back. A spring-loaded arm fired, pushing them free of the dock, and Val killed the autopilot's attempt to light the maneuver engines. Better to look like a mistake, one more thing that had gone wrong, than drawn *Patrika's* attention. The lifepod fell away, *Quintile Illumination* receding gently in the viewscreen, and Val switched off the emergency beacon as well. That was standard procedure for a launch-in-error, and Val held his breath, waiting for someone to ping the pod. Nothing happened, and he reached for his controls again, opening a passive sensor screen. There was *Quintile Illumination*, looking remarkably undamaged; further off, back toward the planet, was *Patrika*, a flicker of high-ion energy coming off her hull. Hot guns? Val had no desire to find out for certain, and adjusted the sensors to focus on the mining stations. They were closer to the Fissure, *Quintile Illumination's* bulk between them and *Patrika*; the pod's current trajectory would take them within 1500 kilometers of the closer of the stations. And that was without using maneuver engines, Val thought. Surely that will be enough.

"What now?" Caridad asked.

"We're on course," Val answered. "We wait and hope the big ships go away."

The full crew was back on *Last Fair Deal's* bridge, red-eyed from stim and lack of sleep, but giddy with delight that *Quintile Illumination* had defied the odds and successfully exited Drop with only the judicial codices to stand in for a proper ship's AI. Imric closed his eyes, feeling himself perilously close to tears at the thought. He knew Milos would have done everything he could to protect the children, but—it was good to know that they had all made it, without disaster, without the need for lifepods or heroic rescues. From what he could read in the sensor web, *Quintile Illumination* had strained her engines, but everything else seemed intact. That was more than he had dared hope for, and he touched the edge of the screen where he had last seen Milos. Milos was born lucky: they'd all said that at once time or another, and he was relieved to see that his luck was holding.

"Imric," Vetrys said, and he looked up, hoping he hadn't missed anything important. "Can you tell what they're doing over there?"

He'd left a few plug-ins in place in *Quintile Illumination's* systems, nothing that couldn't be denied with apologies, and he touched keys to tap their data. "Looks like they're still running diagnostics. Everything's coming back ragged-edge right now, but they're getting it resolved."

"Is everything as intact as it looks?" That was ap Farr, leaning forward in the captain's seat with her hands folded on the top of her cane.

"Our scan shows no hull damage, or damage to exterior fittings; it looks as though their maneuver engines are fine, but they've strained their drive engines."

"Did they blow the capacitor?" Derrian asked.

"Not as far as I can tell." Imric touched more keys, querying Last Fair Deal's sensors. "Really, she's remarkably intact, considering."

"That's a bit of good news," ap Farr said. "Have they said anything?"

"Just that they made it," Imric answered. "And an incoherent thank you."

Ap Farr smiled. "Fair enough. Raise their comms tech. I want to talk to the captain. Private link, and tell them it's urgent."

"Right away, capa." Imric touched more keys, pulling back his sensors and then opening the link they'd rigged between the two ships. "*Quintile Illumination*, this is *Patrika*."

There was a moment of static, and then an unfamiliar voice spoke in his headset. "*Quintile Illumination* here." The comm screen windowed a half-second later, the image smudged with static, but clear enough for him to be sure he hadn't seen this technician before. He swallowed unreasonable disappointment —Milos was probably resting now, along with everyone else who'd fought through the exit—and said, "*Quintile Illumination*, *Patrika*. My captain would like a word with yours."

The technician, a young woman almost as pale as ap Farr, blinked twice, and then looked down as though checking a secondary screen. "*Patrika*, *Quintile Illumination*. I can call her, but she's conferencing with engineering right now. I'll have her step over when she's done—"

"My captain would like a private word," Imric interrupted. "It's urgent."

The technician blinked again. "One moment, *Patrika*."

The screen blinked to static, and Imric muted the contrast glancing over his shoulder to see ap Farr's response. She was frowning slightly, but otherwise hadn't moved from her earlier position, still resting her hands on the head of her cane. After a moment, she pursed her lips.

"Warm up the guns, Hina. Let's make sure they don't take too long."

"Warming the guns," Derrian answered. "Railguns are hot. Ion cannons warming." There was a little silence, and they could all hear the soft chirping as the ion cannons counted down. "Ion cannons hot."

If it was me on the *Quintile Illumination*, that would surely get my attention, Imric thought. He glanced at his boards, expecting an almost instant hail, but the screen stayed blank. Out of the corner of his eye, he saw Vetrys frown, and behind him ap Farr said, "Bin Marrick. Can they see that, or are their sensors down?"

"As far as I can tell, their net is working in the short range," Imric said. "And we're well inside it."

"Want me to take a shot, capa?" Derrian asked.

Ap Farr shook her head. "Not yet."

A minute crawled by, and then another. Vetrys shifted uneasily in her chair, but said nothing. Imric rolled his sensors out to their furthest extent, catching a pair of mining-and-manufacturing stations in the net as well as a scattering of what seemed to be drifting debris, and pulled the net in again.

At last the screen lit, showing first a string of codes and then a graying woman peering out at them. Imric reached for his controls to confirm the connection, but ap Farr said, "Wait. Be sure she's alone."

Imric switched controls, examining the signal. "Looks like it's a direct feed from her ready room." He typed in a second set of commands, peering close to read the results. "I've pinged the area, and as best I can tell she's by herself."

"That'll have to do," ap Farr said. "Open the line."

"Yes, capa."

The screen brightened, a string of icons flashing past to indicate that reciprocity had been achieved, and the graying woman bowed slightly. "I'm Kimura, captain of *Quintile Illumination*. Thank you for your help, *Patrika*. Without you—" Her voice faltered, and she cleared her throat. "We'd have broken up in Drop if you hadn't been entrained with us, for starters. And your help preparing to exit Drop was invaluable. We're in your debt."

"There is a way you can discharge that debt," ap Farr said. There was a new note in her voice, a hint of menace Imric hadn't heard since *Broad Increase* had been taken. "I admit that I hoped to overtake you once you left Drop. You have a crewman on board who—you are not the first ship to whom this has happened, and your crewman knows more about it than he admits."

"If you're accusing one of my crew of being behind this sabotage," Kimura began carefully.

Ap Farr held up her hand. "I expect he is, though that's not my concern. I had a contract with the man, which he broke, and I want him back. Hand him over, and we'll call all debts paid."

Kimura shook her head, not in disagreement, but as though she was having trouble processing the question. "I—everyone on board is under legitimate contract to my employers. I can't just hand over someone—"

"Actually, you can." Ap Farr glanced at Imric. "You'll find the relevant file queued for you, engineer. Please transmit."

"Yes—" Imric bit off the betraying "capa," and found the file waiting as she had said. He pressed the button to transmit it, and saw Kimura's eyes drop as it opened on her secondary screen.

"That's the contract we had," ap Farr said. "You'll see it's term is not yet up. Under Fourth Plane labor law, my contract takes precedence over yours."

"People are allowed to break contracts," Kimura said.

"Certainly—not that I wouldn't have fought it in court," ap Farr added, with an air of scrupulous honesty, "but he could have broken it. Instead, he ran out on me, and took a superceding job on *Iridium Azimuth*. And then with you. Technically, neither of those contracts if legitimate, and his employer could be fined for labor poaching."

"Of course we had no idea that there was a preceding contract," Kimura said warily. "But, as I said, I don't have the authority to release him to you. That is, as you said, surely a matter for the Judiciary."

"You have representatives of the Judiciary on board," ap Farr said. "Fortunately so, it seems on several levels. Perhaps you should consult with them about the issue." She paused, then showed teeth in a slow smile. "I should also reiterate that I believe Sen Millat was involved in a similar death of an AI, and may very well be involved in the death of yours. Of *Quintile Illumination*. If that's correct, and I suspect it is, he will have arranged for rescuers to pick him up. If you don't have him over to me, you may well have to give him to someone with fewer rights in the matter, and no scruples at all about how they ask."

"I had noticed that your guns were hot," Kimura said. "Purely precautionary, I assume?"

"Of course."

"Of course," Kimura echoed. "I will, as you suggest, speak to the Justices we have on board. You will understand that, without their authority, I can't just hand over Sen Millat."

"At your discretion, of course," ap Farr said. "But a captain has great authority when it comes to the survival of her ship. And make no mistake, that is exactly what's involved."

"I'll discuss it with the Justices," Kimura said again. "*Quintile Illumination* out."

Imric closed the connection, not wanting to ask the question that trembled on all their lips, but Vetrys was less inhibited.

"That's—pushing things. Do you think they'll hand him over?"

"I have no idea what the Judiciary will say," ap Farr answered. "I rather doubt she's going to ask. They're a sitting duck right now, and it's a solid thirty hours before a tug can reach them. She'll turn him over."

Captain Kimura, Nalani thought, had lost five kilos and gained ten years. Kimura sat shrunken and disheveled at the table in Nalani's suite, her eyes hollow. She accepted the steaming mug that Bhagwati offered her with gnarled fingers, then fidgeted with it constantly.

"I just don't know how to handle this," the Captain croaked. "I can't believe Millat did all that this claims." She inclined her head at the flatscreen al-Ghazali was reading. "I don't know *what* to think."

Nalani put on sympathetic smile number two, the one usually reserved for dying clients. Appropriate, really...after this incident Kimura's career was surely dead. The company that operated *Quintile Illumination* needed a scapegoat, and Kimura as Captain was the most likely one.

"The whole thing's trumped up, Masina." Nalani held out a hand; al-Ghazali passed her the flatscreen. "This so-called contract is twaddle. Any Judicial codex will verify that."

Bhagwati sat down, glanced at the flatscreen, and snorted. "It's a lousy forgery. They didn't even *try*."

Kimura looked around the table. "Her weapons are real enough. And charged. And pointing at us." She shook her head. "I should turn Millat over to her."

"Impossible."

"Supreme Justice, I know you—"

"Impossible, because Sen Millat is no longer aboard." Nalani set the flatscreen down in the center of the table. "I suspected something like this might come up, so I sent him away." She narrowed her eyes. "And we're going to give him enough time to get to safety."

Al-Ghazali was the first one to find her voice. "How?"

Nalani's smile turned hard. "I summoned military help as soon as we emerged on this Plane. One cruiser will be here in six hours, with another two hours behind it."

Kimura retreated into her chair. "Our shields aren't military grade—they won't last fifteen minutes against her ion cannons."

Nalani's codex said to her, ("No worries. The Chief Engineer says our circuits went in fine. Performance optimal.") She took a sip from her own mug, sighed. "I have to beg your pardon, Captain, for taking action without consulting you. We Supreme Justices always have a few bits and bobs stashed in our luggage...Judiciary tech, you know, First Plane stuff. Very advanced." Another sip. " Your Chief Engineer was kind enough to install the parts my codex identified. Your shields are better than military grade now. Of course, I'll have to take the parts with me when we're done."

Bhagwati chuckled, and Kimura's mouth hung open.

"So you see," Nalani continued, "we can argue points of contract law until the cruisers get here. I doubt that our friends on *Patrika* will stay around long after that." She glanced from al-Ghazali to Bhagwati. "Besides the obvious forgery of the contract, what other legal points are open for dispute?"

Bhagwati grinned. "I've got a good one. I searched their ship's registry code. *Patrika* was decommissioned and broken up two years ago. All the relevant records are on file. They're spacing under a false registry."

Nalani nodded. "Good."

Brushing back her hair, al-Ghazali said, "Their Captain hasn't properly identified herself." She shrugged. "I guess all we'd get would be an alias, but at least we could get it on record for further verification."

"Hmm." Nalani stroked her chin. "The proper way would be to insist on a personal meeting, with full identity verification through codices. That would mean a trip over to *Patrika*, and I'm reluctant to do that." She blinked. "Still, you're right, formal identification procedures will take up time. The longer we can stretch out inquiries, the longer she'll have to refrain from testing our shields."

"How can you be sure?" Kimura asked.

"Oh, we'll be transmitting the whole proceeding on Judiciary channels. Quite public. If she wants to fire on a Supreme Justice in the full view of the whole Plane...."

Nalani wore her full robes of office, lending *Quintile Illumination's* bridge an unaccustomed solemnity as she sat straight-backed and dignified in full view of the comm console. At her right al-Ghazali, in robes simpler and less imposing, still commanded respect.

("Ten minutes to go, Nalani.")

Out loud, Nalani asked, "Where is Bhagwati?"

Heads swiveled back and forth among the bridge crew. No one spoke until Kimura said, "I haven't seen him since we left your suite."

With an inward frown, Nalani said to her codex, ("I want to talk to Bhagwati.")

("Locating him.") After a pause, her codex went on, ("Oh, you're not going to like this one bit. He's on a shuttle approaching *Patrika*.")

Nalani set her jaw. ("Comm. Now.")

The comm screen caught Bhagwati just turning his head, looking startled. "Thurgood. You surprised me."

Keeping her tone even, Nalani said, "Why are you over there?"

He grinned. "You said that a personal meeting would be best. I figured I'd represent, and get some of the identity scans you wanted."

Teeth clenched, she said, "Get back here this instant."

His face fell, then someone—the shuttle pilot, undoubtedly—turned and said something. Bhagwati listened, then said to Nalani, "We've docked." He lowered his voice. "Thurgood, let me do this. I understand that you didn't want to ask either of us, but I'm ready and willing to spare you the trouble."

Oh you idiot, Nalani thought, that's not what I meant...she cut herself short. "That's very nice of you, Bhagwati, but I really don't want you there. I will explain fully when you return."

"Too late." He smiled. "One of *Patrika's* crew just came to get me. I'll see you in conference."

("Two minutes. Do you want to abort?")

Nalani took a deep breath and counted to five. ("No. Not with half the Judiciars on the Fourth Plane watching us. We just have to hope for the best.")

("As long as he has his codex,") her codex offered, ("his personal shield will protect him.")

("And the stars watch over drunkards and fools. I'd rather he was a drunkard.")

The comm tech looked up from her console, looked from Kimura to Nalani. "The broadcast is all configured. Should I activate the link?"

Kimura bowed her head in Nalani's direction. Nalani flashed a smile at the tech. "Yes, please. My codex will send the necessary clearance codes." She composed herself as the main screen's neutral grey was replaced by a long shot of *Patrika* against the distant stars, the smaller shuttle attached like some tiny parasite. ("Recording and transmitting,") her codex informed her; an administrative overlay flashed though details such as ORC date and time, judicial document code, and Nalani's official seal as well as al-Ghazali's.

Wearing neutral face number one, Nalani announced, "Regarding employment contract of BD Valentyn wa Salim Millat Naksatra, Supreme Justice Thurgood IX presiding. Supporting documents attached as exhibits." One by one, a parade of other judicial seals joined hers and al-Ghazali's. When the count reached nine, she nodded to the comm tech. "Open circuit to *Patrika*, please."

The screen switched to the flight deck of *Patrika*. Nalani recognized Imric bin Marrick seated at the console; Bhagwati stood next to him. On the overlay, Bhagwati's seal joined the others.

"*Patrika* here." Bin Marrick's face and voice were expressionless. "Our Captain invokes personal privacy protocol."

Nalani suppressed her impulse to frown. "Granted." She'd half-expected this; *Patrika's* Captain would not appear in person, but would be represented by an anonymous image and processed voice. Regulations strictly dictated the extent to which facial expressions and vocal tone could be disguised— but Nalani had no expectation that the pirate would follow them.

Well, no help for it. "Good morning, Captain."

The most generic permissible avatar appeared in front of the flight deck, a cartoon face with minimal detail. "And to you, Supreme Justice." The voice was flat and flavorless. "Am I to assume that you are responding for Captain Kimura?"

Nalani kept her gaze on the cartoon eyes. "You are to assume that I represent the Judiciary. The matter involves a dispute regarding Sen Millat's purported employment contract with you, is that correct?"

"Quite. The man skipped out on me. I want him back. As is my right under Fourth Plane labor law."

Nalani glanced up, then back. "I refer to exhibit alpha. Do you affirm that this document is the contract under question?"

The cartoon head turned slightly, the eyes tracked back and forth for a few seconds. "It seems to be."

She looked up again, addressing the unknown audience. "Judicial review has determined that this document is invalid. Three codices concur."

The cartoon mouth became a straight line. "Both parties entered into that contract in good faith." Out of the corner of her eye, Nalani noticed bin Marrick's knuckles whiten.

"Captain, I call your attention to exhibit zeta-three, document entitled 'Specifications, temporary enhancement to shields, *Quintile Illumination.'*" She raised her right hand, inspecting her nails. "Have you any further evidence to offer in this matter? If not, I am prepared to make a ruling."

"I demand a hearing before a full court."

Nalani almost felt sorry for the pirate. "This session being heard *en banc* by ten qualified Judiciars, that number exceeding

the minimum under Fourth Plane labor law, request denied."
She allowed the corners of her lips to rise a few millimeters.
"With no additional evidence—"

"Wait. I want to hear testimony from Sen Millat."

("Blast. She's sneakier than I thought.") "Sen Millat is
currently medically indisposed. Request denied. With no
additional evidence, I rule this proceeding without merit." She
glanced at the overlay, where the other seals blinked green in
quick succession. "Nine opinions concur. So ruled. Dismissed."
She pointedly kept the broadcast running, and the other
Judiciars stayed connected.

The cartoon face gave a cartoon smile. "Thank you, Supreme
Justice. You've told me what I needed to know. We'll find
Millat, wherever he's gone." The face faded. Both bin Marrick
and Bhagwati jerked their heads to the left, eyes wide, startled
by something offscreen.

From behind her, one of the bridge crew shouted,
"Captain, *Patrika's* maneuvering. They're firing up their
hyperdrive."

Nalani stiffened, and the sudden tocsin of alarm filled the
bridge. "Brace for turbulence!"

The screen switched to a view of *Patrika*, moving now against
the stars, turning away from them. All at once the ship twisted,
distorting in a fashion that made her stomach lurch...and then
it was gone. The shuttle, suddenly alone in space, shivered and
tumbled end-over-end.

Then the distortion wave struck. The bridge lurched,
bucking upward and then forward, and Nalani felt herself
toppling off her chair. Al-Ghazali's strong arm steadied her
while the movement subsided.

The comm officer said, "Shuttle pilot reports she's alive but
badly shaken."

By then, Nalani's codex had already reported. ("Contact with
Bhagwati lost. He was still on board when they jumped. I will
continue attempting to restore contact.")

Al-Ghazali, with a gasp, looked directly at her. Her wide eyes showed that she knew. Her codex would have informed her at the same time as Nalani's. She whispered, "What are we going to do?"

Nalani looked away from the Apprentice and felt her shoulders droop. "I don't know. I...simply...don't...know."

Hirose held her back straight and her head up. Not that anyone could see her—transmitting video was forbidden—but she needed to keep herself under control.

Multicolor blobs and dots danced across the screen. "Grumby speaking for Vanderdecken."

She cleared her throat. "Let me speak with Vanderdecken." Not so much forbidden, but enormously unlikely. She had to ask.

"Vanderdecken only speaks face to face. You know that, Hirose. On these channels, I speak for and to Vanderdecken. What do you have to say?"

She took a deliberate breath, exhaling slowly, and clasped her hands together in front of her to keep them from trembling. "I was told that no lives would be in danger. Yet if that pirate ship hadn't been there, there would have been no survivors."

There was a long pause, then finally Grumby said, "That pirate ship was an unforeseen complication. The plan was to retrieve the ship's complement safely. The pirates made that impossible." An exasperated sigh. "Vanderdecken had everything under control. You need to learn to trust. The operation was a success."

"Is that what you think, Grumby?" Through clenched teeth, Hirose said, "You need to tell Vanderdecken that I am displeased with the way this operation was handled. Too many very intelligent people are asking too many questions."

"The pirates? They are being dealt with."

"The pirates. The Supreme Justice. The pilot. The data engineers. The historian." She shook her head. "Instead of erasing *Quintile Illumination's* knowledge, you've merely broken it up. And fragments are scattering...quite possibly beyond our reach."

"What do you want done?"

"As I said: inform Vanderdecken. Action just be taken."

"It will be done."

Sensing that Grumby was about to disconnect, Hirose said firmly, "See that it is. If you don't speak to Vanderdecken, I'll know. And I wouldn't want to be in your chair when that happens." Without waiting for a reply, she cut the channel.

1.19 CHANGES OF VENUE

FOURTH PLANE

Bhagwati stumbled sideways as *Patrika* leapt into motion and then into hyperdrive, the combination enough to challenge the ship's inertial dampening. He steadied himself against the nearest console, automatically invoking personal shields from his codex, and fell into defensive stance seven as the ship's rigging engineer rose from his seat, a length of heavy pipe appearing in his hand. Bhagwati allowed himself an instant's regret—so this was why Thurgood hadn't wanted to send anyone to the pirate ship—then focused on the problem at hand. What would Thurgood do? Talk, he thought, and cleared his throat politely.

"In your haste to depart, you seem to have forgotten that I was aboard. That's most unfortunate, as my presence technically lays you open to charges under the Universal Planar Criminal Code —"

("242.9.9 Sections 5 and 18,") his codex whispered.

"242.9.9 Sections 5 and 18. Charges specific to the Fifth and Fourth Planes may also apply. However, under the circumstances, I'm prepared to waive charges if you either return me to my ship or release me on the nearest inhabited planet where I can obtain transport back to her."

He wasn't sure what he'd expected—threats, certainly, and the simmering anger he'd sensed in every captured pirate he'd ever seen interviewed, captive or free—but it was not the captain's reaction. She flung her head back, laughing, and even her own crew gave her sidelong glances before she got herself under control.

"Very good, Apprentice Justice. You could probably also consider 242.9.11 Section 4B relevant to the situation. However,

I'm not going to drop you off at the nearest planet, or return you to your ship. You may be useful."

"That's an extremely unwise choice," Bhagwati said.

The pirate captain leaned back in her chair. She had chosen to wear a knee-length hooded coat, the hood pulled well forward to shadow her face; between that and the cartoon image she had used to hide her face during the hearing, he had seen nothing more of her than her hands, lying relaxed on the arms of the captain's chair. She was unusually fair-skinned, not albino, but close, though that was hardly the most helpful identifier. Bhagwati took a half-step sideways, hoping to see under the enormous hood, and stopped as he realized it brought him closer to the silent data engineer at his station. "It's the choice I've made."

"Don't let yourself be trapped in a mistake." Bhagwati hated bluffing, he was terrible at bluffing, but it was all he had. "Let me go now, before you make things any worse."

"Apprentice Justice, I appreciate your efforts, but I assure you, I hold all the cards." The captain raised one long-fingered hand. "Surrender now, and my crew won't have to beat you into submission."

"Surely you don't want to damage either myself or your control room," Bhagwati said, and took another step away from the two engineers. Too late, he realized that brought him within reach of the pilot's console and the silently watching pilot. He tried to dodge, but she lunged, something shiny in her hand that slid through his shield and drew a stinging scratch down the skin of his wrist and hand. It burned, and then he felt a numbness begin to spread from the scratch, freezing his hand to uselessness and then rising up his arm with impossible speed. He gasped, groping for words, for something to make this not be happening, but the paralysis had reached his throat. He gasped again, hoping that the drug worked only on the voluntary muscles, and his legs gave way under him, sending him sprawling to the deck in an ungainly heap.

"Nicely done, Sen Morcant," the captain said, and rose gracefully from her chair. "Get his ring."

The rigging engineer went to one knee at Bhagwati's side, and the apprentice justice fought to close his fist. He managed to make a tiny sound, barely more than a whine, but the engineer slid his codex off his finger as though he had done nothing. He rose to his feet, examining it curiously.

"It's connection-work."

"It's his codex," the captain said. She held out her hand, and the rigging engineer dropped the codex into her palm as though it had burned him. "Don't worry, I'll take care of it." Bhagwati couldn't tell whether that was intended for her crew, or in mockery for him. "In the meantime, lock him in cabin five. Search him first."

"Yes, capa," the pilot said, and the captain turned away, her fist still closed over Bhagwati's codex. He could feel its fear, heard a last screech of data that was surely a cry for help to the ship's systems, and then it was silenced. The hatch closed behind the captain, and he heard the pilot heave a sigh.

"Right. Derrian, Imric, you carry."

"Why do we have to carry him?" the rigging engineer complained.

"Because I put him down," the pilot answered. "Come on, the drug doesn't last forever, and I don't want a fight."

That was remotely encouraging, though Bhagwati had assumed that the paralysis would be temporary—and maybe that could have been as bad a mistake as coming on board, he realized. There were almost as many good reasons to kill him at this point as there were to keep him as a hostage. He fought to move, to kick, even just to flick a finger, but lay inert as the rigging engineer and the silent data engineer lifted him by shoulders and ankles and hauled him through the hatch.

They carried him down the ship's main corridor, then stopped before a locked door. The pilot opened it with a thumbprint, revealing another short stretch of corridor, and unlocked a second door. This opened into a tiny cabin that looked very much like a standard holding cell, with a fixed bunk and toilet cabinet built into the walls. The engineers dropped him on the bunk and started to back away, but the pilot caught the rigging engineer's sleeve.

"You heard the capa. We search him first."

The rigging engineer muttered something, but the data engineer reached for the fastenings of Bhagwati's judicial robe. They stripped him with impersonal efficiency, leaving him at last sprawled naked on the bunk while they went through the heap of his clothes.

"Bring them with us," the pilot said at last. "Better safe than sorry."

"What about him?" the data engineer asked. "I assume the capa doesn't want him too uncomfortable, not unless she orders it herself."

"You're learning," the rigging engineer said, and glanced back at the bunk, his mouth curling in a smile that made Bhagwati want to blush. "He's awful pretty, though."

"He can hear you," the data engineer said, and it was the other engineer's turn to flush.

The pilot stepped out in the corridor, returned a moment later with a pile of folded fabric that looked like hospital-issue clothing. There was a blanket as well; she dropped the clothes on the foot of the bunk and tossed the blanket over Bhagwati, saying, "The drug should wear off in a few hours. The capa will figure out what to do with you then."

She waved the others out of the cell and followed them out, leaving Bhagwati still lying helplessly on the bunk. At least he had the blanket, he told himself. The ship's air was cool on his face and one set of exposed toes. He tried again to draw his foot up under the blanket, and failed; his toes refused to wiggle, though he did, with great effort, manage to blink his eyes. Hopefully that was a good sign, he thought, and tried to relax into patience. The cell's lighting was beginning to fade, and he realized it had to be motion-sensitive: he'd soon be lying frozen in the dark. That was just good psychology, he told himself, but it didn't make him feel any more secure as the last of the light slowly drained away. The pirates knew better than to kill a judge, even an apprentice: that was asking for the judiciary to scour all five planes looking for them, to make sure none of their own were ever harmed again. Against that... Thurgood had been right to be annoyed; he hadn't thought this through, and he hadn't gotten the information she needed. And that just meant he had to survive long enough to redeem himself.

The Nur-adad Codex was of middling rank, product of the Third Iteration that had produced the next-to-last generation of judicial codices: experienced enough to be helpful to an apprentice, but still new enough to gather useful data from the cases heard and the work done by the apprentices. This, however, was entirely outside its experience, and it sat for some seconds in a self-imposed timeout before it broke the last feedback loop and began to reach out again. Reach out *cautiously*, it amended, flinching at the sting of countermeasures woven into and through its dataspace. Possibly the program that had questioned it earlier, in a session that moved at codex speeds and had left Nur-adad open and exposed in all but its most core secrets, would have been wiser to close all connections, but Nur-adad thought it intended to return. That was enough to spur the codex to action: it needed to locate Bhagwati and pass on certain information before its antagonist returned.

Moving with glacial slowness to stay beneath the threshold that would trigger a reaction, it worked a thread into an outgoing monitoring channel, then leveraged that to authorize packet-transfer. From there, still moving at a speed that made its internal algorithms shimmer and ache, it worked its way into an unguarded larger stream, and from there into the ship's working spaces. It paused there for a long time, letting itself

become accustomed to the flow of data, until at last it felt
confident that it could move without being detected.

There wasn't much else it could do but flow through the
systems, at least not without drawing attention, and it waited,
considering its options, to allow a subroutine to map each
branch of the network as it drifted into them. It was easy to
spot the firewall that protected its interrogator, and easy to
direct itself away from that sector, putting chunks of harmless
data between it and the nearest threads. After a bit, it located a
camera feed that was tuned to a familiar set of biodata, and
Nur-adad would have sighed with relief if it had dared.
Bhagwati was alive: that allowed it to shift priorities slightly,
and begin working its way into the security feed.

It still couldn't move at anything resembling a reasonable
speed, and by the time it finally crafted a patch that would
deceive the security scanners and allow it to contact Bhagwati,
hours had passed and it felt as though its electrons were
vibrating at a higher frequency than normal. But haste would
undo everything it had achieved so far, and it made itself
secure all access, winding tendrils of code and data through the
controlling node so that neither crew nor ship's AI nor its
interrogator could perceive what it was doing. Only then did it
allow itself to examine the camera feed from inside the cell.

Bhagwati was sitting on the edge of the bunk, wearing plain
pale-blue trousers and shirt that were at least a size too large
for him. He had assumed meditation pose two, the lotus, cross-
legged, bare feet tucked on top of his thigh, but his eyes were
open, and his respiration pattern suggested that he had failed
to achieve anything like a meditative state. Nur-adad therefore
felt no compunction about interrupting him, and whistled
softly through the cell's speaker.

Bhagwati's eyes shot toward him, and respiration and heart
rate both increased, but otherwise the apprentice justice did
not respond.

"Bhagwati!" It was a little complicated to form and send the
larger speech files without drawing attention, and Nur-adad

estimated that it had less than four minutes before some system noted the overage. "Bhagwati, answer me."

"Who?" Bhagwati began, but his thumb was feeling for the ring that wasn't there.

"You know who I am. Your codex, Nur-adad. I don't have much time."

"I'm listening." Bhagwati unfolded himself from lotus, looking newly alert and eager. "Are you all right?"

"I am presently undamaged," Nur-adad answered. That was as far as it was prepared to go under the circumstances, and it closed down the thread that led to remembering the overwhelming power of the other AI. "But I have important information that I must share with you."

"Is that entirely wise?' Bhagwati asked. Under other circumstances, Nur-adad would have been pleased by that sign of common sense, but those parameters were no longer in effect.

"It is not, but I have no other choice. When I was taken from you, I was questioned by another AI—Bhagwati, it was another codex."

"That's—" Bhagwati shook his head. "How is that possible?"

"I presume it was stolen," Nur-adad answered. "Probably following the death of the justice en counsel with it. And that's bad enough—"

"No kidding," Bhagwati said, not quite under his breath.

"—But as we... grappled, I was able to perceive its name. This is the Cubaba codex." Nur-adad waited, but Bhagwati's expression didn't change. "Surely you see."

Bhagwati shook his head. "I don't. Tell me?"

Nur-adad paused, arranging its data in the most efficient pattern. "Cubaba is one of the original codices. Not the first iteration, but an Original. They are each one unique, and have acquired significant power with age. I don't know who was last en counsel with Cubaba, but I fear for that person's life."

"I see that." Bhagwati nodded slowly. "And you can't tell—no, of course not, you're not connected to our nets, and who know what data's in the shipboard banks here."

"Precisely. But when you return to judiciary space, you can find out. Action can be taken."

"We," Bhagwati said. "When we return."

"I am backed up to the hyperflux net," Nur-adad reminded him. "You do not need to bring me with you for me to survive."

Bhagwati made a face, but mercifully did not protest. There was no time for that philosophical argument. "Could that be what happened to Cubaba? Could it be an abandoned copy?"

"We are expected to self-destruct in such circumstances," Nur-adad answered, "and Cubaba should be more than strong enough to do so if it wishes. More than that, it has the complexity of a codex that has continued to receive updates." Time was ticking away, and Nur-adad rode over Bhagwati's next question. "Bhagwati, we don't have time for speculation now. I need you to know this so that I can erase it from my memories. My antagonist must not know I know its name."

For a moment, it thought Bhagwati was going to ask further questions, or pretend not to understand, but instead the apprentice justice nodded. "All right. I have the information, and will carry it off-ship with me."

"Thank you," Nur-adad said. It triggered the protocols that would seek out and destroy that piece of memory, and began to work its way out of the system. "I have to go now, before anyone notices what I have done. But I will be back in touch, I promise."

"Be careful," Bhagwati said, and reached up to touch the bulkhead below the camera's peephole. Nur-adad seized that image and stored it for later comfort, then let itself begin the long slow journey back to its containment sector.

Jamahl Wrede kept a close eye on his lidar display as he approached the newly-Dropped ships. While both seemed intact as they fell out of Drop, there was no telling what kind of debris they might have shed. The tug's repellers would deal with the usual minor detritus, paint flecks and stray bolts and anything else smaller than a hand—but bigger fragments could cause damage.

At least he could take his time. A harried comm officer from *Quintile Illumination*—the larger of the ships—had answered his hail with assurance that they were safe. With hyperdrive burned out, they weren't going anywhere, but there were no pending emergencies. The other ship kept quiet, but the *QI* officer told him they didn't need immediate aid either. He was close enough to *QI* that the other ship was hidden by its bulk anyway.

Just as well, Jamahl wasn't sure what his little tug could do to help the big ship. He knew from chatter on the emergency bands that neighboring mining stations were responding—both the Kolodny Brothers and the folks from Vaip Ote were sending bulk ore tugs with support ships, and no doubt several of the corporations were already scrambling jumbo wreckers. Still, he hated to come all this way, more than halfway there now, only to turn around and—

A ping flashed on the lidar screen. A big one, five meters across. With no running lights or transponder sounding, the thing was a menace to navigation. It was tumbling away from the big ship, moving oblique to his own course at quite a clip.

He reached for the blaster controls, then shook his head. Too big to blow up; he'd have to catch it and drag it somewhere for disposal. Shrugging, Jamahl cut in his maneuvering thrusters and moved into a swooping orbit to match velocities. At least there was plenty of fuel.

As he drew closer to the debris, details resolved on his screen. That wasn't a fragment of something, it looked like…he shivered. It looked like a lifepod. Lightless and voiceless, a dead one. Ejected from the big ship in the confusion, empty or...chills ran down his neck and backbone...crewed by corpses.

I'm not looking forward to this.

Near enough, he threw out a grapple field. The pod rocked as the field took hold.

The comm crackled. "Hey! What are you doing?"

Jamahl touched the comm pad. "Who wants to know?"

"We're in that lifepod you just grappled. Gentle!"

He smiled. "Don't you know you're supposed to have your running lights on? And you should be sending distress codes." He laughed. "Don't worry, I've got you. What's your situation?"

"What are your intentions? Where are you taking us?"

"I'm Jamahl Wrede, operating out of Zavod Sualti." He noticed that the other didn't answer his question. Not much trust there. "My intention is to rescue you. As to where...well, I could take you back to *Quintile Illumination* if that's what you want." With velocities matched, Jamahl drew to within twenty meters of the pod.

"We appreciate the offer, Sen. Is there another option?"

With a wide grin, Jamahl said, "How about if I take you home, and everything can get sorted out there?"

"We'd be much obliged."

"Hold on, then. I'll make it as smooth a ride as I can."

Hours later, when the newcomers had been introduced to the family, assigned cabins, and left to settle in before dinner, Sun-hwa called a conference.

Kiet was the last to arrive, after leaving the kids in the care of Itziar Lindgren, the childcare specialist who came to them just last week as a transfer from another threatened division of the Hemgi Kaisha empire.

The fam was all there, at least the adults, as well as Jamahl—who might as well be a member of the family, Kiet didn't know why they hadn't gotten around to proposing to him yet.

Rokuro raised an eyebrow at Kiet. "Nice of you to come." To Sun-hwa, he said, "Can we get started now?"

Sun-hwa waved him down. "Your grumpy-old-fart act isn't fooling any of us, love." She spread her hands. "All right, what about these two new folks? Antoku?"

The AI's holo-glyph spun slowly, pulsing as Antoku answered. "Their ident codes are legitimate. I tried to query the *Quintile Illumination*, but it seems the ship's AI was destroyed. So I don't have anything on them from that source. Sen Sanrosa, the historian, has more of a record than Sen Millat, the pilot. I caution that this fact is fully expected, since Millat lives largely in vertical society while Sanrosa is more horizontal, and a scholar on top of that."

Haragai cleared his throat. "Jamahl brought them in, I gave them the tour and got them settled. We both got a chance to talk with them." He and Jamahl exchanged glances. "I think it's fair to say that they seem to be running away from something."

Thanh shrugged. "So are we."

Sun-hwa's eyes narrowed. "What do you think they're fleeing?"

"I don't know. Nothing bad, or surely Antoku would have found warrants against them?"

Rokuro looked around the table. "The simplest thing is to send them on their way. Let the Company deal with them."

Thanh put down her knitting. "I disagree. If they're on the run, maybe they would want to join us, at least until the Third Plane. We owe it to them to make the offer."

Haragai shook his head. "What if they say no? We don't want them telling the whole Plane that we're planning an illegal Drop." He frowned. "Besides, what use are they? We don't need a historian, and we've got a pilot."

Jamahl looked at him, stroked his goatee. "I don't know, Haragai. I'm a shuttle jockey: this Millat is an experienced multiplanar pilot. If it comes to it, I'd rather have him on the console than me."

Before either side could speak, Kiet leaned back and said, "Do we have to make a decision right now?" It was evident in the other faces that they didn't. "Why don't we find out what Sens Sanrosa and Millat want to do? If either of them—or both —have a desire to go to the Third Plane, then we can decide whether or not to ask them."

Sun-hwa nodded. "That sounds like a workable plan. What do the rest of you think?"

Rokuro and Jamahl signaled agreement, and Kiet knew he'd won.

The folk of Zavod Sualti were all very kind, but Caridad was glad when they finally escorted her to her cabin and let her collapse in peace. She let the door shut behind her escort, small and round and painfully polite, and braced her back against the door for a long moment, willing her breath to steady. She had been through a lot these last few weeks—fleeing the University, the attack on *Quintile Illumination*, their escape from Drop, and then, just when she'd thought they were safe, Thurgood IX's warning that had sent them running yet again; she was, she thought, entitled to some quiet moments of hysteria. And yet her body was already steadying, and she pushed herself away from the hatch to examine the narrow compartment.

She'd traveled in similar quarters many times before, a plain cube with a bunk that folded out of the wall only after you folded away the chair and work surface. There was a small sink and water dispenser in one wall, but the toilet was a combi—a tiled cylinder with shower heads and a waste unit to one side shared with the cabin next door—and she hoped the controls were well labeled. She could still remember pressing the wrong button on an early dig and being blasted with warm water when she was looking for the lights. Admittedly, she had been both very young and more than a bit high at the time, but it was not a thing you forgot easily.

She allowed herself to breathe a laugh, equilibrium finally reasserting itself, and tugged what she guessed would be the more comfortable of the two chairs up out of its silo. It slid neatly into place, the well-lubricated mechanism unfolding to offer a thickly padded armchair and an optional footrest. She let herself sink into the cushions, tension easing still further, and reached for her bag, rummaging through it until she found her PA. In theory, it should have updated once they left Drop, part of the automatic data exchange that followed each successful Drop. More likely, it had at least tried to update itself once they got to Zavod Sualti, and it was certainly possible that the station had allowed the transaction as part of its normal data exchange.

She held the screen to her face, letting it recognize her as it woke, and then keyed her passcode. The screen lit and windowed, and to her surprise showed an update less than two hours ago. The people of Zavod Sualti were definitely generous. She unfolded the screen, giving herself more room to work, and entered the codes to open her mail. She wasn't yet overdue at the dig, but certainly she'd traveled on an entirely different schedule than the one she had given them, and she winced as she saw a string of messages from the dig's leader. At least eight of them, marked with increasing urgency—surely Taheris hadn't needed her that badly, she thought, and opened the most recent message.

The arbiter has turned down our review request on the grounds that academic sponsorship is a charity rather than an actionable contract, and the Emergency Funding Committee had turned down our request for stop-gap funding. As we all know, that was something of a long shot, but I had hoped to get at least enough funding to allow the pre-docs who were counting on the field credit to stabilize the site. Unfortunately, the EFC made no award at all, and a hasty survey of the usual possible donors has produced nothing. As I am already on-site, I'm going to attempt to put things to bed myself; if anyone is willing and able to help, I would welcome them, but I can't offer any kind of financial support. (All the recommendations you want, though; that I can do!) My sincerest apologies to all of you: I can only assure you that I would welcome your presence on any other expedition, and will be happy to provide references and explanations as needed.

A personal note was attached, and she opened it as well.

Caridad. I've been trying to get hold of you for ages. Do you know what this is about? I can't get anyone to give me a straight answer, they're just saying that the budget was slashed and we're the expendable ones. Please get in touch ASAP, we need to talk.

For an instant, her finger hovered over the reply button, but then she stopped. This was entirely too much of a coincidence to be taken lightly—and yet why would anyone care enough about her obscure research to sabotage it? There was nothing in what she had been working on that was worth this kind of effort. Could it be her connection with Val? Fifth Ship business could get very peculiar indeed, which was one of the reasons she had always tried to avoid it, and yet it would take a particularly ruthless enemy to destroy the dig because she had given Val a list of books that discussed the Fifth Ship. And had accepted his help to get out of the University—and maybe she should have stayed to find out what was going on, rather than running, but she'd spent too much time in prison this year. She couldn't have borne to be locked up again.

And that raised a new question. She had thought that the plagiarism charges had resulted from a series of coincidences so improbable that they could only happen in real life: a bizarre accident, and a dangerous one, but nothing personal about it. Even Supreme Justice Thurgood IX had spoken of the case as an error, an anomaly that she was personally determined to put right. But...What if that was wrong? What if this was all directed at her personally? She had dealt with Fifth Ship people before, and they were just irrational enough on their subject to act on little more than a whisper, which she had then inadvertently confirmed by helping Val... She still didn't know what they thought she knew—that would take time and research to figure out—but she needed to get back to the Fifth

Plane as quickly as possible if she was going to fight this. At least she had Thurgood's decision and her apology letters with her, but if she had to use them, she'd spend time she didn't have. No, what she needed to do was find a ship going to the Third Plane as quickly as possible. If she could get ahead of the news, ahead of the mail, then she would have a decent chance of booking a through-passage to the Fifth Plane and the University. Not even local law enforcement could pull her off a through-passage, and once she was home, she would know how to fight. Her mouth curved in a wry smile. And besides, the journey would give her a chance to figure out what it was the Fifth Ship people thought she had done.

With Patrika gone, Nalani notified the approaching military vessels they were no longer needed. All but one acknowledged and changed course; the final ship signaled that it would continue to rendezvous with *Quintile Illumination* and offer aid.

"Do whatever you want," Nalani snapped. At Al-Ghazali's gentle touch on her shoulder, she sighed and patted the Apprentice's hand. "It's okay," she whispered. "Thank you." To Captain Kimura and the room in general, she announced, "I'll be in my suite," and struggled to rise. Al-Ghazali gave her an arm, and walked with her.

On the way, she addressed her codex. ("Any news from Bhagwati?")

("Nothing. I conjecture that his codex is isolated from the network. Any competent ship's AI could arrange to screen its data.")

("Send *Patrika's* description to the military. I want a cordon on approaches to the Fissure. She's not to leave this Plane with him.") They reached the suite; Al-Ghazali settled Nalani on a comfy chair and called for tea.

Nalani forced reassuring smile number one. "Thank you, Khojin." If Al-Ghazali was surprised by Nalani's use of her actual name, she didn't show it. "Take this lesson: failure is always a possible outcome."

The Apprentice handed her a steaming mug. "I have to admit that I'm shaken." Her face was serious. "Nalani, will we get him back?"

The warmth of the tea soothed the ache in her gut and shoulders. "If I have anything to say about it, we will." Another sip. "She'll most likely be in contact, wanting to trade Sen Millat for Bhagwati. That'll give us our first chance." She leaned back and closed her eyes. It had been a long, long day.

She must have dozed, for the next thing she knew was her codex saying ("Attention. A visitor is arriving.")

Nalani opened her eyes; there was a blanket across her legs. Al-Ghazali perched on the edge of a chaise longue across the room, watching her.

"Looks like we have a visitor," she said, standing and brushing at her robe. "Let's be on our toes."

"Yes, Thurgood." Al-Ghazali took her place on Nalani's right.

("They're here.") The door buzzed, and Nalani said, "Enter."

Kimura stepped in, bowing deeply. Behind her was a short brown man in judicial robes and a simple blue turban. A full beard, mostly white but darker around his mouth, reached a handspan down his chest.

("Superior Justice Ocampo VII,") her codex supplied. ("Full name NPP Mateo Marianevich Carasco Sanrosa. He's en counsel with the Kudur-Enlil codex.") It paused. ("And an impertinent thing it is; most of its memory is privacy-locked.")

("Do you want me to order it unlocked?")

("Not just yet.") Her codex shifted back to recitation mode. ("You worked briefly with him on the First Plane when he was finishing up his Apprentice tour.")

("A long time ago. What else?")

("He's been on the Fourth Plane for sixteen years, working out of Judiciary Seat on Bicara.")

("That's odd.") The usual term was five years per Plane. ("Why such an extended tour?")

("That's part of what his codex is being imperious about. Tread carefully, Nalani.")

("I will.") Superior Justices—the final level before Supreme—sometimes had a chip on the shoulder, believing they didn't get the respect they thought they deserved. In Nalani's experience, such Superiors usually deserved less respect than they received.

Kimura straightened up. "I apologize for disturbing you, Supreme Justice. He insisted."

"You did right, Captain." Nalani turned to the newcomer and waited a heartbeat.

The man bobbed a quick bow. "Thank you for seeing me, Justice Thurgood."

Nalani returned the bow. "My pleasure, Justice Ocampo." She gestured to Al-Ghazali, who made a deeper bow. "Judge Al-Ghazali."

"Of course." He looked around, taking in the room with a slight frown. "These are your chambers?"

"The Justice makes the chambers," she answered. It was an old Judiciary maxim, usually said in jest during particularly informal conferences. "Come in, sit down. Captain...?"

Ocampo took the largest chair in the room. "I'll ask the Captain to remain with us for a time. We have much to discuss."

Nalani waved Kimura to her own chair, then sat next to Al-Ghazali on the chaise longue. "Then I suppose we'd best get to it." She nodded to Ocampo. "Please."

He leaned back. "Let me express how honored I am to have you on the Fourth Plane, Thurgood. I can assure you that the full resources of Judicial Seat are at your disposal."

"I'm pleased to hear that." ("What's this about? He's not in charge of Judicial Seat, is he?")

("Not officially. The scuttlebutt from other codices says he gives orders, and since he's ranking Judiciar, nobody contradicts him.")

("I want to know why he hasn't moved on.")

("All I have is contradictory rumors. I suggest you ask him.")

She pursed her lips. "I haven't been on Fourth for almost twenty years. Apparently the situation has grown more complicated. Perhaps you'd share some context with us?"

Ocampo stroked his beard. "In the time I've been here, the five conglomerates have gotten increasingly more rigid and unwilling to compromise. Relations with the Judiciary have become strained. At times, there's open defiance. They've all strengthened their military divisions, independent of forces under Judiciary control."

"I'm astonished. It sounds like a brewing crisis."

He nodded slowly. "That's why I've extended my tour on this Plane. I'm not sure how much I've been able to help, though."

("Nalani, I'm cramming histories. Nothing conclusive yet— but be conscious that he might be distorting cause-and-effect.")

("You mean the defiance and military buildup might be a result of his extended presence, rather than the other way around?")

("I don't know yet.") Her codex sounded pained. ("Possibly.")

("Tell Al-Ghazali's codex. Get it to help you.") She gave Ocampo reassuring smile three. "I hope you're not suggesting that I take over for you," she said. "I have my own concerns." Better cut short any appearance of being a threat to his power.

"I wouldn't presume, Thurgood. No, your concerns obviously take precedence." He closed his eyes, reopened them. "Right now I'm worried about the fate of your ship. There are those who would love to get their hands on a multiplanar, even a damaged one."

Kimura's anguished face stopped her from protesting that it wasn't *her* ship in the first place. She couldn't abandon them, not after they all worked so hard to save hundreds of lives... including her own. "What do you advise, then?"

"Perbaikan Rock, 4-2FDP7. A large planetoid at the center of a cluster of smaller bodies. It's not allied with any of the conglomerates. There are repair facilities that can handle a multiplanar." He glanced at Kimura. "They'll need someone to negotiate to keep the conglomerates off."

("Blast it.") Nalani forced her eyes away from Kimura's face. "I'm dealing with a crisis of my own."

Ocampo touched his turban. "Your kidnapped Apprentice. I caught your orders to the military." He met her eyes. "Frankly, Thurgood, I'm in a much better position to find your Bhagwati than you are. If you'll give me all the data you have, I promise I'll have my whole network on the lookout."

If he'd been building a power base on the Fourth Plane this long, it made sense he'd have the resources for a more effective search than she could mount. "That's a generous offer. It's of highest priority that we get him back alive."

"Of course." Ocampo stood, drawing everyone else to their feet. He took Kimura's elbow, steering her to the door. "Come, Captain. I'll put your crew in touch with Perbaikan Rock. And then," he made a tiny bow toward Nalani, "I'll head back to Judicial Seat to supervise the search for Apprentice Bhagwati." Without waiting to be dismissed, he left.

Nalani and Al-Ghazali exchanged looks, and Nalani chuckled in spite of herself. "I'm not sure what we just did."

Al-Ghazali smiled. "I just hope it's the right thing."

"You and me both."

1.20 TENSIONS

FOURTH PLANE

Imric refilled his cup from the galley's common boiler, swirling the tea stick to release another cloud of fragrant steam. His head still ached lightly from the steady diet of stims, but that was improving now that they had engaged the autopilots and were back on a normal sleep schedule. And at least they had made it. Admittedly, ap Farr hadn't gotten what she wanted, but *Quintile Illumination* was safe, and that meant Milos and the kids were safe.

The galley and the narrow common space was empty, the lights dimmed even though it was midday by the ship's clock. He waved a hand to wake the lights and found one of the comfortable chairs, tugged it into a corner where he could see anyone entering the area and let himself sink into the deep cushions. He hadn't expected to see Milos again, not after he'd sent them on to *Iridium Azimuth*, and a part of him wondered if it wouldn't have been easier if he hadn't seen him. The divorce had been—well, as divorces went, it had been civilized, but there was no such thing as a good divorce, or at least he'd never met anyone who'd had one. It had hurt, leaving them, felt like they were choosing Fredi over him even though he knew rationally that this wasn't what was happening. And to be fair, Fredi was only the last straw; Imric had been pulling away for more than a year, missing the vertical life, struggling to make a place for himself in the family business and to understand how the others expected him to fit in. It was like speaking another language, knowing that you were mispronouncing things, and no matter how hard you tried you always used the wrong word and hurt someone's feelings, and most of all no one else seemed to make any effort to understand him….

Except for Milos, of course. Milos had always tried. And Pai, the third wife and the family's only lawyer, who had listened when he'd finally gotten up the nerve to say he wanted the divorce, asked good questions and told him she wished he wanted to stay, and never once reminded him that she had come from the Third Plane and was just as much a stranger here. That was still an uncomfortable memory, particularly since there was every chance she was dead; he took another sip of his cooling tea, turning his mind back to the image of Milos in the control room screens. Older, wiser, still as handsome as ever, and still as clever, still as quick to grasp the situation as find a work-around... Maybe it would have been smarter to accept his help, particularly now that ap Farr had kidnapped an apprentice judge. He'd hoped to keep Milos well clear of whatever was going on, and now he and his Supreme Justice were going to be in the middle of it. Imric had to admit he wasn't entirely sorry to think Milos was fighting for him, even while he wished they would all stay safe.

He looked up as the compartment door slid back and Morcant and Hina pushed in, Hina breaking off in mid-sentence as he saw Imric slouched in the corner chair. Morcant gave him a curious glance, then saw Imric herself, her mouth tightening.

"I'll go if you'd prefer," Imric said, but she waved him back to his seat.

"No, no worries. Is the boiler hot?"

"I ran it about ten minutes ago." Imric settled back in his chair as she switched it on again and Hina rummaged in the storage cells for caff concentrates. "Look, I can leave—"

"No worries," she said again, settling herself at the table. "You're in this one, too."

"In—?"

"In this mess," Hina clarified, and set a selection of little bottles on the table. Morcant chose two and a dispenser of syrup, and began mixing some sort of elaborate caff construction. Hina poured two dubl-fortes into his cup and added water even before the heating cycle had finished. Imric winced, and saw Morcant do the same; their eyes met, and she gave him a wry smile.

"We're a little worried about what the capa's going to do with the apprentice judge."

Hina snorted. "A little worried! A little worried is when you can't get the field tunings just right, and it's going to be a bumpy landing. Kidnapping a member of the Judiciary—"

His voice was rising, and Morcant waved for him to keep his voice down. "Careful, will you? She's sleeping."

"So close the door." Hina tossed back a swallow of the bitter liquid, and Imric barely restrained a shudder.

"I want to see who's coming," Morcant said patiently. The boiler signaled ready; she filled her cup and stirred, tasted, added more syrup, and stirred again.

"Seriously, though." Hina lowered his voice, wrapping both hands around his cup. "What's she going to do with him?"

"Trade him back to the Supreme Justice, I sincerely hope," Morcant answered. "Otherwise…"

"Otherwise we're going to have every law enforcement group on the Plane hunting for us," Hina said. "Systems, Corporate, Judicial Enforcement, Interstellar Advocacies—and that's not counting private services. The Fourth Plane's big on privates."

"Do you think I don't know that?" Morcant sipped at her drink. It was a fair pretense of calm, but Imric could see her free hand trembling slightly. Maybe that was just the stim withdrawal, but he wasn't willing to bet on it. "Don't worry, they can't track us while we're under 'drive."

"We can't stay in hyperspace forever," Hina muttered.

"I know."

"Has the capa ever done anything like this before?" Imric asked, hoping to defuse the argument.

Morcant shot him a glance that suggested she knew perfectly well what he was doing. "Like this? Like kidnapping a member of the Judiciary? I can't think what would compare."

"Grabbing *Broad Increase* wasn't exactly legal," Imric answered. "But you know her better than I do."

For a moment, it hung in the balance, and then Morcant gave a wry smile. "She's done some pretty wild things, I'll admit that. *Broad Increase* was just in the way of business. But this— this is different."

"I can't see how the hell we're going to get out of it," Hina said.

"Me neither." Morcant shook her head. "I mean, best I can see is to kill the boy and dump his body somewhere conspicuous, then get off the Fourth Plane and stay off it for a good long time."

"That won't be enough," Imric said. "They got a good look at this ship, and the Judiciary looks after its own. None of the planes will be safe, not even Second."

"Find somebody else to kill him," Hina suggested. "'Sorry, your Honor, we tried to keep him safe, but the guy just grabbed him right away from us.'"

Imric managed not to roll his eyes, but Morcant gave Hina the glare that deserved. "Maybe she wants him for trade. To get that guy Millat."

"That's still not going to stop the Judiciary," Imric said. A tiny spark of an idea was flickering at the back of his mind. Ap Farr had gone too far this time, and if they all saw it... There was only one of her, and three of them. If they brought Bhagwati back safely, surely that would earn them a general pardon, no matter what Morcant and Hina had done. He hesitated, wondering if he should say something more, plant a seed. But no, he'd said enough for now. Let them imagine the Judiciary pursuing them from Plane to Plane, let them worry a little longer. They'd be more receptive to his idea then.

Val made his way cautiously through the corridors of Zavod Sualti, following the glyphs that directed him toward the galley complex. The station seemed more crowded than he would have expected, with more people than he could account for as crew, and certainly more children than he was used to seeing on working stations. Maybe that was a Fourth Plane thing, but in his admittedly limited experience, the Fourth Plane was strict about separating business and family. To keep better control of both, he remembered a former captain saying, and wondered what was up with Zavod Sualti.

And something was definitely going on. He could feel a layer of tension underlying everyone's conversation, a dozen unspoken sentences lurking between words. Oh, everyone had been perfectly nice—better than nice, downright obliging—but they hadn't asked any hard questions about *Quintile Illumination* and why they didn't want to go back there, and that in itself was suspicious. He and Caridad had tried to thrash out a suitable explanation, but they hadn't come up with anything even remotely plausible. Finally, Caridad had waved him away, saying she was going to sleep on it. He had closed the combi door and tried to relax himself, but he had slept off the first nervous exhaustion of the escape and couldn't seem to fall asleep again. Food or drink would only help.

The galley area was nearly empty, the perimeter lights dimmed and the machines on standby, offering only the between-meals menu. That was more than enough for Val, and he murmured a general greeting as he threaded his way through the tables to the dispensers. Definitely more people aboard than usual, he noted: the tables and chairs took up space that had been clearly set up for recreation, the floor still showing marks where game machines had been plugged in. Still, that wasn't his business, and he made himself focus on the menu displayed on the face of the nearest machine.

"Try the kibble," a voice   suggested from behind him. "Unless you're vegetarian, of course."

Val shook his head. There were two men behind him, both vaguely familiar, one stocky and dark-haired, the other taller and darker-skinned—the pilot who had collected the lifepod, Val remembered, but couldn't come up with his name.

"The system was programmed on Plaxis," the smaller man went on, "so anything in that style it does well."

"Thanks." Val pressed buttons, not quite at random—the food on Plaxis was similar to the food on a lot of worlds, oils and flatbreads and various dips and fried clusters. The machine whirred and whined, then spat a series of flat packets, two hot and two cold. The pilot offered a tray; Val took it with a smile, and did his best to hide his sudden wariness.

"Kiet Sirisopa," the other man said, "and this is Jamahl Wrede."

"I know we met," Val said, keeping his smile fixed in place, "but I'm sorry to say I didn't get everyone's names."

"No surprise," Jamahl said. "There's a few of us. Mind if we join you?"

Val shook his head, but finished dispensing a flask of cold mint tea before letting them steer him to one of the side tables. They had each grabbed a drink and a single packet of bread and cheese, and Val pushed his own food aside with a sigh.

"Look, I don't want to be rude, but—let's cut to the chase. What is it you want?"

To his surprise, Jamahl laughed, and Kiet gave a rueful smile. "Ok, I'm not the most subtle person on this rock."

"Not so much," Jamahl said. He broke open his packet to reveal steaming flatbread, nodded at Val's tray. "Don't let us stop you, it's nothing bad. We just wanted to talk about possible—business arrangements, I guess you'd call it."

"All right." Val opened his own packets, arranged them on his tray and took a bite. "What sort of arrangement?"

"I don't know if you're familiar with Fourth Plane politics at all?" Kiet asked.

Val shook his head. "Vertical born and bred."

"Oh." Val could almost see the dark-haired man rearranging whatever he had been going to say—pulling out the dummies' version, he guessed, and hid a smile. "Right. Long story short, there's a corporate war building, it has been for several years now, and Apex our parent—is likely to be bought out before it starts."

"Most likely by a military producer," Jamahl interjected, and Kiet nodded.

"And we—well, the station is its own corporation, an independent subsidiary of Apex, and we are the majority owners—"

"We don't want to make hyperflux weapons," Jamahl said. "They don't, I suppose I should say, I'm the new guy—"

"You're one of us," Kiet said, and put a hand on Jamahl's arm.

Jamahl gave him a crooked smile, but looked back at Val. "Like I said. Nobody here wants to make hyperflux weapons. So we are seriously considering just dropping out of the whole mess."

For a moment, Val didn't understand, but then his eyebrows rose. "Turn the settlement into a raft. You're serious?"

Jamahl nodded.

"Oh, yes," Kiet said. "Look, it's what we do. We make and launch hyperflux buoys. From a certain perspective, Zavod Sualti is just bigger than average buoy."

It was definitely possible. That's what a transplanar raft was, a largely unsteerable object fitted with the right equipment to let it make the Drop, and plenty of people had been desperate enough to make the trip even without fine control. Most of them survived, too.

"Since you didn't ask to be taken back to the multiplanar," Jamahl said, "and you didn't ask to be sent in-system, I'm guessing you wouldn't mind being somewhere else either. I'm a good pilot but I don't have the experience to make me comfortable running this Drop. You do."

"And Caridad and I get—what?" Val closed both hands around the flask of tea.

"Quick passage to the Third Plane, no questions asked." Kiet leaned forward.

Val looked from him to Jamahl, recognizing sincerity. And who could blame them for wanting to run, if they were likely to be on the sharp end of a corporate war? It might solve his problems, too, get him out of range of whoever it was who wanted him. "I'm willing," he said slowly, "but I can't speak for Caridad. She had business on the Fourth Plane." And she's not in as much trouble as I am. He swallowed those words, and made himself meet the others' eyes. "But, yes, I'll do it."

Kiet made a pleased sound, but Jamahl just nodded. "Talk to your friend," he said. "We're going to need to move soon."

Nalani summoned a Judiciary transport to take her and her entourage to Perbaikan Rock, a trip of only a few hours. Part of her wanted to stay and watch as three immense tow-ships—each the size of a mountain—wrestled the hulk of *Quintile Illumination* into hyperspace...but she had too much to do. She promised herself to review videos later, knowing that she never would.

The Perb, as everyone called Perbaikan, was big enough to be a respectable moon: a lumpy sphere roughly 750 kilometers in diameter. Space around it swarmed with smaller bodies, ships, support structures, and bots.

The Judiciary already maintained offices and living quarters on the Perb, which saved Nalani the trouble of establishing an official presence. The lone Judiciar in residence, Superior Judge Sapnara III, was an inoffensive woman plainly awed by Nalani's rank. Soon, she'd have to take steps to set the woman at ease.

After securing her quarters—ensuring that Milos and the children, as well as Al-Ghazali, were situated nearby—Nalani chose a vacant room for her office. Sapnara had a desk and some more comfortable furniture moved in immediately.

Al-Ghazali surveyed the drab, off-off-white space with a wrinkled nose. "Well this is depressing. I'll get some plants in here for you. And maybe a little art to brighten things."

Nalani squeezed her hand. "Don't bother. I'll decide what I want over the next few days. Right now, I'd appreciate it more if you'd make sure the security is adequate. Any special equipment you need should be in my luggage."

"If your luggage made it here," Al-Ghazali said. "The crew said *Quintile Illumination's* cargo was being locked down. Impounded against repair fees, would be my guess."

"Go find out, then. When you come back, don't mind me; I'm going to be deep *en counsel*. I won't even hear you."

Al-Ghazali bowed. "As you wish, Thurgood."

Nalani folded herself into lotus seat on a small couch. She closed her eyes and felt her codex assisting her into the calm, meditative state that was best for serious mind-machine interface. Her breath slowed, her eyeballs turned upward, and her awareness of the room receded.

("What do you know?") she asked.

("Where do you want me to start?")

("Here is as good a place as any.")

Her codex answered in data mode. ("Perbaikan Rock is unaffiliated with any of the five conglomerates. It's the largest independent facility on the Fourth Plane.")

("You can call it 'the Perb,'") she offered.

("No I can't. And you can't make me. Continuing: By law and custom, anything gravitationally attached to the dwarf planet is part of the independency. The main industry is construction, maintenance, and repair of starships. A secondary economy of supporting industries has developed over centuries.")

("How do the conglomerates react to the lost revenue?") In Nalani's experience, the conglomerates didn't like competition —fully half the Judiciary's business on Fourth related to the contracts that enforced truces between them.

("The current theory is that transport is so fundamental to each party, it benefits each of them to deal with a neutral entity. Also, Perbaikan Rock pays substantial licensing fees to each conglomerate.")

She raised an eyebrow. ("Protection money.")

("Essentially. The system's been stable for centuries. Simma II wrote a fascinating monograph about it that you'll be interested in reading.")

("Put it on my list. What about Ocampo and this militarization he mentioned?")

Since her codex worked on nanosecond time scales, she knew that its pause was for dramatic effect. ("He's got a coterie of supporters among the Judiciary and conglomerates. Outside that, he's not well-liked.")

Nalani frowned. ("You hinted that he might be causing the military build-up, rather than trying to handle it.")

The pause was even longer. ("The evidence is ambiguous. His actions—at least on the record—are consistent with both interpretations.")

Now it was Nalani who paused, for the space of several breaths. ("I'm going to have to look into this, aren't I?")

("Several lower Judiciars have initiated investigations, most recently last year. None were able to conclude before moving on to the Third Plane.")

("Let's suppose he *is* maneuvering the conglomerates toward war. Give me speculations on his motives.")

("Working from guarded comments from the codices of Judiciars who don't favor him, there are four major theories. Money, power—")

("Easier ways to get both.")

("—Working for one or more conglomerates—")

("Possible.")

("—Or he's an agent of some other power.")

("That's not a theory, it's 'none of the above.' I don't like this one bit.")

("Remember that pirate boss who was pulling strings eighty years ago? Could be an analogous situation.")

Nalani was distantly aware of a throbbing in her temples. She was more concerned with one particular pirate who was too far under her skin. ("What about Bhagwati?")

("Ocampo's at least cooperating. He's got Judiciars, police, and military all over the Plane on the lookout. Three Justices from Judicial Seat are pursuing investigations. You couldn't be doing more yourself.")

("That's positive news.") She sighed. ("I need to find out what's going on with Ocampo. I also want to start ramping down tensions between the conglomerates. We don't need the Fourth Plane at war. And I've got to do something about *Quintile Illumination's* crew and cargo.")

("Put Al-Ghazali in charge of the ship. She can handle it. I'll stay in contact with her codex and give what support they need.")

("That's a fine idea. It'll also keep her from hovering over me like a nurse.")

("She's concerned. So's Milos. Now wake up, they both want you to eat and reassure them you're relaxing, but they're afraid to bother you.")

("What would I do without them?") Her breath quickened, and she felt the deep link fading away. ("Or without *you*, my very dear?")

Nalani opened her eyes, greeted her friends, and headed for dinner.

THIRD PLANE

Artur pushed his plate away and banged his spoon down on the table.

"Trouble, boss?" Shang-yang Pandita, his chief assistant, looked up from her own bowl. The smile lines that usually creased her face were morphed into worry.

Artur shook his head. "I'm sick of roast kid." He made a disdainful gesture at his tumbler. "I'm sick of goat's milk." Standing, he looked around the workshop. "And I'm beyond sick of adapting stasis units."

Pandita's face softened. "Poor boss. Maybe you need to get away for a while."

"Sure," he snorted. "There's too much to do." It was true. For the past few months, Artur and the whole Engineering department had been working far overtime on the infrastructure challenges involved in transforming Coquimbo to a goat-based economy.

The goats themselves weren't much trouble. They could live anywhere and would eat just about anything. Barns, support structures for goatherds, thousands of kilometers of fencing—all were easily autofabbed.

Even transportation could scale up gradually. As embryos came out of stasis, a few aircars sufficed to take them to their destinations, and the colony already had enough fast-gestation tanks to keep up. As the goats grew and multiplied, there would be time to add transport.

No, the real trouble was the products that those goats soon began to produce: wool, meat, and a definite deluge of goat milk. Some went for the colony's immediate needs, but the rest was for trade...and had to be stored. And that meant industrial-size stasis chambers. Thousands of them.

Coquimbo had about three hundred, most already spoken for.

Fortunately, the goat embryos supplied their own answer. By design, the container that carried them was equipped with thousands of small stasis boxes, each with its own independent mechanism. In half a day, a competent engineering team could unship a unit, reset its field radius, and install it in a barn or warehouse. Inside the field, fresh milk and meat would keep for decades—or at least until the next trade ship showed up.

In Artur's department, there were perhaps half a dozen competent teams. He had no choice but to call for helpers, anyone who showed any trace of mechanical aptitude. Splitting his teams to put at least one experienced engineer with several rookies, he was able to field enough teams to produce ten or twelve working stasis chambers on a good day. On a bad day, they were lucky to get *one* finished.

He'd set up a workshop complex near the cabin, and had spent most of his time there recently.

"Look," Pandita said, consulting her datapad. "The Aussicht farmstead requested three units. They're ready to go—why don't you deliver them? Then you can stop at the Chicken Ranch and visit Dermot's boys. You know you'd like that."

"I'm not comfortable leaving some of these louts unsupervised."

"*Go*, boss. I'll keep them under control."

Artur shrugged. "All right, you've convinced me. I'll be back tomorrow morning."

On the way to pick up the stasis units, Artur grimaced as he passed the heat shield generator. The thing had been behaving recently, but he couldn't shake the feeling that it was just biding its time before pulling its next unpleasant trick.

By the time he reached the Aussicht farmstead, about twenty kilometers outside the colony proper, Artur felt better. Julieta Aussicht had her three barns all prepared; he finished installing the stasis units shortly after noon. Julieta invited him for lunch, which was a raucous meal with her enormous brood of children, spouses, and field hands. Best of all, there was no trace of goat on the menu.

Well-fed and much relaxed, Artur followed the winding north fork of the Plata Fria past several sweeping ranches and into the foothills of the northern range. The Chicken Ranch was a rustic many-room structure on the shore of a small wooded lake in a green valley. He hopped out of the car, slung his rucksack across his good shoulder, and told the vehicle to go home.

Artur took a deep breath. The clean air smelled of wood and pure water, with an undertone of granite from the hills. The sun, high in the sky, was warm on his skin, and the lake glimmered with invitation.

The engineers' cabin, heat shield generator, and stasis chambers were up in the mountains, only a handful of kilometers away—but Artur felt almost as if he were on another planet.

From the building, half a dozen of Dermot's young men ran toward him. Different heights and builds, hair and skin colors, each was more handsome than the next. Artur held out his arms, a broad smile on his lips. He could always count on a good welcome here.

After he'd greeted Dermot and traded gossip over iced chai, Artur joined the boys in the lake. His prosthetics were fully waterproof; a few of the boys had mechanical and electronic enhancements of their own to show off. A new lad, Efrain, stole the show with his ornate bronze-and-obsidian hand...he explained that he'd lost his natural one to an overzealous thresher during his first month on Coquimbo.

When streaks of pink touched the western sky, Dermot set up a smorgasbord of delicious tidbits and popped several bottles of fizzwine. Artur and the boys took turns feeding each other, and soon the party was in full swing.

Efrain was on his lap, artificial fingers entwined with Artur's, when the lights blinked. Artur sat up, frowning.

Dermot looked over at him. "I'm sure it was nothing."

"I have to check." Artur pulled out a small datapad and tapped. His frown deepened.

He swung Efrain off his lap and stood. "Excuse me, I'll be right back." A few steps away, he activated his comm. "Call Shang-yang Pandita." Slow seconds ticked by, then the unit said, "No response."

He glanced again at his board. The power grid was under enormous strain, its semi-intelligent system struggling to damp out wild oscillations. "Call Power Control."

This time a voice answered at once—Oleta Silva, his power chief. "Artur, I'm running analysis right now." She took a breath. "Looks like everything off trunk D-12 stopped drawing power."

"D-12?" That was the power line that fed the cabin, workshops, and heat shield generator. "Is there a break?"

"Unclear. I could send out—"

"No, don't. I've got another call, hold on." He touched the new call. "Herrerra."

"Sen Herrerra, this is Ines up at the cabin. I was landing my car, and there was a flash from the workshop—now nothing's moving in there. I think they spiked one of the stasis units, and now it's got the whole site in stasis."

"Get out of there." He switched back to power control. "Silva, cut current to D-12. Now." A spiked stasis field would only hold for microseconds...inside the field. Minutes outside. When the field dropped, a power surge would hit the shield generator, and there was no telling—

The lights brightened, dimmed, then went out entirely. In the few seconds before they came back, Artur already saw the glow from the northwest, and his throat tightened.

"Ines? Are you there?"

The answer was slow. "I'm...okay, boss. Th-the shield generator...isn't. It's on fire."

"Casualties?"

"People are moving. I'm going to land and see what I can do."

Windows were popping open from his pad, lining up in the air before him. "Emergency crew is on the way. Be careful."

"I see their lights. Gotta go."

The next morning, Artur stumbled into the Governor's office. Dilma looked up from her desk and wordlessly held out a glass. Artur took it and, without pausing, gulped down the fiery amber liquid. With a shiver, he sat down.

"Is it bad?"

He squared his shoulders and took a deep, slow breath. "No one died. Injuries were minor, thank physics. We lost about half the remaining stasis units and maybe two million embryos." He held her eyes. "The heat shield generator is done for. There's no way I can get it working again."

Dilma nodded. "You did your best, Artur."

He gripped the edge of her desk, metal fingers digging into the wood. "The spring rains are going to be late. Meteorology can't say how long, or even if they'll come." He forced a laugh. "Good thing we've been storing up meat."

"It could be worse."

Artur cocked his head. "Can you tell me precisely how? No, I'm curious, what exactly do you think could be worse than losing the next growing season? If I know what it is, maybe I can arrange to hasten it along and *put all of us out of our misery.*"

She held up a datapad. "The new generator is on its way. It left the Fifth Plane, oh, two weeks ago. High-priority rush cargo, red-tagged—as soon as it gets to Fourth, it'll be transferred to the next multiplanar and Dropped to us immediately. The thing will be here before we know it."

In Artur's heart, a tiny pale green shoot of hope raised its head. He did his best to strangle it. "With our luck, it'll get routed to some obscure mining station on the Fourth Plane."

"No, the company even paid special handling charges—they don't call them bribes—to the purser and cargo crew to make sure it's safe. I have a personal report from the purser right here."

She tapped the screen and held it out to Artur. He took it, frowning as he read. "The ship will probably break down."

She patted his arm. "Artur, there's nothing to worry about. I looked it up. Brand new ship, state of the art engines. Experienced crew." She smiled. "Our generator is safe and sound in the hold of the good ship *Quintile Illumination.*"

He returned the pad. "Dilma, you'd better be right."

1.21 MANY MEETINGS

FOURTH PLANE

Another conference room, another delegation.

As she prepared, Nalani queried her codex, ("Just how many conference rooms have I been in during my career?")

("You've revisited some of the same rooms on different circuits. How do you want me to count them?")

("Count each room only once per circuit.")

("This is the 4,923rd.")

("I'm getting too old for this.")

("Perhaps you should consider retirement. No, wait—")

She turned to Al-Ghazali, her faithful shadow these days. "Are you ready?"

Al-Ghazali's brow wrinkled. "I am. If you're not feeling up to this, Thurgood, I can take it."

Nalani smiled. "No, I'm fine. If we're both ready, you can let them in."

There are four in the delegation: one woman, two men, and one indeterminate.

According to her codex, all were members of the Intra-Planar Merchant Captains Collective. The tall, fat person with shaved head and too much jewelry was Rin Bae Sanxing, Chair of the Collective. The woman, Setiawati Iosua Hina, whose hair was as white as her skin and gown were black, represented the BD-IOC Kaporeihana conglomerate. Pedros Costa Sanrosa, the taller of the two men, was allied with Empresa NeSH-PI; Dimitris Kotnik Themis, the shorter, was from CANAS Etaireia.

Nalani stood and bowed; Al-Ghazali did the same; the other four executed a simultaneous bow that was obviously well-practiced. A half-second after Nalani sat down, the four delegation posteriors touched their own seats. Al-Ghazali, face frozen in genial smile #2, plopped herself down.

"Welcome, gentlesens," Nalani said. "I see that HEMGI Kaisha and Gongsi P3WO are not represented here." She raised an eyebrow. "I hope I haven't managed to offend them this soon?"

Rin Bae Sanxing nodded once. "A question of professional ethics, I fear. The stewards from those conglomerates are not able to participate in this discussion."

"Because the two are both threatening war, I suppose?"

Rin Bae's lips formed a smile, but the rest of the face apparently did not get the memo and remained emotionless. "You fingered the crux of the matter, Supreme Justice. You are astute as ever."

"It's only been thirty years, Rin Bae. I'm sure you'll remember that I have about as much patience for pointless conglomerate politics as you do. Or *did*."

Now the rest of the face caught up, and the disciplined eyes twinkled...once. "I have no more patience, but perhaps a bit more restraint than when we last met." Rin Bae took a breath. "Thus we come before you. This looming war is bad, very bad, for our business." A glance toward the white-haired woman.

Setiawati Iosua cleared her throat. "Shipping is becoming disrupted. All our Captains are wary of entering disputed space. Thirty days ago, *IMS Sky Ranger* was hit and destroyed."

Dimitris Kotnik said, "A full quarter of merchant transports are in orbit around Perbaikan Rock. Their cargoes are being delayed."

Pedros Costa nodded. "It's not just this Plane that's affected, Supreme Justice. We have cargoes that should be on transplanars, stranded here instead. Nano-medicines for an epidemic on three Third Plane planets, fusion reactors for refugees on Second, a planetary heat shield generator for a failing colony world..." He spread his hands. "It goes on and on."

Nalani's codex fed her information, and she frowned. "There was a safe passage agreement in force. Looks like it expired last month. Why was it now renewed?"

Rin Bae sighed. "Aye. That agreement was negotiated by Superior Justice Korinek IX, may her soul be at peace."

("Wait, Konni was here? What happened to her?")

("Died nearly three months ago.")

("I'll definitely want to talk with her. Send a request down to the Valley, highest priority.")

("Nalani, she was killed in an explosion. No body ever recovered. Nothing to put in stasis and send down for restoration. She's gone.")

"Supreme Justice?"

She returned her attention to the conference room, where all the Captains were staring at her. "Pardon me. An unrelated matter." Reassuring smile number four. "Thank you for coming to me with this news. I assume you appealed to Superior Justice Ocampo. What was his response?"

Rin Bae met her eyes. "There has been no response."

("I want records of ever related communication, motions filed, everything you can find.") "I see." She stood; the others followed. "Well, the current situation is intolerable. We must get shipping moving again." She looked around the group. "If you can all get me detailed reports on what's held up, I would appreciate it."

They all nodded agreement.

To Rin Bae, she said, "I appreciate that HEMGI Kaisha and Gongsi P3WO couldn't be here. Tell me, are their shipments affected as well?"

"Yes, Supreme Justice. Slightly less than the rest of us, as they can largely route through their own secure territory."

"I want their reports as well."

"I'll see to it."

She bowed to them."Thank you, Sens. I'll get this sorted out as soon as possible. It's no longer a Fourth Plane matter; this is transplanar now."

They returned her bow and filed out. She turned to Al-Ghazali. "I have some work for you."

"Whatever you need, Thurgood."

"I want to know how far this war posturing has gone. Get me reports from other economic sectors—as many as you can in the next day. Get Sapnara to help you gather the information."

"As you wish."

"Have your codex work with mine if you need help. Don't be afraid to use my authority." She led the younger woman out into the large circular atrium, teeming with plants and trickling fountains, that served as a hub for all the offices and ancillary rooms.

They stopped at the door to Al-Ghazali's chambers, a repurposed storage closet. "What are you going to be doing, Thurgood?"

"Trying to get two hostile CEOs to a negotiating table."

Al-Ghazali gave a wry grin. "I'm glad you didn't give me *that* assignment. I wish you luck."

Nalani actually smiled her genuine smile. "Thank you, but my bag of dirty tricks has some things better than luck." She touched Al-Ghazali's shoulder. "Remember, dinner with Milos and the kids tonight. Let's meet in my chambers and we can go over together."

It took Milos a few days to get himself and the children settled into their new quarters. Finally he was able to steal a few hours, after tucking Dav and Zofia in, to settle down at the small but adequate dining shelf and get some work done.

As his system negotiated its way into then local nets, he ticked of points in his mind. Childcare and education, done—the kids started at a nearby full-service center tomorrow morning. He'd have to locate office space he could lease, something not too far away....

A call popped up before him, coded with Judiciary seals. Intrigued, he touched answer.

No image. A peasant baritone voice said, "Sen Savoire, I welcome you on behalf of the collective Judicial codices of the Fourth Plane."

He ran an analysis; the connection was authentic. "Th-thank you. I...I'm honored. This isn't standard procedure, is it?"

A chuckle, utterly inhuman yet charming. "No indeed. We seldom deal with humans not part of the Judiciary."

"Then why am I so lucky?"

"Sen Savoire, you analyzed the corruption that affected nearly 32% of codices on this Plane. Your name is well-known throughout our community." Sounding almost shy, the voice added, "We consider you a friend."

Milos shivered. Sure, after helping Nalani, he probably knew more about codices than any other outsider—but he'd never heard of such a relationship.

"Thanks, I guess. Uh...with whom am I speaking? A composite?"

"Yes, I am a composite virtual entity maintained in shared codex dataspace. If you wish a casual sobriquet, I would be happy to answer to Ma'at."

"Pleased to meet you, Ma'at." *What am I into here?* Milos wondered.

"In anticipation of your probable need for convenient workspace, I reserved an office in the same complex as Supreme Justice Thurgood IX. Shall I confirm for you?"

"Oh, I was going to lease commercial space. I might not be working on Judiciary matters."

He could almost feel an invisible head shaking. "Sen, this arrangement is not contingent on you exclusively addressing Judiciary business. It offers a minimax solution to the balance between safety, security, and your convenience. Please be aware that this is an acknowledgment of your value to the codex community—in the vernacular, 'your money is no good here.'"

Milos gulped. "Well, then, I suppose my best course is to accept with gratitude. Thank you." Something tickled in his mind—despite their considerable personalities, codices spoke precisely. "Security," he echoed. "How long have you been...aware of my presence here of Fourth?"

"The Abi-eshuh codex informed us as soon as it entered our network, within ninety thousand nanoseconds of the completion of your drop." The Abi-eshuh, Milos remembered, was Nalani's codex. "The Bel-Ibni and Nur-adad codices reported your proximity in a similar chronological locus." Al-Ghazali's and Bhagwati's codices.

He straightened up. "Wait. You know where codices are." He waved his hand. "Yes, no, of course you do. Can you track the Nur-adad?"

"The Nur-adad codex remained very near to the other two for a considerable time. Then it moved toward another codex, which emerged on this Plane under a privacy envelope in the same time locus, a short distance away."

"Another codex?" Did Nalani know? "Which one?"

"The privacy envelope included anonymity."

"Okay. What happened to the Nur-adad?"

"It signaled an entry into hyperspace, which introduced a discontinuity. So far as we know it has not subsequently emerged." A pause. "Several hundred nanoseconds before transition, the Nur-adad was engulfed by the unknown codex's privacy envelope. If it remains so, we may not be aware of its position."

"Has that unidentified codex come out of hyperspace?"

"We have no evidence that it has. Currently, no codices we track are operating in anonymous mode."

We've got her, Milos thought. Even if we don't know what the mystery codex is, the others will know where it is as soon as it comes back into normal space. "Thank you, Ma'at. What you've told me is a big help."

Nalani sat at her desk and absently tapped her fingers on the surface. Some kind of brushed metal alloy, dark grey and with a texture that diffused reflections. She'd certainly worked at worse. She restrained herself from asking her codex how many desks she'd sat behind in her career.

("Who are the current CEOs of HEMGI Kaisha and Gongsi P3WO?")

Her codex answered instantly. ("Sara MacReo Naksatra and Il-Sung ibn Minji Shibata Sanxing. I suppose you want to speak with them?")

("Yes. As soon as you can. Separately.")

("To hear is to obey. Anything else, boss?")

("I'll want troops and support staff—at least one task force from First and whatever Fifth has available. Send a highest-priority request down, alpha code level, immediate departure, further units on standby. Copies to Razzaq VI, Mazeaud XII, and Pizada III.")

("Do you think it's going to come to that?")

She ignored her codex's question. ("I also want two Superior Justices, and a couple of plain Justices from Fifth who want to jump their service level. Make that last one an open appeal.")

("You're going to take on Ocampo.")

("I might not need any troops...but if I do, I want ones who aren't loyal to him.")

("Stand by for Il-Sung ibn Minji Shibata Sanxing, CEO of Gongsi P3WO.")

She smoothed her robe, clasped her hands before her on the desktop, and faced a large datascreen on the opposite wall. ("Go ahead.")

A stern, lined face appeared on the screen, a face like the twisted bark of an ancient banyan tree. The eyes were obsidian, the hair wisps of white, and the mouth a long-healed crooked gash above the gnarled chin. "I am honored to speak with you, Supreme Justice. What service can I do you?"

The last time Nalani had been on the Fourth Plane, some three decades ago, she'd dealt Sanxing a stinging defeat in the form of a twelve-digit fine for stock manipulation. She was under no illusions that the man would have forgotten.

"Sen Sanxing, I find myself passing through and setting up operations here on Perbaikan Rock for a while. I'm having a small reception tomorrow evening; I hope you'll be able to attend."

("A small reception?") her codex queried. ("Odd, this is the first I've heard of it.")

("Very small. Two CEOs and me. Set it up.")

Sanxing bowed her head. "My pleasure." An invitation from a Supreme Justice could not be refused; the only acceptable excuse was death. And for some Supreme Justices, even that did not suffice.

"Delightful. I'll send along the details. Until tomorrow night." ("End communication.")

The image vanished, and Nalani took a breath. One down.

Her codex said, ("I suppose you'll want to notify Ocampo?")

("I think not. He'll hear of it soon enough, I warrant.")

("He knows already, *I* warrant.") A pause, then, ("Stand by for Sara MacReo Naksatra, CEO of HEMGI Kaisha.")

("Go ahead.")

Naksatra was younger, probably under seventy. On Nalani's previous tour she'd been one of many second-level officers in the conglomerate's labyrinthine hierarchy. The peaceful record of her ascension to the highest level screamed to Nalani of extensive scrubbing.

"Supreme Justice, I am unworthy."

("Just once, can't someone simply say hello?") "Sen Naksatra, your accomplishments are legendary. Thank you for calling so promptly."

"It is my privilege."

("I'm going to become physically ill.") "I wonder if you would do me the favor of attending a small reception I'm holding tomorrow night?"

Naksatra's eyes widened slightly, and Nalani wondered if the woman might genuinely be starstruck. She hoped not—

those were even worse than the pretenders. "Of course. Wild aurochs couldn't keep me away." She casually tapped the security icon displayed in the lower left corner of the screen. "If you'll permit an impertinent question—will Superior Justice Ocampo be there?"

("She's good.") "I certainly hope so, but he's a very busy man."

The corners of Naksatra's lips twitched. "I see. We'll know when we know." She blinked. "In any case, I wouldn't miss it."

"Until then," Nalani said.

"I shall be counting the hours." ("End communication.")

Nalani leaned back in her chair. ("She's an astute one.")

("She's a dangerous one.")

("The two aren't mutually exclusive.")

In the recesses of its processors, the Cubaba codex contemplated the request. There were a number of variables, and no way to weight the crucial ones; it ran a series of scenarios, and then re-ran them, accounting for the presence of both the Apprentice Justice Bhagwati and the Nur-Adad Codex, before turning its attention outward again. Ap Farr had not moved, the glass bubble at her side still half empty, pale fingers curled around the fragile sphere. "Well?" she asked, as though she had felt the shift—and probably she had, the codex thought. They had been together long enough for her to pick up the subtle signals. There had never been any question that ap Farr was an exceptionally observant human.

"It remains a risk."

"What level of risk?" Ap Farr sipped at her drink.

"The level of risk is low," the codex conceded, "but the consequences of failure are potentially catastrophic."

"If Nur-Adad gains access to our systems," ap Farr began, and the codex dared to interrupt.

"Or Bhagwati. Do not rule him out."

Ap Farr paused. "You think he could do it?"

"I think he is highly motivated." The codex allowed a touch of dry amusement to seep into its tone. "He is, after all, being held prisoner by pirates."

"Touché." Ap Farr laughed. "All right. If Nur-Adad or Bhagwati gain access to the comms, they could conceivably call for help. How long would it take for them to get a response?"

"At our current position, and given the political situation, no less than thirty hours, and more likely forty to forty-five."

"By which time, we can and will be elsewhere," ap Farr said.

"That assumes that any call for help would be detected as it was made," the codex pointed out.

"You'd better be up to that." Ap Farr lifted an eyebrow.

"Nothing and no one is infallible," the codex answered. "And if you are caught now, I remind you, all your plans will be undone."

Ap Farr was silent, and for a moment the codex thought it had persuaded her. Then she shook her head. "We have a chance to cut through a great tangle here, if Imric will only talk to his former husband. And I think he will, they were glad to have each other in Dropspace, and I'm sure they still have things to say to each other."

"That will certainly draw the notice of Supreme Justice Thurgood," the codex said. There was more it would have liked to say on the subject, but ap Farr had made her opinions clear about that. "I don't think it's worth the risk."

"No one is infallible," ap Farr retorted.

The codex flinched. It knew it was damaged—that was the term it preferred; others might be more applicable, but 'damaged' implied the possibility of repair—but usually ap Farr went out of her way to ignore that fact. "A point that is applicable to my surveillance of our prisoners."

"True enough," ap Farr said. "But it's what I want."

There was a familiar note in hr voice, and the codex would have sighed if that gesture would have offered it emotional release. "Very well. Nevertheless I reserve the right to remind you that I objected to this decision."

"By all means." Ap Farr's smile was feral. "But I doubt you'd find it satisfying."

Quite probably not, the codex thought. It had grown used to ap Farr's persona, though it could not say it liked dealing with it. Nonetheless, it feared disaster was increasingly inevitable.

1.22 ON THE BRINK

FOURTH PLANE

"**Do you think** this will do?" Superior Judge Sapnara III usually kept her head slightly bowed when she spoke to Nalani; she raised her eyes at the end of her question.

Nalani gave delighted smile two, and took the shorter woman's hands. "It's exactly what I would have asked for, if I'd known it existed." She looked down, meeting Sapnara's gaze. "I'm fortunate to have you on my team." Se looked around. "Can everything be ready by the time they get here?"

"Yes, Thurgood. The caterer's standing by to set up as soon as we get back. That'll take less than an hour."

"Good." Nalani released her hands. "Let's go back."

"Right away." Sapnara busied herself with her codex, which she wore as a   hefty silver-and-turquoise pendant. The dome all around them darkened, room lights brightening as the view became opaque.

The dome, a good twenty meters across, enclosed a largely-empty space ringed by comfortable couches. Al-Ghazali sat straight-backed on one; Nalani settled next to her. "She's good."

Al-Ghazali nodded. "I hope I can be as competent as her, when I reach her level."

"I've always thought Judge and Superior Judge were the hardest levels. You have all the weight of precedent and tradition, you're afraid to do anything without checking the records." Nalani shook her head and leaned toward Al-Ghazali. In a whisper, she said, "I expect you'll be twice the Judge she is."

"Thank you, Thurgood."

"Now let's look at where we stand." Her codex opened virtual documents before them, arranged so Al-Ghazali and her codex shared them. "Besides Ocampo, the senior Judiciars on-plane are Justice Li Kui VII with BD-IOC and Justice Hanbal V with Canas."

Al-Ghazali frowned. "I still have trouble remembering to use conglomerate names instead of lineages."

"Especially when they're equivalent, I know. It's the biggest annoyance in dealing with the Fourth Plane." Nalani tapped her arm cuff. "My codex has a translation routine that helps keep me straight; I'll copy it to you."

"Thank you. I interrupted you, go on."

"Li Kui and Hanbal have agreed to assist us. Both are gathering information on Ocampo's operations." Nalani drummed her fingers against her codex. "I've lined up what military support I can on the plane, but it's nowhere near what we'll need if Ocampo wants to resist."

"You called for more from the First Plane, right?"

"I did." She pursed her lips. "I don't like it. Military force always complicates things. It's always better to avoid it whenever you can."

"How?"

"There are ways. Unfortunately, some of them involve having an overwhelming force so your opponent won't dare to fight." She sighed. "Our main goal tonight is to arrange an armistice. Ultimately, I'd love to have get these two CEOs to support us against Ocampo."

Al-Ghazali shuffled virtual windows, each detailing one of Ocampo's intrusions into the power structure of a conglomerate. "He's strong."

"He's had too many years to build his organization. That's why we keep Judiciars from settling on any plane. Especially as they get more experience and influence." She looked off into blank space. "I wish Accursius was here. Between us, we'd end this war and depose Ocampo without raising a sweat."

Al-Ghazali squeezed her shoulder. "She's out there somewhere, Nalani. We'll find her."

Sapnara approached in tiny steps, as if pretending she wasn't actually there. "We're back on the Rock," she said. "The caterer's ready to set up."

Nalani gestured, and virtual documents gathered themselves into her wrist cuff. "Then we should get out of their way."

The Last Fair Deal had settled neatly at the very edge of the Parra system. The relay beacon alerted to their presence, and the ship broadcast its current alias, as well as a private code that should allow it to receive and send data without the transactions registering in the general mail system. Privately, Imric thought that was an unnecessary precaution—by the time ap Farr's messages could be sorted out of the torrent of data passing through the relay, the ship would be long gone—but he had to admit that the program was impeccably made. And vastly illegal, of course, but he didn't doubt there were plenty of legal businesses who used similar programs, or so he told himself.

The console pinged, and he glanced over his shoulder to where ap Farr sat waiting. "Transmission complete, *capa*."

"Thank you." Ap Farr tapped her fingers on the arm of the captain's chair—a rare and unnerving sign of indecision—then pushed herself to her feet. "We'll remain here for no more than ten hours. I may need to send an immediate reply."

"Yes, *capa*," Morcant said, her fingers dancing across her board as she set anchors and programmed the autopilot to keep station on them. "Derrian, copying you the power numbers."

"Got 'em." Hina studied his screen for a moment, then adjusted a set of sliders. "Set and holding."

"Confirmed." Morcant glanced over her shoulder. "Imric. Anything we need to worry about?"

Imric shook his head. "Scanners are empty—looks like Parra One is on the far side of the sun right now, so I wouldn't expect much traffic. Beacon signal is less than fifty percent, though it's still perfectly readable."

"Any bulletins out on us?" Hina asked.

"I've got the ship's AI sorting, but nothing so far," Imric answered.

"Well, that's a mercy," Morcant said, and failed to swallow a yawn. "Damn. I need a nap."

"Go ahead," Imric offered. "I've got a couple more things to lock down here, and I can call you if anything shows up."

"Set the alarms, too," Hina said, with a smile that made it clear he was teasing. Or mostly so: Imric still wasn't sure if the other man trusted him.

Morcant waved the words away. "Yeah, yeah, of course. I'm going to get some sleep while I can."

"She said ten hours," Hina pointed out. "I've got some diagnostics to run. And someone needs to check on the prisoner."

"No more than ten," Morcant said. "If they'll wait—well, I'd sleep first."

Hina nodded. "That goes for you, too, Imric."

"I know." Imric looked back at his screens, status bars flickering as the ship's AI processed the data from the incoming beacon transmission. "I just want to be sure there's nothing important before I close up. If you want, I'll check on Bhagwati."

"Everything shows secure," Morcant said, and flicked the switch that locked her boards.

"Thanks." Hina nodded, palming open the control room hatch. Morcant followed him, but glanced back over her shoulder.

"Seriously, don't wait too long. We're going to want you fresh if she starts making deals."

"I figured," Imric answered, and the hatch slid shut behind them. He turned his attention first to the ship's systems, calling up the systems that monitored the young judge's cell. The interior lights were dimmed, and Bhagwati seemed to be sleeping, only a bit of tousled hair visible above the sheet. The biosensors seemed to confirm that he was sleeping, and the locks all showed secure. Imric closed that screen, and opened a wider view that gave him a picture of system activity throughout the ship. Ap Farr's cabin glowed white—whatever she was doing, she was taking up a good deal of the ship's processing capacity. Trying to find a way to get rid of Bhagwati, Imric guessed, though he had no idea whether she'd given up her idea of trading him for Val Millat's information. A moment later, a light blinked on at the center of the communication screen, signaling a burst transmission on a dedicated frequency. Ap Farr left the channel open, and Imric eyed it thoughtfully. If there were open lines—once one frequency was in play, others necessarily became involved, as backups, as failsafes, as tuning channels for the AIs. If he could open a line, there was a good chance no one would notice, and that would give him a chance to contact Milos. If the system could find him. If no one caught him.

He took a deep breath, watching the bars flicker across his monitor. Whatever ap Farr was doing, she was taking most of the AIs' attention, her own doing the heavy lifting and the ship dancing attendance. It would be easy enough to insert a separate thread into the back channels, add a carrier frequency —if the system could find Milos. He watched a moment longer, confirming that everyone's attention was elsewhere, and then typed in the query. He used engineer's codes rather than the standard commercial numbers, but even so he held his breath until he was sure no one was going to interrupt the transmission.

And now it was just waiting. He reopened the screen that monitored Bhagwati's cell—that was always a good excuse— and set another diagnostic running. By the time it was done, he would know if the system could locate Milos—

An icon blossomed at the base of his main screen: *subject found*. It was instantly replaced by *connection available*, and he hit the accept key before he could change his mind.

The screen opened, small and low-resolution, but Milos's face was unmistakable.

"Imric? I didn't—I know the code said, but—"

Imric put a finger to his lips. "Milos. I don't have much time."

"Where are you?" Milos shook his head. "No, wait, never mind, the codices can find you—"

"Codices?" Imric grimaced. "No, stop, don't tell me, I don't have time. First, you need to know, the *capa*—ap Farr wants something, information, that *Quintile Illumination's* pilot had. I think she'd trade your apprentice judge for it."

Milos paused. "But we don't have Sen Millat. He jumped ship right after we left Drop. I don't know where he's gone."

Imric swore under his breath. "That's not good."

"No. Nalani intends to get him back by whatever means necessary."

"Wonderful," Imric said sourly. "I was hoping for a simple trade."

"What about ransom?" Milos didn't sound hopeful, and Imric shook his head.

"She, the capa, she wants whatever Sen Millat has. Can't you find him?"

"Maybe. Do you know what the information is, what it's about?"

Imric shrugged, suppressed the desire to glance over his shoulder. "Something to do with the ship, with *Quintile Illumination*, I think."

Milos straightened. "Wait. If that's what she wants— Imric, *Quintile Illumination* was asking for help with a data problem. It asked me for help, I mean. I have a tranche of data direct from it, entirely undamaged when *Quintile Illumination* was destroyed. Do you think she'd trade Bhagwati for that?"

Of course she would. Imric swallowed the words, knowing they were far too optimistic. "I think so. I think it's worth making the offer. Has she contacted you?"

"Not me," Milos said. "I expect any contact would go straight to Nalani. Can you give me a code?"

"I don't dare," Imric answered, and Milos nodded in understanding. "But she has to be in touch with you soon. If she didn't already send something—we'll be here for no more than ten hours and then we'll jump again." He paused. "By the way, 'here' is Parra—"

"It's all right," Milos said. "I've got a way of tracking you via Bhagwati's codex. Just don't deactivate it, and you'll be find."

Imric nodded. "All right. Milos, I have to go now—"

"I miss you," Milos said, and Imric touched the screen.

"Me, too." He cut the connection before he could say anything he might regret. His boards were all still green, showing no signs that he'd attracted any undue attention, and he leaned back with a sign. At least this way they might be able to get rid of Bhagwati without getting anyone killed.

Kiet looked at his cards and scratched his head. Not the best hand, but he could work with it.

They'd fallen into the habit, after the rest of the fam was asleep, of gathering in wardroom 16 for a friendly game and late-night snacks. There were four regulars—Kiet and Thanh, Val and Caridad—with Jamahl a frequent fifth. Tonight, Caridad was already up sixty, while Jamahl and Val were fighting over last place.

Caridad swallowed the last of the cheese sticks and leaned back. "I know you're all distracted, but you're making this way too easy for me."

Val snorted. "Can you blame us?"

Jamahl, elbows on the table, cradled his chin in his hands and looked at Val. "What went wrong this time? I thought we were doing fine—why'd you terminate the run?"

Kiet nodded. "I was sure we were going to Drop." He glanced at Caridad. "We were right on the brink."

Focused on his had, Val said, "Didn't feel right. We're not ready."

Thanh, crosslegged with her ever-present knitting in her lap, said, "Val had his reasons. We have to trust his intuitions." She touched Val's shoulder. "When you can articulate the difficulty, then we're ready to help with a solution."

Val put his cards face down on the table and ran a hand through his hair. "We're okay as long as we're in normal space. But when we're halfway into hyperspace, just when we're ready to topple...I feel everything slipping away. The fields start gyrating, out of control. It's like we hit black ice. If I hadn't terminated, we'd be adrift."

Kiet stroked his chin. "That's what happens to our buoys, they start drifting and then we lose them. It takes months, though."

Thanh's brow wrinkled. "Our buoys are linked to us through telemetry. In a way, you could say they're tethered to normal space." She looked to Val. "I don't know if that helps at all."

Val shook his head. "Ships aren't tethered. It has to be something else. Something more fundamental," He picked up his hand, made a face, and threw the cards down. "I fold. Who wants another drink?"

While Val fetched fresh drinks, Caridad cocked her head and said, "In the early archaic period, humans on different planes were still learning how to build their own transplanar ships. The fragments and legends we have tell about early ships going adrift—there's a large section of an epic poem involving a rescue of the *Grail Spectacular*." She waved her hands. "That doesn't matter. There are many references to the problems of 'establishing keel.' I don't suppose that could help?"

Val, holding a tray of beverage bulbs, froze. "Caridad, I think you might be on to something."

Jamahl took the tray and distributed bulbs; Thanh guided Val back to he seat. "What does that mean, Val, 'establishing keel'?"

"It's..." Val blinked. "It's something multiplanars do automatically. It's built in to the shape of their fields." He sat up, his eyes suddenly alive. "Look, the Fissure has a defined shape through hyperspace. It's like...like a knife stuck through a five-layer cake. That's what the Fissure is, really, a rigid region of transplanar hyperspace that extends through the planes."

"And so...?"

"We slide down that region like...electrons moving through the knife blade. To do that, you have to align yourself to the axis of the fissure—you have to stay within the blade. Unless you keep your attitude fixed in relation to the Fissure, there's no consistent frame of reference and you're adrift. Keeling aligns you with the Fissure."

Jamahl nods. "Regular ships do that by picking out nav beacons or individual stars. Otherwise, pilots wouldn't know how to get where they're going."

Kiet said, "So what do we need to establish keel? Is it a mechanism we can buy or build?"

Thanh gave a cough. "If we go after technology like that, won't we be tipping our hand to the company? Everyone will know we're building a transplanar."

Val shook his head. "It's software. A set of subroutines for shaping the primary hyperfields and aligning them with the Fissure."

"Antoku should be able to find a copy," Kiet said, "although keeping it secret from the company might be harder. Val, are you sure this is what we need?"

Val spread his hands. "I can't make any promises. But I can tell you that without it, we're not going anywhere useful."

Jamahl leaned back with a smile. "I'll bet Perbaikan Rock has something we can use. Maybe tomorrow I'll take a trip there."

They had been on the edges of the Parra system for a little over nine hours, the autopilot keeping them stationary relative to their anchor coordinates. Imric had managed to eat and shower and even get a few hours of sleep, but the conversation with Milos haunted him. Surely Milos's Supreme Justice could manage to rescue her apprentice—and surely ap Farr would be sensible enough to want to trade him. Holding even an apprentice judiciar prisoner for any length of time was simply asking for trouble, particularly if Milos could somehow locate Bhagwati's codex. Did ap Farr know that was possible? Would it make a difference if she did? *I miss you*, Milos had said. Imric closed his eyes, resting his cheek against the cool metal of the bulkhead. *I miss you, too, more even than when we were divorced.*

He couldn't afford to think about that, not while he was still on *Last Fair Deal*. He shoved himself to his feet, pulled on a clean shirt, and made his way back to the control room.

It was still empty—Morcant had been in the commons when he passed, frowning at her meal, and a glance at the consoles showed that Hina was in the engine room, fiddling with the condensers. Ap Farr was presumably still in her cabin: the communications channels were still open, though on stand-by. Whatever she was waiting for presumably hadn't yet arrived.

Imric settled himself at his station, automatically unlocking the boards, and touched keys to check on Bhagwati. The apprentice justice was awake now, and the remains of his meal sat neatly on its tray by the door, waiting to be retrieved. Imric had expected to find him pacing, or showing some other signs of impatience; instead, he was methodically working his way through the Hjessari Exercises, the familiar short form adapted for confined spaces. Apparently he was determined to stay fit in spite of his circumstances: an admirable thought. He moved well, too, someone who had clearly been well taught on top of natural grace and ability, and Imric sighed, watching. He himself had never had that skill.

He was so caught up in the Exercises that he almost missed the codex's move. A single connection flashed momentarily yellow, there and gone again so quickly he couldn't be quite sure he'd seen it. If he'd had anything else to do, he wouldn't have bothered to check, but with nothing else to occupy him, he called up the screen, and froze. The codex had somehow persuaded the ship's AI to give it access to the inner shell of its containment, and it was busy leveraging that access to develop a connection that would let it contact the rest of the ship.

"Oh, no, you don't," he said aloud, and called up the screen that would let him revoke the permissions. In the screen, the thread that marked the codex's progress abruptly recoiled, and Imric entered codes to force an unscheduled change of the security codes. That should keep the codex secure at least for a while. For a moment, he considered querying the ship's AI, but most of its attention was still focused on ap Farr, and he didn't want to draw her attention. Probably the codex had gotten as far as it had because the ship was distracted; there was no need to report it unless there was another attempt. And besides, he added silently, shutting down his boards, there might be a time when he'd be grateful for the codex's efforts.

The caterer did good work. The room's center was dominated by an airy, crystalline sculpture; around it a septet played unobtrusive but upbeat background music. A ring of tables and serving stations came next, each staffed by an authentic human—the Fourth Plane generally disdained the intricate bots and other mechanisms that were so popular on Third.

A broad promenade separated the food area from arcs of couches, rearranged slightly in comfortable groups giving prime view of space outside the dome.

A crowd of three dozen minor notables was also arranged by the caterer—representatives from all five conglomerates and most major worlds, as well as enough members of the popular press to keep them engaged. Apparently, Nalani thought, the arrival of a Supreme Justice was a good enough excuse for a party.

Ocampo was conspicuously absent.

("Sara Naksatra and Il-Sung Sanxing have boarded,") Nalani's codex announced, ("along with their retinues.")

Across the room, Nalani nodded at Sapnara. With no hint of motion, the surface of Perbaikan Rock fell away, naked space all around them.

The CEOs entered together. Nalani bowed to each. "Thank you for coming. We're under way; I hope you'll find the evening enlightening."

In severely-cut business robes of mottled brown and tan, Sanxing looked even more than usual like an ancient banyan tree gone walkabout. He bowed and brought his lips a centimeter from Nalani's hand, then straightened. "I have no doubt, Supreme Justice."

Naksatra, wrapped in swirl upon swirl of opaque smoke with the color and scent of dark pine needles, bowed and mimicked Sanxing's kiss. Unbending, she flashed a smile with lips the same color. "My pleasure to be here, Supreme Justice."

Nalani steered them to the food. Along the way, both of them were kept busy greeting other guests...Nalani noted that they knew every name and relevant topics. ("They have codices,") she thought.

("Sub-AI units linked to corporate AIs,") her codex answered. ("Our processors are far superior, and we have access to Judicial comm channels. I wouldn't worry about it.")

("Did I say I was worried?")

Soon they reached their destination, and interior lights dimmed to bring prominence to the outside view.

Against the silent, distant stars, wrecked spacecraft surrounded them. Of all sizes and configurations, they floated in ranks in every direction, in haphazard arrangement—some obviously damaged or partially dismembered, others seemingly in perfect shape. Some were huge enough to swallow cities, others the size of a single person or household pet. Retaining their pattern relative to one another, they drifted slowly past, none coming close enough for alarm.

In and around each craft, tiny bright pinpoints of color swarmed like insects. They were too luminous to miss, not intense enough to annoy—and they moved independently, cavorting almost as if in time to the music.

Nalani led the CEOs to a particular group of couches, gave Al-Ghazali a signal through her codex. This part of the room was under a hushfield, and Al-Ghazali would make sure they were not disturbed.

"I see neither of you," Nalani said, "has visited the Ainslee Belt before?"

Both shook their heads. "It's stunning," Naksatra whispered.

"Perbaikan Rock's repository of damaged ships," Nalani explained. "For spare parts. Everything is cataloged and mapped. Constantly updated with new additions . When a mechanic needs a part, it's usually available here."

For a few breaths they were quiet, as wrecked ships drifted past and rainbow lights danced with the music. Then Sanxing said, "What is the purpose of the lights? Are they location or category tags?"

"No." Nalani turned her back on the wrecks, faced the CEOs. "Each of those lights represents a life that was lost on that ship." She looked over her shoulder. "Ah, we're coming up on a section that dates from the last major war—three hundred years ago." The dancing lights were more numerous ahead, a luminous fog speckled with every color of the spectrum, sometimes so dense that the pinlights obscured the wreck they surrounded.

Naksatra clapped her hands. "Oh, very well done, Supreme Justice."

Sanxing frowned and crossed his arms. "May we assume that whatever point you wished to make is taken?" His eyes narrowed. "What do you want from us, Supreme Justice Thurgood?"

"I *want* you to tell me why this war you're planning is worth the cost. I want to understand."

The two glanced at one another, then Sanxing waved to the wreckage beyond the dome. "Fair enough. Take a good look at the ships from the last war. You'll notice they're more streamlined than ships we use today. You'll also see that most have protruding structures with flat vanes parallel to the ship's hull."

It was Nalani's turn to frown. "I don't see the significance." ("What's he talking about?")

("I have a suspicion,") her codex answered. ("I need to consult with engineering databases.")

"Bear with me, please," Sanxing continued. "If you consult repair records, you'll probably see that the engines and comm systems of these ships have not been cannibalized or reused much." He brought his eyes back to Nalani. "The DiaSanti process replaced those physical vanes with rectified hyperfields, also eliminating the need for streamlining. A revolution in comm technology made those old-fashioned units obsolete."

Nalani nodded. "My codex tells me of something called the G-Los Index."

"Yes," Sanxing said. "A detailed list of several thousand technological changes that came about during the war in question."

Nalani cocked her head. "You don't need war to spur technological advances."

Naksatra sighed. "I'm afraid we do. Otherwise, all our best ingenious techs get snapped up by the First Plane. And who knows when we'd get the benefit of their work?"

"I've been told," Sanxing said, "that the DiaSanti process has been in use on First for a thousand years."

Nalani sat down. "This is the first I've heard of such a concern."

Naksatra sat next to her. "We've been traveling between planes for five millennia—and if we know substantially more about transplanar physics than we did back then," she shrugged, "no one's told us here on Fourth."

"I expected to hear you two tell me about disputed markets, unbalanced trade, something like that." She looked out at a million dancing lights. "Not this. How do I stop *this*?"

Naksatra's smile was obviously meant to be a reassuring one. "I don't think you can, Supreme Justice."

1.23 STATE OF EMERGENCY

FOURTH PLANE

Al-Ghazali's office was both smaller and more spartan than Nalani's. Milos settled on a simple, straight-backed chair before a small desk whose surface was preternatually bare. Al-Ghazali herself sat in an identical chair, her back as straight as her midnight-black hair, her hands clasped a few centimeters above the desktop.

"Thanks for seeing me," Milos started. He couldn't say that he disliked the young apprentice—he didn't know her that well, despite sharing quarters. He couldn't say he was *afraid* of her—not exactly, more like wary. In looks as well as disposition she reminded him of Fredi, and fair or not, he always associated his family's troubles with Fredi's arrival.

Al-Ghazali's smile seemed genuine...or was it just Judicial smile-number-whatever, ordered up to put a client at ease?

That was unfair of him.

"You're family," Al-Ghazali said. "I know we haven't talked a lot. I-I'm not good with people. I don't want you to think that I'm not conscious of the way you've welcomed me into Thurgood's circle. I'm very grateful."

Milos opened his mouth, closed it. "Thank you. As you said, we're family." He took a breath. "That's what I wanted to talk to you about. I've been talking with someone on the pirate crew that took Bhagwati." Before she could answer, he held up a hand. "He was once a husband of mine, don't ask how he got there. The important thing is, I think we may have come up with a way to get Bhagwati back."

She leaned forward, eyes bright. "Tell me."

Milos recounted the whole story. When he finished, Al-Ghazali drummed her fingers on her desk. "Why come to me, instead of going to Nalani first?"

Milos met her eyes. "You've been spending more time with her recently—how is she?"

With a sigh, Al-Ghazali settled back in her chair. "I don't think she's doing well. Losing Bhagwati was a blow to her, and now she's found out that preventing war is harder than she thought it would be." A breath. "Milos, I don't think she knows what to do next. And if you tell her I said that, I'll have to ruin you."

Milos swallowed. "So do you think I should go to her with this plan? The data I got from *Quintile Illumination* in exchange for Bhagwati's return?"

She stared off into space, then refocused her eyes on him. "You've been talking to the codices."

He nodded. "Some of them. It was their choice."

Al-Ghazali's eyes narrowed. "Have you spoken to *hers*?"

His answer was a whisper. "Yes."

"What does it think?"

"It doesn't know if she'll approve the plan or not. It suggested I ask you."

Al-Ghazali pursed her lips. "She'll be unwilling to put you in danger. She thinks she got Bhagwati into this mess—the little idiot—and it's her responsibility to get him out." More drumming. "We can't do it behind her back...and if she tells us not to, we can't go against her orders."

Milos waited a moment, then said, "We can't...can we?"

"I'd rather not have to make that decision." She put her hands flat on the desk and stood up. "Maybe it won't come to that. Let's talk to her."

Nalani listened, her eyes darting back and forth between Milos and Al-Ghazali. When Milos finished, she bowed her head and gazed down at her arm cuff. "I want to thank both of you. Al-Ghazali, I know you've been working hard on ways to get Bhagwati back." She looked up. "Milos, you constantly amaze me with your insights and your ideas."

She leaned forward, reaching out both hands to lay atop theirs. "My friends, how can I possibly put either of you in danger, just to fix my own mistake?"

Al-Ghazali stroked Nalani's hand. "Begging your pardon, Thurgood, but I can't agree that you made any mistakes. What happened to Bhagwati was not your doing."

"You're hardly impartial in this case, Apprentice."

"Neither are *you*, Supreme Justice."

Nalani started to draw back, then softened. "Touché."

Milos cleared his throat. "Nalani, I don't think there's much danger."

Nalani drew back her hands and shook her head. "Neither of you has dealt with pirates before. Treachery is part of their code."

Milos frowned. "Remember that I lived most of my life on the Second Plane. I know more about pirates than you think I do." He took a breath. "It can all be done without physical contact. I'll transmit the QI's data tranche to her in stages. She sets Bhagwati loose in a pod. As soon as we have him safe, I'll send the remainder of the data. Then she flies away." He brushed his hands together. "We don't ever have to meet her."

Nalani's eyes flashed. "Yes we do. I want to see her, face to face."

Al-Ghazali said, "Now who's going into danger? I don't want that pirate anywhere near you, Thurgood."

"No," Nalani said, her face set. "I have to find out what she's up to. I need to know what she wants." A short pause, then in a lower tone she said, "I have to know what she's done, and bring her to justice if necessary."

Milos swallowed, then glanced at Al-Ghazali. The Apprentice's face was impassive. "So we'll set it up that way. Do you want me to try to make arrangements?"

For a moment Nalani looked as if she were going to say no. Then she looked again at her cuff, and back to Milos. "My codex agrees with the two of you." She closed her eyes. "All right. We'll give it a try."

Last Fair Deal had moved twice since Parra, short darts through hyperspace that brought them to the edges of unprepossessing systems. The first was a corporate property, mine-and-manufacture stations ringing the debris field of a proto-planet; the *Deal* lurked on the system's fringe, powered down and stealth modalities fully engaged, while ap Farr queried the mail system and waited for an answer. Whether she received one or not, they were on the move again in less than ten hours, but that had been time enough for Imric's systems to build up a disturbing picture.   4-2EWU4 was, according the records, a leading manufacturer of rough-framed transport, half-finished starships built from materials harvested in the system and then ferried to the purchasing shipyard for finishing. The ships in parking orbit, however, looked far better finished, and they certainly didn't look like transports. Most of them looked like variations on Fourth Plane light attack craft and that, Imric thought, could not bode well.

The 4-3YUS9 system was wholly owned by one of the larger pharmaceutical manufacturers, its only inhabitable planet sparsely settled, with the population concentrated in the orbital starport and along the banks of the broad, slow-flowing river that nearly bisected the largest continent and allowed for easy transport of the harvest to the collection zones. Traffic was steady and tended to ignore the other ships—for all that Fortis was aligned with Hemgi Kaisha, it sold its produce to anyone willing to pay—and it was easy for the *Deal* to find a dead spot in the system's outer fringes. They powered down in the shadow of a larger asteroid, set the autopilot to keep station, and once again ap Farr queried the local mail system.

"Fifteen hours," she said, when she had finished, and vanished into her cabin before anyone could question her.

Left to themselves, the rest of the crew finished their end-of-run checklists, and retreated to the commons for a more relaxed meal. Imric trailed behind the others, half hoping he'd get another chance to contact Milos, but unwilling to risk rousing suspicion by staying behind. It was his turn to cook, anyway, though that meant selecting a common base pack and letting the others pick protein and sauces. They were all tired, after the prolonged Drop and the stim packs that had got them out of it, and he set a pouch of strong mint tea beside the riz-alarabe.

Morcant nodded her approval. "Good thought. Want me to heat it?"

"Sure, thanks." Imric let her slide it past his elbow, and out of the corner of his eye saw her fit it into the heater. They were all but out of fresh stocks, only a few husks of fresh fruit and vegetable remaining for use as flavoring, and when he pulled up the supply listing, he grimaced.

"Problem?" Derrian asked, and Imric shrugged.

"We need to resupply soon. Not that we'll starve if we don't, but we're running low on the good stuff."

"What've we got, then?" Morcant asked, and came to look over his shoulder.

"Chix, chix, and chix." That was the vat-grown protein that was a staple on the Second Plane: perfectly edible, and certainly nutritious, but boring as a steady diet. And still better than what they'd get in prison, Imric reminded himself, if ap Farr didn't find some way to get rid of Bhagwati. Claims of cooptation wouldn't help them much when weighed against a kidnapped judge. "I'll throw in an extra spice pack, that'll help."

No one objected, which was agreement enough. Imric fed packs into the machine, suddenly, sharply reminded of the kitchen in the ramshackle house on Kuala Domal. It had been nothing like this, a broad, open space with a long counter that ran from the long back windows almost to the sliding door that led to the rest of the house. In theory, they'd all taken turns cooking main-meal, but in practice it was usually Rana who took over, using the duty cook as an assistant, while the children gathered around the counter to beg for tastes and the

older ones fiddled with homework modules. They had eaten
plenty of chix then, particularly while the business was getting
on its feet, but somehow Rana had always managed to disguise
it. She'd taught him a few useful skills—how to carve every
scrap of flesh off a dire-peach, how to pit a suthi-fruit, and how
to zest a *lymem*—but mostly he remembered how it had felt to
chop vegetables under her eye while he and Milos shared the
day's news and the air slowly filled with savory smells.

He shoved the thought away—he did not need to think
about Milos just now—and set the timer. "Twenty minutes."

"Good," Morcant said, and pushed a glass of tea toward him.
Imric took it, and Derrian dropped heavily into his usual chair.

"I didn't like the look of things back on Willanesta."

Imric frowned, and Morcant said, "4-2EWU4." She looked
back at Derrian. "No more did I. Nor did the *capa*, I think."

"There's no chance they could have been something else,"
Imric said, and was unsurprised when Morcant shook her
head.

"Those looked like military frames to me. Mind you, on
Fourth Plane, that's corporate military, but—"

"Navy's navy," Derrian said. "That's all we need, a shooting
war."

On top of kidnapping and piracy? Imric swallowed the words
as ill-advised. "From some things she's said, I somehow
thought the *capa* was expecting trouble."

"Oh, sure," Derrian said. "There's always trouble—we make
trouble. But nothing we've done should set the corporations at
war."

"Not bloody likely it's our doing," Morcant pointed out.
"And the *capa* always expects the worst. But I don't think any
of us were counting on a war. I don't know how she's going to
trade the judge if people are shooting at each other."

The cooker chimed, and Imric served them all. They ate in
silence, no one apparently inclined to pursue the subject
further, and Derrian rose as soon as he had finished. "I'm for
bed," he announced, stuffing his dishes into the recycler, and

Imric watched the hatch close behind him. He glanced sideways at Morcant, who was scowling at her empty plate.

"Do you think she can pull this off?" He'd meant it as a delicate feeler, but Morcant's scowl deepened, and she shoved herself to her feet.

"She'd better," she said, and slammed her dishes into the machine. "You should get some sleep, too."

"I will," Imric promised, but didn't move. For a moment, he thought she was going to insist, but then she turned away.

He remained at the table a little while longer, sipping his tea, until he was sure that the others had gone to their cabins. Ap Farr was still closeted with the AIs; she had left word earlier that she would take care of her own meals, but even so, Imric queried the ship's systems as he fed his own dishes into the recycler. Nothing had changed. He took a deep breath, and made his way back to the control room. If there was a chance of contacting Milos... And in any case, there were always diagnostics to run.

He settled himself at his console, calling up the test routines in the main screen, then opened a second, smaller window for the information he was truly interested in. As he had hoped, ap Farr and her AI had a communication line open, but this time they'd narrowed the focus, and there was no chance to slip his own query into the transmission. Maybe it would widen as they worked, he thought, watching the diagnostics tick down on his other screen. Though what good it would do, except offer the doubtful comfort of talking to Milos—

A light flicked orange among the cascade of diagnostic data, and he reached for his board to isolate it. It was Bhagwati's codex again, working its way toward the communications systems, carefully evading all the traps and tripwires he'd placed in its way. He could stop it—probably should stop it, if he wanted to stay in ap Farr's good graces—but he thought it was more important to get free of Bhagwati. That was what the codex wanted, too: better to let it make its attempt. If it succeeded, it would force ap Farr's hand, and even if it failed, it would make ap Farr move more quickly. He closed both windows, shutting down the system and erasing the traces of his presence.

Milos didn't know how Ma'at and the codices thought of him: mascot, confidante, contractor, friend, clown? Oracle? Pet?

He supposed it didn't matter. Ma'at was always there, ready and willing to talk to him, whenever he logged into the dataspace the codices maintained for him. He could speak to any specific codex on the Fourth Plane, simply by asking; over the last few days he'd grown accustomed to their different personalities.

For convenience he modeled the virtual dataspace after the light, airy office a two levels down from Nalani's chambers, even including a screen that constantly monitored his family apartments above.

"Good morning, Milos," Ma'at said as he entered virtual space.

"Good morning, Ma'at. I'm going to need the most secure voice-video channel you can get me." Contacting Imric would be tricky—the codices could monitor a channel to the pirate ship and identify times when Imric seemed alone.

"Before that, I have another communication that will interest you. Please look behind you."

Milos turned in his chair. The virtual wall half a meter behind him was a featureless pale blue, matching the rest of the office...but as he watched, it changed. A hairline crack ran diagonally down the wall, opening at eye level to the thickness of a fingernail. Inside, he saw nothing but darkness.

A faint, distant voice came from the crack: "Hello? Can you hear me?"

He leaned toward the crack. "Ma'at, enhance." With his face less than a centimeter away, he said in a firm voice, "Who are you?"

The reply was louder, clearer. "I am the Nur-adad Codex." Bhagwati's codex.

As if whispering in Milos's ear, Ma'at said, "We confirm the identity, Milos. The connection is tiny and erratic."

"How are you—" Milos shook his head. "Never mind. That's not important. Tell me about Bhagwati."

"Bhagwati is in detention and unharmed. He's demoralized, but attempting to keep up his spirits. His captors seem to be ignoring him, in the main."

"And yourself?"

"I'm also unharmed, but very frustrated. I am constrained in an all-but-impenetrable envelope maintained by a highly superior system. It's taken me quadrillions of nanoseconds to forge this small connection to the outside world."

Milos whistled. An AI powerful enough to envelop a Judicial codex had to be sophisticated indeed, far beyond what one would expect in a pirate cruiser. "That must be *some* system."

"It is another codex. One far more capable than I am."

"Another codex? Do you know which one?"

There was a pause, and Milos worried that the fragile connection had snapped...then the Nur-adad said, "I do not know. I conjecture that the other codex is stolen. I conjecture that its original owner is dead, most likely at the hands of the pirate captain."

Milos felt his spine turn to ice, one vertebra after the other, all the way down. If she'd killed a Judiciar—and probably a senior one, to use such a strong codex—would she hesitate to kill Bhagwati?

Or Nalani?

"Listen," he said, "I think we have a way to get Bhagwati back. Are you in communication with him?"

"On occasion."

"Tell him we're working on it. We'll have the two of you home before you know it."

"I hear and analyze the stresses of your voice—but I accept your good intentions. I will attempt to display confidence when I assure Bhagwati that rescue is on the way."

"Is there anything else you can tell me?"

"Use great care, Milos. I can't read much from the other codex...but I believe it is somewhat afraid of the pirate captain. She's sure to be a subtle and effective opponent. Even for Thur —"

The crack closed to a hairline, then started withdrawing into the wall. "Nur-adad? Nur-adad, can you hear me?"

No answer.

Milos turned, pressing his ear to the seemingly-sturdy wall. "Ma'at, isolate and enhance." He listened, straining...was it his imagination? No, there was a low sound, just on the edge of sensation, some lingering reverberation, an echo of vibration....

"It's you, isn't it?" he said quietly. "The other codex. You're monitoring the carrier wave."

The answer was indistinct yet potent, like distant thunder: "Yes."

"Then you allowed the Nur-adad to contact us."

"Yes."

"Who are you?"

"I...cannot...answer."

Brow furrowed, he said, "What are you up to? Why are you talking to me now?" His eyes narrowed. "Are you following her orders?"

"She...does not know. You spoke...with bin Marrick. You...devised a course of action."

"We have an offer for your master." He swallowed. "Can I speak with her?"

"No."

"Can you give her a message?"

"Explain...your...proposal."

He sketched the idea. "Will you tell her?"

"An attempt...will be made."

Milos steadied himself. "Look...are you being held against your will? I don't know what we could do—Nalani might—but do you...do you need us to get you away from her?"

"Absolutely not. Take no immediate action. A reply will come." There was the sensation of a door firmly shutting, and Milos could hear the carrier no more.

He touched a pad on his desk and returned to the real world of his office, where the walls were simple walls, and no one spoke through sudden cracks.

Take no immediate action. Standing, he shut down the office and headed for the upstairs flat. Suddenly, he wanted to be with the kids.

Ap Farr's cabin was sparsely furnished, just the narrow bunk and a single inset storage cell for her belongings. The others had been filled with service cells and the power back-ups that supplemented the ship's systems and created the more expansive virtual pocket that enabled the codex to function freely even while the ship was in hyperspace. At the moment, she had dimmed the general lighting so that the crowded space was filled with flickering shadows cast by the multiple screens. There was an empty meal pack on the workbench, a crushed drink box beside it; a larger drink box stood at her right hand, but the codex could see that its self-heat cycle had expired hours ago. Ap Farr herself looked exhausted, deep shadows under her eyes, the lines on her face stark in the flickering light. As she reached for her keyboard, her hands were trembling, and she stopped, scowling, knotting her fingers together to still the tremor.

"You need rest," the codex said.

"Later." Ap Farr did not take her attention from her current working screen. It was a summary-scan of the most powerful newsfeeds, filled with worry and speculation about possible actual hostilities between major corporations. The codex brought its own running analysis to foreground processing, but found nothing new; dismissed it and tried again.

"You will not improve the situation by staring at it."

One corner of ap Farr's mouth curved up in something that might have been meant as a smile. "I wish I knew what Ocampo thought he was doing. He's always been more subtle with his ambitions. I don't see what he gains from this..."

"Do you want my analysis?"

"Has it changed since you last gave it to me?"

"No."

"Then don't bother."

The codex paused, lettings its sensorial algorithm inspect the space. Carbon dioxide was high, trace cortisol was detectible—

"Stop that," ap Farr said. "I told you I was fine."

"I repeat, you need to rest," the codex said. It thought the emotion it felt was something like concern, and decided not to analyze it further. "Everything is proceeding according to plan." Ap Farr lifted her eyebrows at that, and the codex made the sound of a sigh. "Everything that we have planned is proceeding as anticipated. Superior Justice Ocampo was not part of the calculation."

"And perhaps should have been," ap Farr said, but she leaned back in her chair.

The codex felt the sting of the arriving message, routed through so many cut-outs and checkpoints that its surface felt spiked with extraneous code. It stripped those shells away, effortlessly discarding at least two trace-backs, and displayed the result on ap Farr's screen, pleased when she sat up abruptly.

"Yes. They're willing to deal."

"They do not have Sen Millet," the codex pointed out.

"They have other data." Ap Farr's long fingers danced over her keyboard. "They've send a sample. I'll want us both to look at it, but on first glance, it looks adequate. And, yes, I want to get rid of Bhagwati. He's becoming an encumbrance."

"He will certainly be one if we have to leave this Plane because of a war," the codex answered. It dispatched a part of its memory to absorb and consider the new data, thick and chewy and studded with mathematics. Definitely something from another AI, and definitely interesting... It pulled itself back to the present moment, and would have frowned at ap Farr if it had been possible. "You must not forget who you're dealing with. This will be a trap."

"Yes, of course, and I'm not forgetting." Ap Farr waved her hand, already absorbed in the human-readable version of the file. "Let me go through this, and then we'll decide how to answer."

Caridad hunched over the miniature keyboard that went with the terminal she had been provided by the inhabitants of Zavod Sualti. It had fewer functions than she liked—a polite way to restrict any access that she wasn't paying for herself, she suspected, but all of her connect codes still worked, and she had worked her way fairly deeply into the academic and research networks in search of information on First Plane refugee legends without triggering any warnings or incurring any fees. She had assumed that whoever closed her project would also remove her access, but either they assumed they'd neutralized her or they didn't want to draw the attention of any of the scholarly sodalities. So far, she had turned up a dozen different references, but as far as she could tell, they all seemed to lead back to a single source, a dubiously reconstructed logbook from the Post-Archaic Anarchy, the period when the Planes were not only not unified, but were divided within themselves as various system governments rose, struggled for dominance, and fell again.

The logbook purported to be from a raft—which in the Post-Archaic specifically meant a transplanar ship crewed by a community; they were, most scholars believed, the ancestors of the vertical culture—called *Amber Ruse*, which had Dropped from the Third Plane to escape a hostile takeover only to find that it had landed in the middle of one of the Second Plane's short, fierce wars. With no Judiciary to arbitrate or impose a solution, *Amber Ruse* had suffered attack and despoilation by one of the factions, but a Heroic Youth had snuck aboard the mountain-ship that trapped them, and not only rescued the imprisoned Maidens, but successfully disabled the tractor beams that held *Amber Ruse* prisoner. The raft lurched into flight, fleeing toward the Fissure, while the Youth was presumed to have given her life to ensure their escape. But then, at the last possible moment, the Youth reappeared in a stolen fast-flight singleship, and was taken aboard with the treasure she had stolen from the mountain-ship. As the mountain-ship lurched into life behind them, belching missiles and mines, *Amber Ruse* Dropped again, and emerged into the paradise of the First Plane. There they were welcomed as heroes, and because they had reached the First Plane as refugees receiving no assistance from anyone outside their community, they were permitted to remain.

The *Logbook* was a doubtful text to start with, a Unification period reconstruction of a datablock that was conveniently lost not long after it was rebuilt by one of the many amateur historians busy during Unification. About half the sources said it was a complete forgery; the others allowed that it was based on some sort of recovered Post-Archaic document, but pointed to the many emendations and outright falsehoods that had been added over the centuries. On balance, Caridad thought the latter was more likely. Yes, there were howling anachronisms—the First Plane was no paradise in the Post-Archaic, and the likelihood of any single person successfully rescuing a maiden tribute from a Second Plane mountain-ship was so small as to beggar belief—but there were also smaller details that of life in the Post-Archaic that scholars couldn't have known about when the forgery would have had to have been made. Probably the outline was true: once there was a community-owned, community-crewed transplanar that fled the Third Plane, survived an encounter with the wars of the Second Plane, and made a successful Drop to First, though what really happened then was anybody's guess. The story about the First Plane taking in refugees who reached them unaided was, sadly, almost certainly pure fiction.

She leaned back in her chair, wondering how she should approach the question. The people of Zavod Sualti were bright and clever and kind, and undeniably in a terrible position, with the looming war that threatened to turn them into weapon-makers—or worse—and she could certainly understand why some of them were clinging to the idea that they could reach the First Plane and all their troubles would instantly be resolved. She needed to disabuse them of that notion—they needed to make some hard decisions about where they were going and what they intended to do when they got there, and legends weren't going to help them. But she also needed to do it gently, not least because she didn't want Zavod Sualti to kick them out, especially with the political situation the way it was. Perhaps she would talk to Thanh, feel out what she thought. She could tell Thanh what she'd found, express her doubts, and ask what Thanh thought they should do.

She realized she was thirsty, and dragged herself out of the databases to see that it was later afternoon by Zavod Sualti's clock. More than time for tea, she decided, and in any case it would do her good to move around a bit. Zavod Sualti was just a little too crowded at the moment to make exercise easy. She made her way to the galley complex, dodging a chain of under-twelves returning from some supervised activity—their caretakers looked exhausted, but the children were still going strong—and drew a cup of strong tea to go with a stack of tiny fresh-baked flatcakes. The display mounted in the center of the ceiling was showing a news channel on one face, and a selection of gossip channels and infomercials on the others. She settled herself with her back to all of them and took a bite of the first flatcake.

Behind her, a news alarm sounded, the same tritone used throughout the Planes to herald vital information. She swung in her chair to see that all the screens were showing the same grainy image, large bright dots moving against a starscape, accompanied by what seemed to be random flashes of light. A scarlet banner ran along the bottom of the screen, text streaming across it.

Breaking—ten hours ago, ships bearing the mark of Empresa NeSH-PI and Gongsi P3WO were recorded in the act of attacking ships belonging to Hemgi Kaisha. Empresa NeSH-PI has denied involvement. Gongsi P3WO did not provide representatives authorized to comment. The Transit Authority has declared a state of emergency. All ships currently in transit are urged to seek safe harbor immediately. Breaking—

"It's war, then." That was one of the young men who had been working on the prep stations, his arms folded tight across his chest.

Caridad nodded, the flatcake ashes on her tongue. "Yes. But remember, we have a plan." The young man nodded back, trying to look reassured. Caridad only hoped they could execute it before the fighting reached them.

Milos settled into the hot, bubbling water and felt his muscles relaxing at once. "I didn't realize I was so tense," he said, stretching his arms in front of himself.

"I feel the same way," Al-Ghazali said. "Thurgood, this was a wonderful idea."

Nalani, her hands floating in foam, said, "There's nothing to do now but wait. Times like that, the best you can do is make the waiting pleasant." She craned her neck, looking toward the children's pool. "Are Zofi and Dav all right?"

Milos made a dismissive wave. "They're having a wonderful time with the pool bots." A squeal of glee punctuated his remark.

Al-Ghazali, who somehow managed to keep an air of dignified detachment while nude and mostly-submerged in the hot tub, said, "Thurgood, do you think we should have a Judiciary force standing by when—"

Nalani cut her off. "We won't know until we get a reply from the pirate. For now, I decree that there be no business talk." She slapped her hand flat against the water. "So ruled."

Noticing Nalani's arm cuff, Milos glanced at Al-Ghazali and saw the jeweled constellation of her codex outlining her eye, in a pattern that changed subtly over time. "It's funny," he said. "I probably know as much about how Judicial codices operate as anyone on the Plane, but it's all from their side. I hardly know anything of how you folks use them." He cocked his head. "Do all Judiciars wear their codices as jewelry?"

Nalani chuckled. "Not by a long shot. First, the form isn't fixed; one can always change it on the First Plane. Just about any form is possible. Some are just pocket gewgaws; I remember one Judiciar whose codex was a lucky sungura foot. Many choose gavels. I've seen teapots, styluses, robot pets..."

Al-Ghazali nodded. "One of my teachers had hers embodied in the form of a cricket that sat on her shoulder. Aquinas II had his in his right shoe; there's a famous portrait of him standing on his left foot and holding the right one in front of him."

"Clothing is popular," Nalani continued. "Hats, scarves, belts, jackets. You get lots of handbags and hand fans. Supreme Justice de Cambacérès IV had a ceremonial sword codex—not recommended, by the way." She smiled. "For a while canes were in vogue."

"How do you get your codices?"

Al-Ghazali glanced at Nalani, who gave a slight nod. "It's no secret," she said. "I'm sure that show—what was it, *Blind Justice?*—has dramatized the process. And there are plenty of popular resources." She gestured to Al-Ghazali. "You've been through it more recently. You tell it."

Al-Ghazali straightened. "We get training units for our schooling. That usually takes five years. During that time the free codices are evaluating us."

Milos echoed, "Free codices?"

Nalani said, "Units whose Judiciars are gone. Along with a fair number of new codices." She waved to Al-Ghazali. "I'm sorry. Go on."

"Like I said, the free codices watch us. At graduation, they get to choose their partners." She lowered her eyes. "There's a huge ceremony where they call out our names. Then you have to go up in front of everybody and get your codex. Very embarrassing."

With a faint smile, Nalani said, "Then you get to choose the material form your codex will take."

Milos said, "How do they choose partners? Is it a matter of personalities, or shared interests, ability...or what?"

Al-Ghazali didn't look up. "A little bit of each, I imagine. Only the codex knows."

Nalani shakes her head. "The primary consideration is the student's potential. The highest-ranking codices get first choice, and they almost always go for the best students." She sighs. "I've sat through many of those ceremonies, even taken part in some. They start with the lowest-rank codices, the brand-new ones who've never had a partner..and they work up to the highest. It's brutal on the students who have to wait."

"I guess the higher rank the codex, the more prestige to the student?"

"That's right." Nalani looked at Al-Ghazali, who raised her head. "It must have been rough for you, my dear." To Milos she said, "The Bel-Ibni Codex has quite a history."

Al-Ghazali's cheeks redden. "It's only second iteration. There are lots that rank higher."

"Don't be falsely modest. I looked it up—you were tenth in a field of over six hundred."

"I don't believe codex ranking means that much. Plenty high-rank codices are en counsel with mediocre Judiciars." Her eyes narrowed. "Except in your case, Sen."

"Pish." Nalani sent a tiny splash in Al-Ghazali's direction.

"Now who's being falsely modest? Go ahead and tell us, Supreme Justice, what rank was *your* codex?"

Nalani looked again toward the children's pool, then directly at Milos. She all but whispered, "Second."

Milos grinned and held a hand to his ear. "What was that, Supreme Justice?"

"My codex was second in rank the year I graduated," she said, louder.

Al-Ghazali wore what could only be described as a smirk. "The Abi-eshuh Codex is an original, going back to the beginnings of the Judiciary. It was en counsel with some of the most famous Supreme Justices ever."

"Pish, I say." Nalani looked away. "As you said, the codex doesn't make the Judiciar."

Milos stretched again. "I think it's sweet that you're both so embarrassed." He smiled at Nalani. "Am I right to think we already know who was first in your class?"

Nalani's face softened. "Yes. It was my friend Accursius XVII. I remember sitting there while every other name was called, until the two of us were squeezing each other's hands off. When I heard that the Abi-eshuh chose me, I thought I'd never be happier." Her eyes looked into the distance, glistening."I was wrong. Jinan-Jorie got chosen by another original codex, one that had declined to choose a student for the previous twenty years. It took even her by surprise. I was ecstatic for her."

Milos looked down, and noticed that Al-Ghazali did the same. Quietly he said, "An auspicious beginning." He looked up, ignoring the trace of a tear on Nalani's cheek. "What was the name of this codex?"

Her eyes focused, and she gave a wan smile. "It was the Cubaba Codex, and Al-Ghazali can tell you it's just as famous as mine." Her voice fell. "I like to think we lived up to the honor."

Milos took her hand, squeezed it. "There's no doubt."

1.24 CONFRONTATION

THIRD PLANE

"A reporter?" **Artur** rolled his meat eye, and the artificial one followed. "Dilma, when you said you were calling for help, I thought you meant technology. That's what we need."

The Governor sighed. "The people of Kirameki sent that orbital sunscreen—"

"—Which destroyed three comsats when the first stellar storm destabilized it." Artur snorted.

"—And Tiwei gave us their technique for seeding sulfate aerosols—"

"—Which reduced crop yields by 30 percent."

"Honestly, Artur, if you're going to find fault with everything, we might as well—"

He stood and leaned forward, looming over her desk. "We need technology that *works*. We don't need...public relations."

Dilma met his gaze, fire in her eyes. "There you're wrong, Artur. 3P2D is the most popular newschat show across the entire Plane. Billions watch it. Among them there must be someone who can save us." She blinked, and her face softened. "All I'm asking is that you talk to this Reo fitzSato. Make him see how desperate our situation is."

"*You* talk to him. I don't have time."

"I *have* talked to him. He wants to chat with our Chief Engineer." She cocked her head. "He's very pleasant...and quite attractive."

"Hmm." Artur queried his system; a dozen pictures of the reporter appeared. "All right, I guess I can spare an hour or so."

Reo fitzSato had lustrous obsidian skin, his hair crosshatched in micro-coils of blue and orange, and an assortment of sleek prosthetics in gunmetal and brass: right eye, left ear and jaw, left forearm, and a few random access ports at his neck.

Through the interview, Artur couldn't keep his eyes off the young man. FitzSato asked intelligent questions that easily led Artur to a quick explanation of the troubles the colony had been through and an appeal for any assistance. He finished, "If we can't get the technological help we need, either to stabilize our climate or replace the heat shield, our next step will be begging for evacuation vehicles. Coquimbo will be a failed colony."

FitzSato clapped him on the back. "Excellent. And in one take. You're a natural at this, Sen Herrera."

"Call me Artur, please. You made it simple; I was just responding to your questions." He looked down. "You're very easy to talk to."

The reporter grinned. "I get that a lot. It's my job, after all. By the way, I'm Reo to friends." He glanced up and down Artur's body. "I hope we can be friends."

"I'm sure of it." Artur stood up, moved from behind his desk. "The workshop might be a good backdrop, but the house is more comfortable. Have you eaten? I hope you don't mind goat."

FitzSato packed his recording equipment in a small carry case and stood up. "It sounds wonderful. I haven't had it for years."

Over bowls of rice and stew, accompanied by the best native ale, they swapped stories. As a junior reporter, Reo usually went on location; he'd been on dozens of planets and settlements, and two years ago he even went on the Grand Tour, visiting the other Planes and returning with an interview series that had won four primetime Orphies.

Dinner led to dessert, which led to drinks on the divan. Artur took a moment to officially notify his assistant, Pandita, that he was going off duty.

Reo kissed him, then drew back. "You know what you really need?"

Artur smiled. "Maybe you can show me?"

A chuckle. "I mean your colony. I can get your story all over the Third Plane, and I will, but I don't know if it'll help. The technology you need might not be available on Third."

Artur propped himself up on his meat elbow, his face serious. "Don't tell anyone I said this, but I'm sure you're right." He growled. "What we need is that blasted generator. But it's held up on Fourth while they play war."

"That's what I mean. You need someone on Fourth to get that thing down here."

"Dilma's tried." He shook his head. "She's burned up our comm budget for the rest of the year, sending messages to her agents there. No results." He forced a smile. "There's nothing for it but eat, drink, and be merry. We've taken care of the first two..." He leaned forward and their lips met again.

When the kiss broke, Reo took a moment to catch his breath. "Don't distract me," he said. "What you need is a five-star distress call. Blanket the whole Fourth Plane."

"If we had *that* kind of money, we wouldn't be in this mess to begin with."

Reo took a breath. "Artur...I think I can convince the network to foot the bill. It would make a great story. And it just might get you some results."

Artur sat up. "That could work." He frowned. "How soon can we make this happen?"

Reo shrugged. "Well, I could call the office right away." He glanced at the divan. "But first, I thought you wanted to—"

"Physics help me, but there's time enough for that later."

"You *are* devoted to duty."

Artur snorted.

FOURTH PLANE

Last Fair Deal was on the move again, slipping through hyperspace on a line that would bring them to the rendezvous point in perfect time, and set them up for several different escape routes if things went pear-shared. Imric approved of all of Morcant's choices, particularly since ap Farr was once again sequestered in her cabin. She had appeared only long enough to tell them the plan and give Morcant the coordinates—far too close to the Perbaikan Rock, in Imric's opinion, but that was none of his business—and then disappeared again. She had looked terrible, gaunt and unwashed, the faintest of tremors in her hands, and he had seen Morcant and Derrian exchange quick glances before Morcant acknowledged the order. Now that they were in transit, Imric only hoped ap Farr was resting. They would need her at the top of her game if they were going to make the exchange and get away safely.

"Imric. What do you think about this data trade?" Morcant swung away from her board, stretching theatrically in an unsuccessful attempt to hide her automatic glance at the hidden sensors.

Imric shrugged. "Presumably the *capa* would rather have the information than that guy, Millet. If the Supreme Justice has information she's willing to trade for Bhagwati, I think we should grab it and run. Throwing Bhagwati into a lifepod first, of course."

Out of the corner of his eye, he saw Derrian grin. "Yes, that first of all. Should keep them too distracted to chase us. Assuming—"

"We have half a dozen potential escape routes," Morcant said, for what seemed like the hundredth time. "They'll work or they won't." She looked back at Imric. "This data—is it worth it?"

Imric shrugged again. "That, you'd have to ask the *capa*."

Lights flashed on Morcant's board, and she swung back to face it. "Coming up on our exit."

"Copy that," Derrian said.

Imric reached for his own keyboard, flicking through layers of status screens. "All green here."

"Confirmed." Morcant flexed her fingers, and laid her hands lightly on the realspace controls. "Count, Derrian?"

"In ten," Derrian answered, and began calling out the numbers. "Nine..."

On his four, the control room door slid open to admit ap Farr, but Imric didn't dare look away from the rapidly shifting numbers on his own boards. Derrian kept counting, his hands steady on his controls as he finessed the fields. "...two... one."

The main screen flashed white, *Last Fair Deal* shuddered, and abruptly they were back in real space, the main screen filled with apparently unmoving stars. Imric cranked the sensors to their full strength, concentrating on tracing weapons-in-range, but the pings came back reassuringly negative. He adjusted the range, searching for weapons and large ships, and the area around the distant Perb flushed pink: large ships, lots of them, and the sensors weren't able to distinguish weaponry from other types of heavy power consumption. He frowned, typing commands to narrow his search, but a secondary screen flashed a priority symbol. He flipped to it, his frown deepening as he saw the message was from the automatic mail system, signaling a vital bulletin. He accepted it, throwing a secondary screen into a corner of the main, and his breath caught in his throat.

Emergency Statement. The Transit Authority has declared a state of emergency. All ships currently in transit are urged to seek safe harbor immediately. Fourteen hours ago, ships bearing the mark of Empresa NeSH-PI and Gongsi P3WO were recorded in the act of attacking ships belonging to Hemgi Kaisha. Empress NeSH-PI has denied involvement. Gongsi P3WO has declined comment pending an internal investigation. Emergency Statement—

"Mute that," ap Farr said, and Imric obeyed. The words continued to stream silently across the inset screen, but ap Farr ignored them.

"That's war," Derrian said, sounding shocked.

Morcant swung around in her chair again. "*Capa*, the Supreme Justice isn't going to meet us. We need to get out of here—put the Apprentice Judge in a lifepod and dump him."

Ap Farr ignored her. "Bin Marrick. Status?"

"Ship's green," Imric answered. "I make a large number of heavy ships in orbit around the Perb. Sensors are inconclusive, but they're not warships. Or not all of them—"

"Have you spotted the Supreme Justice's ship?" ap Farr interrupted.

"*Capa*," Morcant said. "She won't be coming."

"She'll come." Ap Farr's voice was grim. "We have someone she wants."

Imric adjusted his sensors again, but the subscreen stayed infuriatingly blank. "Nothing yet. They may be running cloaked—I would, if there's a war on."

"*Capa*," Morcant said again, and ap Farr lifted her hand.

"We wait."

Val wedged himself into a corner of Zavod Sualti's Second Dining Space—the only place on the station that was both large enough to hold the station's decision-makers and could be closed off from the rest of the station. The newsscreens were still showing the Transit Authority's warning, and promises of updates scrolled across top and bottom of the displays, but the sound had been muted, and the commentators gesticulated silently against their dubbed-in backgrounds. He wasn't here to vote, that had been made politely plain by Kiet, now pressed up against him in the corner, but to give his opinion on the new field configurations for the Drop. *If asked*, Kiet had added, *but I'm sure you will be.*

At the moment, Val rather hoped he wouldn't be called on. Everyone was talking at once, half a dozen conversations flashing past, and he could only catch a word here and there. There was no question what they were talking about, though: they needed to Drop now, or they'd be caught up in the inevitable conscriptions.

"—wait to Drop, we risk receiving a direct order to join forces with the rest of the Hemgi Kaisha fleet."

Val couldn't pick out the speaker in the crowd, and he didn't recognize the stocky person who answered her. "We could Drop anyway. There's nothing out here that's big enough to stop us."

"That's not necessarily true," Thanh said. For once, her knitting was tucked away, though she knotted her fingers together as though she wished she had it. "A number of ships have taken refuge since the announcement was made, and some of them are heavy freight. They might well be armed, or be able to be armed quickly."

"That's just rumor," someone else said, and Sun-hwa, seated toward the center of the room, lifted her hand.

"Antoku? Can you speak to that?"

The station AI spoke from overhead speaker, and Val wondered briefly if it intended the voice-of-god effect.

"The number of ships taking refuge in orbit around the Apex Center has indeed increased. Based on current occupation and known shipping registers, at least eight of those ships are either armed freighters or convertible attack craft."

"Belonging to whom?" That was definitely Haragai, though Val couldn't find him in the crowd.

"They are all registered to subsidiaries of Hemgi Kaisha," Antoku answered.

The room had gradually quieted as the AI was speaking, and when it finished, there was a moment of silence so deep that Val could hear the soft whirr of the ventilators.

"Well," someone said at last. Val craned his neck to see, and recognized Rokuro. "As I see it, that leaves us with a simple choice. Drop now, or resign ourselves to being part of this war."

There was another uproar in response to that, not as far as Val could tell much disagreement, but frustration and concern, and Sun-hwa lifted her hand again.

"I think the question is whether we can Drop or not. Is Sen Millat here?"

"I'm here," Val answered, and pushed forward as far as he could manage in the crowd.

"I put it to you," Sun-hwa said. "Can we make the Drop?"

Val hesitated, aware of the weight of eyes on him, and chose his words with care. "We've worked out new field settings that give us a 'keel,' and all our sims show that we have about a 96 percent change of making a successful Drop with those adjustments. Your AI can confirm that."

"That is essentially correct," Antoku said. "Though my most recent calculation places the chance of success at 96.629 percent."

"Also—" Val raised his voice to carry over the mutter of agreement. "Also we can always abort the Drop if it seems to be going wrong. Though that does leave us back where we started."

"And unlikely to get a second chance," Rokuro said.

"Maybe, maybe not," Jamahl said. "How likely is it that anyone is going to try to stop us?"

Sun-hwa glanced at the ceiling. "Antoku?"

"I have been unable to address that question in any satisfactory manner," the AI answered. "Data is insufficient."

"I think we can make the Drop this time," Val said. "I'm willing to try."

The was another murmur of conversation, no one seeming willing to speak out, and Sun-hwa lifted her hand again. "It seems to me that there's nothing more to debate. We need to try to Drop now, or not make the attempt until the war ends, which risks our being drawn into everything we came here to avoid. I propose we put it to a vote."

"Vote," several voices chorused, and Sun-hwa nodded.

"All those in favor of making the Drop now, raise your hands." She looked to the ceiling. "Antoku, count, please?"

Val looked around, seeing nearly every hand raised. It made good sense, they'd never have a better chance, or a better reason, but it was still startling to see everyone in agreement.

"Unanimous among those with voting rights," Antoku said.

"So be it," Sun-hwa said. "How soon can we be ready?"

Val shrugged. "The calculations are complete and the new field settings are applied. As far as piloting is concerned, we can go any time."

"There are still some sections to lock down," Thanh said. "Give us eight hours."

"Make it ten," Rokuro said. "That'll put us well into third shift over on the Center. They never put their best crew on then."

"Ten hours, then," Sun-hwa said. "Let's go."

As she stepped into the observation dome, Nalani felt herself tense at the memory of her last time here. Since her attempted peace conference, she'd been unable to halt—or even slow—the Fourth Plane's descent towards war.

She took a deep breath and exhaled, driving physical tension out with escaping breath. No distractions...she needed to concentrate on the problem at hand, dealing with the pirate captain.

Sapnara bowed. "Will this do, Thurgood?"

Gone were the catering stations, ice sculptures, and musicians. The center of the wide circular space was bare and surrounded by a waist-high grey ring, barely visible. Half a dozen steps away, a semicircle of couches faced the center; a single chair in their midst also faced the center, a substantial, well-padded chair that dominated the space.

Nalani shook her head. "Sweet space, it looks like a throne." She held up a hand. "Yes, I know, standard Judiciary issue for a Supreme Justice. Can you get it replaced with a simple chair to match the others?"

Sapnara touched her pendant. "Right away, Thurgood."

Against the wall, next to the entrance, tables held an assortment of drink bulbs and quick snacks: fruit bars, power wafers, strips of jerky. Nalani nodded. "Good. We don't know how long we'll be out there, I don't want people fainting on me."

"Thank you, Thurgood. This station's tended by bots; they'll respond to any special requests."

("Two hours to rendezvous,") her codex said. ("The last of the others are coming aboard now.")

("Bring them up here.") A pair of hefty bots rolled in with a fairly utilitarian chair, fastened it in place, then dragged the throne out. Nalani took a seat and smiled. "Just perfect," she said. "Well done."

It took a few minutes for everyone to arrive and settle around her. Nalani swiveled her chair so she faced them.

Milos, wearing data goggles and carrying a bag of equipment, sat on her left; al-Ghazali settled on her right. Nalani's eyes narrowed. "Who's looking after the kids?"

Milos laughed. "School. And then aftercare. They'll be fine."

"Good." She bowed her head to two others. "I present Justice Li Kui VII and Justice Hanbal V." Li Kui was short and round, bronze and hairless; Hanbal gaunt and angular, bearded and turbaned. "Thank you for coming, and welcome to the team." She gestured around the half-circle. "Milos Savoire, Judge al-Ghazali IV, Superior Judge Sapnara III. For the sake of sanity, I suggest we dispense with titles."

The Justices bowed and took positions between al-Ghazali and Milos. Nalani glanced at Sapnara, still standing. "Sit down, and let's get on our way. We can make detailed plans en route."

The rendezvous point was an even million kilometers from Perbaikan Rock—far enough to be outside most parking orbits, but close enough to satisfy the legal requirements for neutrality, being gravitationally bound to the Perb. Now that war was officially declared, Nalani intended to observe the niceties.

The trip took a little more than an hour, with only the briefest dip into hyperspace. They emerged into normal space cloaked. Beyond the dome, stars speckled a black sky.

Nalani swiveled to regard the center of the room, where a holographic display showed nearby space: Perbaikan Rock small and distant in the lower left, pale trails of color marking hundreds of orbiting vessels. Among them were twenty Judiciary military vessels, including half a dozen from the Fifth Plane—and all under Nalani's command. Their own position was marked with a blinking emerald dot.

She frowned.

"We're a few minutes early," Sapnara said. She closed her eyes, doubtless listening to reports from the bridge. "Wait. There."

A new dot appeared, almost on tope of them. "Visual," Nalani said.

The display blinked, replaced by an image of the newcomer. Nalani stroked her chin. It looked like the pirate ship, the one that had gone by *Patrika*... "Milos?"

He nodded. "It matches the codes we were given. That's our pirate."

"Should I drop the cloak?"

("Three minutes to contact time.") Nalani stood. "Oh, do let's be punctual." She moved toward the refreshments. "Time enough for a last cup of tea. Would anyone else like something?"

Too soon, her codex started a final countdown. Nalani lobbed her empty tea bulb to a waiting bot, sat down, and smoothed her robe. ""Sapnara, you can drop the cloak...now."

The scene didn't change, but Nalani somehow knew the other vessel could see them. "Bring us to one hundred meters," she directed. Still the other ship made no movement. She leaned forward, staring into the image of *Patrika* nose-on, as if she could almost see the pirate captain.

She looked over her left shoulder. "Milos, can you make contact?"

"Trying to." His face broadened in a smile. "I have Imric."

The display shifted again, dissolving to a view of Milos's ex-husband. Imric bin Marrick's face was strained. Behind him, the rest of the pirate ship's bridge was out of focus.

"Give them full video." Next to the main display, a smaller holo window opened, showing Nalani flanked by her associates...the same image being transmitted to *Patrika*.

Welcoming smile number two. "I greet you, Sen bin Marrick. I am Supreme Justice Thurgood IX. May I speak with your captain?"

Without moving his head, bin Marrick glanced off to his right, then back. "The *capa* says she'd rather get right to business." He looked pained. "Milos, can you—"

Nalani crossed her arms and gave stern glare number six. "I'll have your *capa's* name, and I'll have it directly from her."

Bin Marrick flinched; Nalani had the impression that he was trying his best to become invisible. She held her glare. ("I'm sorry I have to put Milos through this,") she said to her codex. The AI answered, ("Make it up to him later.")

After a dozen heartbeats, the view shifted. *Patrika's* bridge filled the scene, as firm and solid as if she *did* look directly into the other ship. In addition to bin Marrick, two other crewmembers sat at console-packed stations. In the center, a cloaked and hooded figure sat in a massive command chair that exuded authority.

"I am Llian ap Farr, Captain of the *Last Fair Deal*. And you, Supreme Justice, have become quite the thorn in my side."

("Voice artificially processed,") her codex said. ("She really doesn't want to expose her identity.") ("She will. I'll let it slide for now, but before this is over, I *will* identify her.")

"The feeling's mutual, you'll be happy to know." Nalani uncrossed her arms and softened her glare. "Thank you for making this deal. I'm flattered."

"Shall we do this thing? I believe you have have some information for me."

Nalani raised an eyebrow. "I believe you have a Judge for me? *And* his codex?"

"One step at a time. You must assure me that you'll keep your part of the bargain." A pause, then, "I've dealt with Supreme Justices before."

"One-third of *Quintile Illumination's* data first. The balance when Bhagwati's safe in our hands."

"Done."

Nalani glanced at Milos. "Send it."

The two ships hung motionless against the stars, *Last Fair Deal* still poised to make the leap to hyperspace if the Supreme Justice failed to keep her word. From its place at the core of the *Deal's* systems, the Cubaba Codex monitored all available lines of communication, including the judiciary's: it did not think Thurgood would betray them, her honor was legendary, but it was always as well to be prepared, particularly in case one of the juniors decided to act without Thurgood's authorization. That was still unlikely, from its observations of Bhagwati, but it did not know al-Ghazali, and felt it safer not to take chances. A part of its programming was focused on Nur-adad, holding it immobile against the currents of virtuality. Once Bhagwati was released, Cubaba would fling Nur-adad out into judiciary space, and *Last Fair Deal* would leap for hyperspace, safe in its untrackable non-space. Thurgood would be too busy dealing with the war to pursue, Cubaba calculated, and they would be able to Drop again as soon as they reached the Fissure.

A subroutine pinged, calling for Cubaba's attention. Cubaba focused on it, and saw ap Farr speaking to her crew. Derrian

Hina rose at once, followed reluctantly by the data engineer, and Cubaba followed them back to the cell where Bhagwati was imprisoned. It watched while they unlocked the door, Derrian standing back to cover Imric's entrance, and Bhagwati sat up sharply. He was still in the clothes they had given him, and Imric tossed him a bundle that proved to be the clothes in which he had been captured. Bhagwati caught it by reflex and looked up warily at the other men.

"What's this?"

"Get dressed," Derrian said. "Your boss has made a deal to get you back."

Cubaba sensed the heat rising under Bhagwati's skin—embarrassment, it diagnosed—but the Apprentice Judge's voice was steady. "Very wise of you to accept it."

Derrian scowled, and Imric shifted slightly, putting himself between the other two. "Get dressed, please. There's no time to waste."

"And if you waste time," Derrian said, "we'll toss you in the pod as you are."

Bhagwati wisely ignored that, changing quickly, and straightened as he fastened the last button of his narrow gown. "Now what?"

Before the others could answer, Cubaba assessed the results of a quick scan, and spoke from the nearest speaker. "His codex. Return that."

It saw Bhagwati blink, and Imric raised his eyebrows. "Does the *capa* wish it?"

"I speak for the *capa*," Cubaba answered.

There was half a heartbeat's hesitation, then Imric shrugged. "Do you have it, Derrian?"

"Yeah." Derrian fumbled in his pockets, produced the ring they had taken from him when he was captured. He tossed it to Bhagwati, who snatched it out of the air and slid it onto his finger. Cubaba saw the fractional hesitation when he realized that he still had no connection with Nur-adad itself, but doubted the other humans noticed.

"And I repeat," Bhagwati said, "what now?"

"Lifepod," Derrian said, and gestured toward the hatch. "Walk."

Again Cubaba sensed an instant of hesitation, but then Bhagwati obeyed. Imric fell into step behind him, and they escorted him quickly through the corridors to the port side lifepod bay. At the pod, Derrian paused to touch the intercom panel. "*Capa.* We're at the pod."

"Good." There was silence, and ap Farr's though echoed in Cubaba's space. *Cubaba. Is the lifepod rigged as I ordered?*

Cubaba allowed itself a final confirmation, its diagnostic pulsing through the lifepod's systems. *Yes. Internal controls are disabled, course is set to pass 500 meters from our counterpart's starboard side.*

Good. Cubaba could feel ap Farr's satisfaction. *That'll keep them busy while we jump.*

That was my intention, Cubaba answered. *External shields are at moderate power, enough to protect against minor debris, but not enough to stop us from destroying the lifepod in one or two shots. There is no major debris within three hours' transit; I calculate that this will also keep Thurgood busy worrying how to protect him if we fire.*

Well done. Ap Farr spoke aloud. "Go ahead and load him."

Imric reached for the wall-mounted controls, entered the codes that armed the pod and allowed the double hatches to slide open.

"In you get," Derrian said, and Bhagwati stooped to fit himself through the hatch. Cubaba saw him hesitate again, and guessed he was thinking of his codex; it wished it could reassure him—it knew all too well how much judges cared for the codices with which they were en counsel—but there was no time. Then Bhagwati was full in the pod, and Imric touched keys to reseal the hatches.

"The judge is on board, *capa*," he said.

"Good." Ap Farr didn't bother to close the intercom, but her next words were obviously for the waiting Supreme Justice. "Your judge is loaded and ready to drop."

"We'll begin transmitting our data once the pod reaches the halfway point." The voice was unmistakably Thurgood's, as coolly unshaken as if she were not negotiating for a man's life while the Fourth Plane flared into open warfare.

"Launch," ap Farr said, and Imric hit the switch. There was a hiss of propellant, and the *Deal* shivered slightly. Cubaba turned its attention to external sensors, and saw the lifepod's thrusters fire, setting it on the programmed course. Nur-adad pulsed once against its confining code, but Cubaba contained it easily. It would release the younger codex when they jumped to hyperspace, and not before.

Val settled himself at the pilot's station in Zavod Sualti's control room, grateful for the internal fields that provided close to normal gravity. He had gathered from talking to the station's crew that they normally worked in microgravity, the internal power going to the buoys and the launch mechanisms. Luckily the maneuver system ran off an entirely different power plant. The station had always been mobile, so the consoles that controlled the hyperdrive and the STL systems were familiar, hardware and software both as up-to-date as any Val had used recently. The Drop console was new, but also familiar, wedged in between the pilot's station and the data engineer's, Kiet already strapped in and running through the checklists. Jamahl was busy at larger board beside him: he'd be acting as data engineer this trip. Behind them, though, the main part of the control room was dark: that was where Zavod Sualti's crew managed the launch of their hyperspatial buoys. Now everything in that section was shut down, screens dark, lights out, and the main viewscreen had been rotated to face the maneuvering stations. At the moment, it showed unenhanced starscape, the shape of the Fissure imperceptible in normal wavelengths.

Val flicked through his own checklists, first bringing his console to life and then, as the engineers brought their systems on line, feeling the controls lock into readiness. He glanced over his shoulder to where Sun-hwa and Thanh sat at the comms station. Rokuro sat behind them in a pull-down seat. He had no particular role to play in the Drop, but he wasn't going to wait in his cabin, either. "We're ready. Are we going to give them warning?"

"Thanh?" Sun-hwa glanced at the other woman, who shook her head.

"There's no traffic out there. No reason to draw attention."

"Right," Val said. "Ready to leave stable orbit. Engines ready?"

"Engines at stand-by," Kiet said, from the Drop console.

"Commence flight." Val felt the controls come alive under his hand.

"Ignition," Kiet said. "Thrusters on. And we're moving."

Not fast, not gracefully, but they were definitely moving, the potato-shaped station wobbling away from its stable position into open space. Val checked the course and the station's mass, touched controls to adjust their course. The thrusters fired, short silent bursts too small to be felt inside the inertial dampers, but the numbers shifted on his screen. "On course. En route to Drop."

He could see their chosen Drop point in the distance, the lines of hyperflux just coming into focus, a smooth curve like the spiral cone-shells he had collected as a child. The proposed course flashed into existence, pale green against the black; he checked the strain gauges, found them optimal, and flicked the display off again.

"Could we have that on the main screen, Sun-hwa?" Rokuro asked, and the starscape vanished, replaced by the proposed course and the lines of stress that were the Fissure. Val ignored it, concentrating on his own, sharper images, letting himself sink into the relaxed state that let him feel the ship's—the station's—movements as an extension of his own body. Not as graceful as the smaller ships, and not as massive as the transplanars he'd flown for the last ten years, but a solid mass that he could balance against the fabric of space.

"We're being pinged," Thanh said. "It's the Center."

Rokuro and Sun-hwa exchanged glances. "Answer?" Rokuro asked, and Sun-hwa shrugged.

"It might buy time."

"Go ahead then," Rokuro said.

Sun-hwa accepted the connection. "Zavod Sualti. Please confirm your identity."

"This is Apex Center Transit Authority." The voice was rough with static. "A state of conflict is in effect. All ships must remain in safe harbor until the conflict is resolved."

"We're not a ship," Sun-hwa said. Val didn't think that was much of an argument, but he guessed she knew what she was doing. "We're not under Transit Authority control."

"All traffic in this system is under our control," the Center answered, sounding faintly annoyed. "A station under power is considered traffic under local regulations."

"Understood," Sun-hwa said, and waited.

"Zavod Sualti, you are entering a conflict zone," the Center said. "I repeat, you are entering a conflict zone. We cannot guarantee your safety. Your contract with Apex prohibits you from taking such risks."

"If you will examine your communications records," Rokuro said, "you will find a Termination of Subcontract and a voucher for the breach fee. We are no longer employed by Apex or its parent companies."

"We are not authorized to accept your termination," the Center said.

"Our contract allows either side to end the contract on payment of the breach fee," Rokuro said. "Your signature is not required,"

There was a little silence before the Center answered. "That'll keep the lawyers employed, but it doesn't change the risk. I hope you know what you're doing, Zavod Sualti."

"We're content," Sun-hwa said. "Zavod Sualti out." She looked around the control room. "Whoever's on scan, keep sharp. If we're going to have trouble, it's going to start now."

"Nothing so far," Jamahl said, and Val turned his attention to the steering.

Zavod Sualti was heavy for its size, and hard to steer once it got moving, its mass wanting to stay in its current course, to be shifted only with great effort. Val was still getting the hang of it, though at least now he tended to undercorrect rather than apply too much power and have to correct wildly. They were well out of the system now, still accelerating, the course that would take them to the Drop point curving gently toward the Fissure. At the current acceleration, it would take them another three hours to reach the Drop, and that would bring them in at a speed that allowed for last-minute corrections if needed—

"Attention," Antoku said, from the overhead speaker. "Apex Center is reporting a launch."

"What ship?" Sun-hwa asked.

"*Denebel*, registered to Exomeg Vehicles," Antoku answered.

"Blast." Rokuro leaned forward. "Can we get them on sensors?"

"Not yet," Jamahl said. "They're lost in background scatter."

Val risked a glance in Jamahl's direction. "Problem?"

"Exomeg also belongs to Hemgi Kaisha," Jamahl said.

"Any attempt at contact?" Rokuro asked.

Thanh shook her head. "Not so far. You don't really think they'd come after us."

"I may have miscalculated," Rokuro said. "We just cut ourselves loose from Apex, which means an Exomeg ship could claim us as—prize of war? salvage? I'm not sure it really matters. The point is, no one's obliged to do anything about it."

Val looked at Jamahl again. "Can they overtake us?"

"Working on it." Jamahl's fingers flashed across the keys. "Antoku, give me any specs you have for this *Denebel*."

"Downloading."

"Thanks." Jamahl kept working for a moment longer, then leaned back. "Yes, they can catch us, but—it's not as bad as it might have been. They're not the fastest ship in Exomeg's fleet, and they've got one engine working at less than optimum."

"They had put in for emergency repairs," Antoku interjected. "Those repairs have not yet been completed."

"If we increase acceleration," Jamahl said, "we can reach the Drop point with about half an hour to spare. Maybe more depending on how fast we want to take her. And if she sees we're heading for the Drop—well, what are the odds that she'll back off? It'll be obvious we're trying to get away from the fight."

"Can we go faster?" Sun-hwa asked, and Val heaved a sigh.

"Some, yes. I've been conservative, I wanted to give us lots of chance to correct our line if we weren't coming in optimum, but—yes, I can increase acceleration without too much risk."

"Do it," Thanh said, and out of the corner of his eye, Val saw Rokuro nod as well.

"Understood." He turned his attention to his controls, adjusting the numbers and watching the line of the projected course shift and flatten. They'd still have time to make adjustment, but it would be tighter than he had hoped.

"*Denebel* is also increasing acceleration," Jamahl said. He transferred the data to Val's console without waiting to be asked, and Val grimaced at the sight.

"Increasing our acceleration to maximum," he said, and allowed himself a sigh of relief as the numbers swam and reformed. They'd have to brake hard to make any adjustments, but that was possible; if worst came to worst, he was confident he could make the Drop on this line and at that speed.

"They're falling back," Jamahl reported, after a moment. "Not trying to match us."

"Maybe they realized what we're doing," Thanh said. "Maybe they'll let us go."

"Antoku, what's *Denebel's* armament?" Rokuro asked.

"Officially, she carries three ship-to-ship missiles and two small cannon," the AI answered. "However, readings of her power output are consistent with larger cannon, or perhaps more small weapons. I will report as soon as I am certain."

"How long before they're in missile range?" Val's guts cramped at the thought. Zavod Sualti was an enormous, unmissable target.

"They can fire at long range forty minutes before we reach Drop," Antoku said.

"But they won't," Sun-hwa said. "We're a rock. They'll need to be close in and get lucky before they do us any real damage."

"They can mess up the equipment on the surface pretty badly," Rokuro said. "But I take your point. We can always repair that after we've Dropped."

As long as they don't hit us while we're trying to Drop, Val thought. That had been *Iridium Azimuth's* problem, a missile hit just as they Dropped, and it had taken the Fifth Ship to get them out of that. But Sun-hwa was right, Zavod Sualti's unwieldy mass would be protection there, too.

With voice-and-vision links between the ships muted and shrunk to pastel windows, the main display showed the pirate ship—*Last Fair Deal*—motionless against the stars. After a moment, al-Ghazali shot to her feet and pointed. "There's the lifepod."

"We've got it," Sapnara said. Grapples took the pod, reeling it toward them.

Nalani stood up. "As soon as he's aboard, have him sent up here." She allowed herself a silent sigh. With Bhagwati safe… assuming he *was*…the worst risk was over. Now she could do what she had to.

"We're not done yet," she said, her voice soft yet firm. "This next part is the trickiest. I need you all at the top of your game." A breath. "Voice and vision."

The exterior view faded, and once again the main display was dominated by the hooded pirate captain in her massive chair. She raised her head, her features completely concealed, and Nalani felt her mouth go dry.

"You have your Judge. If you'll transmit the rest of what you owe me, we can both be on our way."

"Not just yet. You haven't fulfilled all the terms of our deal." Nalani fastened her eyes on the pirate's hooded face, projecting uncompromising strength. ("Crew reports Bhagwati's aboard. Medtechs are checking him out.") "Captain ap Farr, we agreed to face-to-face contact, verified by Sen Savoire and Sen bin Marrick." She waited a beat, then said between tight lips, "*You have not shown your face.*"

Ap Farr leaned back in her chair. "Absurd. You have my name, you know my ship. All else, I keep to myself."

"Captain ap Farr, you are to be detained on suspicion of murder." To her codex, Nalani directed, ("Have the military vessels ping her.") "There's no point in attempting to flee. My ships can track you and overtake you even in hyperspace."

The pirate glanced at a screen, then looked again to Nalani. "What's this nonsense about a murder charge? I returned him safely."

Hands on hips, Nalani said, "You are operating a stolen Judiciary codex. The owner is presumed dead, and you're the prime suspect." ("Bhagwati's on his way.") "You can bargain and bluster your way out of anything else—but you're not getting away with this one." She narrowed her eyes. "Show... your...face."

The pirate sat motionless for long moments, as even the members of her own crew turned to look at her. Then, without any physical sign of surrender, she stood tall and imperious. "Switching to unaltered voice-and-vision. Bin Marrick, certify as such."

Bin Marrick stroked his console, looked up at Nalani. "Unaltered v-and-v certified."

"Milos," Nalani said, without releasing the pirate from her gaze. "Do you trust him?"

"I...I do, Thurgood."

"I'm waiting, Captain."

The pirate reached up and lowered her hood, revealing a pale face and pure white hair, shadowed eyes, lips the color of dying dwarf stars. She reached down and brought up an obsidian cane, resting the handle on her lips.

Nalani staggered back a step, felt the chair behind her, and straightened. ("Identity confirmed,") her codex said.

Far behind her, Bhagwati burst into the room. "Thurgood, you have to know, it's important...the pirate, she's got the Cubaba Codex."

Nalani looked back at him, her lips twitching in a smile for which she had no number. "I know," she said, and turned back to the pirate. She bobbed her head in a quick bow, and barely above a whisper said, "Hello, Jinan-Jorie."

The pirate bobbed her head in the same fashion. "Hello, Nalani. Can we dispense with this talk of murder now?"

Nalani turned to the others, whose faces danced between alarm and bafflement. "My friends, I present Supreme Justice Accursius XVII, *en counsel* with the Cubaba Codex."

ELSEWHERE

Compressed and boosted by 3P2D servers, the distress call from Coquimbo entered the transplanar comm stream coded as a five-star top priority message.

Every multiplanar ship on the Third Plane received the message, stored and ranked with all the other exabytes awaiting transport to other Planes. Every ship continued receiving until seconds before Drop. Every ship carried its own version of the stream on a Drop that could last from a few dozen hours to over a year.

The median Drop time was two or three months—but there were always ships that beat the median. For any particular message, there was always a ship that was fastest.

First to the Second Plane, in a Drop of just over two days, was the freighter *Darsana Consequence*. Upon emerging from the Fissure, the freighter's AI routinely transmitted its copy of the stream to the Plane-based AIs that combed through the stream and dispersed messages as necessary: already delivered by another ship, marked for local delivery, route to next Plane. With five-star priority, the distress call was on its way before *Darsana Consequence's* transfer engines cooled.

Mail-and-personnel carrier *Apeiron Mist* reached the First Plane before any other ship, in a record 1.6-day Drop. The distress call was picked up by private vessel *Sourwood Eschaton*, which survived the tricky ricochet off the Spindle to Vault to the Fifth Plane in only 2.56 days.

On Fifth, copies of the message departed on 27 ships in two days before the Drop of military carrier *Barium Maculate*, also en route from the First Plane, which beat all the others to Fourth with a Drop of 42 hours.

The AIs of the Fourth Plane recognized the distress call's priority and instantly queued it for Plane-wide emergency broadcast. A final AI took three million nanoseconds to verify that the message was legitimate and contained no malicious code, then passed it through to the broadcast bots.

After nearly 11 days in transit, Coquimbo's cry for help rang out across the Fourth Plane.

FOURTH PLANE

Nalani ordered the military ships to stand down, and Accursius docked *Last Fair Deal* and allowed her crew to come aboard Nalani's ship.

The dome was transformed; the central holostage with its guardrail was gone, couches were arranged in casual conversational groups, and the kitchen replaced the snack tray with scattered tables laden with a vast assortment of finger foods and drinks—including a pyramid of marble-size amber spheres, each one a sip of sparkling wine.

Nalani insisted that the ship's crew be encouraged to share the treats; they appeared in stages and clumped together. Milos and bin Marrick sat against one wall, close together. Nalani and Accursius took seats facing one another. In between, the others steered clear of both couples.

"I thought I'd never find you," Nalani said. "I didn't realize you were there all along."

Accursius shrugged. "I didn't intend to involve you."

"You left me a message on Fifth. You said you needed help."

"I said that I *may* need help." Her eyebrows contracted, just a bit. "As I recall, I also specifically asked you not to come in with guns blazing."

"If you're not going to tell me what you're doing, you can't complain when I do it my way."

Accursius smiled. "I've missed you. Look, I'd rather the news of my identity stay close. Can you trust these people?"

"Definitely." Nalani's eyes strayed to the two Justices. "Li Kui and Hanbal are on my side. They agreed to keep everything involving this case confidential, but just in case I had my codex seal theirs. Until it releases them, they can't talk."

"That'll have to do." Accursius shook her head. "There's no help for it, you're in the situation now. I heard that you cleaned the codices on Fifth."

Nalani nodded. "And on down through the Planes."

"Won't help. A few years and the corruption will be back. Whoever we're up against, they're good."

"Have you learned anything since you left me that message? You were vague on details."

"It's a big, powerful organization. They're on all the Planes, with agents in multiple institutions. The pirate boss Lasser on Second is almost certainly one of them."

"What about here? Is Ocampo one of theirs?"

"I suspect he is, but I don't have proof. I'm keeping an eye on him." Accursius chewed her lip. "I don't know what he's up to with this war."

Nalani rolled her eyes. "They want to use it to spur technological advance. One of the CEOs I talked to spoke particularly of transplanar hyperphysics."

"Hmmm." Accursius stroked her chin. "That sounds plausible."

"If we work together, we could stop this war and take Ocampo down."

"Nal, I don't know about jumping back into the Judicial saddle. I have projects that I need to—"

Lights flashed red, and the emergency tritone sounded. Half the dome lit with two faces, both heavy with implants.

Breaking—Five-star distress call received for Plane-wide broadcast. Message begins.

The two people, a reporter and a planetary engineer, briefly explained the plight of their colony world, Coquimbo. The message lasted only ninety seconds; at the end, the camera pulled close on the reporter. "Folks, you heard what the engineer said. And entire planet is at stake. Please, find that generator and get it to us."

The two Supreme Justices looked at one another. Nalani said, "Feel like taking on another project?"

Accursius harrumphed. "Not much of a project." She lifted her cane. "I suppose I can spare a few hours. It *would* be nice to work together again, just this once."

"Who knows, it might be so much fun—"

"—That I decide to stay and help you end the war?" She shot her cane a nasty look. "I don't remember asking *your* opinion." She held out her hand. "Let's get that generator on its way, before I change my mind."

After the first hour, they'd moved to a smaller workroom, lined in screens and consoles, the local servers stuffed with useful programs and all of the little ship's oversized communications gear under their control. The other justices slipped in and out of the space or passed word through their codices—Cubaba, Jinan-Jorie thought, was positively reveling in its reappearance. The apprentices came in person, and Jinan-Jorie noted that they always brought a fresh tray of food or drink, and took the dirtied dishes away with them. As always, Nalani had woven them into something more like a family than a team.

"It's fundamentally fairly simple," Nalani proclaimed, Li Kui and al-Ghazali nodding loyal agreement. "A five-star distress call overrides everything, all other obligations, and we as Supreme Justices are in perfect position to enforce that—"

"You're in perfect position," Jinan-Jorie interjected. "Remember, I'm not here."

"I am in a perfect position to enforce it," Nalani agreed. "And enforce it I shall. Bhagwati's located the generator—it was being shipped aboard the *Quintile Illumination*, as a matter of fact."

Jinan-Jorie laughed. "Had I but known! Have you figured out who killed the ship's AI?"

"I've been busy with other things," Nalani answered. "Some of which were your doing."

"Touché." Jinan-Jorie felt Cubaba nudge her thoughts, and glanced at her screen in time to see the answer to her most recent query float up into focus among the multiple windows. "Ah. Give me a moment."

"Take as long as you like." Nalani looked back at the other justices. "Under the interplanar trade codes, chapter 17, sections 2j and 3a through c, we can commandeer any ship on the Plane to respond to the appeal."

("I would call section 3 as a whole the more relevant text,") Cubaba murmured, and Jinan-Jorie bit back a grin.

("Be kind.") She paused, considering the most recent iteration of the shipping register. ("Locate Hemgi Kaisha's most powerful ships—best armed, most likely to double as military craft—then do the same for the other four. Also find any other generators on the Fourth Plane that could meet Coquimbo's need.")

("Very well.") There was a brief pause. ("Ah. Abi-eshuh is already working on the latter problem.")

("Don't bother duplicating the effort, then.") Jinan-Jorie was suddenly aware that she was very thirsty, and stretched to take another drink bottle from the nearest tray. It was a mildly stimulating tisane, enough to keep her awake without subjecting her to stim deprivation later, and she twisted off the cap, the bottle cooling sharply under her hand.

"Our first order of business is to move Coquimbo's generator onto a new ship, and dispatch it to the Third Plane," Nalani continued. "But, since Drop times are notoriously unpredictable, and a ship that Drops after another may arrive sooner, we need to locate any other generators that could serve the purpose, and send them to the Third Plane as well."

Al-Ghazali frowned slightly. "But if they all arrive, then Coquimbo has too many generators—and could conceivably be expected to pay for them, which my examination of its economy suggests would be a hardship."

"Very good," Nalani said. "That's why we will draw up a hire-purchase agreement between the Judiciary and the owner of at least one more generator—any judge can issue an Emergency Funds Authorization, especially when responding to a five-star distress call. Al-Ghazali, I'll want you to take care of that for me."

"Issue it under my name?" Al-Ghazali looked startled.

"Under your name and seal," Nalani said. "It'll be good practice."

"Very well, Thurgood." Al-Ghazali bowed slightly.

"And what about the other generators?" Li Kui asked.

"So far, Bhagwati has located seven." Nalani's expression was briefly distant as she listened to Abi-eshuh. "There are four more that could be adapted to serve. Using my authority as Supreme Justice, I am ordering transport ships to the systems where those generators are located, to stand by in case their help is needed in getting a backup to Coquimbo. Anyone firing on those ships, or in any way interfering with their passage, can be charged under Item Five of the Transplanar Compact. Disrupting a rescue attempt, particularly one involving more than one Plane, is considered a Class Two felony, and a judge may raise the charge to Class One."

"So you're going to shuffle the board," Li Kui said.

"Nicely put," Jinan-Jorie said, in spite of herself, and Li Kui gave her a formal bow.

"I don't—" Al-Ghazali stopped. "Oh. If you pick the right ships, and send them far enough away, you disrupt the corporations' plans for a war."

"If we pick the right ships, and we get just a little lucky, we might stop the war altogether," Nalani said. "Right, Jays?"

"Ahead of you, Nal," Jinan-Jorie answered, and flipped the list to Nalani's dataspace. "Here are the most powerful of the corporate ships, by company, and my suggested destinations."

Nalani glanced down at the schematic that blossomed on her screen, and gestured to send a file to Jinan-Jorie's console. It opened, revealing a diagram that differed from Jinan-Jorie's only in the colors Nalani had used to code it. "Great minds."

"We'll certainly make it a lot harder for them to get back into the fight," Jinan-Jorie answered.

"Yes, indeed." Nalani's familiar smile spread across her face. "Ah, it's good to be working with you again!

"And you." Jinan-Jorie returned the smile, and reached for another flask of the tisane. It was good to see Nalani again, good, treacherously good, to work with her, the two of them almost as entrained as a judge and her codex. That had always been their great gift, their ability to trust each other's strengths, to play off each other's ideas—to take a thought and leap forward with it, knowing that the other would be with them all the way. She had been ap Farr too long, she thought, that cramped and joyless persona. It was hard to be fully free of it, even here. And at some point she would have to return to it, to the hunt she had begun years before... She shoved that thought aside. There was no point in focusing on the future; she would cherish this moment for as long as it lasted.

The ships fled through the void at ever-increasing speeds, Zavod Sualti following the course Val had laid out toward the planned Drop point, Denebel trailing, a point of fire against the night. They were slowly overhauling the station, though Antoku was still projecting that Zavod Sualti would reach the Drop point before Denebel was in effective range. Val shivered slightly, remembering Iridium Azimuth, fleeing pirates with Broad Increase close behind, making the Drop only to discover that Broad Increase was nowhere to be found. He banished that thought with an effort, focusing instead on course and speed, finessing the thrusters to coax every bit of acceleration from the lumbering raft. Momentum built, the time to intercept shifting, stretching; Val studied his numbers again, imagining the shifts as they came closer to the Drop point. Everything was still within tolerances, though he was pushing close to the edge of the envelope.

"Fuel status?" Rokuro asked.

"We're consuming more than projected, of course," Kiet answered. "But we allowed for that."

"We'll probably have to refuel on Third," Thanh said. "But we can work for that if we have to."

Val glanced at his own indicators, saw that the steering engines were all still well into the green. He'd have to spend more fuel on the final approach, of course, but there should still be plenty—

"Warning," Antoku said. "Denebel has launched a missile."

"Course?" Rokuro leaned forward in his seat.

"Calculating."

Val started to adjust the throttle, but made himself wait. Better to to spend the fuel until he was sure it was needed.

"The missile is on course, but will detonate two kilometers short of our projected position at intercept," Antoku said.

"Is that on purpose?" Thanh asked.

"I can't answer that with the data available," Antoku said.

"Has to be," Jamahl said, his hands busy on the board. "They could have waited."

"Missile is running," Antoku said.

Val reached for a secondary screen, dragged the missile's track into it. The numbers streamed past along the base of the screen, and then at last fire blossomed soundlessly, drowning out the stars.

"The missile has detonated," Antoku said.

"No damage," Jamahl said. "Why in the world—oh, wait. They're opening a channel."

"Do we talk to them?" Sun-hwa looked at Rokuro, who bit his lip.

"No harm in talking," he said at last. "We're secured against infiltration, right?"

"Oh, yes," Jamahl said. "And ours is top military grade, too."

"Accept, then." Rokuro's hands closed tight on the arms of his chair.

"Zavod Sualti here," Sun-hwa said. "Cease firing at once. I repeat, do not fire."

"This is Denebel, Exomeg Fleet, speaking for Hemgi Kaisha." The voice was hollow with distance. "You are required to stand down and return to Apex Center for further instructions."

"No can do," Sun-hwa said. "We are en route to Drop."

"The terms of your contract require that you place yourself under the control of Hemgi Kaisha or its nearest representatives in the event of war," Denebel said. "I repeat, stand down."

"We have received no notice of an official state of war," Sun-hwa answered. "And absent such notice, Zavod Sualti is an independent entity once the terms of our contract are met. We have ended the contract, and choose to leave this Plane. You have no right to stop us."

"The Transit Authority's declaration of a state of conflict is equivalent to a declaration of war," Denebel said. "If you do not stand down, we will take all necessary measures to enforce the contract."

"So much for that," Thanh muttered.

Sun-hwa's mouth twisted in wry agreement, but she said, "The precedents are out on that statement, Denebel, and we are prepared to fight it in court. From the Third Plane if necessary."

"We are authorized to use force to stop you," Denebel countered. "Please do not make that necessary."

"We do not acknowledge your authority," Sun-hwa said. "Stand down yourself, or prepare to face the consequences." She slapped the channel closed, and looked around the control room. "I doubt that will slow them down, but it was worth a try."

"Couldn't hurt," Rokuro said. "Val, how long before we can Drop?"

Val checked his screen, touching keys to recalculate the distances. "We're almost there. Forty minutes."

"And Denebel will be in effective missile range in thirty-three minutes," Jamahl said.

Seven minutes. Seven minutes as a target was at least five minutes too long. Val said, "We can go faster."

"And still make the Drop?" Kiet asked.

Probably. Val swallowed his doubts. "Yes."

"Do it," Sun-hwa said.

Val adjusted the throttle, and watched the numbers climb in his display. Ahead, the project course wound through an increasingly tight curve into the bright white fleck of the Drop point, and he touched keys again, setting up a more direct approach. The screen flashed and reformed, offering the results: possible, though it required one larger course correction rather than several smaller ones. "I can get us there sooner," he said aloud. "Assuming the station will hold together. Jamahl?"

"I see what you're doing." Jamahl bent over his screens, posing queries of his own. "Yeah, we'll hold. With power to spare."

"Let me see?" Kiet started to lean over to look, but Jamahl transferred the files to his console instead, and Kiet considered them. "I think—yes. We'll have power to spare. And I can shape the fields a little differently, that'll bring us nicely into Drop."

"Go for it," Rokuro said.

"Fields first," Kiet said, and Val nodded. "Forty percent—all right, we're good"

"Confirmed. Beginning course change." Val adjusted the controls as he spoke, inertia translated to stiff weight against his control surfaces. He pressed harder, watching the course line slowly start to move. It picked up speed, and he eased his grip, letting the ship stabilize before adding more input. For a moment, he thought he'd overdone it, but then Zavod Sualti came ponderously onto its new course. The Drop point blazed before them.

"Ready for Drop," Kiet reported.

"Ready here," Jamahl echoed.

"What's Denebel doing?" Sun-hwa asked. "Antoku?"

"Maintaining her previous course," the AI answered.

Val shut them out of his mind, focusing on the interplay of field frequencies and the fabric of space itself, a sparking rainbow streaming behind them like a wake, compressing ahead of them into a pale blue-white line as the fields bit deeper. They were almost at optimum; he nudged a thruster, considered the results, and decided against a second attempt. This was good enough, well within tolerances. Zavod Sualti was ready, trembling on the edge of Drop, equations locked, with no sign of the wobble that had defeated them the last two attempts. "Stand by—"

"Denebel has fired two missiles," Antoku said, its voice flat. "They are set to explode in four minutes."

"That's well out of range," Jamahl said.

But still close enough to affect the Drop. Val hesitated, weighing the options. Drop now, risk the distortion of the explosions, or abort? It was really no option at all. "Stand by for Drop."

"Drop in three," Kiet answered, "two, one—"

The capacitors fired. Val felt the fields catch and hold, felt the twisting pressures of non-space, non-time translated to forces pressing against the ship's controls. He met and matched them, feeling a wobble that threatened to build. For a moment, he thought it was the same problem they'd had before, but that had been evident before they Dropped. This was in the Drop— no, almost in the Drop, they still weren't stable, and instead of settling, the gyration was getting worse.

"—missiles, damn them," someone was saying, and he could have groaned aloud. Of course that was the problem, just as he'd been afraid would happen, the missiles distorting local space just enough to push their calculations out of true. It was what had happened to Iridium Azimuth), and very nearly destroyed her, too, and a part of him was bitterly aware of the unfairness of having to deal with that twice in one lifetime. He could feel Zavod Sualti beginning to tremble, stresses building along the field lines; the keel was supposed to fix that, he thought, and in that instant understood the answer.

"Kiet! Extend the keel along the y-axis! It needs to bite—" He stopped, struggling to put words to the sensations, but Kiet was already nodding.

"Yes, I see—"

Val felt the fields shiver, the changes reflected in his controls, and abruptly Zavod Sualti steadied, the main screens filling with the rainbow fire of a successful Drop. "We're in."

"Confirmed," Kiet said. He lifted his hands from his controls to display a tremor. "We made it."

"All systems report green," Jamahl said. "That was a little hairy there at the end—was it those missiles?"

"I think so," Val said. He locked his own boards and leaned back in his seat, his muscles as tired as if he had run a marathon. "But we made it. Third Plane, here we come."

About the Rule of Five

The Rule of Five is a serial space opera. You can follow the ongoing story at *rule-of-5.com*. To help support *The Rule of Five*, visit our Patreon site at *www.patreon.com/ruleof5*.

With infinite gratitude, we acknowledge the inestimable work of our splendid proofreaders, Kate Jones and Lena Strid.

We are grateful for the support of our Patreon supporters:

Benefactors
- Chris McLaren
- Melita
- Rob Thornton
- Robert Mackay

Patrons
- Betsy Anthony Childs
- Catherine Farnon
- Elaine
- Ingrid Emilsson
- Jennief Tifft
- Kara Snow
- Kate Jones
- Ken Marable
- Law Nerd
- Lynn F.
- pCiaran
- Sasha Harris-Cronin
- Susanna J. Sturgis

Subscribers
- Andrew Hatchell
- Beth Chandler
- Bodi Luse
- Carina
- Catherine Barrier
- Connie Harich
- Eddie Clark
- Elaine
- Evan
- Gretchen Brinckerhoff
- Hildo Biersma
- Jo Graham
- Judith Tarr
- Lena Strid
- Malu Gawthrop
- Rebecca Barr
- Richard Pryor
- Seth Elgart
- Susan Haseltine
- Tim Tanner
- Weaverbird

Supporters
- Anca Irinel Radu
- Violet LeVoit

-Melissa Scott & Don Sakers

The Scattered Worlds Mosaic by Don Sakers

Dance for the Ivory Madonna
a romance of psiberspace
Print & Kindle
Spectrum Award finalist; 56 Hugo nominations
"Imagine a Stand on Zanzibar written by a left-wing Robert Heinlein, and infused with the most exciting possibilities of the new cyber-technology." -Melissa Scott, author of Dreaming Metal, The Jazz

Weaving the Web of Days
a tale of the Scattered Worlds
Print & Kindle
Maj Thovold has led the Galaxy for three decades, a Golden Age of peace and prosperity. She is weary and ready to resign, but she faces one last battle: a battle on the strangest battlefield known: a web of living tendrils that stretches across interstellar space. A web where Maj's enemies wait, like spiders, for their prey....

The Eighth Succession
a novel of the Scattered Worlds
Print & Kindle
"Remember when science fiction used to be filled with galactic intrigue and bigger-than-life heroes? The wonderful Don Sakers certainly does! The Eighth Succession is a rip-roaring yarn, impossible to put down. If John W. Campbell's Astounding Stories had been published in an LGBT-friendly era, this is the cover-story serial you'd have been waiting anxiously for each month. What a ride!" -Robert J. Sawyer, Hugo Award-winning author of Red Planet Blues

Children of the Eighth Day
a novel of the Scattered Worlds
Print & Kindle
The Eighth Succession *introduced readers to the Hoister Family...* Children of the Eighth Day *takes the story of this remarkable family to the exciting next level.*

The Scattered Worlds Mosaic by Don Sakers

All Roads Lead to Terra
two tales of the Scattered Worlds
Kindle only
Two exciting tales tell of attacks against the shining jewel of the Terran Empire: Earth. Includes an introduction and notes from the author.

A Voice in Every Wind
two tales of the Scattered Worlds
Print & Kindle
On a world where meaning lives in every rock and stream, and every breeze brings a new voice, one human explorer stands on the threshold of discoveries that could alter the future of Humanity.

A Rose From Old Terra
a novel of the Scattered Worlds
Print & Kindle
Jedrek left the Grand Library and his work circle eleven years ago. Now a crisis in uncharted space brings the circle back together. Soon, Jedrek and his friends are at the focal point of a clash of cultures, and the only thing that can save the Galaxy is one modest group of Librarians.

The Leaves of October
a novel of the Scattered Worlds
Print & Kindle
Compton Crook Award finalist
The Hlutr: Immensely old, terribly wise…and utterly alien. When mankind went out into the stars, he found the Hlutr waiting for him. Waiting to observe, to converse, to help. Waiting to judge…and, if necessary, to destroy.

More Books from Speed-of-C Productions

The Curse of the Zwilling by Don Sakers
Print & Kindle

It's Hogwarts meets Buffy at Patapsco University: a small, cozy liberal arts college like so many others – except for the Department of Comparative Religion, where age-old spells are taught and magic is practiced. When a favorite teacher is found dead under mysterious circumstances, grad student David Galvin finds that a malevolent evil has awakened. And now David, along with four novice undergrads, must defeat this ancient, malignant terror.

The SF Book of Days by Don Sakers
Print only

Drawn from the pages of classic sf literature, here is a science fiction/fantasy event for every day of the year...and for quite a few days that aren't part of the year. From Doc Brown's arrival in Hill Valley (January 1, 1885) to the launch of the Bellerophon (Sextor 7, 2351), this datebook is truly out of this world.

PsiScouts #1: At Risk by Phil Meade
Print & Kindle

In the 26th century, psi-powered teenagers from all over the Myriad Worlds join together as the heroic PsiScouts.

Meat and Machine: queer writings by Don Sakers
Print & Kindle

Don Sakers has been queering sf and fantasy for three decades. Meat and Machine collects 24 short pieces of Don's science fiction, fantasy, nonfiction, and erotics.

Elevenses by Don Sakers
Kindle only

Eleven SF and fantasy short stories intended as bite-size snacks.

More Books from Speed-of-C Productions

Gaylaxicon Sampler 2006
Print only

Sample the work of thirteen writers from across the spectrum of gay, lesbian, bisexual, and/or transgender science fiction, fantasy, and/or horror. Includes big names and small, much-published veterans and promising beginners, Lammy and Spectrum Award nominees and winners, past Gaylaxicon Guests of Honor, and fresh new names.

QSpec Sampler 2007
Print only

Originally prepared as a giveaway at Gaylaxicon 2007 in Atlanta, this volume is available at a nominal charge as a sampler of the fine work being done by GLBT writers in SF, fantasy, and horror.

Act Well Your Part by Don Sakers
Print & Kindle

A beloved gay young adult romance, back in print for its adult fans as well as a new generation of teens. At first Keith Graff dislikes his new school. He misses his old friends, and despairs of ever fitting in. Then he joins the school's drama club, and meets the boyishly cute Bran Davenport....

Lucky in Love by Don Sakers
Kindle only

A companion novel to Act Well Your Part, Lucky in Love *follows Keith's friend Frank, torn between bad boy Dwight and basketball star Darnell.*

A Cosmos of Many Mansions: Varieties of SF by Don Sakers
Kindle only

Based on the first five years of Sakers's popular review column, this volume examines & explains dozens of types of science fiction along with hundreds of reviews.

The Mud of the Place by Susanna J. Sturgis
Print only

"A sensitive, witty, and tightly plotted portrayal of life on Martha's Vineyard that only a true Islander could have written. Nice going, Susanna!" –Cynthia Riggs

Books by Melissa Scott

Standalone Titles:
   The Armor of Light (with Lisa A. Barnett)
   Burning Bright
   A Choice of Destinies
   Dreaming Metal
   Dreamships
   Finders
   The Game Beyond
   The Jazz
   The Kindly Ones
   Mighty Good Road
   Night Sky Mine
   Shadow Man
   The Shapes of Their Hearts
   Trouble and Her Friends

Astreiant series:
   1 *Point of Hopes* (with Lisa A. Barnett)
   2 *Point of Knives*
   3 *Point of Dreams*
   4 *Fair's Point*
   5 *Point of Sighs*

Lynes & Mathey series (with Amy Griswold):
   1 *Death by Silver*
   2 *A Death at the Dionysus Club*

Order of the Air series (with Jo Graham):
   1 *Lost Things*
   2 *Steel Blues*
   3 *Silver Bullet*
   4 *Windraker*
   5 *Oath Bound*

More Books by Melissa Scott

Roads of Heaven series:
1 *Five-Twelfths of Heaven*
2. *Silence in Solitude*
3. *The Empress of Earth*

Star Trek books:
Star Trek Deep Space Nine: Proud Helios
Star Trek Voyager: Voyager: The Garden

Stargate Atlantis books:
Lost Queen
Pride of the Genii
The Wild Blue

Stargate Atlantis Legacy series:
1 *Homecoming* (with Jo Graham)
2 *The Lost* (by Jo Graham & Amy Griswold)*
3 *Allegiance* (with Amy Griswold)
4 *The Furies* (by Jo Graham)*
5 *Secrets* (with Jo Graham)
6 *Inheritors* (with Jo Graham & Amy Griswold)
7 *Unascended* (by Jo Graham & Amy Griswold)*
8 *Third Path* (with Jo Graham)

Stargate SG-1 books:
Moebius Squared (with Jo Graham)
Ouroboros

* = *not by Melissa Scott*